"Hip, sassy, and filled with offbeat characters
who will steal your heart."

—Katie MacAlister, *USA Today* bestselling author

Other books by Naomi Neale:

SHOP 'TIL YULE DROP (anthology)

CALENDAR GIRL

NAOMI NEALE

MAKING IT®

January 2005

Published by

Dorchester Publishing Co., Inc.
200 Madison Avenue
New York, NY 10016

ISBN 0-8439-5470-1

The name "Making It" and its logo are trademarks of Dorchester Publishing Co., Inc.

Printed in the United States of America.

Visit us on the web at www.dorchesterpub.com.

ACKNOWLEDGMENTS

For all their help on this book, I really must thank my three best girlfriends in all the world. Lydia Cisaruk kept me sane on weekends by dragging me to karaoke, making me eat Jiffy Pop, and swapping stories about our past hobbies. Patty Woodwell overflowed with moral support and helpful criticisms when I most needed them. And Tahirah Shadforth, founder of the original Elizabethan Failure Society, has long been a dear friend and an imaginative dynamo. This one's for you, ladies!

CALENDAR
GIRL

DECEMBER

Mercer-Iverson Department Store
(a pitiful $7.75 per hour)

Every Who down in Who-ville liked Christmas a lot. But the littlest Who with a man's hand on her fanny . . . did not.

I expected the typical masher. Perhaps a standard-issue divorced dad, or a middle-aged businessman boasting a comb-over, a leer, and a winking eye. The white-haired gentleman behind me, though, could have headlined the "Jolly Old Grandfathers" section of a talent agency's casting book. "Heidi, observe this fine specimen!" he exclaimed when I whipped around. "We've discovered a prime example of the famed North Pole Elf!"

All afternoon, visitors to Mercer-Iverson had lined up by the hundreds to sit their children on our Christmas Grinch's lap. Lucky me—my job required being nice to all of them. The evil overlords of Who-ville demanded compulsory cheeriness, including to sleepy-looking girls and their lecherous grandfathers. I was even luckier because Mercer-Iverson had seen fit to stuff its seasonal workers into uniforms that brought a new dimension to the word *tights*. The millennial fabric squeezing all oxygen from my bloodstream seemed to have been genetically modified with the DNA of a boa constrictor.

Bending down to talk to little Heidi in tights two sizes too small made muscles pop to places they were never intended to go. I suddenly seemed to be wearing my bum as a backpack. My fingers clawed at the elastic while I tried to stretch a smile across my face. "Hi there, sweetheart!"

Heidi backed away in a hurry, eyes wide. I was used to her reaction. I too would be frightened of a crazed woman grabbing her own butt, wearing a smile rarely seen on anyone not overdosed with Zoloft. "You're not an elf," she accused with narrowed eyes.

"That's right! I'm a Who."

"A what?" Her grandfather leaned down and cupped his ear, not quite hearing me.

"A Who."

"A who? A what? Who are you?"

"Nan Who!" I pointed to my name tag, emblazoned with Seussian lettering.

"And what, pray tell, is a Who?"

When I straightened back up again, the bottom half of my buttocks sprang down to the back of my knees as if strapped to a bungee cord, while the top half remained firmly in place. Pain made me stagger sideways. "Why, a Who is a citizen of jolly Who-ville," I forced out, clutching my lower back with one hand and gesturing to the Christmas fantasy village with the other. Crap. Something was seriously wrong down in the antipodes. It seemed as if I had four butt cheeks instead of two. Had I given myself a horizontal Who-wedgie?

"Jeez! Stop holding up the line!" yelled a woman with a thick Jersey accent, a dozen feet away. The long row of parents lining the Astroturf approach to the lair was restless. Some of them had already waited for over an hour to see the only department-store Grinch in Manhattan.

I clutched at my behind, trying to pry out the elusive elastic buried inches deep in my flesh while I soothed the savages. "From this point you may expect a fifteen-minute wait. . . ." The groan rising from the crowd drowned out the rest of my sentence.

"*Excusez-moi. Parlez-vous français?*" A short man with horn-rimmed glasses plucked at my fur-trimmed Christmas Who-jacket.

His request warred with all the others. "Where's the god-damned restroom? If I leave for the god-damned restroom will I lose my god-damned place in this god-damned line?"

"Fifteen minutes is outrageous! Who is your manager?"

"How much are photographs?"

"What's a Who?" I heard once again from behind me.

I closed my eyes. Why, oh why, had I given up smoking two years ago? For my health? What had possessed me to want to live to the age of twenty-eight? What was the point, I ask?

That's when I felt the hand again.

"Ex-*cuse* me, sir!" It was the closest I could come to a re-buke without betraying my anger. Grandpa only winked when I removed his wandering digits from my quadruple Who-crack. "Reena Who, I'm on break," I called out to the woman guarding the cave door. Ignoring the crowd's groans and threats and the fact that I wasn't due lunch for another thirty minutes, I hobbled to the multicolored entrance of our break room.

Inside, the Whos down in Who-ville were crabby as Sneetches. They wrenched their Who-groins and their Who-out-of-reaches. The interior of the Who-ville Postal Office was alive with the hiss of fingernails across nylon when I stepped through its petite front door. After the latch clicked shut, I broke the sound barrier throwing myself to the break room floor, where I squirmed until I'd managed to get my control-top candy-striped tights down around my knees. Of course, the sonic boom could have been the sound of my butt rebounding into its proper shape. I wanted to weep with relief. "Oh thank God!"

Not one of the dozen other Whos seemed to think it out of the ordinary for me to be flailing on the floor, legs in the air, tights in a twist. Safdar Who stepped over me on his way to one of the rickety benches along the wall, tugging his Who-ass and his Crotchamacallit without giving me a second look. Plunk a sticky margarita glass in my hand, smear my lipstick, and hang a cigarette butt from the corner of my mouth, and I could've been my alcoholic roommate from three years ago who stuck me with three months' worth of back rent.

I craved a burger. I needed a drink. I needed St. John's wort to get my black mood back on balance. Most of all, I wanted a muumuu. A nice, loose muumuu.

With her Who-bootie, Amanda Who nudged me from where she sat on a bench. Her mouth busily assaulted a wodge of grape-flavored bubblegum I could smell even above the faintly antiseptic smell of the floor wax. I'd heard she was trying to quit smoking. Like me, she wore her tights around the knees. "Nan, Damien's looking for you," she said without greeting.

Damien was not what I needed. Not at all.

"That's nice." We Whos were a gossipy crew. After two weeks of the same relentless routine, everyone knew everyone else's business. I'd heard from Reena, for example, that Amanda had received a demotion of sorts when she'd been caught slipping her phone number to one of the single dads waiting to see the Grinch. Amanda had been yanked from line duty so fast, Reena had told me, that her departure had left tread marks on the perfume aisle floors. Instead of greeting guests at the entrance to Who-ville, Amanda was on Max patrol now, cleaning up after the dour and placid antler-wearing hound who posed with kids for photographs. Rumor was that it had embittered her.

"Mmm-hmmmm, must be nice."

From her tone, doubtless Amanda knew that Damien and I were something of an item. Yet we weren't. Not really— only in the past tense, and past imperfect at that. "Where is he?" I asked, trying not to sound too interested.

Amanda pointed one of her neatly-trimmed nails in the direction of the Porta-Potty. We Whos were not permanent Mercer-Iverson employees, a fact the department store reinforced at every opportunity. As subcontracted workers, we were not allowed to roam the store in our costumes, nor were we permitted in the Mercer-Iverson employee lounges, the Mercer-Iverson lunchroom, or any of the department store restrooms reserved for the use of customers or staff. Because Mercer-Iverson had restricted our access to one mere small room and a back hallway to the exit, Who-ville was a sparkly, snowy ghetto unto itself—like a gracious plantation facade nailed onto a one-room unpainted shanty.

"So." Amanda elongated the word, savoring it as if it were one of the smokes she craved. "What exactly is up between you guys?"

It was less a question than a land mine. No matter how casually it had been tossed out, I knew I had to tread carefully, here. What Damien meant to me, past or present, was none of her business. Yet refusing to answer would only guarantee me top billing in that afternoon's murmured gossip: *That slut thinks she's better than us, you know? Like we don't all already know she's boinking someone else's boyfriend? Bitch, please.*

"Oh, you know." I lay flat and, as much as it pained me to do it, hoisted my tights midthigh so I could walk again. I couldn't pull off the tricky act of fielding Amanda's inquiries while lying down on the break room floor, writhing around like a slug sprinkled with salt.

I'm not a tall woman. In my Who-niform, with my pale hair sticking out in a *That Girl* flip from under a Who-hat that brought my altitude no higher than five feet and five inches, I looked more like a scrawny middle-school student than a composed and unruffled adult. I still tried to appear as dignified as possible, though, when I struggled from the floor and took my place on the bench beside my interrogator.

"Confidentially?" We both knew the murmured word to mean *Listen, I know you're going to spread what I'm about to tell you as far as the outer boroughs, but you're going to get the scoop, so you'll keep that in mind when you attach your byline to the story, right?* I took a moment to adjust my jumper, as if considering the one best way to phrase it.

In anticipation, her jaw ceased its chomping motion.

"I like to think of Damien as more of a . . . *hobby*. I think you catch my drift."

Chomp. She thought that one over. *Chomp chomp.* She nodded once before her mouth resumed its steady mastication. "Yeah. Oh yeah!" She grinned at me. We were of a type, now. Girls in charge. Women who enjoyed sex and went after it on our own terms. We weren't prudes or Mrs. Grundys. We weren't sluts who couldn't keep our knees together. The two of us were degreed women who made adult choices only partly based on surreptitious reading from the self-help sections of the best bookstores, knowing that we had to skim quickly, because we would never buy any volumes that would look lowbrow next to our old college Oxford annotated editions of *To the Lighthouse*. Even if we could afford to.

In a rare display of good timing, Damien exited the blue cubicle, hands still smoothing the fit of his costume. He didn't lift his eyes and look around until he'd made sure his goodies were snug and his tunic pulled around the tops of his thighs. From my perch across the room I watched as his eyes flickered in the direction of an Asian Who sitting near the door. Up and down they moved, drinking in the girl's perfect posture, her bland smile, her exquisite legs crossed at the knees. The cover of her magazine featured a stern woman in a purple leotard and bun, which didn't surprise me in the least. Damien loved his dancers.

Should I have been jealous of the way he watched her? To be honest, I didn't feel any more upset at his prowling than I had at Billy-Boy, the old tomcat my parents kept when I was a kid, who used to sit on the fire escape and whip his tail around as he watched unsuspecting birds. Once in a while the old cat would rouse himself, quiver his loins, and pounce. Although it had usually been my job to dispose of Billy-Boy's broken victims, how could I despise him? The cat had only followed instincts programmed by nature. Any pity I felt at that moment was for the poor, unsuspecting dancer.

"He any good?" Amanda asked out of the side of her mouth. She had been watching him too.

"Good enough I haven't had to buy batteries in a couple of years."

The insinuation got a loud enough cackle from her to attract Damien's attention. I waited for his stare to finish lingering over Amanda before moving on. Finally our eyes met—and there was his slow grin, this time reserved especially for me. It was the only thing of his I could claim for my own, that confidential smile. Two years ago, when I'd known all Damien's secrets—things he said about his never-present girlfriend, names of the women he flirted with, names of the women he'd slept with—I had thrilled to that smile. As recently as a year ago I might have obtained satisfaction at bringing it to his lips.

These days, I was beginning to feel a hobby could become an inconvenience.

In one of our costumes it takes a self-confident man to imagine himself a sex god. Somehow Damien pulled it off. When wearing street clothes he appeared scrawny, even undernourished, but tights highlighted his ropy muscles. The brim of his off-kilter hat rested just above his dark, thick eyebrows, lending him twice his usual sexual menace. His eyes were what hooked most women, though. They were of so deep a shade of brown that I could never tell where the color ended and the iris began, and his impossibly curly lashes opened so wide and big that he looked as if he had stepped out of Japanese anime. It was impossible to suspect those glistening eyes of insincerity, even when you knew him as well as I once had.

In his candy-striped costume straight out of a children's book, Damien Morris looked like some kind of sextacular Seussed-up super-stud. If Mercer-Iverson's Christmas village ran its own red light district, Damien would have been its most successful pimp; he was Who-ville's own Prince, circa *Purple Rain,* a short, pouting bundle of glossy hair and narrow hips, looking to cruise down Mulberry Street in his little red Corvette. I'd known Damien through his long manes and Caesar cuts, from grunge neglect through fussy platinum-blond streaks. I'd witnessed his facial hair in every configuration, manscaped into goatees, carefully maintained stubble, long and sculpted sideburns, and soul patches. Not once had he ever managed to escape genes that made him look essentially female, though not feminine. Many were the times I'd told him to face facts: nine times out of ten, he was *prettier* than any of the women in the room.

"Look at him strut," Amanda murmured to me. "Cock of the henhouse."

"If not the whole Frank Purdue factory system," I said with meaning. She raised her eyebrows, and I nodded. "Oh yeah. Big things in little packages, if you know what I mean."

"Really!" She gave him a speculative glance below the tunic as he eased closer. "Well. That's my cue. Break's over anyway. See you out on the floor," she said, rising and pulling up her own tights. I noticed she fanned herself all the way from the bench to the door back out to Who-hell.

Truthfully, I was glad of Amanda's exit. I'd hated the way I'd sounded with her. Sometimes it seemed as if I wore mask after mask. Out on the floor when I kept the crowds in their lines and dispensed candy and photograph order forms, my body wore a costume and my face was a mask painted with a smile that never wavered. With the Seasonal Staffers management, I wore another that boasted wide and attentive eyes. The mask I'd worn for Amanda had appeared confidential and cold-blooded, and just as false. Take a fingernail and *tap tap tap* against any of them and you'd see how hard and artificial they were.

"Hey there, foxy lady," Damien murmured, sounding like a stock character from a blaxploitation film. He lowered himself next to me, knees on the edge of the bench, and let his hand slither between my thighs. "I like it when you have your panties already down."

"Oh, very nice," I said, pushing him off and struggling to my feet. When you work thankless jobs on your feet, you learn to take every opportunity you can to sit. Standing only further numbed what already felt like aching stumps, but I disliked being toyed with in front of a crowd. "Molest me in front of everyone, why don't you?"

"Ooh, mother, may I?" Damien had a gift for making the most innocent phrases sound lewd. As I'd expected, he followed me to one of the two curtained-off areas the men and women used as dressing rooms. I didn't have to look over my shoulder to know that every eye in the break room followed us. I could imagine the dancer Who, her magazine's top perfectly aligned at the bridge of her nose, peering at Damien's butt with approval, then at me with the mental codicil of, *what does he see in her?*

It's not that I was hideous. I wasn't grotesque, the kind of person others made a mockery of when her back was turned. It's just that I looked like a child. Our two-person parade could have been Little Red Riding Hood followed by her lupine stalker. I'd always resembled a kid—I could still wear outfits I'd owned in ninth grade. My hair was pale and wan, like weak tea. Depending in what light I stood, it might take on a washed-out blond, anemic brown, or blanched red hue. Few days went by when I wasn't mistaken for someone half my age; I was regularly asked for identification to get into R-rated films. When I used to smoke, outraged do-gooders would march up to me and ask if my mother knew I was addicted to those filthy cancer sticks. When I looked at myself in the dressing room mirror now, I still resembled nothing more than a thirteen- or fourteen-year-old dressed up for Halloween. I'd thought our Who-fits were darling when I'd seen them on the hangers. At the moment, I yearned for something less confining and infinitely more comfortable—a whalebone corset cinched tight, or an iron maiden with extra spikes would do. I hauled up my tights and grimaced at the pain. "Do you think these costumes are cute?"

My answer was a pair of lips on my earlobe and Damien's pelvis grinding my rear. "Let me show you how cute I think you are," he murmured.

"Show Alycia," I said, pretending to ignore him. "She's your girlfriend."

"She's in Ohio this week," he murmured, nibbling his way down my neck. On my rear, I could feel his hardness pressing into my skin.

"Too bad, so sad." I tried to squirm away.

Damien was in one of his more torturous moods. "Aw, come on, Nan," he complained somewhere in the vicinity of my nape. I gasped; my neck was my shivery spot, and Damien knew it. "She's been gone a week."

"She'll be back soon."

"She'd want me to be happy."

"She'd want me," I said, finally wriggling out from his entwined arms, "not to be fooling around with her boyfriend."

"But we used to have a thing." I held up my hands and closed my eyes. I'd had enough. I liked Damien. Part of me craved Damien still, but all this flirting was too rich a banquet for a girl on a sexual diet. I didn't open my eyes again until I heard him say, "All right, all right."

He had retreated a couple of steps. "All that teasing's so unfair," I said. "We've been over this issue!"

"Too many times. How long has it been?"

"Thirteen months."

"Dang, has it really been over a year since you and I . . . ?" He sounded incredulous. Not, I suspected, at the length of the time, but more at the notion that anyone could resist him for so long. Once again he wrapped his arms around me. "Friendship hug, friendship hug," he swore, when he felt me tense up. Damien kept his hands squarely around my middle, away from any dangerous spots.

"No wandering fingers," I warned. He rocked me in front of the mirror, his head over my shoulder. Fending off Damien's continual barrage of propositions over the months hadn't been easy. Fast-forwarded in my memory, all those successful deflected passes made me feel like Wonder Woman, repelling German bullets with her magic bracelets.

"So why don't we break that streak sometime? Hmmmm?"

It amazed me how badly I sometimes wanted to. Sex with Damien was like having Internet access on a temp job. It was easily available, distracting, chewed up time, and let me slip out of my head for a little while. Yet that didn't necessarily make it good for me. "How many times have I told you I don't want to be that kind of girl any more?"

"Okay then. What kind of girl do you want to be?" The buzz of his voice in my ear made me shiver. I smiled. This was the Damien I liked best—the one who had talked to me late at night, either in my bed or on the phone, asking questions and imagining possibilities. "Do you want to be a good girl? I have a thing for good girls. Especially if they're in those Catholic schoolgirl uniforms. Hot!"

He was joking, though only barely. I laughed and swatted at him. "No. Not that kind."

"Then what?"

I only thought for a moment before I replied. "The kind of girl designed to be kissed upon the eyes."

We swayed to some internal rhythm of his own. "You've been listening to *The Fantasticks* too much."

I laughed, surprised. "You recognized that?"

"A musical runs for forty-odd years, you hear some of its songs occasionally. Go on. What else?"

"How about a solvent girl, then?" I asked. In the mirror I could see one of the other Whos peeking around the curtain behind us. Her head quickly vanished. "A girl who knows where she'll be getting money from after Christmas? How about the kind of girl who can go out for dinner at a real restaurant and go to the movies and shop in a department store like this one, all on the same day, without fretting about where the cash will be coming from? That's the kind of girl I want to be."

I looked at my reflection, opposite us. I don't know whether it was the light, or the oddness of my mood, but for a moment I didn't recognize myself. Small wonder—is this where I'd pictured myself being at twenty-eight? That reflected face, so small and alien in an outlandish costume, belonged to someone else. The girl I once thought I'd become would never have taken up with a player like Damien, much less dragged him along as a liability, year after year. What happened to all the things I used to plan for myself? The smart and clever little jobs I thought I'd hold? The intelligent, eligible men I thought I'd meet?

I'd thought my refusal to find a corporate, soulless career used to be part of my cuteness. I had enjoyed the oddball positions I'd taken fresh out of college—they made good dinnertime conversation. At twenty-two my employment pattern had been quirky and charming. At twenty-eight, I seemed simply shiftless and desperate.

And yes, when I'd taken this job, it had been out of desperation. *Just one more month,* I'd promised myself. *It'll be fun. You'll be bringing smiles to kids' faces.* After the first week, when I'd remembered that at Christmas the children were unhappy, the parents were unhappy, and all of us Whos were the unhappiest of all, I'd made bargains. *Compromise a little. Tough it out. You'll find a real job in January. A job you'll like.*

How many of those promises to myself had I made over the last several years? Lately I'd held one bad seasonal job after another, wearing costume after costume. How many pieces of myself had I bargained away with every compromise?

Enough, obviously, that I barely recognized myself. Where did those pieces go, once you set them loose? Could I get them back? I wanted them back. My tired-looking eyes and slumping shoulders made me look depleted.

A nasal voice startled me off the depression train and back to reality junction. "Cheer Facilitators? Attention, Cheer Facilitators! I'm looking for Nancy Cloutier. Has anyone seen Nancy Cloutier?"

"Crap." What did DeeDee Camillo want now? Was I in trouble for taking an early break? The woman had a knack for making me feel like a total child. Although we had to be the same age, around DeeDee, her managerial clipboard, and her even more regimented bow ties, I felt like a seventh grader sent to detention. "She's going to want me to be Cindy-Lou Who," I growled, suddenly realizing why she'd been looking for me.

"What's wrong with that?"

"Damn it, I *hate* window duty. I'm here!" I called out the last two words over the curtains while I batted away Damien's hands.

"She's *undressing*," I heard someone outside say. A chorus of titters, both male and female, followed the comment.

Damien's pink tongue busily flicked at the corner of his mouth. "We've never played Grinch and Cindy-Lou Who, you know. Could be kind of . . . *saucy*."

"Stay here and shut up," I warned Damien, dimly aware that thanks to his comment, I'd never be able to read Dr. Seuss to any of my future children. Assuming I could still have any after a month of Who-tights cutting off all circulation to my kiddie-bearing parts. Damien crossed his arms, gave me a lazy grin, and leaned against the wall while I gave my tights a final wrench so I could limp out of the dressing area.

"Attention, Cheer Facilitators. Attention!" Amazing how DeeDee could turn her head to look around the room, and yet never manage to make accidental eye contact with anyone. DeeDee was my same height, only her rotundity made her somehow much more imposing a figure—to me, anyway. To everyone else, she was still a short woman trying to compensate with bushels of words delivered at top volume. "While we're all waiting for Nancy to make an appearance, I'd like to make a reminder: Cheer Facilitators extracting chewing gum from audience participants before their visits to the Mercer-Iverson Grinch are required to use the sanitary plastic gloves posted in appropriately concealed spots throughout the in-character area. Per health codes, I cannot stress enough the necessity of *changing* your gloves and *properly disposing of them* after each and every successful extraction of—oh, there you are, Nancy. I was hoping . . ."

I knew exactly what she was hoping, and I didn't want any of her Cindy-Lou Who madness. Window duty was an awful way to spend an afternoon. "It's Nan," I told her.

The two words brought DeeDee to a halt. Her lashes flickered madly, as if I'd finally gotten the nerve to tell her that everyone called her "The Armadillo" when her back was turned and that we were all also wondering if she'd heard of a marvelous new dentifrice designed to improve the quality of oral hygiene? Called toothpaste? And maybe she should use it, once in a blue moon? "Beg pardon?" she asked, smiling in a way that didn't imply any pleasure or amusement.

I despise people who affect phrases like *beg pardon?* or *excuse?*, but only half as much as I dislike being known as a *Cheer Facilitator.* "My name isn't Nancy," I told her from across the room. "It's Nan."

"But it says Nancy on my shift sheet."

I'd gummed up the works. Sometimes I seemed fated to be the pebble in the cogs, the sticky wheel on the shopping cart, but I'd only been standing up for myself. Again DeeDee fluttered her eyelashes. The dozen other Whos on break watched in silence. We were all twenty- or thirty-somethings with spotty job records and a healthy disrespect for supervisors who mistook volume for authority. No one looked directly at me, but I could sense that more than a few people were glad I'd stood firm on my name. Maybe my name was one of the few things left I wasn't willing to compromise. "I'm sorry for your shift sheet. It's Nan."

"Please excuse." DeeDee's nostrils flared. "Nanc—Nan, I wanted to assign you to . . ."

A blast of air drowned out the rest of her request. Whenever the break room door opened, it let in noise and a jet stream of hot, sticky air from the Who-ville exhibit. It took DeeDee a moment to realize that she'd been out-babbled by the crowds. By the time the door shut, it was too late. Old Mr. Andrew Iverson had stepped into the room and absorbed whatever attention we'd been giving our supervisor.

I liked Mr. Iverson. I wasn't exactly sure what his role was among the many Iversons who ran the Mercer-Iverson empire, but he'd charmed me with his habit of walking around the department store with both hands clenched behind his back, like an elderly tutor of Latin from an old novel. With sartorial habits that included rumpled shirts and flyaway collars and practical yet ugly shoes, he reminded me of several old college professors I'd enjoyed. "Heaven forbid I interrupt," he said, bowing slightly at the waist as if he were a Freon-filled Dippy Bird. "But do any of you happen to speak French?" No one replied. "There's a young girl without who wishes to speak to Santa Claus, but neither she nor her guardian are conversant in English. I thought perhaps—"

"I do!" I swear on a bidet of holy water I don't know what possessed me to speak up. It's true that during my twelfth grade French class trip to Montreal, I managed to distinguish myself linguistically by sneaking a group of kids from our hotel after curfew to order *le pizza de pepperoni et bière* from the Pizza Hut across the street. It's true I survived the caper without the waitress laughing at me (or, for that matter, carding me), but that one accomplishment and a hazy memory of how to play the Mille Bornes card game scarcely qualified me to act as Mercer-Iverson's international good will ambassador. Anything, though, had to be better than incarceration in one of the frigid Seventh Avenue showroom windows for an afternoon, miming surprise at the sight of a Grinchy Sandy Claws rifling presents from my Who-tree.

Mr. Iverson peered at me through wire-rimmed spectacles. With his tweedy gentility, he reminded me of an aged Bob Crachit from a community theatre production of *A Christmas Carol.* "How extraordinary," he murmured, looking me up and down. Had he really never before noticed our eye-popping costumes? Perhaps not. After all, he seemed to think that the green-faced actor outside was good old Saint Nick.

"Beg pardon." DeeDee firmly planted her nose where it didn't belong. I should have expected it. "I was *hoping* that Nancy might lend her *considerable* talents to our display window, Mr. Iverson."

"Oh, I see, I see." Mr. Iverson gave me one final scan, brows furrowed as if I were a particularly devilish clue from the Sunday *Times* crossword. "I didn't mean to override any of your decisions, Miss . . ."

"Camillo," DeeDee supplied, displaying a maximum number of teeth with a minimum amount of cheer.

"Yes, certainly, Miss Camillo. How dreadfully absent-minded of me to suppose that merely because I am the individual who subcontracted the services of your company, I thought I might take the liberty of extracting one of your people to assist a young girl who is waiting for—"

All of us knew that DeeDee had been hoping to parlay her Seasonal Staffers position into a full-time job with Mercer-Iverson. A crap managerial job is better than a crap job as a seasonal Who, but to me crap smells the same whether you're wiping it off Converse or Blahniks. She reversed gears from obstructive into obsequious in less than half a second. "Please excuse, but as I was saying, sir, I think it would be better for our Nancy to accompany you. 'Tis the season, after all, and I'd hate to keep that poor young girl waiting any more. *Zhoyoo noel,* no?" DeeDee backed away, bowing slightly. She would have made a grand Elizabethan court flunky.

I tucked away the phrase. I'd been trying to remember how to pronounce the season's greetings in French. "Shall we, my dear?" asked Mr. Iverson, cocking his head.

"Yes, sir," I assented.

I trotted behind him out the door of the postal office and back into Who-ville full of minor misgivings. Who the heck was I to translate a little girl's Christmas wish list? Was I insane? Before I could work myself into any full-fledged regrets, much less confessions and pleas for my job, Mr. Iverson turned and looked over his shoulder. "How long have you been an elf here, my dear?"

"A week now, sir," I replied, speaking up over the crowd noises. "We're really Whos, you know."

"Eh?"

Mr. Iverson had to be at least of retirement age. I felt obligated to address him with formality, even if I did want to rumple his hair like I would my own grandfather. "Ms. Camillo likes to call us 'Cheer Facilitators,' sir," I told him.

The information immobilized our progress. There might have been a hint of maliciousness behind my sentence, but I had said it matter-of-factly. "Cheer Facilitators?" he said, scrutinizing me first through, and then over his spectacles. "What utter rubbish. Come along." We began walking once more.

Something about Mr. Iverson's stance and slightly ceremonial manner of greeting the floor workers reminded me of days long vanished. He obviously belonged more to the Manhattan of Edith Wharton than of *Sex and the City.* When we passed by molded plastic decorations and electronic price scanners and computerized checkout screens, or as we ducked under a metal detector festively disguised as a bank of mistletoe and had our every step mapped by surveillance cameras overhead, Mr. Iverson seemed at odds with his surroundings. He should have been surrounded by wood paneling and thick velvet curtains, I decided. I could see him consoling women about the silk stocking shortage during the Second World War, or touting turn-of-the-century developments in electrical gadgetry. In a store laden with every kind of modern technology, he seemed an antiquated afterthought.

"And here she is," he said, smiling at the little girl sitting on what we Whos laughingly called "the puke bench." Mr. Iverson bent over and spoke in the loud voice that some people affect for children and non-English speakers. "Our little foreign visitor! Isn't she a dear?"

The little girl stared at Mr. Iverson, then at her father, a short man with thick glasses who blurted out a single word: *"Français?"* The pair had been separated from the main line and perched alone on a stretch of seating where we rested children whose overexcitement at seeing our department store Grinch brought their stomachs to turmoil. I vaguely remembered having seen the father in the line before my break.

"Ah, yes," Mr. Iverson continued at top volume. "I've personally found for you a translator. *Parlez-vous français tres bien,*" he commented, clasping his fingers together and looking quite pleased with himself. He beamed at me. "Mademoiselle . . . er, ah."

"Cloutier," I supplied, smiling. "Nan." The father appeared delighted. He waved his arms and let loose with a speech entirely in voluble, rapid French. Armed with my glossary of twenty phrases, half of them curses, I could understand none of it. It was as if I'd pulled the arm of a slot machine and my triple-seven jackpot was coming out in French vocabulary, so I bobbed and smiled and cocked my head and tried to appear utterly delighted while it poured on and on and on.

"My goodness, what a quantity of verbiage. What the devil is he saying?" Mr. Iverson wanted to know. He had plastered a broad smile on his face to appear amiable.

"He's very pleased to be here in New York and especially at the world-famous Mercer-Iverson department store, and his daughter is excited as well, and he wanted to thank you for finding someone to translate." I was making it all up, but the man didn't seem angry, and the praise pleased Mr. Iverson, so what harm could I do? Was it too late to claim the man spoke a dialect I couldn't understand? Probably. I didn't want to let poor Mr. Iverson down. Maybe it was for the simple reason that he trusted me, but something about the old guy made me not want to disappoint him—and I didn't have the remotest skills to succeed.

I'd have to bluff my way through. "We're next, okay?" I called up the stairs to the Whos standing outside the faux-Grinch's lair.

"You'd better come on, then," Melba Who called back down. "He's got one heading out now."

I smiled broadly at both the father and daughter and held out my hand to the girl. She was a pretty little thing with long blond hair spilling out from under a black beret that matched her long black coat. She couldn't have been more than six or seven. Together we marched toward the cave opening, leaving the adults to circle around behind the cave. Once her father and Mr. Iverson were mute but smiling figures at the bottom of the ramp, I spoke. "You look exactly like me at your age! Are you ready to see the Grinch?"

My mood was infectious, and she'd understood exactly one word: *"Le grinch?"* Over her face fell an expression I'd seen on hundreds of kids in the last two weeks: happiness multiplied by fear. Had my family visited Santa at Mercer-Iverson when I'd been the girl's age? My mother had sworn by Macy's, so I couldn't see her shopping in one of the city's smaller and older department stores. Santa had been something like God, back then. He saw us when we were sleeping. He knew when we'd been bad or good. Only, in my day, if a girl played her cards right, Santa could give her a Ker-Plunk and a new doll a heck of a lot more quickly than God could cough up answers to prayers. No wonder the poor kid looked sick to her stomach. "Don't worry," I said with a squeeze of my fingers. "Everything will be all right."

We had three actors playing the Seussian icon, all of them in green-face and a traditional red Santa costume trimmed with white fur. I was glad to see that afternoon's actor was Alvin. I'd worked with Alvin Melbourne a couple of Christmases ago. Side by side we'd passed out samples of summer smoked sausages to passing crowds; he'd gone on to win an Obie for an Off-Broadway drama the following spring. From the way he scowled at me, sprawled out on his chair within the garlanded cave, I could guess he felt his return to the seasonal work wasn't, well, quite so triumphant.

What a costume, though. "I've seen cakes wearing less frosting, buddy boy," I told him. When Alvin furrowed his eyebrows and shook his head at my familiarity, I shrugged. "She doesn't understand, poor little sweetheart."

"Oh, she's the French one?"

I'd always pictured the Grinch's abode as a spartan bachelor pad, but with all the ribbons and swags of holly and wreaths and candles, this particular interpretation had apparently been dreamed up by the entire staff of *Martha Stewart Living* after an all-night binge of sniffing lines of uncut potpourri. The girl looked around the brightly lit cavern with interest, but mostly stared shyly at the faux Grinch. When Alvin extended his arms in the girl's direction, she burst into a wide smile and instantly ran forward to leap onto his lap. "*Je veux . . .*" she began excitedly.

"*Arrêt,*" I begged her in a terrible accent. Hey, spending my youth playing hazards on my brothers in Mille Bornes had done me some good after all! She stopped talking and obediently waited. I peered over Alvin's shoulder through the window where parents usually hovered to eavesdrop on the conversations between their kiddies and the kelly-colored actors. The niche was only a few feet away from the head of the line, but the girl's father and Mr. Iverson had been delayed by the long circular route from the puke bench. Only when I saw both pairs of spectacles glinting through the window did I signal her to start again. *"Allez!"* I hoped that was right. I said it softly, just in case.

Alvin had waited patiently until that point. "Merry Christmas, little girl!" he said in a loud, booming voice. "You look like your heart is three sizes too large!"

He looked at me to translate. *"Joyeux Noël!"* I told the girl. She laughed. It might have been at my pronunciation.

"And what's your name?" he asked, glaring at me for reducing his in-character speech to a two-word sentence.

"Uh, *nom?"* I ventured when the little girl looked at me.

It was a word she recognized. *"Je m'appelle Bina."*

"Her name is Bina," I informed Alvin.

"I got that, thank you very much," he replied between gritted teeth. "And what do you want for Christmas, Bina?"

The girl looked at me. I had no bloody concept of how to translate that long a sentence, but I was under the gun to say something. I could see Mr. Iverson craning his neck around the corner. Very softly, and as nasal as I could get it, I made some French-sounding noises. *"Fwah fwah fwah fwah vous pour Noël?"*

"Man!" Alvin whispered, shocked. "You are going to be so fired!"

"Shut up," I hissed back.

Bina stared at me as if I were mad, but when Alvin cleared his throat and gave her an encouraging lift of the eyebrows, she got the idea. *"Je veux une Barbie,"* she started.

"She, um, wants a Barbie!" I was pretty sure on that one.

Alvin nodded and smiled with encouragement. "A Barbie!"

"*Et je veux un Game Boy avec Pokémon.*"

"Something about a Pokémon Game Boy!" I was caught up in the excitement of the moment. Thank God for capitalist conglomerates and brand names that transcended borders!

"*Et je veux une roue de poterie, et je veux une balle de disco tournante.*"

"Um, she wants some curtains and a CD player?" I was less sure about those.

Bina's face screwed up in concentration as she obviously attempted to remember her memorized list. "*Et je veux un sac à dos de Hello Kitty, et je veux une boule huit magique, et je veux Le Jeu de Vie.*"

"And she wants her own wine cellar and a telescope and some socks."

Alvin glared over the girl's head at me. "You don't understand a word she's saying!" he accused, sotto voce.

I had to bite my lip. "You're right. I've got nothing."

Bina, however, had one more item. "*Et!*" she announced loudly. "*Et je veux un poney!*"

"And a pony!" I crowed, this time with enough volume to carry across the room past Alvin to Mr. Iverson's ears. "Bina wants a pony." For all I knew, *un poney* was some kind of special spoon the French used to eat their snails, but the hell with it. It sounded like she wanted a pony, so by gum, a pony I'd claim for her. Had anyone—besides rich girls in Connecticut and ranch girls in the west—ever gotten a pony for Christmas? Somehow I highly doubted it. Her father would understand what all that had really meant, and that mattered more than my feeble translation.

I'd first noticed the sneezes while Bina had been rattling off her wish list. It was while Alvin and Bina hugged in some kind of wordless show of approval that they began to issue forth with the regularity of a clock's chimes. "Oh my," I heard Mr. Iverson say with a sniffle. "Excuse me, do."

Alvin leaned back and peered through the window

while he helped Bina off his lap. "Are you all right, sir?" he murmured.

"Oh dear. Oh my! I can't think why—'*tchoo!*" Mr. Iverson's sneezes were as dainty as his interjections. "The only thing— '*tchoo!*—to which I'm—'*tchoo!*—allergic is—'*tchoo!*—dogs."

"Max," Alvin and I said, looking at each other.

"*Max?*" Bina asked, now so radiant I could tell her happiness could not be more complete. "*Le chien Max?*"

"You'd better step through the next room quickly, sir," Alvin advised through the window. I think it pained Alvin's Method sensibilities to break character in front of one of the children, even if she didn't understand a word he was saying. The well-being of a genuine Iverson was always first priority, though. "Max the dog sits there for photos with the kiddies."

Bina became more excited at another mention of Max. I took her hand and leaned around Alvin. "Mr. Iverson, sir, I'll deliver Bina to her father. You can—"

"No—'*tchoo!*—no, I'm fine, my dear, I'll—'*tchoo 'tchoo!*— muddle through somehow."

Poor guy! "We should do lunch sometime," I told Alvin on my way out. "You might wanna do something about that complexion problem, though."

"Hey, it ain't easy being green." He grinned after me. All the same, I think he was happy to see me go.

I didn't have to be Nancy Drew to notice three clues to Mr. Iverson's allergy mystery when we stepped through the cave door and into what was supposed to be Max the Dog's house.

1) There was no dog on his chair. In fact, there was no dog to be seen anywhere at all.

2) There were, however, a pair of striped Who-tights sticking straight up into the air, and another pair sprawled lazily between them, as two Whos were engaged in wild and passionate Who-monkey-lovin' right there on Max's little sofa.

3) Actually, there was no number three. I was too much in shock over number two to notice anything else.

"Damien?" I couldn't believe my eyes. No—my eyes I believed. I really couldn't believe my friend's *nerve*. Damien leaped up and turned at the sound of my voice. A lazy smile played over his lips before he wiped them on his forearm. "Amanda!"

"What in the—*'tchoo!*—dickens!"

"Crap!" I heard Amanda growl, as she tried to struggle to her own feet. I was relieved to see their costumes were intact. They hadn't been doing anything more than some tongue wrestling.

I was too appalled at the sight of the two Whos to observe the entrance behind me of Mr. Iverson and Bina's father. Bina seemed completely unfazed. Maybe people in France dry-hump all the time. "Why, this is completely—*'tchoo!*—unaccepta—*'tchoo!*—ble be—*'tchoo!*—havior!"

I didn't care about Damien putting moves on Amanda. Screw that. What bugged me was that I'd gotten him this job with Seasonal Staffers—how could he repay me like this? That alone made me angrier than I had been in months and months. When I heard a crash and cry behind me, I worried I'd had a Carrie White moment, striking out with a telekinetic flash. When I turned, though, all my rage evaporated at the sight of Mr. Iverson sprawled on the floor, the tops of his feet lying across an antler-wearing bloodhound busily engaged in licking its privates.

"*Max!*" Bina ran across the room to kneel down by the pooch, her juvenile concern only for the dog's well-being. At the same time, her father and I ran to kneel down by Mr. Iverson's prone form. Bina's father heaved Max's heavy bulk from under the old man's legs, sending the dog trotting a few paces with his lead trailing behind.

"Are you all right, sir?" I asked.

"My—*'tchoo!*—glasses . . ." I found them a few feet away, and helped put them on his face. "My goodness—*'tchoo!*—what a tumble!"

"I'll help you up," I suggested, shooting glares at the guilty couple across the room. Amanda appeared as if she wanted to run from the store all the way back to New Jersey, while Damien merely looked sheepish, but not particularly sorrowful. "We'll get you back to your office."

"Ah, no need, no need, my—'*tchoo!*—dear." He shied away slightly when Max lowered his head, gave him an experimental sniff, then licked the side of Mr. Iverson's face. "Straight to the hospital for me. I—'*tchoo!*—believe I've had the misfortune to—'*tchoo!*—break my arm."

Malamute's Bar & Grill
(beer: $9.00; unlimited stale popcorn: free; three mournful R.E.M. songs on the jukebox: $1.50)

I gazed deep into my friend Ambrose's hazel eyes. "Did I ever tell you I used to love that man?" From our long table I made a sloppy gesture to the familiar front door beneath its panel of blue and green stained glass. Emmett, the man in question, lounged against the wall, blond and smiling, speaking to one of the old regulars. His hands were clasped around a tall mug of the same lager I'd been drinking for the previous half hour. "I used to love that turtlenecked, square-jawed . . ."

"Unshaven."

"Unshaven," I echoed. "Unshaven and stubbly . . ."

Ambrose rested his nose and cheekbone on the knuckles of his right hand and followed my gaze. "Muscle-y."

"I used to love that turtlenecked, square-jawed, unshaven, stubbly, muscle-y man," I agreed. "In college."

Ambrose patted my hand. "Yes, you talk about it before nearly all of our meetings. You loved him and never told him, like Patience on a monument, smiling at grief, and afterward you were glad of it."

"Glad!" I agreed, emphasizing the point by slamming my empty mug on the table. "That's right. And you know why I was glad?"

Without a pause, Ambrose reached out and refilled my glass from one of the pitchers of the red-brown beer. "Because he dated girls who were total losers, especially that blond Irish bitch Kristen, who toyed with his feelings and never could commit and played him like a violin."

"Like a Stradivarius!"

Although the bar was chilly and grew colder with every rush of air and flying snow the front door let in, Ambrose still had the sleeves of his sweater pushed up to his elbows.

"Hey, what is it about you big, goateed guys that always keeps you warm in rooms that make me shiver?" I suddenly asked him. "Is it your body fat? Because I've got plenty of that and I'm still freezing."

On any given visit, it only took two tall mugs of Malamute's amber lager to make me feel like all was almost right with the world. Tonight, it was going to take three. Maybe four. On Avenue A's boulevard of bars, Malamute's was one of the few that didn't attract the NYU coeds or would-be hipsters from above 14th Street. Its unadorned brick walls, vaultlike ceilings, and deep but narrow capacity drew a mixed crowd of locals who came for the specialty beers, greasy burgers, and low-key atmosphere. Our Elizabethan Failures Society had met there for years. "Let's both pretend I wasn't offended by that comment," Ambrose chuckled. He never minded what I said to him. "Do you want my coat?"

"It's the beer talking," I told him. As if to prove the point, I belched. "Sorry," I said, waving my hand in front of my face.

He pushed the white paper basket of popcorn toward me. "Try to eat a little something, would you? The meeting hasn't started yet."

In a gesture of obedience I stuffed my mouth full of the salty kernels. "Wath it inthenthitive of me to thay dat about Emmett to you?" I asked, managing to keep the spew to a minimum. "I mean, with you being in love with me and everything."

"Honey, it's nothing I haven't heard before," he said.

"I'd love you back if you weren't gay, you know."

"For the thousandth time: I'm not gay."

I swallowed and opened my eyes wide and made my voice sound credulous and dopey. "Oh-kay!" He only smiled and shook his head. "I know gay. You're gay. You might not admit it yet, but you're gay. My brother's gay. I *know* gay." When he opened his mouth to make the usual protest, I interrupted him with a triumphant pointing of my index finger. "You said Emmett was muscle-y! You did! You wouldn't have noticed that if you weren't gay!"

"Nan, the man wears skintight sweaters so *everyone* will notice how muscle-y he is. You don't have to be gay to see he could crack a walnut by flexing his pecs."

"Is Nan insisting you're gay again?" Maya Jasper, as ever clutching an oversized book to her chest, sat down in the chair opposite me. She smelled of cold weather. Beads of water sparkled among her cascades of dark, tiny braids; it must have started to snow more heavily since my arrival an hour ago.

"Of course she is," Ambrose said, leaning over and giving Maya's brown cheek a kiss while she removed her coat. "It wouldn't be a Society meeting without accusations of buggery."

"They're not accusations! I'm not judging! I'm just saying, is all." I grabbed another handful of the popcorn and started sucking off the salt until the pieces softened. "Besides, Ambrose is being patronizing and treating me like the cute little drunk I am."

"Oh Nan." Maya finished unwrapping her scarf. She paused a moment and let it rest in her lap. "You're anything but cute when you're drunk."

"Ergo, she must not be drunk yet." Ambrose grinned, and from his seat at the table's end reached over and brushed a hank of hair from my face. "Because she's still very cute indeed."

I cupped my hand to my cheek and mouthed the word

gay! at Maya. She smiled back at me indulgently. I used to sneer at anyone who proclaimed another person was her "best friend in the whole world." It's such a fourth-grade concept. I liked to remark that my friends bring different qualities to my life; they lent it texture and depth. How can you pick out any single one and claim him or her to be the best? And yet, Maya was my best friend in the whole world. We'd roomed together in college our junior and senior years and had been friends ever since. We bickered regularly, saw bad movies together when one of us had enough money, and hunted free entertainment when we didn't. "She's all right," Maya said, refusing to stroke my ego. "Where are the others?"

"Pinball," Ambrose told her, jerking his head backwards. Jack and Clark, members of the Society, hovered over an old Cirqus Voltaire game across the room at the far end of the bar counter. Both their faces were illuminated from beneath by its green flickering lights. Jack leaned on a miniature ATM, watching Clark demonstrate his body English on the game's bulk. "That makes everybody, but Emmett's waiting for someone."

"He told me, when I came in." Maya had finally extracted herself from her winter gear and draped it into padding for her chair. "Any idea who?"

"Mmmm," is all that Ambrose said. I saw him glance at me sideways.

"Oh, yeah, probably." Maya's eyes flicked in my direction as well, then back again, as if she'd thought the better of it. "So what are you working on this week?"

Maya spent her days either poring through old books and records in archives, or else scanning the Internet at home in her bathrobe. She called herself an information broker, and had regular clients looking for all kinds of arcane facts. "Some more genealogical research for that guy I was telling you about last—"

"I'm not stupid," I interrupted. "I know what you're trying

oh-so-hard not to talk about. He's waiting for some girl." Maya fell silent. She and Ambrose exchanged guilty, expectant looks. I grabbed more of the popcorn. "I'm not *still* in love with Emmett, you know. It's a thing of the past. A fait accompli. *Finito.* Ziparoonie."

"We know." Ambrose squeezed my hand again.

"Have we gotten to the part with Kristen, yet?" Maya asked. "That's always my favorite."

"Been there," Ambrose replied. "Done that. Posted the digital pictures on my Web site."

I scoffed. "Mock if you like, but it's over. Pffffft." By the door, Emmett Dunnigan laughed and flirted with Rosie, the seventy-year-old Malamute's regular whose claim to fame was having been in the original chorus of *The Pajama Game.* I meant my words, too. There wasn't any room in my heart for Emmett anymore. There hadn't been in years. I was feeling especially maudlin this evening about something that never was because . . . well, because . . . never mind. I'd figure it out when my blood alcohol had diminished.

I'd never been convinced we would have worked as a couple, even if I'd had the courage during college to tell him of my feelings. I'd more enjoyed the drama of unrequited love for an unattainable guy. Sometimes I'd spent evenings in Emmett's dorm room bed, cozy among dirty sheets that smelled of Polo and of him, watching him construct miniature stage sets of plays no one had produced in over a century. Sometimes I would pretend to do my homework while he leaned over from his roommate's top bunk and read to me long speeches from the original *Lady Audley's Secret,* acting out the different roles with varying English accents, hamming it up to make me laugh. How he'd loved those accents! I'd always return alone to my own room and lie awake until early in the morning, thinking about how special our time had been; yet my stomach would squirm over the mere idea of telling him what I felt.

At heart, all along I knew it was an utterance I would never make.

"How about I order you a burger?" Ambrose asked. When I tried to protest, he shook his head. "My treat. You need something a little more substantial than popcorn, I think."

I enjoyed the idea of my friends thinking I was drunk when I was really only the tiniest, slightest bit tipsy, though it was as much a fiction as my unrequited passion for Emmett. "You're always looking out for me, Amby. I'm going to pee," I announced. The urgency of my bladder, at least, was a feeling I couldn't deny.

Malamute's isn't a grungy place, but the toilet seats of the women's room left much to be desired. After disinfecting myself at the sink, I spent a few moments gazing at myself in the mirror again. Earlier that day in the break room, I'd thought I'd looked depleted, somehow. I still did. My oversized sweater didn't much belie that impression. With its hem nearly reaching my knees and my little pink fingertips barely poking out of the too-long sleeves, it looked as if I'd thrown the sweater in the wash but I'd been the one who shrunk. Could everyone see those blue crescent moons underneath my eyes, or were they merely something brought out by the fluorescent bulbs overhead? Did I always look so wan? Mia Farrow at her most anemic had more color than I.

The restroom door opened with a mighty creak of its hinges, admitting a rush of the back hallway exhaust from the kitchen's vents, acrid and smoky. The woman joining me was one of those professional, classy types dressed from head to toe in stylish casual wear selected from the racks of Carolina Herrera or Escada or one of the other Fifth Avenue boutiques. And what a head, too. I snuck a few looks in her direction as she leaned forward to apply a matte lipstick in a deep, deep burgundy shade. Her blond mane had been razor cut with such precision that in the airless bathroom, her hair looked as if it were blowing in a gentle tropical breeze. I could tell the color had been expertly assisted to its champagne perfection, mainly because her eyebrows were so dark. Those suckers didn't merely arch, either. They winged straight up and out in the direction of her temples. If Mr. Spock had married Linda Evangelista and the gene for pointy ears had proven recessive, this is how their daughter might have turned out.

I could picture this woman careening back in her wheeled leather chair at the end of her long workday and crossing her long, elegantly clothed legs so she might change from a pair of work-practical Taryn Rose pumps into her Kate Spades, cell phone glued to her ear as she made dinner plans at some uptown eatery. What did she do? In my imagination, I made it something that revolved around long, complicated phone calls and apple martini lunches. Perhaps an event planner? She seemed the kind of woman who could spend entire afternoons calling caterers and ordering chiffonade salads, Peking duck spring rolls with pineapple-wasabi dipping sauce, and roast racks of lamb *boulangère* by the hundreds. The kind of woman who knew what *boulangère* meant, in fact.

I hated her, I decided. Oh, I disliked thinking that, even to myself. I always disapprove of women who on principle hate other females merely because of the way they're put together, or how thin they are, or because they think the other woman is sexual competition, or whatever spurious reason they've created to justify the emotion. It's stupid. As dumb, in fact, as hating someone because of their lack of beauty or their age or skin color. Still, I hated her—although in a theoretical, intellectual way that didn't involve any actual investment of emotion at all.

I could easily picture Blondie sitting in an oxygen spa, firing a bunch of sad-looking hourly workers like me over her cell phone and laughing about it with—whoops. She'd caught me staring at her reflection. The woman pursed her lips and, in a way that left no doubt that she had, pretended she'd not noticed. I turned a deep, deep red. Pale as I am, I flush easily; it didn't take a mirror to confirm that I'd turned roughly the color of a baby new potato. The only thing I could think of to do was smile, then pretend I had something wedged in my teeth that had to be pried out using the nail of my little finger.

Classy, that.

It wasn't until the blonde turned and stalked out, disapproval wafting in her perfumed wake, that I stopped picking at imaginary spinach and regained my normal pasty color. Why in the world had I felt so suddenly inadequate in front of her? That wasn't in the least like me. I shrugged, checked my hair, and walked back down the dingy hallway to our usual table.

I could accept I wasn't wealthy enough to don her kind of duds anywhere outside a dressing room. I recognized my life wasn't about expensive hair and designer shoes and text messaging and catering. Every woman who wafted through Mercer-Iverson in the last two weeks would have hammered home that lesson to me if I'd never learned it before.

What I couldn't accept, though, was that Blondie was sitting at our table. Next to Emmett. Leaning into him, in that intimate way couples adopt when they're trying to announce to the world they're an item. I halted for a moment, stunned. The person Emmett had been waiting for—she had been that scented and pampered creature? What—why—how—when?

I turned off the journalism-student questions and stumbled forward. My Converse-clad feet seemed more unsteady than only a moment before, as if during my stopover in the restroom, somehow the bar had been loaded onto a cruise ship and set adrift on seven-foot waves. Maybe I had indulged in a little more of that amber lager than I cared to admit.

Although I hadn't spoken at all to Emmett since his entrance into the bar twenty minutes before, I studiously ignored him as I lowered myself into my chair, spine stiff. Maya raised her eyebrow. "Everything okay?"

"Fine," I replied. "Wonderful. Absolutely peachy, thanks." I pretended not to notice when Maya and Ambrose exchanged glances, instead extending my mug. "More beer please?"

I believe Ambrose would have intervened in my quest for the perfect buzz, but Clark was only too happy to grab one of the pitchers we'd ordered and give me a refill. Good old Clark! I'd already swigged down two big mouthfuls of the stuff, Clark nodding in approval and matching me gulp for gulp, when I heard Emmett clear his throat from the other end of the table. "I see we're all here." I knew he was referring to me, but I only gazed through amber depths to the bottom of my glass. I hadn't been the one who'd held up the meeting by hanging around the front door, waiting for my blond ice princess like some old hound dog hoping to be tossed a scrap from the kitchen counter. Nosiree. "I hope you don't mind," I heard him say, "but I've brought a guest to our meeting tonight. Isobel LaPlatte, these are my friends, the members of the Elizabethan Failures Society."

All of Emmett's speeches managed to sound rehearsed; this one more than others. I could picture him practicing it to himself, the way he had used to memorize long passages of the dense century-old plays of which he had been so fond— lips pursed to release the flavorless vowels of the blond girl's name. Isobel LaPlatte, indeed. It sounded fake to me.

"Charmed," I heard Isobel say. Only it came out sounding more like *chormed*. My heart sank at the accent. It was unfair that the girl should be beautiful, well-clad, *and* British. Then again, Emmett really liked his accents, damn him.

"You're from England?" Jack asked, leaning forward to gawk at the girl.

"London, surely." Maya leaned forward and put her chin in her hand, fascinated.

"West London, actually." *Erkshully.* From the emphasis she gave it, I gathered the west was supposed to outclass any other directions.

"Wicked witches come from the west too, you know," I muttered to Ambrose, soft enough so that no one else should have heard me.

"Isobel's parents sent her to Godolphin and Latymer," Emmett told us in the same manner that I always thought a car salesman might stress a model's leather interior with driver's side cold-weather seat-warmer. "And later to Oxford."

"Godolphin and Latymer's an English public school, isn't it?" Where did Maya come up with these facts? "What college at Oxford?"

"Lady Margaret Hall." *Leddy Murgret Hurl.* To listen to Isobel I had to switch on that part of my brain I used whenever I saw a new film adaptation of a Jane Austen movie. My internal translator sucked in the syllables that dropped like pearls from Isobel's superior, polished lips, and after a two-second delay whispered the interpretation to me.

"She's a fashion editor for *Charisma.*" Emmett seemed proud of this particular fact. Oh, a fashion editor. That explained lots. Peachy, absolutely peachy.

"Emmett, darling, won't you introduce me to your Losers Society chums?" *Durling. Lursers.* I was so busy envying her high-class tones that it took me a moment to realize Isobel had insulted us.

"Hey!" I protested in a growl. Ambrose reached out and put his hand on mine. I looked past Jack to where she sat, blandly unaware of how deeply she'd offended anyone. Hadn't she offended anyone else? Jack—unshaven, dressed in shabby overalls, and unaware that the wind outside had blown his thin hair awry—sat hunched over, hands between his legs, knees touching, like a kid who'd forgotten to bring a present to a classmate's birthday. Clark, whom I'd never known to be anything less than confident with women, openly gaped. Maya studied Isobel with restraint, drinking in every detail of her clothing and face, unconsciously imitating the way Isobel draped her wrist and allowed the tip of her index finger to rest ever so gracefully against her honed chin. And Ambrose—well, I didn't look at Ambrose, because I knew the warning I'd see in his eyes, if I dared.

"That's Jack Kleinsmith beside you," Emmett began, extending his hand. "He's a painter."

"Hi." Jack waved his hand and managed to spit out a single weak word. Isobel merely nodded.

"Clark is the actor of our group—can't throw a stick in New York without hitting an actor, you know."

"*Hah!*" Clark barked out a single syllable of amusement so loud that from the corner of my eye I could see Isobel rear back in her seat . . . if that well-bred, gentrified retreat qualified as rearing. Clark looked mortified at himself. He smiled nervously, ran a hand over his ponytail to smooth it, and tried pretending he wasn't there.

"Maya's next to him. She's an information broker." Maya mouthed a pleasantry, smiled, and nodded, still not looking away. "And Ambrose—well . . ."

"Ambrose works in a coffee shop." Ambrose spoke for himself, without hesitation or excuse.

"He's a fantastic playwright, though," Emmett declared. It sounded as though he were awarding a consolation prize.

"Ambrose hasn't had a play produced in years and happens to sling frappucinos in a coffee shop. Nice to meet you, Isobel."

"And Nan—"

The moment Ambrose had spoken, I'd decided to take the same tack. I didn't want to hear the apology in Emmett's voice when he attempted to fit me in a neat little pigeonhole and explain me away. "Hi," I said, looking directly at Isobel for the first time. "I'm Nan. I'm a Cheer Facilitator with Mercer-Iverson. I'm sure you've heard of it." I couldn't discern a flicker of recognition in Isobel's eyes. I didn't think the bogus job title would spark anything, but I thought the name of the department store or at least the memory of our meeting in the ladies' room might.

"Nan is our little literature lover." I cringed at Emmett's justification of my life. "Former English major."

"American literature, actually," I reminded him, before Isobel could decide we had a common bond in the letters of her homeland.

"She's our little Thoreau, our Nan."

I wanted to smack him.

"Thoreau?" Isobel's reaction was polite, but put off, as if she thought Thoreau might be some kind of venereal disease.

I tried to pretend I wasn't really listening, but Maya spoke up. "Thoreau was a nineteenth-century writer who rejected the notion that life was all about working. He decided to live as simply as possible, on as little money, so he bought a cabin by Walden pond for twenty-eight dollars and worked only enough for his most basic needs, so he could spend the rest of his time understanding his life and the world around him." Is that what people really thought about me? That I was spending my life in introspection by the edge of some vast urban cesspool? Admittedly, reading *Walden* had been one of the big formative experiences of my undergraduate career—that and the massive crush I'd had on the blue-eyed professor who taught the course—but had I ever, at any point, mentioned Thoreau to these guys? Had I ever made an explicit connection between my minimalist lifestyle and the mighty Thoreau? Or had my friends fabricated a polite little fiction about me to justify my spotty employment record?

"How is that little apartment, Nan? Nan lives in the strangest apartment you've ever seen," he told Isobel. "It's over a bakery, and—"

"We've only had three murders on the block this week, thanks," I said with cheer that was both forced and feigned.

"Nan's always joking," Emmett said. I couldn't tell if he was smiling or gritting his teeth.

"And I nearly helped kill one of the Iversons of Mercer-Iverson today, too."

"Charming friends you have, darling," commented Isobel. *Chorming.* "I can't at all see why they're losers." For a flash I wanted to smack her, too, but at least Isobel's hostility didn't arrive in the form of apologies. How could I have forgotten Emmett's need to put down his friends around a new woman?

I downed what remained of my lager and held out my mug for more. Jack, however, was too engrossed in stealing glances at Emmett's new fling to oblige, so I poured for myself. "They're not losers. They're Elizabethan Failures," Emmett explained. "We all are. It's a society." When Isobel merely assembled her features until they were as blank as a birthday card for a boss hated by his office workers, Emmett hauled out one of his favorite old crusty speeches and put it to eloquent use. It was reserved usually for curious Malamute's patrons and occasional Society guests; my brothers both had complained of having to sit through it on more than one occasion. "To explain what an Elizabethan Failure is," he began, "let us contrast it first with what may appear to be its natural opposite: the Elizabethan Success. Take, for example, that all-around Renaissance man, Sir Philip Sydney."

"Who?" Isobel looked as if she was attempting to remember if perhaps she had run into Sir Philip at the Ascot.

Emmett hastened to explain. "Sydney was the very embodiment of grace, courtesy, and heroic virtue, the fine flower and ornament of the English renaissance. He was also a scholar, a poet, and a man of action, who died young in battle. Legend has it that in his last moments he insisted that the cup of water offered him should be given instead to a dying soldier nearby. Such is an Elizabethan Success." The others raised their glasses of lager in a toast. I grudgingly followed. Emmett was in fine oratory form now—it was a shame to deny him his due.

"An Elizabethan Failure, on the other hand, is a sprightly offshoot whose contrariety from an Elizabethan Success is simply a degree of artful realization. The Elizabethan Failure writes poetry, drama, and letters—yes—but he doubtless will never know the joyful stamp of a printer's press. The Elizabethan Failure may engage in battle, but the blow that fells him will most likely be an accidental one. And the cup of water so gallantly offered will, at the last moment, slip from his weak grasp, thus rendering two people thirsty instead of one." He paused to raise his mug again. "To the Elizabethan Failure!"

"Hear hear!" we all cried, me less enthusiastically than the others.

It was right at that moment that one of the bar guys slapped down the dinner Ambrose had ordered for me—an enormous burger stacked to castle-like proportions with cheddar, bacon, onions, and horseradish sauce, surrounded by a veritable moat of fries. When I looked around in embarrassment, Emmett smiled at me indulgently. Isobel merely curled her lip. If that dame was a food Nazi, I was going to have a fit. "Do you have any salads?" she asked.

"Sure, lady," said the bartender. "What kind of dressing? We got French, ranch, Italian, lowfat bleu cheese, and thousand island."

"No dressing. Just endive, please, with mandarin orange slices."

The bartender only stared at her. Perhaps he thought she'd called Malamute's a dive? And if so, would he tell her off? Please?

"They don't have endive here," Emmett told her at last, before taking over the ordering. "She'll have a side salad. No dressing."

I caught the bartender's arm before he retreated. "My dinner is so huge. I'm not going to be able to eat all of it," I told him at a volume a shade louder than normal, so it would carry. "Could you bring me a box?"

I cut off a third of the hamburger and delicately placed the larger portion in the polystyrene container he provided, then lifted my plate and made sure everyone could see me scooping all but a small portion of the greasy fries inside. I was starved, and this was free food, but there was no way I was going to chow down on a three-quarter pound burger in front of Twiggy. I'd take the rest home and eat it the minute the door shut behind me. I was well practiced at this particular deceit; I used it on those infrequent occasions I'd score a dinner date, so the guy wouldn't think that he'd be saddled for the evening with a hungry-hungry hippo.

What was left of my hamburger would give me only four mouthfuls. I snapped off two of them like a piranha offered Amazon-dipped tourist fingers and followed them up with alternate mouthfuls of lager and fries while the others began asking questions. How long had Isobel and Emmett been dating? Three months? That long? Emmett, you dog, where have you been hiding her? How long had she been in the States? A year? Did she have any family here? Only some distant Greek cousins? Isobel's replies were largely monosyllabic. When I wasn't regarding the steam still issuing from the seam of my take-home box, I snuck looks at Emmett, so proud of his latest catch.

"I certainly hope we'll see more of you," said Maya, beaming. I could have pointed out that Maya's accent had become unusually clipped and laden with consonants, like Madonna after her move to the UK, but I refrained.

"Oh, you will." Emmett grinned, and reached across the table for Isobel's hands. "Should we tell them, love?"

Even though I'd moments before downed a scalding French fry, my stomach went icy cold. "Emmett and I are pre-engaged," Isobel announced without prelude or fanfare. Cue delighted babble and effusive congratulations. They lasted for about ten seconds, and then vanished as everyone tried to absorb the news. During the stunned silence, Isobel stared at her platinum watch. "Darling, you did say we'd go dancing tonight?"

Emmett, Ambrose, Maya, and me. We were the original quartet who formed the Elizabethan Failure Society six years ago. Emmett was the expert on Dion Boucicault, Shaw, and Wilde; Ambrose wrote plays; Maya covered the classics and philosophy, and I was literature. Other members had joined as we met them after college. We'd had actors and art historians and novelists and artists and all manner of people who couldn't afford to practice what they'd been educated in, but the core four of us had always met, month after month, to catch up, to drink, and to share. And now . . . My plate was empty. I contemplated my fingernails for dessert.

"We'll go dancing in a bit, darling," Emmett said. "I still have some catching-up to do." They exchanged smiles.

Isobel turned her long, lovely neck until she faced Jack. Aware of the scrutiny, he cleared his throat. Her lips parted. "You're a painter, then?"

"Ah, yeah, that is, yes ma'am, I mean, yes," Jack stammered. He toyed with his paper basket of popcorn, then suddenly put his hands back into his lap.

"How fortunate. I've bedroom walls that want a redo," she remarked. "Are you available?"

"He's not that kind of painter, love," Emmett told her, laughing lightly to smooth over the faux pas.

Damn right Jack wasn't that kind of painter. I waited for his affronted reply, mentally urging him to give it to her good. "That's okay," he stuttered out at last. "I can do that kind of painting too."

The hell! The absolute, bloomin', bloody hell! Barely able to see with my blood pressure elevated to the boiling point, I rose to my unsteady feet. All eyes turned to me. "I . . ." Really, I should have planned what I was going to say in advance. I wanted it to be witty. I wanted it to be cutting.

What came out was neither. "I gotta go." I grabbed my fleece pullover and wrestled with armholes that seemed to have disappeared. My head emerged a moment later. Everyone still stared at me, save Emmett. He seemed absorbed by his beer. "Em." I addressed him directly, to make him look up. "I'm really happy for your pre-engagement. I'm sure it will be a *Masterpiece Theatre* wedding with vicars and choirboys and . . . stuff. Here's hoping the two of you will enjoy a happy pre-marriage. I mean, marriage." I hefted my mug into the air and waited for the others to follow suit. They did, although slowly. Then I downed what was left of my lager. "And now I have to go. Enjoy your *dornsing*. I mean, dancing."

I grabbed my box. I might not even wait to get home before I started to scarf down the fries. If it wasn't too wet outside, I'd eat them on my walk home. "Lovely to meet you, pip-pip," I said in Isobel's ear on the way out. Then, to Emmett, I added, "She's a keeper, Em. A fine bit of stuff, wot?" Our glances met for only a moment, and then his blue eyes slid to Isobel. He was already preparing excuses for my behavior.

"Why don't I walk you home?" Ambrose suddenly was standing behind me, his leather jacket already on and his scarf wrapped around his neck.

"Should I come?" Maya groped for her coat, her voice concerned, but relaxed when Ambrose shook his head.

"She's a little light-headed. Been on her feet all day, and she's had a little too much to—" I didn't wait to hear the rest of what he had to say. I was already out the door, my face and ears stunned by the cold. Snow pattered against my dry skin, each flake stinging like a small, smart slap. Behind me, I heard the door swing open almost immediately. "Wait up!"

"I don't like you apologizing for me, too," I complained. The carryout box squeaked when I opened its nubs and helped myself to a fry.

"You were a little bit rude. And you're not half as drunk as you're pretending to be."

"Me, rude! Didn't you hear how *awful* Eliza Doolittle was to Jack?" I couldn't stand still and argue. I needed motion and activity. Chunks of salt bounced around my boots as I started to stomp down the street. I nearly collided with two students exiting Hi-Fi wearing only long-sleeved T-shirts. Idiots. "And no one said anything!" I half-shouted, picking up my train of thought a moment later. "Not one of you!"

"Sweetie, you know how Emmett is with women. It's not the first time he's been engaged."

"Pre-engaged!" I shouted. "Pre-engaged to Posh Spice! What in hell is a pre-engagement, anyway? Engagement is supposed to be the *pre*-part!"

"He was engaged to Kristen—"

"And she was a bitch."

"And then to . . . what was her name?"

"Catriona, the dumb bunny who thought it was sooooo wonderful a coincidence that Jesus managed to be born on Christmas day so people could celebrate two things at once during the holiday season?"

Ambrose laughed. "Gawd. His women are so ridiculous. Why do you *care?*"

"Because—" We continued our brisk walk up the street while I thought about that one. The cold was making my teeth chatter. "Because, because, because, because, because of the wonderful things he does," I finished.

I knew the answer was lame. So did Ambrose. He stopped me and hugged himself tight to keep warm. "Seriously, Nan. Because what? Do you still care for him?"

"No!"

"Then why? Tell me."

I stood there, unable to conjure up an adequate response. "You three are all I've got sometimes," I told him. "The only sane things, anyway. Everyone's moving on and leaving me behind."

"I'd never leave you behind." At that moment I couldn't bear to look in Ambrose's eyes. I knew they'd be too serious for my mood. Too yearning. For a moment more we stood under the flickering and gently percussive front light of some other bar that wasn't our Malamute's, not saying a word. As if by mutual agreement, we started walking again.

"I really don't care for him anymore," I repeated. It felt true, but for some reason I still resented Isobel's intrusion on our set. "Not beyond the standard-issue set of caring responses, anyway."

"I'm sure you don't."

I suspected Ambrose was humoring me. "Anyway. Here's the Cock." I gestured to the bright neon rooster that marked one of the many Avenue A boy bars. Music poured out through the open front door. "You can go join your fellow Friends of Dorothy if you want."

Ambrose chuckled again, this time with a little more weariness. "Sweetie, I've told you oodles of times, I'm not gay."

"Oodles!" I crowed, triumphant. "You said *oodles!* That's *so gay!*"

"It was an ironic employment of the word *oodles*. I used to write. I can do that. Besides," he said gently. "I said I was walking you home, and I am."

"But you're freezing," I pointed out. "What happened to all that body fat?"

"You've got cocoa at your place, right?" I nodded. "That'll do me. And we can reheat the rest of that dinner you're pretending you don't want."

"If you think you're getting your hands on my burger, gay boy, you've got another think coming." I laughed when he whipped off his scarf and flicked it at my butt. "Stop it!" I shrieked.

"You stop!"

Although we were older by a few years than many of the kids prowling the boulevard of bars, from the way we loudly splashed our way down the glistening sidewalks, no one ever would have guessed it.

Panda Pagoda
(lunch for two, including egg drop soup, egg rolls, ice cream, and a carryout order of sweet-and-sour wontons: free; pack of Listerine breath strips: free; newspaper: free; cab fare to the Upper West Side: free.)

"Wrap up what's left of the Mongolian beef, the shrimp with cashews, the Hunan lamb—no wait, she ate all of that." He lifted up two more lids, one with both hands, to see what was left inside. "And these pan-fried noodles. Do you want the rice, baby? Wrap up the rice too, would you? And don't forget that the young lady has a take-out order." The waitress nodded and with all the practiced ease of someone shuffling a pea under walnut halves, swiftly maneuvered all the dishes onto her rolling cart and wheeled them away. "Eat your fortune cookie."

"Thank you, Daddy." It had taken my father a few years, but he'd learned that if he outright wrote me a check I wouldn't cash it. If he hid money in my coat pockets, he'd find it tucked under his Palm's cover at our next lunch, or returned to his apartment via the U.S. mail. In the last months, however, he'd discovered that if he took me out to lunch or dinner and ordered too many dishes for two people with normal appetites, he could send me home with food enough for several days. He got the satisfaction of knowing I was eating. I kept my dignity. And the managers of all the Chinese restaurants had the satisfaction of appropriating a considerable chunk of my dad's American Express credit line. "What's different with you?" I asked him.

He was too busy tucking away his receipt to look up. "Nothing, why? Read your fortune, baby. Let's hear what it says."

"Something about you's been bugging me for the last hour." I sighed and cracked open the vanilla-smelling cookie once I'd wrestled it from its crinkly cellophane. "*You will be reunited with good friends who will guide you to happiness . . . in bed.*"

"Spare a father a heart attack from fortunes like yours, baby. Wipe your mouth. No, the other side. That's right. Let's see." He split open his cookie with a single hand and tossed the remnants into his soup bowl. "*You may catch more flies with honey than vinegar.*"

"In bed," I added automatically. "No, honestly, what is it about you? There's a difference."

The waitress rattled back right then and lifted from her cart a plastic shopping bag full of white boxes printed with red dragons, the plastic handles twisted into a tight knot. On top of it she placed a smaller bag containing only one hefty box, warmer than the leftovers. "Have a Merry Christmas," she said with a smile.

That was our cue. Lunch was over. Our topics of conversation had been the same as ever. He spent his portion complaining about faculty politics within the university's history department and about an honor code violation, while I spent my time telling him funny stories about my latest job—namely, my three-week incarceration in Who-ville. Dad and I always kept the conversation light so we didn't find ourselves mired down in the questions that might cause friction between us: on my side, *When are you going to get a girlfriend already?* and on his, *When are you going to get a real job?* It wasn't until we both had slid out from the overstuffed comfort of the Panda Pagoda's round booths that I pinpointed what was unusual about my father's appearance.

"You shaved! That's it!" For as long as I could remember, my father had sported a scruffy beard, more pepper than salt. It had clung like a weed to places where most men trimmed their beards, like his cheekbones and the lower reaches of his neck. Now the hair jungle had been whacked away, reducing it to longish sideburns and a tidy little goatee. Enough was left to trick my eye into thinking the beard hadn't gone away, but I realized I was looking at the pink skin of his cheeks for the first time since I was six.

He seemed a little embarrassed to admit it. "I might have spruced up a little. We'll share a cab," he informed me before we stepped out through the restaurant's front door into the midday noise and congestion outside. It was less a suggestion than a command. I knew he planned to drop me where I needed to be so I could save on car fare. "Carry those handles firmly, baby," he said when I sauntered out behind him, staggering under the weight of all that Chinese food. "And put them in the refrigerator first thing when you get home, so that they don't spoil. You might want to freeze what you're not going to eat right away. The average shelf life . . ."

"Dad," I interrupted, shouting over the roar of a passing truck. "I know how to freeze leftovers."

The rest of his lecture on home economy was lost on me when he raised his hand and flagged down a cab. Forget his Ph.D., forget his distinguished teaching honors, forget his tenure with Columbia's history department. Cab hailing is where Dad's real talent lies. Were my father ever lost on a Himalayan glacier, far from any village, the rest of his climbing team lost to avalanches and frostbite, his own brain addled from lack of oxygen, and he managed to raise his right hand into the air, Nepal's only big yellow taxi would suddenly loom up out of a crevice, headlights blazing through the mists, driver ready to take my father to the nearest Irish pub. "Get in," he ordered, holding the door open. "Tell the driver where you need to go, honey."

I ducked under his arm and gave the cabbie an address on West 88th. "Are you wearing *cologne?*" I wanted to know. I'd inhaled a mouthful of the stuff during our brief moment playing London Bridge. Usually Dad had that . . . well, *dad* smell. Kind of a mix of twice-worn shirts and a trace of shaving cream, sometimes with Old Spice thrown in on special occasions.

"Avoid Columbus Circle if you can," my dad ordered the driver, once again not answering my question as he slid next to me on the seat. He rattled off a long list of directions that would get us both where we were going, closed the door, and rearranged the Tower of Babel I'd constructed out of my takeaway boxes. "You should keep the center of gravity low. That way they'll be less likely to tip."

"Hello." I knocked at his skull with my knuckles. "Anyone home?"

"Don't be mean to your poor old daddy, Nan honey."

"I'm not being mean! I was only wondering what's up with—oh my God, is that a new coat?" It had to be. It was made out of wool! My dad had been such a friend of synthetic fibers that the last time he'd been near wool was at a fourth-grade excursion to a petting zoo. My bags rustled as I leaned over, seized the lapel, and looked inside at the label. "Jhane Barnes?"

"Sweetie."

It was too late. I flipped over his tie. "Ferragamo?" His shirt collar was crisp, ironed, and bore no trace of frayed edges. "Ralph Lauren?"

"Honey. Ow!"

His head banged against the window as I wrenched up his pants cuff—a cuff! On my dad's pants!—and looked at the bottom of his shoe. "Good God! Kenneth Cole!"

"Baby!"

"Don't baby me! What's going on?" On instinct I ran my fingers through his hair. "You're wearing *gel!*"

"Not gel," he said, his tone stiff. With hurt dignity he

smoothed down his tie so it lay flat on his shirt. "Gel is too stiff. I apply a texturizing pomade after my morning shower."

My father could have admitted to a secret drinking problem and I wouldn't have batted an eye. He could have confessed to a love of Internet porn and I wouldn't have thought twice. Nothing in the world, however, could have prepared me for the shock of hearing those two words from his mouth: *texturizing pomade*. "Baby, when a man reaches a certain age, he has to think about his skin and hair care regimen or else . . ."

"Okay. Stop it. Stop it right there," I told him, totally aghast. "You are not my father. My father's skin and hair care regimen consists of shampooing twice a week with Head and Shoulders and using the suds to wash his face. My father's last pair of shoes were a pair of decade-old penny loafers with a hole in the sole—a pair of loafers my poor late mother bought him from Land's End. My *real* father's idea of fashion is a grey cardigan with brown slacks and blue socks."

"Don't tell such lies about your daddy." Dad sported an expression I recognized. I'd worn it myself on a few occasions when I was the victim of a particularly bad haircut and still had to make appearances in public despite a personal conviction that I should spend the following month at home with a pillowcase over my head, comforting myself with Cheetos. It was an expression that combined wounded self-respect, fear, and pride. "I never once in my life wore blue socks with brown slacks. I've never owned blue socks. Driver, don't go down here, take . . . well, hell."

We turned down the forbidden street so abruptly that I was flung back sideways. Dad cursed—whether at me or at the cab driver, I couldn't tell. "Well, well, well," I told him. "What's gotten you so interested in . . ." I gasped an honest-to-God, lung-sucking, long gasp of understanding. "Are you seeing someone? Are you seeing a *woman?* Who is she?"

"I'm not seeing a woman." His hands roamed over his texturized hair, fluffing it back into shape.

"Then who gave you this makeover?"

"It's not a makeover," he said. "It's a make-better."

I stared at him. "You're a pod person, aren't you," I stated. "You're like, a pod person from the planet Fashionista and you've planted little pod spores in my shrimp with cashews and tomorrow I'll wake up and find I'm a pod person too with a deep and immediate hunger for a facial."

Dad ignored my jibes. His eyes flicked over my forehead, and then back to my cheeks and chin. "A facial might do you good, Nan. A good moisturizer would keep your skin from drying out. You're so fair you should find one with a good SPF for daily use, actually. And eye cream, tapped on below your lower eyelid, would reduce those circles."

My hands flew to my face. My skin was indeed dry and fair. And damn! I *knew* people could see those circles! "Where did you pick up all this stuff?"

"I'm an educated man." He spoke with a hint of defensiveness. "I can read! And I ask questions at the stores."

"Has Mitchell seen this . . . this . . . this transformation?"

"We went to Barney's together last week, but I don't think he's seen the goatee." Dad leaned over in an attempt to see his facial hair in the driver's rear mirror. "I think it looks good, don't you?"

I did, but I wasn't committing myself just yet. "You guys went to *Barney's?* Did Mitchell pick out that coat?" My older brother Mitchell was the sloppiest dresser of the family. Maybe Barney's had stimulated his dormant gay fashion sense.

"No. I did."

"It's worth more than all the rest of your old wardrobe combined."

"It's an investment piece."

I could tell from his tone of voice that I'd vaulted past

wounding his pride and was venturing dangerously close to attacking it with a jackhammer, so I backed off a little. I really wanted to know where he was picking up terms like *investment piece,* though. "You really do look very nice," I told him. "You look different—not wildly different. Different enough that you don't really notice how good you look." His lips pressed together. "No, no, I mean, you look *good,* but it's not an in-your-face kind of thing. It's subtle. I like it."

I had to sit through a very long pause before he graced me with a simple, "Thank you, baby."

"You're welcome." I looked at my made-better father for a minute or two. For one of the rare moments in his life, he seemed tongue-tied and uncertain of what to say. "What about Brody? Has he seen all this?"

"You know Brody."

The three words summed up a lot. Yeah, I knew Brody. My younger brother was so busy with his family and his career that if we saw him once a year, we considered ourselves lucky. "He's still coming to New Year's Day dinner, right?"

"I assume. I talked to him on my cell phone yesterday and he sounded like he'd be there. Kylie has some kind of croup, poor kid."

I was staring at Dad again. "Good God. You have a cell phone now?"

"Honey."

"Are you *sure* you're not seeing someone? You know I don't mind. I know Mitchell wouldn't mind. Brody would, but don't let him tell you not to get on with your life, because I think . . ."

"Baby," he said.

"I'm just saying . . ."

"We're here."

Oh. I looked through the foggy window. Sure enough, we

were sitting outside the Moroccan. "Swanky place," my dad commented. "Who do you know here?"

From anyone else I might have taken the comment as a little bit of an insult, but Dad seemed genuinely curious. "A boss," I said. "Kind of."

"Boss? At his apartment? In the middle of the afternoon?" He puffed out his cheeks and blew out a column of air. "Nan, you're going to give your daddy a heart attack, making him drive you to your . . . your nooner. Have you thought this through? Don't be having an affair with your boss. It won't help you climb the ladder of success."

"Daddy! I'm not!"

"It's not very good practice to put yourself into situations that can be misinterpreted," he said, only slightly appeased. "Do you have pepper spray?"

"The guy's old, and he's an invalid," I told him. "I've been reading to him and it's paid off. He's going to hook me up with a babysitting job for his grandson, which is spot on what I need, since the Who gig ends day after tomorrow."

I have to give my dad credit. At the mention of my job's end, his hand automatically groped for the jacket pocket where he kept both wallet and checkbook. Before he made the fatal mistake of withdrawing either, his fingers quickly walked, spider-like, right back down to his lap. "I hope that works out for you then, honey," he told me with admirable restraint. I tried to gather my multiple packages so I wouldn't have to see the worry in his eyes. "Now, make sure you take the bags by the *handles*. And get them into a refrigerator as soon as possible. And don't let them spoil." I might not have liked the notion of taking his money, but I did love when my daddy fussed over me. A few moments later, when my feet were safely planted on the concrete, he stuck his head out the window and issued his final instruction. "And listen, if he dares to lay a hand on you, don't be afraid to kick him in the uglies."

"Yes sir." I don't think he heard my agreement. As the window hummed back up, I could already catch the sound of him rattling off instructions on how the driver might best avoid Broadway traffic on the way up to 116th Street.

Apartment 1907, The Moroccan
(one copy of *On Her Majesty's Secret Crevice*: $0.99; lost pride: too high a cost to mention)

" '*So, my saucy vixens.*' *The secret agent cleared his deep-voiced throat with potent meaning while the square-cut diamonds of his gold cuff links sparkled in the red-wine glow of the tropical Fiji sunset. 'Are you fine young fillies aficionados of the socks-first approach to a fine fellow divesting himself of his Savile Row finest, or . . .* ' *The agent's masculine lips curved, catlike, into a supple smile of heady promise. 'Shall I remove my trousers?*' "

Mr. Andrew Iverson shook his head and interrupted my recitation. "I cannot abide a man who first removes his trousers. I find it unseemly, a gentleman lounging about in little else other than his socks and garters. What do you think, my dear?"

I thought it was a little bizarre we were having this conversation at all, that's what I thought. "From the nude-guy sightings I've had in my apartment, I assumed your entire gender was born with black feet and ankles," I deadpanned.

"Oh my." For a minute I worried I'd shocked the old fellow, but when his chest started jiggling up and down and a soft whuffing noise issued from his mouth, I realized I'd amused him. Good. A couple of weeks stuck in this hole, and I'd need a little amusement, too. "Oh, my!" he wheezed, until I handed him a tissue.

Not that I wouldn't want to live in such a hole, mind you. *Chez Iverson* made my apartment look like the outhouse from *Li'l Abner;* all I needed was the crescent moon on my front door. The living room here had been decorated long ago with dark wood paneling. Everything was dark, in fact—the paneling on the walls, the planks of wood on the ceiling, the furniture, the mounted antlers and swords and deer head and other accoutrements of manly aggression. All of them somehow made the place look like a dressed movie set for a private gentlemen's club, or maybe John Steed's bachelor flat from *The Avengers.* Mr. Iverson's only concession to the casual nature of our afternoons was not to wear a necktie; the plaster cast beneath his tweed jacket made a considerable lump.

Maybe it was because of the dreary setting that I really enjoyed making Mr. Iverson laugh. "Okay, back to the story," I said. "Mind if I—?" I pointed to the bowl of the sweet-and-sour wontons I'd brought for his lunch. I helped myself from the take-out box when he shook his head. " *'Långbyxorna!'* moaned innocent Annika, the blonde seductress with cheeks like rosy apples. 'Strumporna!' cried sophisticated Hedwig, the red-headed Jezebel with the come-hither bedroom eyes. Then, simultaneously, 'Bege två!'* They're Swedish, you see," I explained to him. "Vixens are always Swedish in these novels. I collect pulps, you see. It was an early sixties thing, Swedish women who could barely control their own hormones. If you see a Swedish sexpot in pulp fiction, you can bet there'll be sex after the raclette."

"Ah, but I do believe raclette is Swiss, not Swedish."

"Meatballs then." I was about to recommence reading when Mr. Iverson cleared his throat. His nurse had abandoned the soaps on TV to perform a cursory check on her patient. I nodded understanding, turned the page of the larger book enclosing the paperback pulp I'd picked up on a table outside a used-book store, and began reciting. *"My sister, Mrs. Joe, with black hair and eyes, had such a prevailing redness of skin that I sometimes used to wonder whether it was possible she washed herself with a nutmeg-grater instead of soap."* It was a description that could have applied as well to the day nurse, with her frizzy hair, sour expression, and her ruddy, raw complexion. I patiently read aloud from the leather-bound edition of Dickens while she took his temperature and sniffed at my offering of Chinese food. At last she waddled once more to the den and *All My Children.*

No sooner had the door shut behind her than Mr. Iverson leaned forward and in a hushed undertone hissed, "That woman is a spy!"

We'd covered this territory the previous times I'd visited. "I don't think anyone wants to spy on you," I reassured him.

"My dear, you've no idea how many younger family members would love to hear an official medical opinion that I'm unsuited for work. They're like wolves. All of them—the Mercers, the Iversons, the Mercer-hyphen-Iversons, the Iverson-hyphen-Mercers—to see me gone they'd all give their left—pardon me for the phrase, my dear—orb of manhood. Even the ladies." I'm not usually one who takes a great deal of pleasure in another person's paranoia, but I can't deny I got a kick whenever Mr. Iverson got excited enough to let down his gentleman's guard and let loose with the oaths like "orb of manhood." It gave me the heady sensation of being in a West Point locker room, circa 1892.

The doorbell rang. When I made a move to rise, Mr. Iverson motioned me to stay still. "Let the nurse get it. Nurse! As if I need nursing! I've never had a day's illness in my life! I told my cousin I'd rather be taken out to pasture and have a rifle placed to my head than endure the patently false concerns of someone who—ah, thank you, Margarita. What a treasure you are!" he called out as the nurse trundled by. Only one more peep of outrage passed his lips. "Nurse, indeed!"

While he muttered, I closed the larger book firmly around

On Her Majesty's Secret Crevice. Nothing against Dickens, but there was no sense in giving away the old man's secret that he preferred my brand of literature to his own. Particularly to family. The fellow who wandered in behind Margarita certainly bore the family resemblance. The nose that seemed scythelike on the older Iverson looked merely slightly hooked on the younger. Though Mr. Andrew's 'do was silver and tamed with a comb, and while the younger Iverson possessed a few wavy inches of black fuzz adding to his already considerable height, both generations had equally thick hair. They were both tall and angular, and ever so slightly hunched in their posture. Watching them embrace was like witnessing Dorian Gray hugging his own portrait.

They definitely were related; the younger version of old Mr. Andrew flopped down on the sofa and immediately put his Converse All Stars on the oak coffee table as if he'd done it a hundred times before. Was he Mr. Iverson's son? Very probably. It made sense that the father of the grandson I'd be babysitting would want to interview me. I checked out the young guy as he removed his leather jacket. With his thick horn-rimmed specs, wild hair, and stubbly face, he seemed the type of guy I sometimes saw haunting the back corners of coffee shops grading student papers or hunkering over a book printed with actual footnotes. Good-looking, if you like those offbeat types. And I surely did. "Colm is an artist," Mr. Iverson explained.

"Painter," said Colm, sitting up and putting his feet on the floor. I liked him immediately. Painter? Couldn't resist them. Looked like he listened to alternative radio? Oh yeah. Totally wrong for me in that underpaid, under-washed way? One hundred percent, you betcha! That's why I found myself wishing I'd met him at Malamute's instead of over a job interview.

"We've only just managed to bring him back into the Mercer-Iverson fold after a short bout of personal liberty."

"Short and decidedly impoverished." Colm cracked a grin

that exposed a row of slightly crooked upper teeth. So maybe he wasn't underpaid. I still found the guy attractive. "It is a sincere pleasure to meet you. Nan . . . am I correct? The old man here has told me about you."

Shaking Colm's outstretched hand was a little like parking an economy car in an airplane hanger. His fingers alone had to be six inches long. The guy had artist's hands, pianist's hands, the kind of hands that could stretch round a cantaloupe. I had Mickey Mouse hands—round palms, stubby fingers. This was an employment meeting, I reminded myself. Despite my businesslike resolution, I still couldn't help but notice he wore no wedding ring on his other hand. Small wonder the guy needed a babysitter, going back to work in the family business after a stab at creative independence. "Absolutely. Nan is absolutely correct. Yes, absolutely." Ouch. Already I was babbling like an idiot. Business, I reminded myself. This was supposed to be business!

"Have I made my daily inquiry concerning your fracture?" Colm asked his dad. Even his way of speaking echoed the older Iverson; it was slightly formal, slightly clipped. Though the accent was decidedly American, it sounded as if he read from some *Brideshead Revisited* script.

"Oh, it's still quite, quite broken," Mr. Iverson assured him. Colm nodded, then smiled at me. "Young Nan has been quite the Florence Nightingale. She's been reading to me."

"Delightful." It takes some kind of guy to make a declaration like that without sounding totally like a wine critic. Or gay, if the two aren't redundant.

Colm smiled; Mr. Iverson smiled. I blinked uncomfortably under their twin scrutinies and finally cleared my throat. "Maybe we should get down to business," I suggested in what I hoped was a professional manner.

"You're direct!" Colm chuckled. I liked his throaty laugh, but in the awkward pause that followed, he didn't seem to want to take the lead. Perhaps he was as inexperienced at hiring an *au pair* as I was at being one.

Fine. I could show him how direct I was. I'd take charge of everything. It would be a pleasant change from being at the mercy of small-minded idiots like DeeDee Camillo. "Do you want to talk about rates?" Was I being too abrupt? I thought I saw Colm blink at my question. Rushing to reassure him, I said, "We can talk about payment later if you want, but let me say I believe you'll find my fees competitive and commensurate with my experience."

"Oh. That's only fair, I suppose." His words sounded quizzical. "Are you . . . very experienced, then?"

"Why sure! I mean, the last three weeks alone I've handled . . ." How many kids daily passed through the turnstiles of Mercer-Iverson's Who-ville? I looked in Mr. Iverson's direction for guidance, but he didn't seem to be following the conversation. "Hundreds? So yeah, I'd say I know what I'm doing."

"I should say so!" said Colm, blinking rapidly at first, then nodding.

Great. I was getting him on my side. I could tell from how his teeth glinted in a grin. "I didn't prepare much of a résumé, but I've brought some references who can tell you I'm the best." While I continued talking, I reached into my bag and pulled out the list. "They'll tell you I'm friendly, but not a pushover. I believe in setting limits. In case you're wondering, I don't spank."

"Good." Colm took the paper I'd slid across the coffee table. "I must draw the line at spanking."

"I'm glad to hear it." The interview was a little unorthodox, but it was going great. "No spanking whatsoever."

"I suppose caning's out, as well?"

Mr. Iverson had been looking from one of us to the other and back again, but at Colm's question he pulled open his mouth in outrage. I was one step ahead of the guy. "Oh, absolutely. You didn't *want* caning, did you? That's a little extreme."

I felt better when he assured me he did not. "What other

qualifications do you have, Nan?" Colm used a finger to push his glasses up the bridge of his nose, a gesture that charmed me instantly. Hoo boy, did he ever have a nice smile.

"I always show up on time. I'm a stickler for punctuality. After this week I'm available whenever you need me. Anytime after the first of the year, actually. Only not New Year's Day. I host a gig for family and friends at my place that day. Oh, and I'm a stickler for washing hands. I hope that's not a problem. I've got a germ phobia."

"Oh no, no, I suppose you would have, in your profession." That struck me as an odd statement. "Now. About your . . . rates?"

"I'd prefer an hourly fee, at least to begin with. We could negotiate a flat fee per day after that, if we're both happy with the situation."

One of his nails rapped against Colm's front teeth. "Hmmmm."

He sounded doubtful. I didn't want to lose him. "Of course, it would all depend on what you need me to take care of. How big a boy are we talking, eight? Nine?" I took a guess at the kid's age. Colm didn't look any older than me. "I don't have much in the way of experience with over twelve."

"Who does, Nan? Who among us does?"

Again, the reply was strange enough that I paused to study him a moment. Was he making fun of me? I felt uneasy, as if I somehow was the butt of someone's joke. "Nan," I heard Mr. Iverson interject. "My dear . . ."

"Old man?" Colm spoke in that choked half-grave manner people use when they're trying not to break out into laughter. "I feel compelled to give you credit. You know how to find the cutest hookers."

"Excuse me?" I can't say I've ever stood beneath a shower massage nozzle spewing lava and brimstone, but I imagine it feels a bit like the scalding flush that poured from my neck down to my toes.

"Nan," repeated old Mr. Iverson. "For the life of me, I cannot imagine under what misapprehension the pair of you are laboring, but—"

If Mr. Iverson thought I was *that* desperate for cash, he had another think coming. "You told me you wanted me to take care of your grandson! I was trying—I thought—*babysitting!*—I'm *not* a—good God!"

He patted his hands against an invisible pillow of air to simmer me down. "Colm is my grandson, and as childishly as he can behave, he's no more in need of babysitting than I am." His lips pursed with displeasure in the direction of Margarita and the den before he resumed. "You're both of an age. I was hoping for more of a mutual meeting of kindred spirits, as it were, than—"

Already my mind was zipping a dozen miles ahead, though. Mr. Iverson had been trying to set me up with Colm? And I'd—oh hell's bells! As if at the scene of a brutal traffic accident, part of me wanted with ghoulish fascination to pick over the bloody remnants of our conversation to see how bad it had been, while the other half wanted to run away shrieking.

I was two of the most miserable women in town. "Oh God," I mumbled, clutching the book on my lap. It was my mantra for the next half-minute. "Oh God. Oh God. Oh God."

"Nan." Mr. Iverson tried to sound gentle.

"It's all right." Colm was still grinning at his joke, his marvelous, marvelous joke at my expense. Oh, ha ha ha. Very funny, that joke. "I'm seventy-five percent sure you haven't been with hundreds and hundreds of guys in the last three weeks."

What did that mean? I wasn't pretty enough to be a streetwalker—albeit a short and flat-chested one? Instantly my defenses rose. I was about to assert that there was no reason I *couldn't* have had hundreds of guys if I wanted when I realized I was only going to dig my hole deeper. "Oh my God," I stammered again, trying to do that flappy thing with my mouth and tongue that people called talking. "I'm not a hooker at all. I am a nice girl! And I resent any implications otherwise!"

Unfortunately, I forgot about my leather-bound volume of Dickens. It tumbled from my lap. When I tried to recapture it, my sudden twist made it bounce from my knees and onto the coffee table, where it fell wide open to the pages that concealed the decidedly less highbrow exploits of Agent Double-O-Sixty-Nine. My used paperback of *On Her Majesty's Secret Crevice* slid across the wood as if pulled by invisible Swedish sex magnets, until finally it came to rest at the table's edge, right in front of Colm. His eyebrows flew up in perfect arches as he mouthed the title.

That was the only cue I needed. I grasped for my bag, considered retrieving my novel, abandoned the idea, and then scuttled across the floor. I was dimly aware of Mr. Iverson trying to call me back, but all I wanted to do was get home as quickly as I could and soothe my burning face under my cool pillowcase. And then maybe move to the Dominican Republic where no one could find me. Ever.

Right before the door closed, I heard Colm's voice ring across the living room. "Very nice indeed!"

"Thank you," I called back, wondering why in hell I even bothered.

In bed

"Giiiiiiirrrrrrl." Thanks to the wonders of cellular technology, I was able to hear every nuance of Maya's annoyance, down to the last drawn-out growl. "It's . . . five-twelve A.M."

"I'm sorry." I don't know why I felt compelled to whisper. There certainly wasn't anyone in my apartment to wake. As if I could make it all better, I added, "Merry Christmas!"

"It's five-thirteen. In the A.M.," Maya stressed. "Are you okay? What's the matter?"

"I don't know." Maya knew me better than that. She waited in silence until I spoke again. "How did I get here?" I didn't mean the living room sofa, where I'd woken. Apparently I'd fallen asleep there the night before. My cheeks had absorbed the cushion's nubbly texture.

"Are you in trouble?" Genuine concern colored her voice. "Did you go out drinking last night? Did Ambrose walk you home? Don't you remember?"

"I'm fine." Calling had been a mistake. In the very early morning hours there's a moment when I'll wake and can't tell the difference between the silent darkness and my closed eyes. It's a quiet moment in which everything's held in suspense. "My life's a mess," I whispered, sitting up and clutching a pillow to my midsection. I twisted the switch on the lamp by the sofa, blinking at the sudden light. Above me were my shelves of books—old college texts mingling with the fifty-cent pulps I loved, fronted by snow globes I'd collected over the years.

Maya's pause was so long that I wondered if she'd gone back to sleep. I was about to disconnect when at last I heard her voice in my ear once more. "Come with me to my family's dinner. You know my mom would love you there."

Centered on the lowest of the shelves above me was a small porcelain figurine of Kwan Yin, the bodhisattva of compassion. It had sat on my mom's desk for years, and was the last thing she'd ever given me before she died. Looking into that sweet, smiling face only made me more sad. "Thanks, but—"

"You shouldn't be alone today. Come on. She's making turkey, and potatoes, and dressing, corn, greens . . ." I heard a loud intake of breath.

"We'll see each other later this week. I'll be okay." Her yawning was contagious. My own mouth stretched open wide.

"Buttermilk . . . pie . . ."

"Merry Christmas, Maya."

"Merry Christmas, Nan. Love you."

I slipped the phone back into its cradle, turned off the light, and blinked several times as I settled back down on the sofa. It didn't make a difference—eyes open or closed, everything still seemed dark, silent, and empty.

JANUARY

My apartment above Przybyla and Sons Bakers (olives, pickles, and assorted relishes: $19.89; one twenty-pound spiral-sliced ham: –$3.42 after daddy rebate)

"The best part of potluck is that it spreads the cost around. Right? No one has to take too much of the financial burden to feed, what, nine, ten people, right?" My dad stuck his head around the corner of the alcove I called my kitchen. "Very smart. Very economical, baby. So how much did that monster ham run you?"

When Dad started digging through his wallet, I shared a rolled-eyes moment with Mitchell, who leaned against my harvest gold refrigerator as if it were some kind of giant crutch. "None of your business," I said sweetly. "And there's only enough room in the kitchen for me."

"Take this fifty. That'll be daddy's contribution." He attempted to stuff a Ulysses S. Grant into my sweatshirt pouch.

Daddy's contribution had already consisted of several bottles of decent wine, a six-pack of hard apple cider, and—though I could have sworn the closest the man had been to a kitchen in the last ten years had been when he greeted the guys making his pastrami sandwiches at the local deli—a homemade flan. I was having none of his charity. "Keep your shekels," I told him, retrieving the bill and dropping it down the front of his shirt. It was impossible to miss the mushroom cloud of warm cologne that wafted up and into my face.

"You really should have that oven checked out, honey," he told me, retrieving the bill from the vicinity of his collarbone and pretending to hide it away in his pocket. "I worry about you setting this entire place on fire. Doorbell. Should I get it?"

"Yes, Dad," I replied mechanically.

Once he was out of sight, Mitchell stuck the tip of his little finger into his ear and wiggled it around. "You know that fifty dollars is going to end up in your sock drawer."

I loved my big brother dearly, but when he pulled his finger from his ear and inspected the tip, I winced. "What do you think of his transformation, hmmm? Did you notice that shirt? Imported, thank you very much. And that cologne?"

"Oh, it's not that big a change."

"You've got to be kidding me, Mitch," I said, putting my oven-mitted hands on my hips. "Did you see those duds? I spent the last month working across the aisle from men's dress shirts and I would swear on a stack of Bibles that his is imported. He smells like some kind of fancy-boy brothel. I could've bought four hams with those shoes!"

"So what, you begrudge him spending a little money on himself? That's not like you."

Mitchell missed the point. "What's the thermometer on the ham say? And you know it's not a money issue at all. Something's up. Remember how we used to have to *beg* him to buy new socks because he'd slice through them with those awful toenails of his and then walk all over the place with his toes sticking out like worms? Oh! That reminds me! Work story!"

"Not one of your silly work stories! It says one-twenty-five," Mitchell informed me, standing up from the oven. "I think it's supposed to be one-forty before you can serve it."

"Turn it up fifty degrees," I ordered him, then leaned back to tell my anecdote. "So there was this Who at Mercer-

Iverson . . . Nina was her name, though that's not important. Okay, and Nina had beautifully manicured fingers, but she was like, this *total* toenail-biting fiend. I mean, I never saw her pull off her tights and munch on them or anything, but one day someone was looking for a mint and there was a tin of Altoids lying on top of her purse, and when he shook it—because it was really light, you see—it made a little clicking noise. Like, a tick-tick-tick. So he opened it. . . ."

"Nooooo!" Mitchell's eyebrows peaked in the middle over where his hands covered his eyes.

"And it was filled with *toenails!* Hers . . ."

My brother had his palms over his ears by this point. The tiny kitchen alcove resounded with his sing-song "La la la la la la!"

I pinned my six-foot-three, two-hundred-pound big brother to the wall and wrenched his hands from his head for my triumphant conclusion. "*And her mother's.* For calcium snacks!"

There's a noise that Charlie Brown always let out in *Peanuts* strips whenever "good grief" couldn't express the anguish. I enjoyed my brother's version: "Auuuuuugh!"

"True story!" I shouted over his cry, as I hugged him and spanked his butt with my wooden spoon. Helpless giggles cut through both our shrieking. It wasn't until my dad's disapproving face appeared in the archway that we calmed down some. He carried what looked like a long cone of paper.

"Son, you know if you don't react she won't taunt you." How many thousand times had we heard that exact phrase growing up?

"Whatcha got there?" I asked, still clinging to Mitch's safe bulk.

"Flowers?" If the resurrected Messiah had done a tap dance in front of the Apostle Thomas, the disciple's voice would have been only a fraction as doubtful as my dad's right then. "For you?"

"It could happen," I informed him, putting down my spoon and grabbing the bundle. Though on the outside I was trying to be Blasé Girl, the kind of woman who gets flowers all the time from admirers, inside I was all a-quiver like a Victorian old maid upon whom the unwed vicar has bestowed a nosegay. Flowers? For me? Really? How utterly cool, and yet . . . who?

Once the arrangement lay on the rickety metal baking table that served as my only counter space, I ripped through the thick white paper and was greeted by a strong, sticky floral scent. Sprays of lilies, actually, interspersed with baby's breath and greenery.

"Who died?" Ambrose had poked his head around the corner at some point. He munched on a carrot stick. He stared at the flowers as if they were his mortal enemy. "By the way, I've been sent to ask when's dinner. You've got a bunch of hungry savages in what you call your living room."

The arrangement was a bit funereal, I had to agree. "Soon," I promised, trying to create an air of mystery as I maneuvered the vase so that no one could watch me read the card. If it was from whom I thought, I'd want to keep it to myself. "We're trying to get the ham to a non-germy temperature."

"Maybe if you didn't have to do your cooking in an Easy-Bake Oven," Ambrose suggested, causing Mitchell to bark out laughter.

I ignored them both. The envelope's flap opened with a small tug. When I read the words computer-printed on the card inside, I discovered my weightless excitement suddenly leaded with reality. "Oh. They're from Brody." Trust my younger brother to pick out something expensive, but strangely inappropriate. "It says, 'Happy New Year!' " I don't know why, but I'd expected the flowers to be a belated sorry present from Damien. Though I'd cut off our physical relationship long ago, he had a habit of sometimes presenting me with the types of presents you'd sometimes give a girlfriend: dopey cards, mix CDs, and once a half-wheel of provolone. I suppose I'd hoped it was him because I wanted a little intrigue in my life. Flowers from your brother was—well, flowers from your brother. "That's nice. They obviously cost him a bundle."

Ambrose grinned. I knew my imagination hadn't been overactive; he'd been outright jealous of those flowers until I'd opened the card. Maybe lilies from Brody was the best possible resolution to a potentially sticky situation. Swear to God, next life, I wanted to be one of those people who didn't feel a need to tiptoe around people's delicate feelings. Either that or a mongoose. So much less stress. "Could you put these on the table?" I asked Ambrose, right as the doorbell sounded again.

"I'll get it," said my dad, wandering off.

"Okay, take me out of my box and comb me because I'm officially wigged," I announced to Mitchell, mentally ticking off all the things that had to be done before I could serve dinner, starting with getting the ham warmed. "What's the temperature situation?"

"He gets more adorable with every year." Mitchell sighed.

"Dad?"

"No." He seemed to think I was deliberately playing stupid. Annoying my big brother came easily, but I honestly hadn't been trying. "Your friend."

"Ambrose?" I asked in genuine surprise. "Seriously?"

"He's like a big teddy bear."

"*Ambrose?*" I thought about it for a moment. Maybe it would be a good thing for Mitchell to start seeing someone again. "You should ask him out."

Immediately I got that closed-off, shut-down expression Mitchell would affect whenever anyone dared suggest he resume a normal love life. "For one thing, he's not gay." Before I could argue otherwise, he added, "Nan, I've known Ambrose ever since you first brought him home for Thanksgiving your, what, freshman year?"

"Sophomore," I said, grumpy at both him and the ham. One-thirty. We were *never* going to eat.

"The man's not gay. Never has been. Never will be." He sighed again, this time longer. "I wonder if he needs a roommate?"

I had something to say to that remark, but my dad once more entered the alcove with another triangular bundle of paper, stapled at the top. "You know, it occurs to me that being a florist would be a good, steady job. I mean, look, they're even working on a holiday."

"Hint taken," I informed him. "But I'm not interested in the floral arts." Who could this second delivery be from? My curiosity was piqued. Brody again? Probably not—these came from a different florist. "Daddy, could you, um, take the salad out to the table?" The big aluminum container could sit out there just as well as on top of my refrigerator.

Dad made no signs of moving. His arms slowly crossed in the same suspicious way as when stoners and skateboarders used to come pick me up for dates at our old apartment door. Despite whatever midlife crisis he was going through, I guess some things never changed.

When I ripped open the paper this time, the card protruded over spikes of dried flowers. "Is there no privacy anymore?" I complained as both my family moved closer. All I needed to complete the picture was Ambrose and his hangdog face. "Big Brother is watching me? Is that the deal?" Once again I had the faintest sense of hope and anticipation as I unsealed the envelope, and then like a soap bubble bursting, the faintest spray of discontent. *"For your many kindnesses this season with best wishes for a most profitable new year, regards from Andrew J. Iverson,"* I read aloud. "Happy now? You. Ham. Get it hot," I commanded my father. "You, salad, follow me," I added to Mitchell.

Avoiding gouging my face with those fragile and aromatic dried spears was no mean feat, but I managed. It had been awfully kind of Mr. Iverson to send me something, particularly since the last time I'd seen him, I'd bolted from his home as if I were the last bat out of hell. "I don't know where she got so bossy," I heard my dad complain. "Your mother and I were never that way."

My apartment . . . well. Starting a sentence with those two words was where imaginations usually went astray. When most people think of the word *apartment,* they picture a collection of connected rooms, more or less scattered with magazines and shoes, in which dwells a person, couple, or family. They don't think of a warren of hallways and rooms running off a large storage area that looks like Willy Wonka's factory ten years after the Oompa Loompa riots. Deserted machinery filled the largest room on the second floor of the bakery; some of it dated back to the early 1900s. Anyone walking into my place for the first time immediately assumed they'd come to a scrap yard.

But no. I'd carved out disconnected living spaces throughout the floor, making my little kitchen in an alcove near an old pretzel-maker. To find my bedroom, one had to wend one's way through an alley of old stacked loaf pans and distressed wood-burning ovens to the far end, sidle through a narrow unfinished hallway, duck, and crawl. Originally a Dutch door separated my sunny bedroom from the rest of the second floor, but over the years the upper half had been nailed and painted shut. The tiny entrance made where I slept feel a little like a kid's clubhouse.

The living room lay right on the other side of my bathroom, making it tricky for any guests trapped in there while someone had a gastric episode. Those in the know, though, could make an escape by stooping down and entering the oversized and nonfunctional fireplace, standing up again, and walking down a narrow passage and through a door into the main machinery room. It had been that feature alone that sold me on this place when I found it after college—that and the steep cut in rent if I worked in the bakery on Saturday mornings and listened out for burglars after dark. That fireplace corridor always made me feel like Miss

Scarlet traipsing the secret passageway from the conservatory to the lounge.

Once we were halfway across the machinery storage room, our steps breaking the trapezoids of light that fell slantwise through the peaked skylights above, I hissed at Mitchell, "What do you mean, roommate?"

He shrugged. A tomato chunk toppled to the floor. "I've got to find a place by the end of the month."

"Why? I thought you loved your place!"

"Simple reason. I can't afford it without Ty."

With my older brother, everything lately centered around the rough breakup of his relationship. "There've got to be other . . ."

"It's not my home without Ty. And Ty's not coming home." Words burst to my lips—calming words, soothing words. Mitchell must have smelled their insincerity before I spoke. "Don't tell me it's going to be okay. I hate that." I felt vaguely guilty. Hadn't we all assured him, after his boyfriend's desertion, that everything would be all right? The more he hurt, the more we had come up with bland reassurances. "So."

I didn't have much of a dining room. Usually I ate on the sofa in the living room. For my annual New Year's dinner, I would cover an old baking table with massive sheets of wrapping paper that Mrs. Przybyla would donate, then I'd top it off with my mismatched silverware and thrift shop plates and the disposable containers of food that everyone would bring. The flowers were a nice, festive touch. "I'm sorry," I apologized. It was no use telling him Ty might change his mind; he had called me after he vanished to confess he'd met someone else. Ty had known Mitchell would never tell any of us what happened, otherwise. "No, really, I'm sorry," I added, when I saw him shrug again. "It's not fair of us to pretend that Ty might come back when the reality is that he's not part of the family anymore."

My brother used to love telling a story about how Dad lost him in a Sears in Paramus when he was five; Dad had wandered across the aisle to watch a college basketball game in the TV section and had forgotten that Mitchell was still staring with fascination at the fishing lures in sporting goods. Eventually Mitch wandered out into the middle of the aisle, lost and confused, not seeing Dad a dozen feet away. For ten minutes he stood there until finally Dad turned around when Mitchell burst into tears. For Mitch, the point of the story had been that he'd been abandoned and neglected— until Mom died, he'd always said it was the saddest day of his life. After his partner of seven years had disappeared six months ago, leaving only a half-assed note saying that things had been bad between them for months and he was doing them both a favor by trading Soho for WeHo, he'd never mentioned the old hurt once.

For me, though, the whole point of the story had to be the reunion at the end. I could easily picture my dad's startled "Hey, buddy!" I liked imagining his open arms and the look of relief on my brother's face when they finally embraced. Mitch saw the Paramus adventure as *Oliver Twist: The Workhouse Years*, where I saw it as the first verse of "Amazing Grace." It was a fundamental difference between us. Nothing could change that. For months I'd trampled all over his feelings with my perky, sometimes offhanded platitudes, but saying the outright truth aloud hadn't served me any better. I thought he might sob when I said that Ty wasn't part of the family anymore. "Oh, hey." I squeezed him tight. "Hey!"

"I'm all right."

He wasn't, though. When would he admit that Ty had done a shitty thing? I could hear the wetness in his heaving chest. "You are lying through your teeth, mister. I'm a big dope. I'm sorry."

"I'll be okay." He snuffled a little, pressed the heels of his hands to his cheekbones, and nodded. "Just give me a minute. You've got stuff to do anyway."

"Yeah?" Part of me was anxious to get away. When

Mitchell's pain was palpable, my first instinct was always to distance myself. I didn't know how to cope with his burden of hurt. When he nodded a second time, I gave him one last quick hug, then ducked through the bathroom into the living room.

"Sorry about the h—" I stopped cold. My guests sat around all four walls, either on futons or pillows, silently glaring at each other. Only my Kwan Yin maintained an expression of serenity. A few glances flickered my way, but everyone seemed intent on studying each others' faces. Had they gotten into an argument? Had the lack of anything but carrot sticks sent them into a food coma?

"I'm dead," said Ambrose, falling backwards onto a pillow. When he laughed, I relaxed. Murder was a silly game we all used to play in college, usually when we were really, really drunk. After everyone drew little slips of paper from a baseball cap and sat in a circle, the person who unfolded hers and found a black dot became the secret murderer who would knock people out of the game by winking one eye at someone, hopefully when no one but her victim would see her. The victim would count to five, announce that he was dead, and then the game would continue until someone caught the murderer in mid-act. "I haven't thought about Murder in *years*," I said. "Who thought of playing?"

"We were talking about that old roommate of yours who told us we were going to hell for playing a game about killing each other." Ambrose's voice rumbled from where he sprawled on his back.

"Veronica," I said, then stopped. "Monica?"

"I thought it was Erica," said Clark in a monotone. He was staring around the circle intently, trying to catch winks. Or was he trying to murder someone?

"*I'm* Erica," said his blond date, breaking her concentration to glare at him.

"Oh, sorry, baby."

"It was Monica," said Maya, talking through her teeth.

"Now shut up." We all knew that Maya took her games very, very seriously. She once actually phoned Milton Bradley to clarify a rule and retroactively declare herself the winner, after a particularly vicious late-night Scattergories skirmish.

"Veronica was the one who ate nothing but cereal." Ambrose's hand drifted to his tummy and began rubbing it. "She had bad teeth."

"I'm dead," said both Clark and his date simultaneously. They looked at each other, giggled helplessly, and fell back onto the cushions.

"It's Maya," I informed Jack and his ponytailed girlfriend du jour. When they both looked up at me in surprise, and Maya's eyes burned with hatred, I knew I'd been right. "You can always tell when she's the murderer because it looks like she's chewing gravel. Emmett's the only one of us who could ever pull off being murderer without a tell." And where was Emmett? Not at my party, for the first time in five years.

"And since *you're* not playing and *you two* didn't guess, I'm the winnah!" Maya whooped, bounced on the cushion, and did a little sofa dance. "The grand winnah! Re-cog-nize! And FYI, Mandy was the one who ate nothing but Apple Jacks and Count Chocula, three meals a day. Veronica was the so-called model who turned tricks."

"Oh yeah," mumbled all my friends, while the two dates goggled at me like I ran some kind of Alphabet City brothel.

"I've had some bad roommates," I told them, trying to sound light about it. I'd had the smokers, the tokers, the looking-for-a-midnight-pokers, the living deads, the pregnant-and-unweds, the neat freaks and the computer geeks, the users and abusers, and more than my share of the outright losers. Whenever I'd extended to them the second floor key, the best thing about any of my roommates was that they (mostly) had their half of the rent and that I was (totally) sure they'd be gone within three months. Part of me liked that they left so quickly. It sent a message to the Przybylas that my second floor haven was some kind of uninhabitable rat trap and that I was the only person crazy enough to live there. And that kept the rent affordable.

Affordable-ish, anyway. I had a thought. Would it be so bad to invite Mitchell to live with me? As a temporary arrangement, of course. He could have what I always thought of as the pipe room—the space where all the building's plumbing intersected and nested along one wall and the ceiling. It might be a hard sell. I could only invest so much enthusiasm in: "It's way bigger than my own bedroom! And it mostly hasn't smelled of urine since my last alcoholic roommate moved out!" Wouldn't it be a good thing to offer, though, even if he didn't take it? All these months I'd tried to soothe Mitch with dozens of hoary old banalities. Maybe I could actually *do* something to help him.

"Dinner's nearly ready, guys," I told the crowd. Once again, the shrill clang of my doorbell reverberated through the floor. "Jesus."

"Maybe it's more flowers." Ambrose rose, obviously prepared to find out.

Maya looked interested. "Nan's getting flowers? From a man?"

"From her brother."

I ignored the scorn in Ambrose's voice and sailed from the living room. "It had better *not* be more flowers or I'll be getting a Daddy Scholarship to the nearest florist's academy."

To my horror, my voice echoed around the vast expanse of my bathroom, the second-biggest area on the floor after the machine room. "A Daddy Scholarship to where?" asked the daddy in question.

"Never you mind," I told him, making a silent New Year's resolution to keep my mouth firmly shut for the next three hundred and sixty-five days. I was dimly aware that everyone had followed me from the den, probably roused to their feet by the mention of food soon. They were going to be disappointed to find their ham warmed only somewhere between room temperature and Ebola fever spike. "Damn it, I'm *coming!*" I snapped in the direction of the big entrance. Whoever was on the other side had apparently died and gone into rigor mortis with his finger still on the button.

Only when I'd chucked loose the big bolts at the top and bottom of the iron door and swung its heavy bulk back did the metallic blast cease. Standing at the top of the staircase were two men, but all I noticed at first were the flowers they carried. No one had given me flowers since the fraternity dance date in college to whom I'd lost my virginity. Now all of a sudden I was swimming in them. Finally I looked up from the plastic-wrapped roses directly in front of me into the eyes of my little brother. "Brody?" I asked.

"Did you get my flowers?" he asked, looking from me to the group of people gathering behind. "I see it's the usual suspects, huh? So did you get the flowers? I sent flowers. You wouldn't believe what they cost, but hey—you're my sis, right?" When I gaped as he shoved the roses into my hands, he added, "But I got more in case they didn't get here." He pushed his way in and immediately began taking off his coat. "God, this place is a *dump*. Think the Lexus'll be okay outside for a few?"

"Happy New Year, Nan," said the other man. He carried a smaller bundle of yellow daisies. I loved daisies. They were bright and much more cheerful than either of Brody's bouquets. A row of crooked teeth gleamed at me as the bearer held out his gift. I recognized the horn-rimmed glasses and the mossy chin stubble immediately.

The flopping sensation in my gullet either had to be my heart, or a live guppy I'd inhaled when I hadn't been looking. I swallowed, cleared my throat, and tried to remain calm. "Oh shit," I said before I could stop myself. "Colm?"

Around the dinner table
(four arrangements of flowers: free; one box of Claritin allergy medicine: $12.98)

"The thing about raw tomato is that though ninety percent of guys won't eat it, most women will." The blond girl—what was her name?—pointed across the table with her fork at her date. "He won't. Cooked—he'll eat it cooked. But not raw." Clark grimaced. A small pile of tomato chunks sat on the edge of his salad plate. "How about you?" she said to my younger brother, who could barely be bothered to hide his sneer.

"Raw tomato disgusts me," Brody told her.

"It's the texture, right?" she asked. Brody and Clark both nodded. From my seat at the far end of the table, I shifted uncomfortably. My little group was used to talking about movies and shows and books we'd read or pretended to read, and here we were letting some little chatterbox monopolize the dinner conversation with garden produce? Then again, a little blessings-counting might be in order. At least I wasn't having to direct the conversation myself. With a nearly total stranger across the table from me, that would have been disastrous.

Funny how all my guests had abandoned my seating suggestions mere moments after Brody and Colm had arrived, adding extra chairs for them both and positioning Colm and me at the end of the table. Funny like a laugh riot. As if reading my mind, Colm smiled at me with closed lips as he munched lettuce. My eyes instantly flickered back to the conversation so I didn't appear too interested. I was way too attracted to Colm to let down my guard.

"That's part of my theory. How about you? Do you eat raw tomato?" the girl asked my dad, leaning diagonally toward him and—hello! Making some pretty hefty crop circles on my table with her D cups!

"Not really, but of course it depends on who's feeding me." My dad fixed her with a charming smile. For my science requirement in college I had opted for the easy B of geology instead of the uncertain challenge of biology, and as a consequence I've never been sure of the exact location of my hackles. Wherever they were, that smile made them levitate into the stratosphere. Dad was flirting!

"What if it was me?" The playfulness in her voice was unmistakable.

"Mmmm, then I'd certainly reconsider my stance."

Brody, Mitchell, and I dropped our forks onto our plates simultaneously. It's hard to describe the queasy sensations I felt as I watched Clark's date spear a few red cubes from his plate, lean across the table, and brandish them in my father's general direction. I can unfortunately verify that watching my father lean forward, lock gazes with the wench, and wrap his lips around her fork, gave me the same shivers I get from nails dragged across a chalkboard, or from someone squealing sweaty hands over a latex balloon. At the sight, Mitchell rubbed his eyes as if he suddenly didn't want them anymore. "Not bad," said my father.

"Dad!" I complained. My family's patriarch was too busy slurping to heed anything I had to say. Colm's glance mingled with mine once more as he wiped his mouth; he had been laughing at the entire thing. One more funny story to carry back to the art department at Mercer-Iverson, I guessed. What *was* the girl's name, again? And why wasn't Clark reining her in? "So what's your theory, Monica?" Instantly I knew my guess had been wrong.

"Veronica," suggested Ambrose, catching my goof. I caught a vague vibe of hostility in his correction.

"*Erica.*" At least she only looked mildly annoyed. "Veronica was your old roommate who used to turn tricks."

"Ha! Ha! Ha!" I said loudly—too loudly—across the table to Colm, though I didn't meet his gaze. "Yes, yes, that was Veronica all right, and yes, she did, but I didn't! Nope! Never turned a trick at all because you have to be a prostitute to do that and I'm not one." From what I could see out of the corner of my eye, the younger Iverson seemed to be silently convulsing in laughter. I curled my lip and shut the hell up.

"So I have this theory," Erica said directly to my father, "that guys who don't like raw tomato are the same guys who don't like oral sex." The words *oral* and *sex* had never before been juxtaposed at a dinner with my family; they collided into the dinner table like a Scud missile. Brody's mouth opened and closed as would a goldfish; his already-bulging eyes protruded further. "Not receiving. I mean, who doesn't like getting it, right? They don't like *giving* oral sex. Take Clark. He won't go down there at all." Clark froze with his fork raised halfway to his mouth, his skin suddenly splotchy with color. When no one around the table said a word, she continued to explain. "I think they don't like the texture of either. Or maybe the moisture."

"Oh my God," Brody muttered as he threw down his napkin and rose to his feet. "Excuse me, please."

No one said a word until Brody slammed the door to the bathroom. "That's telling. His poor wife," Erica whispered to Dad. Maya, caught mid-sip, began to choke on her wine; Ambrose rubbed her back. "No, seriously, I'm just saying that I've noticed that guys who eat raw tomatoes are the ones who have no problems really going to town down there when you need it most."

I wanted to apologize to someone—anyone—for the conversation. No, for the entire dinner. This was going down in history as the most disastrous New Year's party I'd ever thrown! There was absolutely nothing that could make it any wor . . .

Oh, how wrong I was. Colm, across the table, waved his plastic fork. All four of its tines, from tip to base, were covered with as much tomato as he could find in his salad. While he maintained unblinking eye contact with me, he plunged the fork into his mouth and sucked down its contents, chewing and smiling while he waited for my reaction.

Caught off-guard, I shivered. The bum had actually given me a spinegasm! "Why are you here?" I was suddenly moved to ask. Colm chewed and attempted to swallow, his thick eyebrows raised at the question. "Yes, you with the cute glasses and the stubble and the hair. Why are you *here*, aside from your thinly veiled attempts to lure me into oral sex?"

"Um, excuse me." My older brother tossed his paper towel napkin onto the table, stood up, and walked off in the direction of the bathroom.

Even my dad seemed to forget little Miss Erica. "I'll . . . why don't I . . . kitchen," he mumbled, making a beeline away from the table. What? Oh crap, had I trampled over his hope I had my flower of maidenhood intact?

My friends, however, remained motionless, as if they hoped I'd not notice their curious, excited expressions. I was having the kind of confrontation you could dine out on for weeks. Clark still wore his fight-or-flight face from moments before. I felt a little odd about having this— argument? discussion?—out in the open, but it would have been more odd to take it behind closed doors. I barely knew the guy. Why give this conversation any kind of legitimacy? "I mean, you arrived uninvited. I don't know how you knew I was having a dinner today—"

"You mentioned it when I met you," Colm responded without anger or rebuke.

Oh. "Or how you found where I lived—"

"When your grandfather has ample access to the addresses of subcontracted employees, it's a fairly painless process," he said with an immense good humor that made me want to slap him, or pucker up and kiss him. I wasn't sure which.

I shook my head to rid it of the traitorous thoughts. "Regardless!"

"I wanted to apologize. My behavior at my grandfather's was . . ."

"Absolutely appalling and highly sexist?" I suggested. "Both grotesque and utterly unpardonable?"

"How about abysmally inappropriate and inexcusably unseemly?"

"That'll work," I snapped. Was he making fun?

Colm leaned forward. "Will you go out with me?"

It was the last thing I'd expected him to ask—and yet, I couldn't deny it pleased me greatly. "What? No! What? Why?"

My rebuff didn't faze him at all. "I see two reasons. One, it would please my grandfather immensely." He ticked off the point on his index finger.

"So your grandpop softens me up with dried flowers and then you drop by with gorgeous daisies simply so you can do that sweet old man a favor, hmmm? And how did you know that daisies are my favorite? Was that in my personnel file, too?" The petals were a bright gold with yellowy-green centers. Typical for fate to send my favorite flowers clutched in the long, sensitive fingers of a guy only interested in asking me out on a pity date. "You can tell your grandfather he's been reading too much *Great Expectations*. He should know these Miss Havisham set-ups never work. It's all fun and games until someone's wedding gown catches on fire and then boom, it's all self-immolation and misery." I was glad he cracked a grin at that remark. I liked a guy who could keep up with me. "And what's the second reason?"

"It struck me that you seemed exceedingly interesting."

Oh, so he was giving me *that* one, was he? He thought he could waltz in here and sweep me off my feet with his deep voice and dark eyes and charm me into a date by giving me compliments? Well, I would have to show him that he could totally get away with it. Eventually. "I hope you're not still entertaining any false hopes that I'm a call girl," I informed him stiffly. "Because I do *not* get paid for the stuff I do."

Ooch. Those words sounded so much better in my head. "Excuse me," said Ambrose, rising from his seat. He clutched his napkin to his mouth as he ambled off in the direction of the kitchen.

Before Colm could respond, I turned at the sound of Brody's voice. "Um, Nan?" he called out. "Could you come here a sec?"

"Excuse me for a moment," I told Colm, gesturing to where Clark and his date were holding a stifled argument at the other end of the table. "If you get impatient, you might want to talk to Erica, down there. She might be interested to know about your raw tomato obsession."

"I can wait," he assured me.

With its expanse of ceramic, a huge old-fashioned water-pressure-be-damned showerhead hanging from the center of the ceiling, a drain in the floor's middle, and its tiny toilet cowering in one corner, my bathroom had always reminded me of a cavernous abattoir where one could slaughter a cow and then rinse away the bloody residue. I'd once made the mistake of telling that to Maya; she'd subsequently nicknamed the room "Dahmer's Kitchen." "What is the deal?" I barked, then instantly regretted it. Any sound in that completely tiled room echoed and reverberated until the most innocent noise ended up resembling two T-rexes fighting to the death at a well's bottom. Small wonder my friends always refused to void when they visited.

"Who invited *that* guy?" Brody hissed.

"His name's Colm Iverson, of the Mercer-Iverson Iversons, and he came to ask me out, okay?" Both my brothers stared at me with no expression on their faces, which of course made me want to pummel one onto them. "Oh, it's so easy for you guys, isn't it? Brody's got his wife and brood of children and Mitch, you've got—well, you had it, anyway. I know you guys both see me as the jerky middle kid who's never married and whose longest relationship is an on-and-off love affair with *All My Children*." My hisses came out in a fury. "But you know, it's certainly *possible* that I can interest someone and it's certainly *possible* that he might want to ask me out, and yes, it's even *possible* that he could find me physically irresistible. Every old sock meets an old shoe, you know. Isn't that what Mom used to say? I'm not asking for much from you two. Stop the adolescent sniggering and give me a little support. Is that too much to ask? Oh, and for the record, Brody, no one invited that guy, but then again, you weren't exactly invited either. You always spend New Year's with your own family and what's with you suddenly showing up, anyway?"

Both of them reacted to my guttural proclamation with stunned silence. It was a full thirty seconds before Brody cleared his throat and said, "I didn't mean the geek. We figured he was one of your weird dates. I meant *that* guy. The hippie with the ponytail." The three of us leaned our heads out the doorframe simultaneously.

"Clark?" My exclamation drew the attention of Colm, who smiled and waved in my direction. With haste, I pulled my head back in. "He's been in the Elizabethan Failures for years! You've met Clark!"

"Did he grow his hair out?" Mitchell looked dubious.

Brody shot him a pained look. "The point is, why isn't he keeping that girlfriend of his under control? She's throwing herself at Dad like some kind of—" He waved his hands around, groping for a phrase. Finally he gestured to me and finished the sentence while looking at Mitch. "Cheap slut!"

I took a moment to scan my brother from bottom to top in a pointed manner. "Excuse me? And anyway, what century are you living in? We don't have leash laws for girlfriends nowadays, Mr. No Votes For Women. I'd like to see you try to keep that pit bull of a wife of yours under control."

Brody knew I really had nothing against Marcy, his girl bride. In a similar way, I have nothing against hungry barracudas, when they're several thousand miles away in the depths and I'm high and dry in my apartment. Just don't expect me to cozy up to one, thank you very much. Still, the twitch around his eyes was unmistakable when I mentioned her name. Was my baby brother having problems at home? Brody wasn't a confider—he wouldn't tell me if I asked. Was that why he'd shown up out of the blue, bearing gifts? Instantly I wished I'd kept my mouth shut. The three of us might treat each other like dirt, but at heart we don't mean any real harm. "What's with Dad, anyway?" Brody demanded, moving right ahead. "He's all fancied up and reeking like a department store."

I spread my hands in Mitchell's direction. He'd been the one to witness Dad's transformation the longest. "Dad's exploring his metrosexuality," Mitch sighed. "There's nothing wrong with a guy his age trying to look his best."

"Exploring his *what?*" My younger brother has always had a cartoon face: you could draw a simple caricature of him by giving the capital letter U some short curly hair and the biggest dark bug eyes imaginable. When Brody was disgusted or annoyed, those big eyes shrank to tiny slits. He crossed his arms. "This is *Dad* we're talking about. That's *disgusting*. What have you been teaching him?"

Now it was Mitchell's turn for upset. "Metrosexuality, stupid. It's a catchphrase. It has nothing to do with sexual orientation."

Brody had already turned his back. "I don't wanna hear about it. I don't wanna hear. I'm a family man."

Instinct nearly made me leap into the argument on my older brother's side. I've always wondered if other people felt the same as I when their families convene. On my own, I'm a normal, rational person who lives a perfectly grown-up life—not always happy, not always unlonely, rarely solvent. But it's my life and no one else's. After ten minutes in the presence of my family, I'm trapped in some prescripted drama in which I've had an ensemble role a hundred times before. I've always imagined that stage actors feel the same way about their plays, after many performances: déjà vu mixed with sleepwalking. Maybe each of my scenes was improvisational, but in them I'm always billed in the same part of Overlooked Sister Whose Life's Such a Mess That Her Opinion Doesn't Matter.

Well, this time if they were going to overlook me, they could do it without my being there. In their subdued bickering I doubt they noticed when I slipped under Mitchell's arm back into the machinery room. The cooler air there—nippy, actually, since I preferred not to jack the thermostat too high—cleared my head. Poor Colm. For a moment I actually felt sorry for him, huddling for warmth at the lonely end of the table. At least my friends knew me and my penurious habits well enough to fortify their outfits with sweaters from home.

Colm hadn't yet seen me standing there by the bathroom door; he unfolded and reached out to stuff back a wayward daisy into the water glass serving as a vase. His arms were so thin that if I had collected the fabric with my finger, it would have outlined little more than bone. I decided to put him out of his misery. Sighing, I grabbed an old roommate's abandoned wool shawl and approached. He looked up and smiled when I flung the small wrap his way, managing to catch it only at the very last second. "Thanks."

"Because I am not fond of being a familial obligation, I

have decided to, um, decline your offer of a date," I informed him while he covered his shoulders. All my friends grew silent at the announcement. Ambrose, hovering nearby, nodded with satisfaction. Maya made crazy-wild eyes at me and began to shake her head furiously. I ignored them both. All my attention was on Colm. For a moment I thought I'd seen disappointment at my pronouncement, and that was enough to give me satisfaction. "However. I am willing to extend to you an offer. *You* may go on a date with *me*," I told him. What was it about Colm that made me want to talk in his own multisyllabic cadences? It struck me that maybe I really wanted to impress him. "Because I find *you* interesting."

Colm bit his lip. For a moment I feared he might turn me down, and then I'd know he was only asking me out of pity, after all. Or could he be one of those creeps who didn't like a woman who took charge? If that was the case, then he could give back the shawl that made him look even more like his granddad and—what? He was nodding. "Yes," he said, setting my world right again. "I'd like that."

"Fine." I took my place across from him at the table.

"Fine." He seemed to be finding enormous satisfaction in my formality.

"But I name the time and place."

"That's fine too."

"And we're not doing anything that requires a lot of money. We're dating on my budget, not yours."

"Whatever you say," he said with an amiable expression.

In the silence that followed, I thought I could hear audible sighs of relief from my friends at the other end of the table. Then my father leaned out of the kitchen. "Honey?" he asked, his voice meek. "Reassure your daddy before he has a heart attack here. You're not really a call girl, are you?"

American Folk Art Museum
(salami sandwich and a Diet Coke: $9.27.)

"So what's the plan? Am I supposed to spirit you away after a set amount of time? Are you going to throw me a signal if the chemistry's not right? Clue me in." A tornado of steam rose when Maya uncapped the Styrofoam cup in her mittened hands and raised it to her mouth.

"There's no plan." Infusing my words with scorn might distract from the fact that she had nailed me, and good. Even as she spoke, I'd been vacillating about whether or not to arrange some kind of emergency signal. I hated the thought that I was so predictable, but the truth was that I'd already relied upon Maya to help me out of awkward dates for many a year. Too many a year, apparently. "I don't make such plans."

Judging from Maya's reaction, I should have been making a living in stand-up comedy. "Don't tell me you called me away from work on the day of your big lunch date only so I could drink potato soup in the street like a *dog.*"

I shrugged.

"Girl, you make bad liars look pro."

"Okay, *fine.*" The crowd had already begun to get thicker on 53rd Street. It wasn't all that difficult for anyone with a practiced eye to pick out the people who were there for the upcoming event; they were the passersby attempting to appear relaxed as they strolled in the direction of the museum. I nodded very slightly at one of them, a blonde I recognized from several of the previous happenings. She tilted her head in return, then immediately hugged tight the collar of her coat and moved on. "So I'm a pathetic loser who relies on her friends to help her out of pathetic messes with pathetic guys. Sue me. But I've got no plan. What time is it?"

Maya recapped her soup before looking at her watch. "Eleven fifty-six," she told me. "Colm didn't seem all that pathetic to me. Where is he, anyway?"

I nodded to a storefront across the street. "I sent him to get a sandwich for his lunch. Speak of the devil." The moment I'd opened my mouth, he'd emerged through a door and onto the street, blinking and looking around in an uncertain manner. It was as if he didn't see much in the way of sunlight. "Do you think he looks funny?"

We watched him jog slowly in the direction of the crosswalk. "Not really. I would have sworn he was your type, if anything," said Maya.

"Maybe." Colm struck me as a line-straddler. His thick hair, which seemed to have been matted down with sleep and then combed only with his fingers when he woke, reminded me of the artists and artist wannabes who covered the chairs and tables of local coffee shops like a biblical plague of frogs. The expensive wool overcoat struck me as strictly corporate. So did the shiny dress boots. Yet the thick-rimmed glasses spoke of hours spent trying to find the clunkiest, ugliest, thickest frames available, all in the name of appearing careless of his appearance—and how could a girl like me not find that little touch of vanity absolutely adorable? I cringed as Colm edged between parked cars to cross the street and nearly stepped out in front of a speeding cab. He made a weak gesture of apology as the driver honked and cursed out the window. "He *is* awfully sexy."

Maya's attention had wandered to the front of the museum, where some of the stragglers had begun to accumulate in an aimless clump. "I thought you usually brought Ambrose to these flash mob things."

I held up a hand before she could say more. "Please. *Flash mob* is so two years ago."

"Okay, Miss Finger on the Pulse of a Generation. What is this, then?"

"A smart flock."

"And the difference is?"

I ignored her, primarily because there was no difference other than the fact that flash mobs were out, out, out, and smart flocks were in. "Besides, you can't expect me to have Ambrose tag along on a date. I'd sooner bring my maidenly aunt. Ambrose would make disapproving noises every time I turned my head in Colm's direction. What a buzz kill." I glanced at my watch. "We're supposed to be looking for someone dressed like a Vietnam veteran," I reminded her. We both scanned the crowd. A number of the smart flockers had already polarized their attention to a fellow wearing shabby camouflage who sat in front of the museum in a wheelchair, but they were offhand in their approach. Smart flockers didn't mob the organizers. "Is that the guy?" I took a big mouthful of my sandwich.

"No, I'm here." Colm suddenly loomed up behind the both of us, startling me. My mouth had been busy attacking a huge hunk of extra-thick salami. I ducked my head and tried to conceal my chewing with the back of my hand. "What?"

"She meant the guy who's here to hand out our instructions," Maya explained. "I'll go investigate." She warmed her nose and lips with the soup's steam and marched off in the direction of the museum's patchwork facade of blue-grey stone.

Meanwhile, my mouth had decided to conduct a symphony of drool. The salami had been salty and tangy enough to shoot my salivary glands into overdrive, and the slippery tomato and lettuce wedged in my cheeks wasn't easy to chew quickly. My jaws already had that tired, achey sensation I usually only get from attempting to chew a stale caramel. "Fowwy," I said, waving my hand. He patiently sipped from whatever was in his cup—coffee, by the smell of it—and waited for me to swallow.

Which, of course, made chewing all the more difficult. I'm not one of those phobics who has difficulty eating in public, but usually when I'm out with a guy I'm the girl taking dainty little bites, pretending she doesn't want or need bigger ones. What kind of guy can watch a new date shoving a grinder down her throat without imagining half his future paychecks going to grocery bills? "Oo own't af too ftare," I growled, giving up. In another ten minutes he'd mutter a polite excuse about getting back to work, I'd courteously tell him I had a great time, then we'd draw this entire awkward mess to a civil conclusion.

"Drink?" He offered his coffee. It was impossible to read his expression, though I tried. Any Magic 8-Ball could have informed me the likelihood he was laughing at me lay somewhere between *You may rely on it* and *Better not tell you now.* I waved away the offer, and continued my uncanny imitation of a rabid dog trying to swallow its own tongue. All the while, he continued to watch me with that inscrutable, maddening expression his face. Finally I held up a hand in the universal sign language for "Stop! in the name of love!", turned my head, and choked down the rest of the salami.

"Good lord," I muttered to myself. I would never chew again.

"Are you recuperated?" he asked.

Genuine concern colored his tone, which touched me. "Yes, thank you. But you didn't have to stand there and *watch!*"

"You really are an interesting person, Nan." His dark eyes were all I could see of his face as he drank from his coffee.

"Interesting?" I wanted to know more. I couldn't deny that physically I was attracted to the guy. What I hated was that every time I saw Colm, I wanted to be the smart, snappy version of me I liked imagining I could be, but instead came out resembling the total goober that in my worst nightmares I feared I really was. "Like, I want to get to know you better interesting, or look at these cancer cells under the microscope and how quickly they metastasize and devour the healthy host interesting?"

"Ah. Perhaps you mean, I'd like to take you to a nice restaurant interesting, or my goodness look at that five-car fatal accident interesting?"

"Something along those lines, yes."

He thought about that one for a moment. "Like a cactus, interesting," he finally said.

Wait a minute. What was that supposed to mean? I didn't have a chance to ask; Maya had returned bearing three miniature paper U.S. flags affixed to toothpicks. "I thought the point of a flash mob was that we're supposed to act like we don't know each other," she commented.

"Flash mob?" Colm asked. It was the first time I'd seen him nonplussed.

"Hi." Maya flashed a smile at Colm, and then widened her eyes at me. "You didn't tell him?"

"What's a flash mob?" Colm looked up and down the street as if he expected the Sharks and Jets suddenly to pop out from the manholes and swing into a rumble choreographed by Jerome Robbins.

"For one thing, this is not a flash mob," I insisted. Nothing in the world would have made me take another bite of my sandwich, hungry though I was, so I wrapped it up in its paper and began to shove it into my bag. "It's a smart mob. A smart flock," I hastily amended.

"Smart flocks are what they're calling flash mobs this year," Maya told Colm. Oh, she was bringing the snark today.

I could tell. "Here," she said, distributing the toothpicks. "I dropped a quarter in his cup and he gave me these."

"I thought perhaps we were going to the museum," Colm said. "I love the Folk Art Museum."

"I love the Folk Art Museum too. But the Folk Art Museum charges nine dollars for admission, and our deal was that we were going to go on my kind of date. Which means free-wheeling fun for free. Maya and I are experts at getting the maximum fun from the minimum flow." I waited for Colm's response. Maybe I was testing him, a little bit. Most guys, if I'd taken them to something strange like a flash mob—*smart flock*—would have protested with weak apologies for my lack of cash. *I would have paid your admission,* maybe, or *Hey, we can make this on me.* But nuh-uh. This was my kind of date, and he'd have to hop on the train or get left at the station.

Colm didn't bat an eyelash, to his credit. He stared from Maya to me, then twiddled the little flag between his thumb and forefinger so that it spun around with a whirr. "Fun! So what do we do?"

I was one step ahead of him. "See the instructions on the back?" Was he severely myopic? Did he have some kind of genetic ophthalmologic deficiency he was going to pass on to future generations of department store heirs? I couldn't believe how closely to his face he had to hold the flag—but then, the instructions had been printed on their back in six-point type. "Follow them."

"One thousand two hundred and one, approach museum. Face front," he read aloud.

"That's twelve-oh-one in layman's terms," I assured him. The perplexity written in the creases of Colm's forehead made him so boyishly adorable that it was all I could do to restrain myself from rumpling his hair. The last thing I needed to do, though, was to give into impulse and embarrass myself again, or leave the impression that I was his cheek-pinching aunt, likely to lick her finger and wipe a smudge away from his face at the slightest provocation.

"Which is now." Maya nodded her head at the scores of people leisurely making their way down the street. It was always possible to pick out the newbies—they scampered too quickly, looking over their shoulders to see who might be following. Their excitement and anxiety was all too clear. Those of us who'd been through this routine a few times before (or in my case, dozens) knew better. We sauntered. We dawdled. We strolled, slowly, pretending we weren't doing anything out of the ordinary. I daresay there was a bit of mosey in my step.

"I'm afraid I've no real comprehension of what we're doing." Colm still peered at the instructions on the flag's reverse as he trailed behind. "Might I ask you to explain?"

"Act nonchalant," I informed him. "Pretend like you don't really know me."

"I've no difficulty there. I barely *do*."

This banter wasn't getting us anywhere. Public stunts require a certain level of discretion. If I didn't want to get blackballed from the next smart flock, I had to explain, and quickly, before we approached the hot zone. "Smart flocks are a kind of public performance art," I explained. "They involve the cooperation and creative energies of citizens from all walks of life in a carefully choreographed, um . . ." I paused to recharge my vocabulary. Much as I wanted to impress Colm, keeping my conversational style from sounding like the normal, typical, one-syllable me took more energy than a single badly masticated bite of a salami sub could provide. "Um . . ."

"My girl here must have sat on her grand-daddy's dentures, because she's talking out of her ass," Maya informed Colm. I didn't mind the slam—it only hurt because it was true. What I minded was that Maya looked right at Colm! She was breaking the cardinal rule of the smart flock! "Flash mobs are a great big frat house boy joke thought up and perpetrated by a bunch of fools with too much damned time on their hands."

"A carefully choreographed unison of mutual energies," I finished triumphantly. "Plus they're fun. Don't listen to Maya."

"I didn't say they weren't fun," said my friend to her soup.

"Here." My hand shot out from the cuff of my favorite secondhand vintage Sears-Roebuck mohair coat. The sleeves were much too large for me, but I managed to free myself enough to begin wrestling my fingers into his. "Hold my hand. Pretend we're together."

Colm's fingers were still slightly toasty from clutching his cup of coffee. "So I'm to pretend we're together and hold your hand on our first date? I think I can manage that."

I felt slightly abashed at that. What was wrong with me? I knew this was supposed to be a date, and yet here I was, marching Colm through hoops as if he were some sort of inert croquet ball who needed a few smart smacks with a mallet. When I was with a guy, I wanted him to see my best personality—clever, smart Nan. What if that person didn't exist? What if all there was to me was superficial, bossy, loser Nan? Colm had to think so far that all evidence pointed to the assumption that she was the only Nan out there. I squeezed his fingers with mine. "I'm sorry," I told him. "You'll have fun. Honest."

Though little more than bone seemed to lie beneath the skin of Colm's fingers, his clutch was strong and warm. "It might not have occurred to you," he suggested, "that perhaps I already am."

It was the kind of declaration that made me not want to let go.

Up until right before the event, we were merely several dozen or sometimes several hundred individuals with nothing more in common than a postcard in our mail boxes or a text message on our phones giving us a date and an address. Any casual passerby looking at us as we window-shopped or loitered or examined our bags would think we were any random sampling of New Yorkers going about our daily business.

Then there was always a moment when these smart flocks, or flash mobs, or whatever they were calling themselves, would coalesce. Everyone suddenly has purpose and drive. I didn't care what Maya said; it was a thrilling and magical moment. By the time the three of us reached the museum, there were already a good eleven or twelve dozen people assembled in front, all of them facing the entrances. From the corner of my eye I could see non-flock people standing on tiptoe, trying to see what we looked at. They walked away, puzzled, when they found us staring at nothing in particular.

Nearby, several people checked their watches. A lot of people had gotten into the habit, on flock days, of setting them as closely as possible to an online atomic clock. Less than a minute ago there had been only the slightest electricity in the air. Now suspense tingled through the crowd, and every one of us could feel it. Even Colm's grip tightened.

Twelve-oh-three and fifty-seven seconds. Twelve-oh-three and fifty-eight seconds. Twelve-oh-three and fifty-nine. . . .

"All right," I heard Maya sigh. "Let's get this over with."

I let go of Colm's hand so I could attend to business. "One thousand, two hundred, and four," I heard him read from the back of his flag. "Remove shoes and . . ." Like a wooden Bavarian clock set into motion by the chiming of the hour, the hundred-plus of us assembled bent over, hiked up our jeans and trousers and slacks if we had them, and began shucking our footwear. I gave myself silent kudos for wearing sneakers. After the first time I'd been instructed to lie down with thirty other hardy souls on an Avenue A sidewalk with my legs in the air and to pretend I was riding a bicycle for thirty seconds, I had learned to dress as comfortably as possible for these events.

It only took a moment to collect both my shoes and hold

them over my head, as per the instructions. Maya, I noticed, bobbed up only a moment after me, having put both her bag and her soup on the ground. Colm, poor guy, was still struggling. He was going to miss everything.

There was a long moment of expectancy when those of us already brandishing our footwear waited for a majority of the others to catch up. In addition to the crowd of gawkers gathering behind us now, there were people within the museum watching us as well. A couple of suited men and women pulled out cell phones, punched out numbers, and inserted fingers in their open ears so they could hear to talk.

Somehow it felt as if I had been waiting forever when someone near the front of the crowd began banging the soles of his shoes together in a rapid, steady beat. It was difficult to imagine that several dozen people on such impromptu percussion would make a loud sound, but each thud was pretty considerable. Soon everyone had joined in. Someone shouted an okay from the front. Did I remember the instructions correctly? The only way I'd know would be to jump in. All at once, everyone shouted in unison,

"WHO'S YOUR DADDY? JAMES *BROWN'S* MY DADDY!"

I looked over at Maya. Her grin was one of the broadest I'd ever seen. Frat boy prank or not, she was enjoying herself to the max.

"WHO'S YOUR DADDY? JAMES *BROWN'S* MY DADDY!"

When I tried looking over my shoulder, I didn't see Colm. Was he still down on the ground?

"WHO'S YOUR DADDY? JAMES *BROWN'S* MY DADDY!"

That was it. Three times and we were done. There was a brief spate of applause, probably from the newbies, and then suddenly what had been a crowd acting as one splintered into scores of individuals beetling off in any number of directions. Some paused only briefly to slip back on their shoes; others walked off with their footgear in hand. The baffled observers behind us were the only ones who seemed tempted to remain.

And Colm, of course. The poor guy was still sitting on the sidewalk, wrestling with his laces when Maya and I had already managed to shuffle our feet back into their original coverings. I'd stood up again when suddenly I found him looming over me, flourishing a single shiny black boot. He looked around, utterly mystified. "Where'd everyone go?"

A trio of strangers watched the three of us without shame—a standard-issue overweight middle-aged tourist Mom and Dad, accompanied by a sweet-faced little girl of no more than ten. Both the mom and the girl wore foam rubber Statue of Liberty crowns; the girl carried a matching torch in her right hand. "What in heck were you folk doing?" asked the dad as he removed his plastic trucker cap and scratched his freckled head.

I don't care what people from outside New York say about those of us who live here. I know we have a joke reputation for being unfriendly. Yet whenever I'm confronted by someone with a thick Midwestern drawl and a quizzical look on their face, I'm always the poor fool who will stand there for eons and gesture in the direction of the Empire State Building and the nearest bus stop, or who'll scrawl down abbreviated instructions to the Rockefeller Center on the back of someone's Lonely Planet map of the city. Part of me, I suppose, wants visitors to the city to go back home and tell their Aunt Sylvie about the nice girl who helped them out of a tight spot. I liked being a one-girl chamber of commerce.

But not now. Not when I had Colm standing beside me half shod, half in stocking feet, turning around and around in place as if he expected the crowd to come back and give him a second chance. "It was a smart flock," I told the tourists, before addressing Colm. "I'm sorry. You kind of missed out."

"I'd only occupied myself with my shoes for a moment!"

Maya seemed to feel sorry for him, too. "You kind of have to be quick on these things," she told him.

"A smart flock?" Midwestern Dad repeated the words as if I'd spoken them in a particularly obscure dialect of Urdu.

"But . . . !" Colm held up his boot again. "These are a mite hard to remove!"

"Um, Nan." Maya tapped me on the shoulder and nodded in the direction of the nearest intersection, where a vehicle sporting flashing lights rounded the corner. New York's finest were approaching. "You can handle yourself from here?"

"Well," I began, not sounding certain.

"Maybe I wasn't clear. That was not a question." Maya slung her bag over her shoulder. "Colm, I hope I see you again. I'm heading back to the library." Maya widened her eyes and gave my arm a squeeze as she passed. "Call me," she murmured.

"It was enjoyable," Colm called out. He waved his boot in farewell.

I looked around. Perhaps a touch of vamoosing might be in order. My grasp of the legality of these sudden public gatherings was shaky, if by *shaky* I meant *nonexistent.* Surely the goofy things we did at them were nothing more than a nuisance at worst . . . but if that were the case, it occurred to me, why were the organizers always so secretive about the next happening? I jerked my head in the direction of the squad cars. "Can you maybe . . . ?"

"Oh." Colm looked down at his feet. "I suppose I look like an utter fool."

"I wouldn't say *utter*," I said in a halfhearted attempt at a joke. "Want to lean on me? Would that . . . oh heck." Barely had I spoken the words than Colm rested his elbow on my shoulder in a struggle to pull back on his boot. "Give me a warning first."

"You're a good size for that," commented Midwestern Mom. "A little thing like you looks almost made for it."

"Gee, thanks," I growled. Wait until the next time some out-of-towner asked for help. My one-girl chamber of commerce would be closed for good.

"Sorry," said Colm. Then, as he lost his balance and propelled me sideways, "I'm so sorry."

Midwestern Dad couldn't drop his original subject. "So what's the purpose of this here . . ."

"Smart flock," I supplied. If I had to visit a chiropractor, I was sending the bill to Mercer-Iverson's invoices department.

"Yeah, whatever, it seemed kind of . . . I dunno. . . ."

Although he still hopped up and down on one foot while attempting to shove his foot back into his boot, Colm managed to breathe out, "Smart flocks are a variety of performance art in which the cooperation and creative energies of citizens from all walks of life are merged . . . sorry about that . . . in a carefully choreographed unison of mutual . . . there we go . . . no we don't . . . energies." I wanted to kiss him right then and there for having memorized my improvised definition.

"Oh. She means a flash mob," said Midwestern Mom to her husband. "I read about it in *Vanity Fair*, honey."

A pair of cops had emerged from the squad car. One of the officers had made his way to the museum entrance, while the other began listening to the gawkers' stories. "Okay," I told Colm. "We've got to get out of here. Now."

"Why?"

"Because . . ." There was no time to argue. Although most of me didn't seriously believe we'd get into any trouble, I definitely didn't want our first date ending inside a holding cell. "Drop the shoe. Come on!"

It was with the utmost reasonableness that he pointed out, "I'm not leaving behind my shoe. I only bought these last month." He did, however, stop bobbling back and forth as he stood up and tucked his boot under the arm of his coat. "Lead on," he commanded. "This is your date, after all."

"Try to look inconspicuous!" We both laughed at that one. The only way we could be more conspicuous is if we were guiding the Underdog balloon from the Macy's Thanksgiving Parade. We walked a few steps away from the direction of the museum, I with my head held high, he with—well, with a pronounced limp, given that one of one of his soles was a good inch higher than the other.

"Only in New York," I heard Midwestern Dad say as we left them behind. "Only in New York. D'ya have the camera?"

"You're doing that deliberately!" I accused from the side of my mouth, barely able to keep from giggling.

"Correct me if I'm faulty on this point, but aren't you the one who wanted me to walk in one shoe?"

"Yes, but you don't have to . . . you're exaggerating. You're like John Cleese doing the Ministry of Funny Walks shtick." At that, he kicked his leg into the air, took three steps, then kicked again. "Stop it!"

"I shall if you agree to go out with me again."

"You're blackmailing me." I told him, but it was very obvious to us both how very much I enjoyed being blackmailed.

"I like you very much, Nan." High step, low step, high step, kick. "My only condition will be that next time, I choose the venue," he said. Before I could protest, he added, "I assure you we'll go somewhere inexpensive. Nothing fancy. No caviar, no wine. My choice, however."

Kick. High step, low step, high step. Kick. If we weren't attracting the cops' attention, we were surely attracting everyone else's. The flocks of late lunch-seekers streaming past us either pretended not to notice, or veered away as if we shook leper's bells. Where did Colm learn to high kick anyway—in a previous life as a Las Vegas showgirl? "Say yes," he wheedled. His next punt nearly smacked a businesswoman in the head. "Sorry," he assured the woman, whose eyes practically spun around like numbers on an old-fashioned cash register to end up on the total of *I'll sue!*.

"Okay, okay! Twist my arm!" I grinned at him. "I like you a lot, too. Despite being interesting like a cactus."

"Good," he said, once the businesswoman had scampered away. He shook his boot at me. "And I personally am quite interested by cacti." So it was a compliment, after all. "I am well pleased. Saturday, then?"

"Sounds great to me." I'd never before really felt so at ease with a new guy. His silly moments were something I'd never experienced. God knows I'd laughed at other dates, but not *with* many.

Colm looked at his watch. Ouch. Is there a single gesture more likely to kill a mood? "I fear I'd best return to work."

"Oh. Okay." Sometimes it's hard for me to remember that when I'm between jobs, few of the people I know have the same long blank days to fill. My friends and family are all busy people. When they chip out hours to see me, it's always with the expectation that I'll be available whenever they have the spare time free. The sad thing is that usually they're right. "So . . ." I felt a moment's awkwardness. Was he expecting a kiss? Should I shake his hand? Apologize again? What? All this uncertainty made me remember why I rarely ventured from the safety zone of my friends to meet new people.

He gestured with his shoe. "So . . . I'm going to put this back on, now. Saturday?"

"Oh. Yes, Saturday. Bye." I plunged my hands deep into my pockets, prepared to keep my lips to myself before I scuttled off. Maybe next time. "It was fun, huh?"

"Without doubt." I thought he was raising his arm to give me a hearty wave, but his hand shot out and pulled me close. A quick kiss landed on my lips; unfortunately I was too surprised and overjoyed to return it. "Saturday," he reminded me again, backing away. High step, low step, high step. Kick. "One for the road," he winked.

I couldn't wait.

Przybyla and Sons Bakers
(two loaves rye bread, slightly stale: free)

God bless Zofia Przybyla, the only woman in the western world of the opinion I should fatten up. Outside of the rare times I stumbled into an eighth grade museum tour group, she also was that rare person I could look in the eye without having to crane my neck. "Eat more!" she commanded. "You will get sick in that hole upstairs! You need extra layer of fat! Like whale bloober! To protect you from cold!"

I smiled and leaned against the wall and let out a delicate cough. If I had aspirations for an acting career, I could easily have won the part of Mimi in any *Bohème* with that meaningful, tubercular cough. "Oh, I'm fine, Mrs. Przybyla," I assured her. "Really. I don't mind the cold. Or damp. Or leaks." Or the bargain pity-rent either, but I kept that one to myself.

The baker's wife wore an oversized sweatshirt printed with a stern bald eagle, a Harley-Davidson chopper, purple mountain majesties, a fruited plain, and the stars and stripes waving over a Manhattan skyline. The words ALL-AMERICAN GRANDMA blazed across the collage. I kind of hoped she hadn't picked it out herself. "You promise me you don't go on low-carb diet," she said, rapping with her knuckles the loaves I carried. She let out some consonant-heavy curse. "Low carb will put you in your grave, and carry me with it! Pfaugh on low-carb diet! Bread is stuff of life! Screwing you, Doctor Watkins!"

"At," I said faintly, worried that she might work herself into a coronary. "Atkins." She was already staggering against the back stairwell door as she shook her fist.

I wanted to call out a hallelujah of thanks when outside the solid steel security door that I held open I heard the slam of the rental van hatch and a crunch of feet on debris. Mitchell rounded the opening, struggling under the weight of two cardboard boxes, both labeled *Misc*. Nearly all Mitchell's boxes so far had borne the same label. His intentions might have been good at the start; when he had dropped off the first of his worldly possessions the night before, some of the boxes had been marked with perfectly accurate legends like *Books* or *Bath*. Very quickly, though, the *Miscs* had begun to multiply until the spare bedroom was nearly filled with them. I knew if I opened one, I was likely to find a haphazard assortment of flotsam from Mitchell's ruined life: a blanket, a frying pan, an emptied pencil can, and perhaps a framed photograph of Ty. "Thanks," he told me, edging by, exuding an aroma of sweat. Then, to Mrs. Przybyla, "Hi."

Zofia waited until Mitchell was halfway up the stairs before stage-whispering, "You have *boyfriend* living with you now?" So transparent was her expression of outrage that had it been an outfit, Britney Spears would have demanded to wear it on tour. I could tell she was mentally envisioning some sort of orgy pit right above the table where she made her babka.

Keep it light, I reminded myself. I wanted to be the most unobtrusive, unremarkable tenant ever. "Oh, Mrs. Przybyla, you've met my older brother Mitchell before. He's just gone through a breakup and needs someplace to stay. Say hi, Mitch," I called up the stairs.

He turned, already wearing the I-said-that expression I expected. "Hi," he repeated. "I hope the van's not blocking the alley."

Flustered, Mrs. Przybyla wiped her hands on her sweatshirt and unconsciously fluffed the curls around her ears. "Oh, very nice for you, having big brother around to protect," she commented, approving.

My last round of door duty was done, so I let the heavy steel slam shut and began to follow Mitch up the stairs. "Thanks for the bread!"

"You eat!" she reminded me, stepping forward enough to call up after me, but not so far forward that she would lock herself out of the back bakery entrance.

"Have you considered doing something about this mess?" Mitchell dumped the boxes atop the others that sat right inside the door. Most of his furniture had gone into storage; the few pieces that hadn't now cluttered the room's edge. I knew what he meant, though. The mechanical monstrosities. The hulking, lethal-looking contraptions that could have been owned by Sweeney Todd during a bullish pie market. The antique hardware abandoned by generations of bakers who'd occupied the shop below.

"It's too heavy to move. A lot of it's bolted to the floor." It was a bit of a lie. The stuff certainly looked unwieldy, but I hadn't actually attempted to shift any of it since—well, ever. I simply didn't want to.

Mitchell took a long look around the room as if the sight offended him. In the late afternoons the sun shone slantwise through the skylights and cast long shadows among the mechanisms. They looked more imposing than they really were. Poor Mitch. In the patch of wan winter sunlight where he stood, he once again looked like a lost kid. "Let me put this bread away. We can take a break for a few before returning the van. If you want to, that is," I told him.

He shrugged. "Sure. Whatever."

A few minutes later I found him in the living room, trying

to find a clear channel on my television. "Your TV has a *dial*," he stated. Was that supposed to be news to me? I raised my eyebrows. "A *dial*. We never even had a set with a dial growing up. Are you some kind of tree-hugging PBS-watcher or something?"

"When I want to see some TV, I go down to Malamute's," I explained to him. I didn't run a five-star hotel. The closest thing to a creature comfort in my place was the warm spot under the radiator where I once spied a grey mouse napping. "They change the channel for me if there's something special I want to watch."

"I could've left mine out of storage if you'd told me! It's three times the size!" He crossed his arms, seeming to fold into himself like a deflating balloon. I could tell he was already having second thoughts about this temporary living arrangement. Was now a good time to tell him that if he had brought his set with him, chances were that without cable or a satellite dish the only channel we'd receive was the 24-hour Snow Network? Probably not. For the hundred and twentieth time in six months I found myself groping for words that wouldn't make me sound insensitive, and for the hundred and twentieth time they wouldn't come. I made a silent appeal to my Kwan Yin figurine, hoping she'd bless me with compassion. What would our mom have done?

I perched on the edge of the sofa where he had sunk and, on impulse, reached out and ran a hand through his rumpled hair. Mitchell was the only one of us who came out tall and handsome like Dad; Brody and I were both shrimplike and big-eyed. Why was it, then, that Brody was the brother obsessed with clean shirts and combed hair and neat (if ho-hum) clothes, while my other brother concealed himself in oversized army surplus duds? If hiding from the world was what he wanted, he'd chosen the perfect temporary shelter for it. "So what is there to do?" he said at last, breaking the silence between us.

"Mitch, you know my neighborhood. Do what you want!

There are movies you could see. You could hit a bar, get some drinks, people watch?"

"I don't really do bars."

"Not even gay ones?" He shuddered. "Okay. What else do you do?"

He stared ahead, silent. Time passed—seconds, minutes, long seasons, aeons in which polar caps could have grown and receded—until he finally raised his shoulders and let them fall, heavy with weight. During those centuries I had time to consider my immediate future with Mitchell. The one thing I'd liked about my other roommates, besides their inevitable impermanence, had been that I didn't have to entertain them. They had their own lives, their own boyfriends, their own AA meetings to attend. Mitchell had only dozens of framed photos of a lover who might as well no longer exist, furniture crammed in a storage closet somewhere, a crappy room in his sister's crappy apartment, and . . . what exactly else did Mitchell have? "Don't you hang out with friends?" I asked.

"I had a lover. I didn't need friends."

"A person should have both! Didn't you used to—" What did my brother do away from his media librarian job at the private school where he worked? All I could remember of Mitchell's hobbies were the endless model cars that in high school he used to fashion and then finish with little bottles of Testor's paint. I cast a line into the murky waters of my memory, hoping to fish out one of his other activities. Not a nibble. The silence between us began to grow uncomfortable; every second that passed plummeted into a emptiness that neither time nor we could fill. "Set construction!" I said at last. "You used to work in a scene shop for that community theatre."

"Eight or nine years ago. Before Ty."

I had my own empty hours to fill. How was I supposed to share the burden of his as well? Did Mitchell not realize that every mention of Ty numbed me? Perhaps he did. Perhaps that's why he kept returning to the hurt, picking at the scab to make it scar over and toughen. "So what do you want to do?"

Once again, he shrugged as if weighed down by the gravity of a larger, denser planet. "I thought maybe I could hang out with you and your friends now. If you don't mind." A lost little boy in a Paramus shopping mall looked up at me from my sofa, waiting to be rescued.

How could I walk away from him? "Yeah," I said, then tried to invest an enthusiasm I didn't feel. "Sure. That'd be loads of fun."

Calabash Lounge
(beer: $10 a pitcher; Cheetos: $1 a bag)

"Do you want to hear my theory about karaoke?" The little wooden table between us was already distressed by years of battering and wear. With our mugs and pitchers, the two of us had managed to create some abstract artwork of sticky overlapping circles across its surface. Colm leaned in and nodded, his head cocked so he could hear over the din. I raised my voice. "No, actually, it's kind of the same as my whole theory about New York. You want to hear my theory about New York?"

"Sure."

"I can't *stand* this song," I said, gesturing toward the little karaoke stage, where the loudspeakers blared out an off-key imitation of a Red Hot Chili Peppers tune. I plucked out a Cheeto swimming in the last quarter-inch of beer, and popped it in my mouth. The top half was still crunchy, anyway. "Okay. Nan Cloutier's theory of New York! It's a big city."

"Do you really think? Eight million people?" Colm peered at me over the tops of his adorably thick glasses. "I have a theory that in Manhattan everyone knows dozens of people impossible to avoid; and a handful with whom they hope to connect, yet their paths never quite cross."

"Ours crossed."

"And I'm glad of it. Go on, tell me your theory, Holmes."

I loved the way he flirted with deadpan humor. I cleared my throat, feeling a little heady with pleasure. "New York's a big city. Living here's a lot like going from high school to college. What were you in your high school class, like, top ten percent?"

"Salutatorian, actually." He plucked another Cheeto from my bag and dropped it into the pitcher, knowing I'd go after it. "I had to make a speech."

"Stop! You're wasting precious snack foodage. Sometime I'll tell you my theory of how orange processed foods are a major, if not foundational, food group. Okay. So you were salutatorian in high school. Which is a big deal. You were probably like, one of those kids all your teachers thought would go far. Maybe you thought the same yourself, right?" He nodded, probably not so much to agree with me as to indicate he was still listening over the racket. "Then what happens? You get to college and suddenly you're surrounded by kids as good as you. Chances are they're even better. They've got the same grades, the same credits. They've not only been in the top ten percent of their classes or salutatorian in your case, but they've been the vale-damned-dictorian." I stabbed the Cheeto in his direction. "Suddenly you've gone from somebody pretty special to just one of the crowd, maybe to the depths of the lower percentiles. No matter what you want to do, there's going to be someone faster, someone cleverer, someone hungrier going after it and getting it before you. That's the way of the world. It's the same for this place. There's always someone who'll do better than you."

Was I making sense? My thoughts sounded fine in my beer-sodden brain, but spilling them out seemed to take longer than I expected. "This karaoke bar?" he finally asked.

I stared at him for a moment, then laughed. "No! Yes, but no! There's always someone who can sing better than you at karaoke, but I meant this." I gestured broadly with my hands. "This island. Manhattan. New York City. Why get so hyped up and competitive when there's someone younger and a whole lot betterer who'll . . . Betterer?" I asked doubtfully. It didn't sound right, somehow.

"Is this part of your Thoreauvian life philosophy?" Maybe I was slightly buzzed, but my guard instantly went up. This was the second time in a month I'd heard someone compare me to the bard of Walden, and I wasn't all that sure it was intended as a compliment. Colm must have seen something on my face reflecting my sudden dark mood, because he held up his hands in placation. "One of your friends told me about it on New Year's. Clark?"

I made a sound that sounded like *hmfph*. "You know, Thoreau wasn't completely crazy," I told him. "He simply believed in subsistence living as a viable alternate lifestyle. He lived by Walden Pond because he didn't buy into the whole postindustrial, rat-racy, keeping up with the Joneses thing. Living the way he did was a statement for him, a whole way of thumbing his nose at the world and saying, 'Fuck you guys, I'm taking my life by the horns and riding this train until I snag the gold ring.' "

"Perhaps if I looked about for a shoehorn, we could wedge one more metaphor in that sentence of yours." Colm said the words without malice, and softened them further by refilling my mug from the newly delivered pitcher.

This is what I liked about Colm: he got me. He didn't tease my silly theories. He didn't try to compete to see who could be cleverer, or balk at anything I threw his way. I'd never before dated anyone who felt like an old friend after so short a time. Is it any wonder I wanted more of his company?

Onstage, the singer finally finished his travesty with a half-wailed, half-warbled flat note. When the music ceased, remaining Red Hot Chili Peppers fans around the world—both of them—cheered with relief. "Let's give it up!" said the KJ into her microphone as the bar burst into scattered and tepid applause. "Great job, guy! Next I need Sandra to come to the mike! Sandra?"

"Boooooooo!" I yelled at the previous singer through cupped hands as he stepped down from the platform and made his way in our direction. *"Dude! You suck! Booooooo!"*

His voice a study in mildness, Colm inquired, "Nan, you are aware that was your brother singing?"

"Well yeah! You think I'd tell a perfect stranger he was rancid?"

My brother was in earshot for the last three words. He tilted back his head, glared at me through narrowed eyes, and plopped down next to me on the bench. "Thanks so much for the support. And least I'm *singing.*"

"I don't do karaoke. If any part of this date involved me having to climb that stage and sing, I don't know, 'Smells Like Teen Spirit' . . ."

"Funny," Colm said, his hand on his chin. "I pictured you more of a 'Heart of Glass' kind of girl."

"See what they have in the book by George Michael," Mitch suggested, obviously still stinging from my catcalls. He pushed in Colm's direction the sticky three-ring black binder resting neglected on our table. "She'd definitely know the words to all his stuff."

"Liar. You are such a liar. You are liariffic. Your secret agent name is 'Liar. James Liar. Shaken, not true.' " My George Michael obsession had taken place thirteen years ago, thank you! It took several blinks to clear the bleariness from my eyes; I tried to coerce my uncooperative mouth into working with me so I could say as much, when I noticed a familiar figure crossing from the entrance hallway to the bar. The posture was what I spotted first—how the man's leather jacket fell from his slung-back shoulders, his entire torso seeming to follow in the wake of his hips' slow gyrations.

Panic only inflamed the prickly sensation spreading from under my arms down my sides. What had Colm been saying only moments before, about a handful of people it seemed you could never escape in this city? Of all the bad luck . . . or was it luck at all? I lurched to the side, caught Mitchell in a headlock, and growled in his ear. "Damien Morris is here."

"Yeah, I know!" He tried to wrench out of my vise grip, but the beer made me persistent. "Didn't I tell you he was coming?"

It was perhaps the best of timing that Colm decided to rise right then, probably thinking that Mitch's revelation of my former George Michael obsession had caused some family friction. "I'll let you two duke this out," he announced, "while I visit the facilities."

Until he was out of eyesight I continued playfully to hug my big brother tight. Then I turned into a boa constrictor. Mitch would never fight back. He was much too well-bred to hit a girl. Even his sister. "Damien *Morris* is *here*," I repeated.

"Ouch! Holy crap! You're breaking my neck!"

"What do you know about it?"

"Let go of me and I'll tell you!" Once I'd loosened my elbow from around his glottis, I allowed Mitchell a moment to recuperate. He helped himself to my mug, ran a finger around his collar, and gasped for air. When I feinted another lock, he dropped the drama queen act and began talking. "He called this afternoon. I thought he was a friend of yours! Wasn't he at that, you know, last year?"

Damien had been at so many you-knows in the last three years that there was no way in hell I could pinpoint the one Mitch meant. Yes, I got his message—Mitch had met Damien before. All my friends and family had, at some point. Neither my father nor brothers knew he'd been anything more than someone I hung out with, though. I didn't discuss my former sex life with them. "Yes, he's a friend," I halfheartedly agreed. Across the room, Damien was already clutching a vaguely red cocktail, the recipe for which he'd no doubt given the pretty bartender himself. His dark eyes busily wandered the room. "But why is he *here?*"

"He sounded like he wanted to hang out. I knew you and I were doing karaoke with Colm, and he said that sounded like fun, so . . ."

"So you invited him," I finished, getting a nod for an answer. "You invited . . . !" How could I finish that sentence without incriminating myself? *You invited my former sexual hobby on my first real date with a nice guy in months?* How about *You invited disaster down upon me in a manner that has not been witnessed since the last summer blockbuster disaster flick?* Or *You invited an ass-kicking on yourself, mister!*

"Damien," Mitchell said with a great deal of big brotherly patience. "I invited Damien. You had too much to drink, little sis?"

God. There have been many times during my life I've wished that fratricide wasn't punishable by law. At the age of twelve, I'd seen blood for the first time when Mitchell announced to all his male classmates that his little sister was wearing her first bra. I'd lain awake nights wishing horrible multiple deaths upon him at the discovery he'd been reading my juvenile diary; he'd announced at one of my parents' academic dinner parties that by the time I was thirty, I wanted to have married all the boys from *Saved by the Bell*. Including Screech.

Over my lifetime I've thrown things at him, yelled at him, cried because of him. But never before had my older brother absolutely stunned me with such insensitivity. Pain and confusion and rage seemed to tangle together in a white-hot ball that burned between my eyebrows. I couldn't berate him the way I wanted, though. Call it part of my campaign to be a better Nan, or call it my contribution to the effort to make my brother's life a little better, but I tried to remain calm. He hadn't known. I rubbed at my forehead, suddenly feeling very old. "You invited another guy on my date, Mitch. On my male-female date with potential kissage at the end."

"Oh. Oh! This is a real date? Crap. I didn't know! Why didn't you say something? I could've stayed home!"

Would I go to hell for ripping off one of my brother's ears with my teeth? The fleeting moment of savage satisfaction would be worth a lifetime of guilt, right? "I wouldn't want you to do that," I managed to choke.

I'd been investing so much effort in keeping my voice level that I totally failed to notice Damien's arrival at the table. He was leaning over the wooden divide, watching me—except Damien never really indulged in the standard postures of ordinary people. He didn't merely walk. He sauntered. While others stood, he remained poised. And instead of leaning, Damien had draped himself over the rail like a limp-boned cat, his hands folded to provide a soft surface for his lolling head. Those deep brown eyes I'd once enjoyed and now dreaded looked into mine, and his lips parted. "Hi, Nan."

I tried to ignore the teasing, familiar tone. For a long time I've wondered if men really understand how we feel when they flirt with us, even without serious intent. I've rarely been able to relax fully with a flirty guy. Questions bubble to the surface of my brain, faster and faster. *What's his intent? How should I react? How's my tone? Am I matching his playfulness? Is there something in my teeth?* By that point my head feels like thick syrup at a roaring boil, my stomach kicks in with clenching and clutching. I start to feel sweaty around my hairline and behind my ears, and sometimes a little faint. For me, flirting is a full aerobic workout—and I was already busily building new muscles with Colm. "I'm on a date," I told him, pointedly refusing to play his game.

"Hmmm. Someone special?" How in the world could two words be so insinuating?

"I might never know. You see, I haven't had a chance to be alone with him." Damien got the hint, all right. He simply ignored it.

"Alone with whom?" Colm eased himself back into the chair across from me, his hands rubbing against each other. "No paper towels in the restroom," he explained when he caught me watching.

"Colm, Damien, Damien, Colm." I hoped the barest of introductions might shorten my misery.

It took only a quick glance to notice that each sized up the other; Damien's eyes flicked in Colm's direction, lazily traveled the length of his torso, and then smiled at me. Colm, in the meantime, cleared his throat and held out his hand. "How do you do? You're one of Nan's many friends?"

"Work friends, actually." For a moment I thought Damien might ignore Colm's friendly gesture altogether, but at last he straightened up and allowed his hand to be shaken. "Nan and I have worked together for many years."

There had been the slightest undertone to the word *worked* that I didn't like. I cleared my throat and started to speak, but Colm was a step ahead. "Will you be part of the Seasonal Staffers St. Valentine's display, then?"

Damien's lids seemed weighed down and heavy. His lips curled at the ends. I recognized the look: Years ago he had employed it to great effect to lure me against my better judgment into bed. How *unfair* that he used it against me now. "Seasonal Staffers and I have not seen eye to eye recently, but how could I miss that? Maybe I'll play Cupid."

"Hey Damien, buddy, let's go get a beer and play some pinball." My brother rose from his seat and planted his hand on my torturer's shoulder. "Sound cool, bro?"

Damien responded to the fake heartiness with a roll of his eyes and an equally false reply. "Sure thing bro, old buddy, old pal."

"Fantastico! You go on ahead!" Once Damien had begun his slow promenade to the bar, Mitchell leaned over to give me a bright smile. "I'll keep him occ-u-pied so you two can get to know each other bet-ter," he hissed in an exaggerated stage whisper. A lip reader could have followed the sentence from two counties over.

"O-kee-do-kee!" I said in the same dopey tone.

He loped off with a big grin, probably thinking he'd done me a huge favor. "Interesting fellow," Colm commented once we were alone. We both paused to clap for the girl who'd finished massacring "Harper Valley P.T.A."

"Oh, he's only pulling the protective big brother thing," I said. "Honestly, I promise he doesn't invite himself on all my dates."

I really liked Colm's laugh. It's easy to be turned off a guy because he snorts like a walrus or guffaws too loudly or peeps out reedy little titters. Colm, however, only parted his lips slightly to let out a low rumble from his chest that made his shoulders heave. I could live with that laugh, I decided right then and there. "I didn't mean your brother," Colm said. "The other one. Damien?" Oh. Crud. "What's he, an old boyfriend or something?"

Was there jealousy in his sideways look? I didn't know Colm well enough to tell. Part of me thrilled to think he might secretly be threatened at the thought of my other swains. Heck, if he credited me with possible other swains, that would have been satisfaction enough. "No. God no! Not even. Damien's had a girlfriend ever since I've known him. Which has been what, six years?"

"I see. Are they cohabitating?"

Was it the tone-deaf bellowing out "I'm Too Sexy" at the top of his voice at the room's far end? Or was it the lovely beer fog? My brain took its sweet time to decipher the five-syllable word. "Living together? No."

"Are they engaged?"

"No." I wasn't sure where this was going. "Why?"

"Far be it for me to presume." Colm wrapped his long fingers around the mug before him, and looked at me. "I simply wondered."

I really had no idea what he was getting at. I gathered my wits and took a dignified stab. "Are you implying a girlfriend of six years to whom he's not proposed and with whom he's never lived indicates that he is the sort of guy up with whom a girl should not put?"

After a slight pause, Colm gently moved the pitcher away. "I think you've had enough, my dear."

"You sound pretty judgmental for a guy who has been flirting with me since day one."

After pushing them up the bridge of his nose with a finger, he peered at me over the tops of his glasses. "Do you think I've been flirting with you?"

"Yes!" I thought about it. "Definitely!" When he didn't reply, I thought some more. "Haven't you?"

"Most assuredly. With intent."

Feeling smug, I leaned back in my chair. "Hah. Thought so. So why don't you have a girlfriend already, Mr. Casting Aspersions on My Friends?"

His foot brushed against mine under the table as he shifted positions. Much to my disappointment, it didn't linger. "I suppose it's a valid question, but it's also one I could ask you."

"I'm a real catch—next-to-no-job, bad apartment, a brother paving my personal road to hell with his good intentions. It's a real mystery why they're not beating down the door. Now you." Across the dark room, Mitchell and Damien leaned against the bar, drinking together. Although Mitchell's jaw flapped, Damien didn't appear to be listening. I felt small unwanted electric shocks every time his eyes flickered in our direction.

Behind the hand on which his chin rested, Colm's smile showed through his fingers. "Let's see. Where to begin. A few years ago I was deeply involved with someone. April. I nearly married her."

After that statement followed a pause long enough to

drive through the entire Ringling Bros. and Barnum & Bailey Circus. "You didn't, obviously."

"No, I did not. I wanted to, or thought I did, but it wasn't right." When he saw by my raised eyebrows that I wasn't going to let the cryptic statements pass without explanation, he laid his hands on the table and explained. "She thought I wasn't good relationship material. She said I lacked motivation."

"Because you were an artist? Maybe you both had different definitions of the word *motivation*. One of my friends is a painter too, you know."

"That was part of my problem. The old man tells people I was a painter, but I didn't really have a medium. I don't know that I was much of *any* kind of artist. I dabbled at sculpting, at painting. For a few minutes I thought I might be a performance artist—don't laugh." Too late. The notion of Colm standing half-naked in front of an audience smearing his torso in chocolate pudding while reciting Ginsberg made me snicker. "I said it was only for a few minutes! Basically, I was more entranced with the notion of being an artist than in really getting my hands dirty. April was right. I didn't have motivation." I could picture April in my head: one of those whip-crackin', latte-totin', book-clubbin', women's-magazine-quiz-takin' women who lived four to an apartment in Chelsea until she found the right guy and upgraded her abode. "So she left. I can scarcely blame her."

Over the past couple of weeks I'd seen Colm the flirt, Colm the joker, and Colm the hapless, but I'd never really seen him speak so honestly and at such length, particularly about himself. I leaned in, suppressing a yawn, wishing I dared more closeness. "Then what, you went back to the Mercer-Iverson empire so you could impress her?"

He laughed, almost embarrassed. "No, nothing that craven. For a year I was self-appointed King Mope, spending my days walking around Morningside Heights looking for some sort of inspiration, hoping to prove her wrong. I appropriated money from my grandfather at regular intervals. Then one morning I woke up and realized none of it was really working for me. I wasn't the kind of person who could cope with unlimited time and freedom."

"You should've known me then. I could've shown you how to whittle away that time." Something in his description struck me as quite lonely. Perhaps it was my sleepy, beery state, or perhaps it was sincere emotion moving my legs and arms, but I found myself sliding from my chair into the one next to him so that the table no longer divided us. "So then you went back to the Mercer-Iverson empire . . ."

". . . To give me structure, more or less," Colm finished. Ever the gentleman, he had set aside his own mug when he'd moved mine. He now picked up both and set them on the table behind us, so we could both rest our elbows close. When he resumed talking, his mouth was close enough for his breath to stir my hairs and tickle my ear. It was a pleasant, nuzzly sensation. At that moment I wanted nothing more than to lie down with him somewhere comfortable and warm, so I could listen to his voice and feel his breath against my skin. "I think the experience taught me that I'm not inspired unless I have constraints to work against. On my own, I do nothing."

"But when your time belongs to a company . . ."

". . . I'm full of inspired ideas and projects I want to try and visions of things I want to invent. It's the essential human conundrum, isn't it? Without an impasse to tackle, I'm uncreative and dull. I'm one of those people who needs an oppugnant force. Something to *strive against*. Don't you find?"

I loved the way Colm talked—the old-fashioned choice of words like *oppugnant*, the deep-chested, rounded vowels that softened his consonants into little phoneme pillows so downy and inviting that I wanted to rest my head on them. "Oh, I'm not artistic at all," I told him, covering my mouth only a scant second before it stretched into a wide, skull-shaking yawn. There was no way I would ever, ever tell him or anyone else about my life's sole creative output, when for two weeks as a sophomore I mistakenly decided that the world was aching for a modern retelling of *The Decameron* written entirely in rhyming couplets. I closed my eyes to rest them a little. "I don't have anything . . . to strive . . . sorry . . . against." I covered my mouth again as yet another yawn racked my neck and jaw. "Don't you miss having the time to work on . . . your art?"

Through my drooping eyelids, I saw him lean in. "I think I'd rather be full of ideas and to feel alive and not have time to act on them, than have time and yet feel . . . empty."

"It sounds so sad to me. I don't want you to sign away your soul to Mercer-Iverson."

"You're good to talk to," he said in a murmur. Despite the anarchy of a pair of young guys laying waste to Hot Tuna through the loudspeakers, his lips were so close to my ear that he could barely have whispered and I still would have heard every word. Had sound ever been so erotic to me, with other men? Or had I simply been so long without that I would have been aroused by any stimulus? As much as I wanted Colm at that moment—his fondness for tomatoes had never left my mind—I would have settled for quiet, and stillness, and more of his words curling in and around my ear. "But I think we'd better get you home." He planted a quick peck on my cheek as a consolation prize.

"Noooo." I opened my eyes at my protest's end. "Home to bed?" I asked. I'm not sure what about the question struck me as funny, but I giggled slightly. Perhaps it had been the slight surprise in his eyes, or the way he appeared to consider the offer for a few seconds afterwards.

"Simply getting you home will do for a start. A gentleman never takes advantage of a lady in her cups." I was drowsily aware that he had risen from his seat to pull on his leather jacket and scarf.

"You talk like your grandfather," I laughed.

"I believe he would say the same thing as well. Whoops-a-daisy."

"What am I, two?" My eyes cracked open enough to assist him in lifting me to my feet. For a moment or two we engaged in an awkward coat dance while I groped for the armholes and he attempted to meet them with my hands. "I'm not really that drunk," I assured him. "Just tired. It feels like I hit a brick wall a couple of minutes ago." Maybe he was right. All I really wanted to do right then was lie down. I still wished Colm could be beside me, but I felt my fantasy of our first night together mellowing from a vision of unbridled lust to the simple pleasures of talking, touching, and maybe sleeping next to each other.

"All the more reason we get you home, then. Aren't you working tomorrow?"

"Yes, I am." I'd not had anyone button up my coat since my mother, back in grade school. The gesture made me grin. "Listen, I'm fine. I can walk."

"You're sure?"

To prove the point, I wrenched open my eyelids and managed to walk in a more or less straight line away from the table and down two stairs to the main floor. "See?" We took a few steps more. The volume of the mens' caterwauling decreased once we'd passed the stage and its loudspeakers; I didn't turn my head when the woman running karaoke called out a friendly farewell. In fact, it wasn't until we were nearly at the end of the long entrance hallway and near the outer door when I realized I'd forgotten something. "Mitchell . . ."

"I'll go tell him I'm escorting you home. Can you lean here for a minute?"

"I can do leaning." Leaning sounded like a very good thing indeed. I could lean like a pro. If a reporter needed to call a local expert for a hot news story on leaning, I was his girl. I let Colm slump me against the plywood paneling, where I rested my head between two very dirty St. Pauli Girl posters fixed to the wall by thumbtacks and stains. "Tell him . . ."

As my eyes shut once again, I felt Colm's lips tickling against my hair. "I'll tell him you're tired and I'm taking you home and he's not to worry. Now, don't go anywhere."

"No," I murmured. "I won't." I couldn't have fallen asleep, not on my feet there in the narrow little hallway, but it seemed like only seconds passed before I felt a pair of hands grab my waist and pull me away from the wall again. Colm's hips gyrated back and forth in time with the music, encouraging me to give in to the rhythm. "No," I murmured into his shoulder. My cheek felt warm against the leather. "Seriously. Don't dance with me now. This will be our first dance and I don't want to spend the rest of my life telling people 'Eve of Destruction' is Our Song."

My partner was insistent, moving my body to the beat. To him it must have felt as intimate as dancing with a dress-maker's dummy; I loosened up some, finally allowing my self to be led. A hand brushed my forehead, smoothing the hair that fell over it. His fingers continued down to my cheeks, my neck . . . then slipped through an opening be-tween my coat and my blouse to glide over my left breast, where his finger traced my nipple. Even through the layer of cotton and the nylon of my bra I could feel the circle it left as it moved around and around, a complete closed circuit of tingling electricity with a voltage that increased with every passing second. I didn't dare open my eyes, fearful he might stop.

I wanted Colm badly. I had visions of leaping up and wrapping my poor sex-deprived loins around his hips and pinning him to the wall, but I'm not especially athletic. In-stead, I let his musky cologne scent my own skin while I blindly let my lips work their way along the strong bone of his jaw. They wrapped around his chin and continued their climb until at last our mouths met and parted. His tongue shot forward as if spring-loaded, probing the roof of my mouth, the insides of my cheeks, my gums. I couldn't help but groan. Colm's kisses sent flames licking across my skin in all directions. He seemed to know exactly how I liked to be tasted and where I needed to be touched. It was as if we had made love before, long ago, and as if we both still remembered after many months exactly how the other liked it.

Like a bucket of ice water, a possibility chilled me. No. He wouldn't have!

When my sticky eyelids wrenched open, the pain stung like ripping a Band-Aid from a sore spot. "Oh shit," I said, stumbling back. My hands flew to my mouth. The light and noise penetrating my brain instantly gave me a pounding headache at the front of my skull. How stupid I'd been! How stupid, and dumb, and naive, and . . .

"Don't stop, baby," murmured Damien, his lips still moist from my own. "You don't want to stop."

But oh, I did. Because behind Damien, stock-still in the doorway leading to the bar, stood both Mitchell and Colm. My brother's mouth hung open.

I couldn't look at Colm. I didn't dare. The look of hurt and shock he would be wearing would only wound me more deeply. Damien backed off, his damage done, and glanced over his shoulder. He didn't at all seem surprised at our audience.

I couldn't stay. I couldn't explain. I'd told Colm that Damien wasn't an ex—how could I justify what I'd done right there in plain sight? I rubbed at my mouth with my palm, trying to erase the kiss. Then I turned and ran from the bar. My feet thudded over the pavement and down the street in the direction of home.

I hoped against hope to hear someone calling my name, begging me to stop. No one did.

FEBRUARY

Mercer-Iverson Department Store
($7.75 per hour is but the mildest of balms unto my impoverished state)

"Shower your sweetie with Muchas Smoochies?"

The woman with the ragged platinum hair and dark roots didn't turn her head. "Screw off."

Fair enough. I, too, would probably balk at anyone dressed up as a giant magenta heart-shaped box who lunged at me with a plate of candy lips. But I, Nan Cloutier, was a weathered employee of Seasonal Staffers, Inc. Cursing left me undeterred. Without hesitation, I turned to the next shopper strolling past the Muchas Candies display, strategically located on the busy aisle leading from lingerie to the up escalator.

"Give your loved one Muchas Smoochies for Valentine's Day?" The middle-aged matron assumed a pleasant expression and pretended not to see me, using the bun of her hair as a deflector as she walked by. I might not have possessed creative genius, or a degree in anything that mattered, but as anyone who'd ever sat across a Scrabble board from me could attest, no one was as competitive as I. This dame looked like she'd dipped her hand into the candy jar more than a few times. Once I got her to sample the goods, sending her home loaded with caloric chocolates would be a cinch. "Would you like to sample Muchas Smoochies?" I cooed, proffering my sample platter. The woman's neck stiffened, as if I'd been a construction worker commenting on her nice tuckus. "Perhaps . . ."

Persistence might be rewarded in some alternate universe where perhaps an alternate me held down a nice office job and lived in a nice, quiet, brother-free Brooklyn apartment, but what did I get for my initiative and gumption? The woman wheeled around, squinched tight every muscle in her face, and thrust her middle finger in my direction before flouncing away.

"Perhaps you'd like to plant Muchas Smoochies on my *big fat ass,*" I growled at her backside.

If anyone deserved a break, it was the girl in the candy box. Although my arms and legs protruded through flexible nylon holes, the heart-shaped cutouts that sandwiched my front and back were unbelievably unwieldy; my face peeked out approximately below the heart's center, where the Muchas Candies logo curled in gold script letters. The heart's curves flared out several feet to each side of me and met a good foot and a half above my scalp, so every turn made me feel like Joan Collins at her most severely shoulder-padded, flouncing away from the ColbyCo board room in a high dudgeon. "Please tell me this horrible day is almost over," I muttered to my coworker.

"It's more fun to watch you suffer." Either the good folks at Muchas were test-marketing a nicotine-scented candy, or Amanda had lost her battle to stop smoking. She reeked of tobacco. "You look like crap, by the way."

As if I needed to be told. "I am never, ever, ever drinking again."

"Hung over, huh?" I was, but the headache with which I'd woken that morning was nothing compared to what I felt whenever I replayed the previous evening's events. You can hydrate a headache and feed it analgesics; there's no tonic for utter stupidity. "What I don't get," said Amanda, her arms flapping helplessly from her round yellow candy-box uniform, "is why they have us cut the samples in quarters. They're shaped like lips! Once we get the toothpicks in them and put them on a tray, it looks like we've been interning with Jack the Ripper."

Eating candy from our own plates was strictly forbidden. We helped ourselves to samples from each other's. "It's *gritty,*" I complained, discarding my toothpick behind a stack of display boxes.

"Oh, Muchas is crappy stuff. Makes a Whitman's sampler look gourmet. You know what I like? See's. You had See's?"

"Oh my gosh, I *love* See's!" Candy nostalgia helped to lift me out of my depression for a moment. "Whenever my younger brother goes to Las Vegas, I always make him bring me back a box of See's chocolates."

"It's the peanut brittle that gets me going."

"Peanut brittle!" We both sighed. Amanda and I weren't friends—in fact, I could barely endure standing next to her now that she smelled like someone's old pipe—but at least for that brief moment we were united in our mutual admiration for the brittle.

Until, that is, from behind us we heard, "Ahem." Not a clearing of the throat, not glottal syllables. DeeDee Camillo was the sort of woman who tried to command attention by actually saying the word *ahem* aloud, without irony. It took us a couple of moments of turning in place and avoiding each other's costumes before we could both face her; by then I'd managed to run my tongue over my teeth to check for traces of chocolate and compose my face into a smile. "Slow day, ladies? No customers?"

"We were restocking our Smoochies," Amanda suggested, more as a test balloon than anything else.

"If you've finished, then perhaps you could go do what you were paid to do." Thank goodness I'd not said a thing.

DeeDee's scorn for Amanda's blatant lie was palpable. "In other words, *work*. The fact that I'm heading to lunch does not mean you two can slack off."

Inwardly I rejoiced that my poor tired head could take a half hour off from a forced cheerfulness it certainly did not feel. "We'll hold down the fort!" I enthused, earning a nod of approval.

DeeDee still scowled at Amanda. "I've got eyes everywhere, you know," she told her. The Armadillo made several entirely unnecessary adjustments to the display rack of candy boxes while she waited for us to return to our posts.

"Yeah, I knew she had an extra pair in her butt from keeping her head up there," Amanda whispered as we started to sidle around again.

My right heart wing collided with her left side. "Stupid costume," I fumed.

"Yeah, well, at least yours doesn't make you look like Ms. Pac-Man."

No, but mine had the unfortunate effect of frightening small children and sending adult shoppers veering away in order to avoid me, as if I had an invisible perimeter etched in an eight-foot radius around me. "Muchas Chocolates is proud to present their novelty-shaped Smoochies," I crowed to anyone who passed. "Free sample? Free sample, ma'am? Free sample, sir?"

A hunched-over man in casual business dress swerved away in the same vector as everyone else, his shoes skittering over the polished tiles. I've never been able to tell the age of men with completely bald heads; to me, they could be either very old, naturally hairless and young-looking, or youngish and older-looking because they've shaved their domes. "Some Valentine's chocolates for your sweetie?" I called out in his direction.

He paused in midflight to stare for a moment before smiling in apology. "Candy is dandy, but liquor is quicker," he quipped, as if he'd thought of the line himself and as if I'd never heard it before.

"Ha-ha-ha-ha-ha-ha-ha!" My fake laugh sounded like a rapid-fire machine gun, or maybe an amused Elmer Fudd if he were an alto. "Ogden Nash was a stitch, wasn't he?" The amount of condescension I got in these jobs sometimes absolutely amazed me; customers wanted me to be a blithering idiot with only enough wits to bounce their jokes against. Yet whenever I let a little intelligence show, they ran. They were a lot like men in that regard, weren't they?

Only the night before, I'd been the one to run.

No, couldn't think about last night. Couldn't think about that at all; it was already nerve-racking enough being in the same store as . . . Nope, that topic was off-limits too. Best to get it out of my head as quickly as possible. And what better remedy for private embarrassment and personal mortification than throwing myself into the everyday embarrassment and mortification of my job? "Muchas Smoochies for your swee . . . Ma'am, would you like to try a Smoochy from Muchas choc . . . High-quality candies for . . ."

A short, wirehaired man had backed into my aisle from the lingerie section, obviously lost or looking for something. Even as I began my pitch, I assembled in my head directions to the most likely spots a man his age and apparent income bracket might wish to visit: Men's Accessories, Shoes, and the little boy's room. "Hello, sir, wouldn't your wife appreciate—oh crap." The directions all vanished when the man turned. I found myself face to face with my younger brother.

Brody had always been self-conscious of the seeming acres of white visible around his enormous eyes. In his teens, he obsessed in the bathroom mirror to the point that you would have thought he'd been born resembling Little Orphan Annie. At the sight of me, his normally wide peepers bulged visibly. His lips twitched. Once. Twice. The third time, I scowled. "Don't," I warned. Too late. Brody slapped a hand over his mouth and doubled over. All I could do was grit my teeth and endure his mirth-induced convulsions. He wheezed and huffed and generally acted like a thirteen-year-old nuisance instead of a grown man scuffing the knees of his Paul Smith suit on a department store floor. "Get up," I growled at last. I tried rotating my magenta bulk to see if DeeDee had left yet for her lunch break. I seemed to be safe. "Get *up!*"

"Where's my camera phone?" Wiping tears from his eyes, Brody straightened up and began to fish in his coat. He held several frilly garments dangling from hangers. They bounced as he patted down his pockets. "I've got to get a picture of this."

"If you take a photo of me in this getup, I swear to God I will kick you so hard in the 'nads that you will never walk upright again." My threat—and memories of the countless tussles we'd had growing up—paused his roaming hand. Why was he there? My family knew they weren't welcome when I was on the job. Brody's appearance on the first day of the Valentine's promotion, frankly, stunk of fish. "What are you doing here?"

For a moment I thought he was going to undergo another fit of laughter, but he managed to pull himself together. "Oh man. Oh man oh man. You're hilarious!" he said, wiping his eyes and nose. "I was getting some Valentine's shopping done. I didn't know you were working here, honest, swear on the Bible. Total coincidence." From somewhere in the depths of his coat, a beeper went off.

"Uh-huh." A little-known fact about my baby brother: He calls or visits my dad four times a week, ostensibly to talk, but mostly to keep tabs on any little ups and downs that any of us might have experienced over the week. Ever since at the age of twenty-two, when he surpassed both Mitchell's and my own yearly income thanks to a career in advertising accounting, Brody has delighted in being the most financially successful of the Cloutier spawn. On the day he topped Dad's salary two years later, he could have been assaulted by a gang of thugs and pushed in front of the E train and died the happiest man in the world. The beeper for which he groped was merely one of his several accoutrements for success, along with the cell phone clipped to his belt, the BlackBerry no doubt tucked into one of his suit pockets, the Palm, and the laptop he lugged between work and home. Some part of him was always buzzing, bleeping, or chirping to let the rest of us know that he was wanted. "You had no idea I was working here starting today, hmmm?"

Brody blinked multiple times. "No! Seriously! Nuh-uh!"

Another little-known fact about my baby brother: He is a very bad liar. Not for one second did I believe that he happened to have been in Mercer-Iverson the afternoon I started my latest indignity. He had an agenda of some sort, I knew; catching me in my diabetic's-nightmare drag was merely a bonus prize. I played along. "What're you buying?"

"Oh nothing." He edged away, not quite hiding the frillies in his hand.

I couldn't grab at them, as he seemed to expect. There's only so much maneuvering a girl can do when she measures five feet at her widest part. Was I supposed to inquire about the naughty things he and Marcy were doing in bed? Were they seeing a new marriage counselor? "Drop the coyness, little bro. When it comes to brothers buying women's lingerie, I would've sooner expected to see Mitch here than you. What's the occasion?" As part of his act, his eyes darted floorward. "Getting wifey a . . . what is that? A wee teddy. Clingy! And what's this?" He closed his eyes and blushed as with my magenta-gloved hand I toyed with the skimpy concoction of stretch lace. "Valentine's Day mischief! Why Brody, you naughty little . . ."

I halted. My brother's wifey was anything but wee. Unless Marcy had suddenly lost ninety pounds on the Atkins diet that haunted Mrs. Przybyla's waking and sleeping dreams, there was no way in hell she could squeeze into the sleazy black lingerie Brody bashfully displayed. "Oh my God," I said, reaching to cover my mouth with my hands. I banged my forearms on the edge of my costume and nearly sent several dozen quartered Smoochies flying from my platter. "Oh my *God*," I repeated. Those duds of sin were intended for someone much smaller—someone Brody's own size. Suddenly it all made perverted sense: the shopping alone, the lingerie, him showing up obviously with something he had to say. Oh hell.

"Yeah." He swallowed quickly and looked at the damning evidence in his hand. "Nan, I know what I'm going to tell you is going to come as kind of a shock, but . . ."

"No!" I gasped. Damn this heart! It gave me throes of nostalgia for my old Who-niform. At least in my tights I could easily have slapped my hands over my ears and run off screaming. "Honestly, Brody, you don't have to explain. What you do behind closed doors is nobody's business but your own, okay?" The same went for whatever he wore beneath his Paul Smith.

"I'm so glad you agree." I hadn't expected the amiable tone. "And I'm glad we can talk about these issues like adults."

Before he went into details, I gabbled out, "But we don't have to talk about it at all if you're not comfortable. I swear, I won't say a word about you—your—your . . ."

"I was hoping sometime you could meet her."

"H-h-her?" I stammered out in absolute horror. His dress-up persona?

"Melissa." Obviously he wanted some kind of response, but my lips wouldn't cooperate. Why weren't there ever any practical classes to cope with these crises? Why didn't someone publish emergency manuals to cope with how to behave gracefully when your brother announces he's a—a—I couldn't even think the word. My brother watched my mental stuttering with confusion. "Missy. The woman I've been seeing."

"*You're seeing another woman?*" I spat, only modulating it down from a squeal at the very last moment.

"Yes, that is what I've been telling you. Weren't you listening?" Brody employed the broad vowels and careful consonants he used to speak to the hard of hearing, small children, and foreigners who didn't understand English.

Is it bad that for a few moments in my head I hosted a catered shindig celebrating my most sincere joy that my brother was not a cross-dresser who called himself Melissa, once snug in a lacy thong? No? Good, because I nearly threw myself on my knees and sang the entire damned "Hallelujah Chorus" as an a cappella solo before my instincts for self-preservation took over and I remembered that any sudden movements might send me flat onto the floor. "Why is your face so weird?" Brody asked at last.

I stammered out what I hoped might be an appropriate reply, mentally performing an emotional lambada between shock and relief. "Th-this is a lot to deal with, Brody." He looked up at me expectantly.

"It's true love. I never had that with Marcy. I mean, I love the kids and all, but . . . well, you know how Marcy is." Yes, I knew Marcy well enough to predict to the minute when she'd excuse herself from a family gathering and lock herself in the bedroom with a shaker of martinis for the rest of the evening. "It really is love, Nan. I can't tell Dad or Mitchell. They wouldn't understand."

He fondled the legs of the thong in a way that could have been really disturbing if I hadn't been focused on the wistful droop of his eyelids. Brody was confiding in me. For the first time I could remember, he was actually letting me in on a secret, and trusting me to keep it. Was that why he'd come today? For my approval? "And I take it . . . Marcy doesn't . . ."

"What do you think I am, crazy?" he spat out in an entirely normal tone. "No, she doesn't know. She can't find out. Not that she'd listen if you told her. She doesn't like you." That revelation was about as much news to me as the earth's alleged roundness, but it was still something of a stunner to hear it said aloud. "I met Melissa on the Internet."

"Brody," I interrupted. It was obvious he'd staged this announcement so he'd get some kind of endorsement from me, and yet I wasn't at all sure I could support him the way he wanted. Irony of ironies—the girl who'd let just about anyone slop down on her lips in a karaoke bar was giving herself moral airs over her brother's cybersex adventures. "I know these chat room acquaintances can really seem persuasive and powerful."

"That was only the beginning though, Nan. She's very smart. You'd really like her. She's beautiful in person, too, and knows how to talk about, oh, things. She likes the finer things of life too, like me." Both our gazes fell to the scanties he held. I commanded my face not to betray my doubt. Not one widening of the eyes, not one twitch of the lips, and certainly not a smart remark. Once the tension had eased and I'd apparently passed the Easter Island stone face test, he continued. "I wanted to bring her to your party, but she wasn't ready."

To my party? That was weeks ago. "How long has this been going on?"

"It's been four months since we first met in person." Oh crap. This wasn't merely some chat room flirtation. My little brother was waist-deep in a serious slice of real life, and I didn't know in the least what to tell him.

I half-resented his confidence. Why couldn't he have talked to Dad, who had instructions and directions for every situation? Why not Mitchell, who at least could have told him what it was like to be the mate left at home while the other ran off chasing his dreams? Then again, maybe I had my answers right there. Brody didn't want instructions or chastening. "Listen," I finally spoke at last, choosing each word carefully. I didn't know exactly what I wanted to say. "You're my little brother . . . and I guess no matter what I think, and to be honest, I'm not really sure what I think right now . . . I want you to be happy, because life's too short to spend it all in misery and with people who won't talk about . . . you know. Things." He regarded me as if he truly wanted to believe what I was telling him. "Okay?"

"Yeah," he replied. "Okay. You're all right, Nan." Brody had been the only Cloutier ever to sport orthodontic appliances; when he suddenly bared his teeth at me in a kid's grin, I felt disarmed. Today was supposed to be my day for self-recrimination and misery, not for unexpected utility. Feeling good again, even for a moment, threw my guilt into jagged relief. "I'd offer to hug you, but I'm afraid I'd kind of hurt myself."

"That's all right," I consoled. "Have some chocolate lips."

While he munched on a Smoochie, I debated whether to press for more answers while his guard was down. It felt a bit like looting a store during a blackout. "So, are you going to be leaving Marcy?"

"I don't know," he responded, sounding miserable. "I want to, but . . . the kids. It doesn't seem fair."

"Neither does lying. You're not doing anyone any favors with lies." When had I become such a moralizer? To my utter horror, I realized that I sounded like—I sounded like my *dad!* Wasn't it bad enough I inherited his nose? Surely I wasn't going to be afflicted with pontification, too? If I started getting his ear hairs, I was throwing myself off the Brooklyn Bridge.

"Hey." Brody snagged two more toothpicked chocolates from my platter. "Isn't that your weirdo friend over there? The one from your party?" The time it took me to turn in the direction of his pointed finger was the slowest several seconds I'd ever experienced. The unsettled feeling deep in the pit of my stomach only added to my panic. "What was his name? Colon? *Hey, Colon!*"

"Creeping crud," I rasped out. Colm stood with a group of suits near the brassieres, a sketch pad clutched to his chest as he pointed up to the ceiling with the eraser end of a pencil. They were planning a display of some sort, I guessed. "He can't see me. Don't let him see me." What could I do? Where could I go? I couldn't leave!

"I think he heard me," Brody said. "Whoops. Was that bad? What's up with you guys?"

Panic started to overtake my poor tired brain. "I can't see him right now. Or ever. Just . . ."

"Turn around. Sit." Brody reached out, grabbed the side of my costume and the edge of my face hole, and shoved me down. I heard something crack slightly as I hit the floor. The plywood? My butt?

"I can't sit! There's a point where my seat is." His response was to roll me slightly to the side, so that I perched on the right half of my ass. "What's he doing? Where is he?"

From above, Brody's voice sounded confident. When bossy, my brother was in his element. He grabbed my tray, sending Smoochies raining onto me with sudden percussion. "Your buddy gave me the 'hold a second' finger. Draw up your legs. Lean forward a little. Okay, you kind of look like part of the display. Do something about your arms!"

I pulled them in. Was this going to work? Could I pass as part of the decorations? "This is insane!" I hissed. "What's he doing?"

"He's finished up talking to the others and he's headed this way. What's the matter? Did you and Colon have some kind of fight?"

"None of your business. If he asks, I'm not here," I snarled. My kneecaps smarted from the weight of the heart resting against them. "And don't ask him questions. It's none of your business. And if he asks you anything, pretend you don't know. And it's Colm, not Colon. No one is named Colon!"

"Anyone ever told you you're bossy?" Brody sounded highly put out. He thought for a moment. "What about that general? The one who was like, you know, the President's secretary?"

"That's *Secretary of State Colin Powell,* not *colon* like the intestines, you mor—"

As reward for my correction, I got a mighty shove. Brody hefted his weight against my back and rested there, as if leaning against a display decoration. "Hey, Col . . . m," he finally said. "It's Colm, right?"

"Yes, hi," I heard. Colm's voice was muffled. I turned my head and stuck out my ear through the face hole so I might hear better.

"Not Colon?" Brody, probably clinging to one last shred of hope that he'd be right and I'd be wrong, sounded almost disappointed. If it hadn't guaranteed my discovery, I would've reared back and sent him sprawling.

"Brody, isn't it? It's an odd thing. I was hoping I might run into your sister. Not that seeing you isn't an unqualified delight," I heard Colm say. What color was his tone? Sorry-your-sister's-a-slut blue? I'm-sorry-it-isn't-working-out-it's-not-your-sister-it's-me red? Who-was-that-guy-and-what-does-he-mean-to-Nan green? For the life of me, I couldn't tell.

"Yeah." Brody sounded unimpressed. "So what's up?"

"She—I mean your sister—she's working here, isn't she?"

The long pause that followed nearly gave me a heart attack. *Say something!* I willed my brother. *Anything!* "Um, here's the thing. She's not here right now." Not good enough! I didn't want to be on edge for the next two weeks, worried that Colm might loom up at any moment to offer his polite apologies and withdrawal! I shoved backwards a little. "I mean, she quit a few minutes ago. She upped and quit. Yeah. Made a really big scene too. She's like that."

"Nan?"

"Yeah, she's always up to something, always causing trouble." No! Brody was giving the entirely wrong impression! Yet it was no worse than I'd made last night, was it? Maybe sending Colm off thinking the worst of me would save him the pain of finding it out for himself, when next time I messed up again. "Black sheep of the family. A little bit . . ." He made a noise that sounded like *woo-woo-woo!* I made a mental note to strangle him later. "Want a chocolate lip?"

"Ah. No. Thank you all the same. Well."

Another long pause. Brody began rocking gently from side to side, each time jabbing the sharp point of my heart costume into my upper thigh. Finally, after one *to*, I leaned into the *fro* and felt him topple. The swaying stopped suddenly. "Yeah, so. Good seeing you."

"Yes, very good to run across you again."

"Oh hey, you know that sensitive hippie thing?" Oh lord. What was Brody going to say? "Not so smooth, guy. I'd lay off that in the future. Chicks dig a polished, masculine dude. Mano to mano, right, muchacho?"

I wondered how Colm received that advice, delivered by a man carrying an armful of black lingerie. "I'll . . . keep that in mind."

"Okay man. Don't worry about me. I'm going to stand here for a while and finish off these lips." Another pause. "Later, bro."

Afterwards followed the longest pause of all. I tried to concentrate very hard on not moving or breathing too deeply. A minute passed. What was happening? Had Colm left? Did he go away without a word? Could he be still standing around? Two minutes passed. Was Brody still there? Was I sitting all alone on the floor like a big idiot? Wait a minute, was my brother actually taking this opportunity to eat all my damned Muchas Smoochies?

"He's gone." Brody's sudden sideways appearance in my blinkered vision caused me to yelp. "So what'd he do? Sleep around on you? Is he married? If he's married, I'll kick his . . ."

"Third floor: housewares, toasters, small ironies," I

snapped at him, sticking my arms back out their holes. "I can't talk to him, that's all."

For a few seconds we both struggled to haul me to my feet. My costume seemed none the worse for wear. The Smoochies were entirely gone.

"You're not doing anyone any favors with lies," Brody echoed. Could he look any more smug? Somehow I didn't think so.

I thanked him with the time-honored words with which generations of sisters have thanked their brothers: "Shut the hell up and get out of my sight."

Cask & Carton Home Goods
(total estimated cost of entire bridal registry list: in the low six figures)

The bleached entertainment center bore quite a price tag for two unadorned doors hinged to one large opening. We both studied it thoughtfully for a moment, bookend images of bemusement. "Seventy-five hundred dollars for a box?" I asked aloud, finally. "For a wooden *box?*"

Ambrose wrestled with the thick registry printout. "Out of our price range."

"Duh! You think?" I stared at the overpriced crate once more. "Okay, let's guess."

"Nan . . ."

"Come on, guess. Play the game!"

"I don't *want* to play the game. I've been playing the game for an *hour*. The game has lost its charm for me."

"Play!"

My friend crunched his fist against his neck to crack his knuckles, a nervous habit in which he indulged whenever frustrated. "I don't want to!"

"The!"

He glared at me, wearing stubbornness like a shroud.

I was determined to induce a good mood if I had to kill him to do it. "Game!"

"For Pete's sake, all right already." Ambrose conceded. I clapped and danced to make a little show of my pleasure.

"I'll guess . . . her choice."

"Nope. Obvious compromise."

Poor Ambrose. He absolutely sucked at the Guess Who Put What on the Registry? Game, and he knew it. I tried not to gloat as he squeezed shut his eyes, shook his head, and sighed. "I don't get it. Sometimes you say that the glass and steel modern stuff is Isobel's. Sometimes the wooden stuff is hers, and other times it's his. This is wood. Why in the world is it a compromise?"

"Sweetie, you can't go just by the material alone. It's all about the *style*. All the Arts and Crafts style stuff that looks as if it were lovingly hand-hewn a century ago by craftsmen who read Walter Pater in their spare time—that's Emmett. Isobel is the one who picks out the fussy colonial styles and the dreadful sleek modern crap, vacillating between her Golddigger and Laidalot education—"

"Godolphin and Latymer." Ambrose had the patience of a saint.

"—and her keeping-up-with-the-other-editors/*Architectural Digest*/what-I-sat-my-thin-white-ass-on-today-at-the-fashion-show pretensions. This . . . this *box* is neither one nor the other. Thus, I say it's a compromise." Once I really got going, I was unshakable in my convictions. I adopted an exaggerated accent to nail home my point. "Oh Emmett, dorling, I really corn't stand your selections but I will pretend to cormpromise on this multimedia center until I scratch off the veneer with my forked tongue and replace it with something forbulous of my own choice!"

"Nice." Ambrose ignored my passion play. "And you've arrived at these conclusions how?"

"Through adept psychological observation. I am a scholar of human nature."

"A scholar of human nature. Interesting." Ambrose had turned away from me by that time, so for that remark I didn't have the benefit of being able to see his expression. Was he upset because he was losing the game? "Shall we move out of Fantasyland and see if there's anything we can afford in the kitchen section?"

Going in together for a gift for the soonlyweds had been a grand idea. Isobel's Greek-American relations might have been able to spring for this stuff, but neither Ambrose on his coffee shop wages nor I on mine could manage anything solo. After an hour of wandering around the upper floors of Cask and Carton gawping at the extortionate prices of the more extravagant items, I don't think either of us expected to afford anything with our money pooled, either. At least we'd be able to not-afford it a little more easily, together. I envied the young, well-dressed couples we passed as we traipsed down the stairs. They smelled of colognes and fat leather checkbooks. Emmett and Isobel had been one of those couples, when they'd visited here to assemble their list. They'd probably fit right in among the pretty people. Even the store itself was probably a concession: not exactly the tip-top premium establishment Her Blondness would have preferred, but not horribly out of the reach of his dirt-poor circle of acquaintances. It bothered me to think of the discussions they must have had to arrive at the compromise.

Dorling, do your Elizabethan Loser friends have to come? They'll only bring down the tone.

Of course they have to come, love, they're my friends, but we'll have the ushers sit them in the back.

No, I didn't want to follow that train of thought. Bad enough that my acceptance of Emmett's upcoming nuptials was so grudging it made the Hatfield and McCoy situation look like a love-in. I already felt petty pouring so much scorn on the girl marrying the guy I might have married in an alternate universe. That is, an alternate universe in which he regarded me as more than a kid sister. No, best to drop the subject of the future Mrs. Dunnigan altogether. "Maybe I should've sung at that karaoke bar," I said, tracing back to the topic we'd been discussing previously.

"Why?" Ambrose didn't look at me as we rounded the landing. "You won't do karaoke because you're not perfect at it."

"No, because I suck at it."

"You should loosen up and have fun. It's only karaoke."

"That's exactly what you said when you've taken me bowling!" I complained. At the bottom of the stairs, arrayed on shelves facing broad aisles of high-gloss wooden floor, acres of less-expensive merchandise beckoned. Apparently the powers that be in the housewares industry had decided that kicked-up pastels were the "in" hues this year, and they might have had a good point. Customers were flocking to the lively bowls and vases and pitchers and matching implements as if starved for color after such a blah and gray winter. "Loosen up and have fun. It drives me crazy. How can you have fun if you're throwing nothing but gutter balls? Same with karaoke. How can you have fun if you totally suck at it?"

"Don't you have fun at your jobs?" he asked, stopping in front of a carousel of salad spinners and consulting the list.

Ouch. "I don't suck at my jobs!"

Did I detect an eyeroll as he shook his head? He pulled a melon-colored spinner half off the shelf and pushed it back again. "I didn't say you do. But you've managed to cultivate oddball jobs into an art form. For two or three weeks at a time you throw yourself into some temporary thing, no matter how weird. I mean, last Halloween you were a ghost—"

"Witch."

"Same difference."

I begged to differ. The witch was a featured character. Seasonal Staffers hired just about anyone for the ghosts.

"You don't mind dressing up in weird costumes or not knowing where your income's coming from next, yet you're afraid to do karaoke because you're worried how you'll look if you mess up?" He began pulling out other spinners randomly, obviously keeping his hands busy so he didn't have to look at me. What had I said wrong?

"Did a customer yell at you earlier or something?" I reached over and halted him from yanking out any more salad spinners before he drove me nuts. "Because you are seriously crabby."

Ambrose shrugged, managing in a simple spasm of his shoulders roughly to double my annoyance level. What was up with him today? "Okay, fine. Tell me. Why should you have sung last week?"

For years I'd always counted on Ambrose for advice. Knowing that he was merely humoring me by having the conversation made it less enjoyable. "Because my adrenaline would have been up, I wouldn't have been so woozy and sleepy, and then I wouldn't have let Damien mouth-rape me and I could've avoided the entire misunderstanding."

With a noncommittal grunt, Ambrose moved away to a rainbow array of KitchenAid mixers. He fiddled with the knobs. "Seems to me if this guy had any kind of decency he would have tried to phone you or something after."

"He has!" In the first few days following that awful night, the phone had rung several times a day. True, I hadn't answered it and I'd forbidden Mitchell to pick it up on my behalf, but I'd known it was Colm, looking for answers or an apology. Maybe even seeking a little bit of revenge, in letting me know I'd disappointed him. I couldn't bear the thought of having the conversation that would bring to a close a relationship I'd really hoped might work.

In college, when I'd get back from a professor a test or a paper on which I'd been a little bit shaky, I used to accept it with a smile and tuck it away in a notebook without a peek at the grade scribbled on the front. I couldn't bear to see the incontrovertible evidence I'd gotten a grade that was less than perfect, even when I knew the subject wasn't my strong point. Sometimes I'd leave the paper untouched until a couple of weeks later, when the doubt and the hurt had worn away and I could look at my C or C-minus without feeling anything more than numbness. The guilt I felt over Colm went so much deeper. I couldn't contemplate a future when I might be able to examine it without hurt. "He has," I said, running my finger along the smooth, shiny bases of the mixers in an attempt to ignore the lump in my throat. "I don't pick up. You know how I am. What should I do?"

"Move on already." Ambrose whipped away, rustling the registry list. "What do you think about the Calphalon?"

"What do I think about the *Calphalon?*" I took quick steps to catch up with him. He pretended to find the registry engrossing. "Move *on?* That's all you can say? I'm pouring out my heart to you here and the best you have is to tell me to get over it?"

"Emmett's listed this infused anodized steel . . ."

I hated the way Ambrose ignored me. "Colm was the nicest guy I've met in *years*. He was offbeat and sexy and . . ."

For the first time since we'd begun our shopping trip, Ambrose turned and faced me. He set on the floor the plastic basket he'd been carrying on his forearm. Into it he threw the curled list. His jaw jutted out, angry. "Yeah, I'm telling you to get over it, Nan. Either do something to fix it up, or get over it and find someone who really appreciates you. The choices seem pretty obvious to me."

When I spoke, overtones of hurt made me sound shrill. "Why are you being so mean?"

"I'm not being mean. I'm being honest."

"You're being *mean*."

"You just don't get it, do you?" Though he wasn't yelling, the force behind Ambrose's words made some of the other wandering couples turn, look at us, and then pretend we'd not broken the hushed domestic sanctity of Cask and Carton. "You know how Maya's been hashing around this theory that you're like the modern Thoreau, living a minimalist lifestyle, engaged in self-study? It's total crap."

Though my feet didn't move, it felt as if I lurched backwards. "I never asked her to say any of that."

"Probably because you knew what bullshit it really was." He had his arms crossed now. His eyes never left mine. "Thoreau wanted to know himself. He really did want to become a scholar of human nature—his own nature, at least. He wanted to become a better person. You—" There was no good way this sentence could end. My lower lip began to tremble. I sucked it in so it wouldn't show. "You know, most people take temporary jobs like yours as a supplement to real ones, or because they're waiting to find something better. They don't make a habit out of them. They don't take them because they make cute stories or because they're funny over dinner conversations. They're not a way of living for most people. Avoidance is not a valid life choice! You can't pull it off forever!"

He was upset with me because of my *jobs?* Did he think I was going to saddle him with my half of the total? "Why are you being such a prick?" I could barely suppress the quaver in my voice. "Do you not want to go in on the present with me?"

"You just . . . don't . . . get it."

"I don't get what?" I couldn't trust myself to speak more than a short sentence without bursting into tears. I'd never seen Ambrose this infuriated.

"I don't want to be your girlfriend!" he barked. The words seemed to echo through the store. In a softer volume, he continued. "I can't do it. I can't do it anymore, Nan. I can't listen to you talk about your dates. I don't want to hear about how sexy you think guys are. I can't listen to what you do with them. Not anymore. It's too much."

"I—I—" All I could do was stammer. It was no secret that Ambrose had pretended a crush on me for years and years. I'd assumed it was simply that: pretend. "You're not a girlfriend."

He tilted his head and stared at me. *Oh come on,* said the gesture. "You tell everyone I'm gay. Now, I don't particularly care whether other people think I am or not, but you desexualize me every chance you get. I'm not a man to you. I'm only . . ." He shrugged. "A eunuch. Harmless. Another girlfriend."

"That's not true!" I protested. What could I say to make him understand that I loved him, but in a completely different way than what he wanted?

"It is. And I'm sorry, Nan, but I can't take it anymore." A clerk scurried around us with an armful of Cask and Carton totes. I imagined he was probably trying to determine whether or not he needed to call Security. Our face-off of silence lasted for a moment more until at last Ambrose reached into his jacket pocket and fished out his wallet. "Here," he mumbled. "Take a car home. I know you hate crying on the train."

"Don't," I said, already wiping tears from my cheeks. "Don't you dare be kind to me after you've been so mean." I wanted to hit him back—to hurt him as badly as he'd hurt me moments before.

Ambrose stuffed the bill into my breast pocket and leaned over until his lips grazed my cheek in a soft kiss of apology. The short hairs of his goatee scraped my skin. "Fix things up," he murmured to me. "Or move on. For your own sake. Please. I can't do it anymore."

"Ambrose . . . !"

"Not even for you."

Then he was gone before I had a chance to think of an answer. "You're a bastard," I finally whispered. "You're a fucking bastard!"

No one heard me. Surrounded by the artifacts of a happy life my friend had just told me was out of my reach, I was utterly alone.

Mercer-Iverson Department Store
(1,550 halfpence an hour still doesn't sound worth it)

"Lips." Speaking the one word took tremendous effort. In two weeks I'd learned that if I slightly pulled in my arms, I could rest my elbows on a strap inside this bloody costume. After a while my circulation would falter, but numbness and potential gangrene and amputation were a damned sight better than having to use my nonexistent muscles. "Want lips?"

In an ironic twist of semantics, I had discovered that while absolutely no one wanted to accept sample Smoochies from a manic, overachieving chocolate pusher, they had absolutely no problems whatsoever approaching a surly midget with candy. "Delicious!" said one of the women who'd stopped for a late-afternoon snack. She was so stick-insect thin that I worried the tiny quarter-chocolate might cause a visible lump in her throat as she swallowed. I guessed her to be younger than me by at least three or four years; a little Vuitton clutch hung from her elbow and she pushed an expensive Bertini stroller accessorized with an infant whose blond hair matched her own. On moral grounds alone I should have despised her, but I couldn't muster the emotion. "Where can I find a box?" After I jerked my head over my shoulder in the direction of the candy counter, she thanked me and walked away with a clip-clop-clip of her tiny heels. "Happy Valentine's Day!"

"Yeah, whatever." I'd be chirpy too if I lived a designer life, complete with Malibu beach house and a Ken doll of a husband.

"Not to be critical?" Mitchell adopted the tone of someone with criticism plainly on his agenda. "I'm only a lowly media librarian, but it's always been my impression that customer service was one of those areas that required a little bit of courtesy to the actual customer?"

"You sound like Dad. Besides, you're not supposed to be talking to me, remember?"

My brother adjusted his work shoulder bag and inspected his watch for the dozenth time in five minutes. "It's five fifty-seven. What're they going to do, fire you for talking to the brother who's picking you up for dinner with a friend in two minutes and thirty seconds?"

"Lips?" I hoped the elderly couple at whom I shoved my tray would stop, breaking the direct line of sight I had with Mitchell across the aisle. They didn't. "You're right. Perhaps I should thank you for stopping by to witness the dexterity with which I aid others in their quest for higher serotonin levels. Maybe on my resume I should list this gig as 'Authorized Tryptophan Dispenser.' You think? Would that make it sound more like a real job?"

My costume stank. When I'd first donned it, the interior still had a vaguely spicy scent of sawdust and glue, but two weeks of stumping around in an overheated department store during a stretch of above-average temperatures outdoors had left it smelling of BO and crotch rot. No matter where I powdered or what I ladled with antiperspirant, at the end of every day I ended up stinking like a new cologne from the Calvin Klein collection: *Repulsion.* As eager as I was to get out of my costume at the end of the day, I dreaded having to smell myself on the lengthy trip out.

"Tonight's supposed to be fun, okay? You've been in a really pissy mood lately," he told me.

I didn't care to comment on my mood. Some of us simply didn't wear our freakin' hearts on our freakin' sleeves all the time. "I'm doing everyone a favor by not spending all my time whining about how wronged I am, okay? People get sick of it awfully quickly." I didn't have to look at him directly to see his posture deflate. Damn Mitchell for taking that remark personally—though somewhere in the back of my mind, in some passive-aggressive way I'd meant it to sting. What kind of an awful person was I, anyway, to want to strike out like that? "I'm not talking about you, I'm talking about me," I told him, still irritated at having to lie. "Who're we going out with, anyway, Maya? I thought she was working late all this week. Smoochies?" The highly perfumed young man sashaying by ignored me.

"Not *that* late. She's usually done by six-thirty."

"You'd know better than me, these days." Since Mitchell had moved in, my friends were now his. It was as if I'd outsourced to him what pitiful social life I'd originally had; he'd taken over keeping up with their doings. Two nights ago he'd even gone out for burgers at Malamute's with most of the gang when I'd pleaded tiredness from having to shoulder my damned costume all day. It hadn't entirely been a lie—total exhaustion was the price I paid for a daily workout to my trapezoids. Mainly, though, I hadn't wanted to show my sorry hide. I wasn't sure when I'd be able to face any of them again, after my argument with Ambrose. The thought of having to defend myself to Maya that evening made my stomach sizzle and pop like bacon in the microwave. "Where are we meeting her?"

Mitchell's lips twitched. "We're not."

"She's meeting us?" Instantly I was wary. I didn't say a word when a few children took several toothpicks apiece. "So it's not Maya? Who are we meeting, then?"

Mitchell raised his hands and patted the air. I recognized

the gesture; when we were growing up, he'd use it when he was trying to calm me down. "Don't get upset." I was sure a *but* was coming. "Some amends need to be made, and it's really all my fault, so I've kind of taken the liberty . . ."

Ambrose. He'd set up something with Ambrose, although my former friend had made it pretty clear he wanted nothing to do with me. The closeness of my costume only added to the claustrophobia I felt at being ambushed. Somehow it felt as if the temperature had shot up another twenty degrees.

It actually took several seconds of panic before I remembered a little thing called free will. It was quitting time. I didn't have to go through with my insane brother's plans. All I had to do was escape to the dressing room, take off this hateful costume, and run home to refuge. "That chapter's over for now," I told him in words divested of both nonsense and patience. "I'm going home. You and Ambrose have a nice girl-free evening, okay?"

"It's not Ambrose," said Mitchell, red-faced.

I had already started to stalk away. DeeDee hovered right outside the break room door at the very back of the seasonal section, looking from me to her watch with increased irritation. Another minute and I'd have to endure a lecture about padding my time card. Fine. Whatever. I could console myself later with a library book and ice cream. "Then who?" I demanded.

That's when I saw him. It really wasn't *right,* how I could recognize merely his feet and legs as inch by inch the escalator eased him down in my direction. There was no disguising the shiny boots and the awkward posture of his legs, or the jut of his hips. Within a few seconds his face was in view—and then it was too late. "Nan?" he asked, his surprise audible from twenty feet away.

"Colm," I whispered. Was it possible to be feverish and frozen at the same time? My skin was suddenly a red-hot surface drenched with chilled sweat, and where the two met I felt nothing but raw pain.

Our eyes held each other for a moment. Then I took a deep breath, turned, and ran. In my flight I accidentally struck my brother with the right half of my costume, temporarily wrenching it from my shoulder straps and going blind when my face hole twisted around to my ear. I staggered for a few seconds while I readjusted the costume, then limped off in the direction of ladies' accessories.

I heard someone calling my name, but with my face hole pointed in the opposite direction it was hard to hear whether the voice was masculine or feminine, angry or sad. All I knew was that I had to get away. I was stupid for working in this department store when I knew that at any minute Colm could round the corner. I was stupider for trusting my brother.

Stupidest of all was my flight. Oh, I realized that the moment my legs started bolting for the nearest exit. Exactly where did I think I was going, all six feet high and five and a half feet wide of my giant magenta self? Why was I still holding the damned candies like they would protect me from what I most feared? Did I really think I could simply run out of the store? How in the world would I get through the revolving door? Even if I had my Metrocard to get home—which I didn't—I was way too wide to fit through the subway turnstiles, and there was no way I could get into a cab.

In the battle of instinctual imperatives, why did flight have to win over fight? Was I really that kind of person? Around me, people veered while I scuttled along the store's broad aisle. Conditioned by several years of reality TV, they invariably all looked around to see where cameras might be hidden. Only when I rounded a corner and nearly slammed into the back of a woman pushing a stroller did my legs stop moving. My magenta slippers skidded along the tiles like a cartoon character. All I needed was an Acme anvil to drop on my head to make my miserable Wile E. Coyote existence complete.

I coasted to a halt within inches of the woman's back. She

hadn't seen me coming, but apparently I created enough of a breeze for her to turn around. Once again I was face to face with Lady Vuitton, she of the luxury stroller. She blinked, startled.

"Nan?" I heard from some distance behind me.

"Here." I brandished my tray. To my eyes it looked as if I'd lost roughly half my Smoochies during my flight—I'd left a little chocolate trail behind me, like some kind of demented purple Hansel and Gretel—but her eyes lit up at the sight of the remaining candies. Honestly, what is it about free samples that attracts the upper middle class? Hand out little squares of box-mix angel food cake in an upscale grocery, and the well-heeled suddenly start a monster truck demolition derby with their shopping carts.

I didn't have time to ruminate. "Here." With a shove, I made the woman take my tray.

"Why, thanks!" Although she had two boxes of the stuff wrapped and tucked under her arm, the woman immediately began grazing. "Did I win something?"

"Customer of the day award," I gasped out, drawing in my arms through their holes. "Congratulations. Bye."

"Oh. All right." I saw her blink in astonishment right before I yanked my head inside and disappeared. The smell was rank and overpowering, as if someone had managed to spray essence of high school locker room inside, but I'd have to endure. There was no way to conceal my legs. They'd have to . . . stand there.

"Hello?" A shadow passed my armhole. Why was I so terrified? Why was I so *stupid?* As I stood there, flattened pancakelike between plywood slabs, I knew how ridiculous I was behaving. "Nan?"

All I had to do was poke out my head and talk to him. It was that easy. But—well, it was like when I was a kid and I kept some library books out three weeks past the due date. My dad discovered them sitting on my desk and insisted we take them back, but I was too mortified. Although I begged and pleaded for him to do it for me, even to take double the fine as a courier fee, he made me return them myself. Both then and now, I dreaded the certainty of the lecture I'd receive. I couldn't take the stern looks, the reproaches, the guilt—the things that struck chords of fear in me louder than any fine or punishment.

Impossible though it sounded, I hoped Colm would simply disappear.

"Nan?" His voice was louder now. Motionless though I tried to be, he moved around to my front. The collar of his shirt was right about level with my face hole. "Are you in there?" He wasn't disappearing. With every passing second I was more cramped and squished and miserable, inside and out. "Hello?"

His face blocked out most of the light when it suddenly appeared in the face hole, but left enough so I could see him looking sideways in my direction. "No one's here," I rasped out.

"Are you playing at being a turtle?"

"Yes. The biggest pink holiday turtle you've ever seen. Can you—?" I sighed. "Do we have to do this?"

"We could perhaps do it more comfortably over dinner or at least a drink."

Comfortable for him, maybe. "Do we have to do it at *all?*" The costume's interior muffled conversation. I knew that he had to smell my skunklike stench. Plus, I needed an Altoid.

"Nan, I don't want you to regret—"

And here it came: the polite start to the recriminations and the blame-laying. He didn't want me to regret the fact that he couldn't see me anymore. It was him, not me. He had standards that I lacked. Or some such nonsense. Basically he would be telling me that I'd regret not hearing him outline all my faults in that adorable clipped voice of his, that I'd regret not letting him rip into me . . . that I'd regret it when he turned and left in a self-righteous blaze of glory. I couldn't bear to hear any of it.

"Don't talk to me about regrets," I told him, angry. I hated having my faults analyzed. "You're the one who's traded in all your artistic ambitions so you can hang banners from the Mercer-Iverson ceilings. One of these days years from now, when you're cleaning out your closet and you run across that last painting you were working on and you think back to the days before you sold your soul for that train pass out of Morningside Heights, then you can come back and talk to me about regrets. Got it?" Fresh air and light struck my face; he had moved back away from the hole. "I know I owe you an apology. I really am sorry. But I don't have to hear you tell me in a hundred different way how I fucked up when I already *know* I fucked up. So let's . . ." I couldn't finish my sentence.

For a long time I stood there, trapped in my costume heart, listening to Colm shift from side to side. My breathing echoed in the darkness. At last I heard his voice once again. "My grandfather would very much like to see you." Regret sliced through me at the words. Never in any of this mess had I intended to slight old Mr. Iverson. "He misses your company."

The declaration made me shuffle my shoulders back into their straps. "I miss him too. . . ." I started to say once my face was exposed to the air. Colm was already walking away. What apology could I offer now?

"I'm sorry." The words were as soft a whisper as ever had left my lips.

My brother was nowhere in sight. For his sake, it was probably a good thing. DeeDee Camillo met me on the threshold between leather accessories and lingerie on my slow trudge back to seasonal items. I scarcely heard a third of what she said. ". . . clearly irresponsible . . . attitude adjustment problems . . . problem since the start. . . ."

Her words made my already pounding head ache even more. On and on she rambled, clutching her clipboard as if its presence gave her an authority she craved. Every insult thudded against me and bounced off. I wasn't buying any of it. "Listen, you little piss-pot tyrant!" I yelled.

She reared away, frightened by how vicious my voice sounded. Even I was taken aback by the violence I'd heard in the insult; I was terrified to know that right below the surface, waiting to explode, was a fiery force I wanted to unleash. I wanted to make her cry, and beg for mercy, and send her running for cover. I wanted to see DeeDee smoldering and in ashes.

Yet it wasn't her I was angry with. Not at all. I didn't like DeeDee, but she didn't deserve any of my anger. I was both the offended and the offender. I needed to reserve it for myself. "You know," I said at last when my head's throbbing reached an unbearable point. "I quit."

My previous blow had been a mere glance; this one struck her squarely between the eyes. "You can't quit! It's Valentine's Day tomorrow! And besides," she added, seeming to remember that I'd seconds ago called her a piss-pot tyrant. "You're fired!"

"Will I get unemployment if I'm fired?" A ray of practicality shone through my gloom.

"No!"

"Then I quit. Sorry for the insult, DeeDee, you didn't deserve it. But I've had enough of this crap." I think everyone has at some time in their life imagined telling their boss off and quitting on the spur of the moment. It's so romantic and Norma Rae, so "Take This Job and Shove It." Somehow, though, it didn't feel at all liberating. I didn't feel happier for doing it. With so much ugliness in this world, I hated adding to it. "Let's be frank. You don't like me being here, and I don't like the job, so let's call it a draw with no hard feelings."

"Can't you work at least tomorrow?" she pleaded. "It's a peak sales day."

"You couldn't pay me enough. I'll leave the costume in the break room for whomever you find, but you'd better warn them it stinks. The company can mail me the check.

Okay?" My last glimpse of my former supervisor was of her chewing her pencil. She hated me, but what could I do? I didn't begrudge DeeDee at all for telling me off. If I'd been in her place, I'd have done the same. I was a lousy candy box, a worse Who, a terrible witch.

I needed to do something real with my life. I was tired of costumes.

MARCH

Top Dawg's Clubhouse
(strawberry milkshake: $8.50; meat loaf: $22.95; pillow mints: free)

"So what is it you do exactly, huh?"

I stared across the table at the long-nosed woman sitting next to my brother, straining to hear her over the tourist noise that filled the chain restaurant. All my life I've envied girls with long faces and noses and narrow, smooth foreheads. Especially if, like Brody's companion, they sported lengthy manes of hair. My own face seemed so round and squat whenever I looked at it in the mirror; I could only imagine what it was like to possess such a patrician profile. And here was my brother's mistress, hiding hers beneath a pair of enormous lilac-colored spectacles and about a pound of foundation. Next to me, I heard my dad's chest rumble as he sprang to answer before I could. "My daughter's situation is a bit unique. You see, she . . ."

"I'm between jobs, Missy," I announced briskly. I wasn't being confrontational—Missy was the woman's actual nickname. I don't know why I felt compelled to use it to end all my sentences, however; it sounded as if I were constantly rebuking the woman. Wasn't "between jobs" what people said, in these situations? Maybe not. Brody and Dad exchanged glances of complicity right as the waitress arrived bearing food.

"Oh my gaaaawwwwwd! That's incredible. That's why I love this place. They give you so much food!" Missy was certainly right. My plate was roughly the size of the platters on which whole turkeys are usually served. Flying buttresses of garlic-cilantro mashed potatoes supported a towering castle of meat loaf slices, each an inch thick. Atop those were piled crenellations of onion rings. The entire ten-pound affair was, improbably, crowned with a toothpick-speared olive. "So much food" was right. I was staring at dinners enough for the rest of the week. "And the presentation! It doesn't get better than this location."

The expression with which Brody stared at Missy made me uncomfortable. I tried keeping my eyes on my tower of meat loaf, but not before I glimpsed my brother's pride at Missy's . . . well, I would be kind and call it connoisseurship, though professing an expertise on a nationwide chain like Top Dawg's seemed a little like proclaiming oneself the Iron Chef of Big Boy's. Brody glowed. No, he seemed to soften around Missy. The crisp lines of his expensive suits rumpled; the ramrod posture he affected to make himself look taller no longer seemed as rigid. Even his eyes relaxed around the edges and seemed less prominent. "You two go ahead and eat," he assured Dad and me. "We'll get a drink and then be on our way."

It embarrassed me to catch the glances my brother would shoot Missy whenever she opened that prim little mouth to speak. I couldn't imagine her as a romantic figure to anyone, with those oversized eyeglasses and that bridge-and-tunnel bray. What in the world was my dad thinking about her unexpected presence? "Oh yeah, oh yeah, eat!" she said, waving her arm so that her twenty wire bracelets jangled against each other. "I'm so sorry about us being late. We were in the office and I told Bro, 'Hey Bro, we need to get going. We're gonna be later to dinner than a hooker to a convent square dance.' And you know what he said to me? You know what he said?"

Dad jumped when she swatted him. He stopped toying with his lamb chop branches sticking out of a foot-high burial mound of mint-sage stuffing and looked vaguely alarmed. "No, what did he say?"

"He said!" Missy's red-taloned tips formed jazz hands that shook with excitement at her upcoming punch line. "He said, 'Okay, Sis!' Get it? Sis? Bro? Get it?" She dabbed at my father. He flinched. "You get it?" she asked me.

"Ha-ha-ha!" I pretended enjoyment. Oh, I was getting it, all right. From the way Brody convulsed with laughter, I guessed that in about an hour and a half, he'd be getting it, too—right after Marcy would be getting a phone call that he'd be staying late at the office that night. My father and I had spent over forty minutes waiting for Brody to arrive before we'd gone ahead and ordered—and no one is more of a stickler for punctuality than my father, particularly when it comes to his food.

Melissa's appearance at our planned dinner for three had been a bombshell, though in retrospect I ought to have expected it. Brody had orchestrated the entire evening, choosing the restaurant and asking the two of us to meet him there. He simply never mentioned bringing a guest. I suppose he thought he could get my private opinion on his . . . whatever she was . . . by springing her on me. God only knew what my dad thought of the strange woman still sitting across from us in her puffy pink overcoat, prodding his son with her press-on nails. She suddenly twitched as if he'd pinched her. "Stop," she teased Brody.

"No, you stop," he murmured back.

"No, *you* stop."

"No, *you*."

I cleared my throat, sickened by the display. "So I've submitted several résumés—"

"Melissa, you're working at Melano and Fruschette with

Brody?" Dad and I had both spoken at the same time, eager to break up their private argument. We looked at each other, both plainly uncomfortable, before diving into our food.

"Oh yeah, I'm an analyst and *he*—" She built suspense at her upcoming joke by extending her hands toward the table's middle. "And *he's* just *anal!*"

With my steam shovel–sized fork, I moved an embankment of mashed potato into my mouth. Anything to keep from commenting. "That's what she said the first day we worked together!" Brody chortled, wiping a tear from his eye.

"How about that." My dad seemed speechless.

"No, no, seriously, Mr. Cloutier, your son is real professional. Everyone in the office says he's one of the company's up-and-comers. Don't they, Bro?"

"Aw, I don't know about that . . . Sis!" After a beat, they broke into a mutual peal of laughter.

Why had I given up drinking for Lent? Did it make me an alcoholic to wish right then for a little airplane bottle of vodka to slip into my milkshake?

"I want to hear about Nan's résumés," Brody said at last. He hooked his elbow over the back of the booth's bench, took a deep drink of his beer, and smiled at me with indulgence. Dad, in the meantime, seemed grateful for a change in topic. He brandished his chop like a conductor waves his baton, encouraging me. Missy leaned back in her chair, cracked her knuckles, and closed her big mouth.

"Well," I began. I felt a little shy, suddenly to have everyone's attention. "I wrote up a nice cover letter and fixed up my résumé on Mitchell's laptop, highlighting my—"

Brody interrupted with an aside to Missy. "Nan has *a liberal arts degree.*"

"—flexibility and—"

"You're kidding!" Missy's voice dropped to a funereal hush, as if my brother had said *uterine cancer.* "Why?"

My father cleared my throat. Out came his lecture voice.

"A degree in liberal arts provides one not merely a single course of learning, but teaches one *how* to learn, so that—"

Much as I appreciated my father rising to my defense, I could handle myself. "I've highlighted my flexibility and communication skills, assets that would make me invaluable in any—"

"A BA in English," Brody confided to his girlfriend. Code for *loser* in Accountant-speak, I guessed.

When Missy raised her fingers to her lips, horrified, I instantly lost what had been a healthy appetite. If she started to wave those jungle red tips in the vicinity of her eyes to fan away tears of sorrow, I was going to get up and leave without a word. "Honey," she said at last, reaching across the table to drape her hand on my wrist. "Why don't you go back to school and get yourself an MBA?"

Brody nodded. "Melissa has one from NYU."

"An MBA from NYU . . . BFD, right?" She hooted with laughter. "I kill myself! I do!"

"You know what, Missy?" I made a mental note that I had to stop doing that. "I'm very glad you have an advanced degree," I said, hoping I didn't sound surprised she had more than a manicurist's certificate from Mr. Bela's School of Beauty, "but there's absolutely nothing wrong . . ."

"Karaoke book?" Our waitress had appeared at the side of our table, a stack of ring binders in her arms. At all our astonished glances, she pointed up through the atrium at the floor above us and explained. "We have karaoke here on Thursday nights on our third level. You'll be able to hear from here. It's a lot of fun!"

Brody looked around the table, then shook his head. "None of us do karaoke," he said with finality, shooing her away. "No thanks."

"I—" Part of me was astonished to hear the word come out of my mouth. I had to swallow before I proceeded. "I'd like a book, please." The waitress handed it over and vanished with a promise to refill my dad's iced tea.

The book's cover stuck to my hands; the inside was more soiled. "You hate karaoke," Brody said. "She hates karaoke," he repeated to Missy.

Yes. I hated karaoke. I hated the idea of getting up on the stage and opening my mouth and yowling some half-remembered ditty to which I could only summon the chorus. I couldn't deny that the thought of people laughing at me behind their hands as I fumbled and stumbled my way through a song made my stomach clench. Yet I don't know what had made me ask for that book. Perhaps it was a melancholy, juvenile side of me wishing I could travel back in time to the night where I'd let everything go wrong—though I suspected my life had gone wrong long before that night. Long before I'd met either of the Iversons, even.

Brody added, "You'd *suck* at karaoke."

I wrinkled my nose and tried to pretend I didn't mind. "You're right."

"Can you believe her? I actually thought she was gonna, for a minute." Missy looked at Brody, jaw askew in astonishment. "I actually thought she was gonna! What a hoot! Bro, you've got some weird family!" Dad and I both bristled at that remark, sitting upright in our seats as if we planned to defend the Cloutier family honor as the two Musketeers. "In a totally cool and fun way, of course," Missy added, not noticing our erect postures.

Brody, however, wasn't so immune to our mood. He looked at his watch, sucked down the rest of his beer, and tapped Missy on the shoulder. "We'd better get going," he told her. "I know you have to . . . ah, get home to your family, and I know I have to get home to mine." Excuse me? Melissa had a husband of her own? Why had I not—oh, there was the ring, sparkling on her finger. An enormous square-cut diamond that in my confusion I'd not noticed. Quite a rock, that was. Unless she'd bought it on her own, something told me that Missy's cuckolded husband was probably making quite the salary.

"Oh." Melissa looked surprised to learn she was going home. She recouped gracefully. "Oh! Yes, I've got to be getting the train. Busy busy busy, you know. No rest for the wick—weary, huh? Well, nice to meetcha, yeah?"

From our side of the table, my father and I both received Brody's air kisses. "Yeah, Nan, good luck with the job hunt, okay?" he said to me, winking.

"You know what you should do, Nan." Missy stopped at my side and patted my shoulder. I could feel her claws through my sweater. "Think about temping. All my BA friends do it. Okay? Call me sometime and I'll give you a few good agencies. See you, Mr. C.!"

Mr. C. sat next to me in stunned silence for a few minutes after the couple weaved their way through the crowded tables and disappeared down the stairs. Over the railing I watched them walk, both careful not to move too closely to each other until they were out of sight. "Nan, baby," Dad finally said, once more ferrying a lamb chop around enough stuffing to feed a small native Peruvian village for a week. "I don't want to put ideas in your head. But didn't you think your brother's relationship with that woman . . . well . . ."

I couldn't look up from my plate. "You think he's maybe having an affair?" I wanted to talk to someone—anyone—about the secret I'd been carrying around for weeks. It had been bad enough all that time to remain silent. After seeing Missy, I wanted to have it out in the open.

Dad chewed for a moment. "Nah." My heart sank. He took another bite. "Your brother's not the type. She's a very odd woman, that's all. Did you want to sing a karaoke song, baby? You should put in your request now so they can get around to it by the time we've finished our dinner. Do you want to move around to the other side of the booth? More room? I'll call over the waitress. Or we can just turn around your plate—"

"I'm fine," I said. My fingers stroked the cover of the karaoke book for a last time. Finally I tossed it across the table. It landed in the empty bench with a thump. "Let's finish our dinner."

"No? You don't want to sing for your daddy?" My brother's absence seemed to have brought back Dad's appetite. I wish I could have said the same for mine.

"No. Brody's right. I'd suck at it." I picked up my fork. "Only an idea I had, that's all."

The Metropolitan Museum of Art
(admission: free; coffee for two: Maya's treat)

Down in the courtyard, not two dozen feet away from where I sat warming my stiff fingers around a cup of coffee, splinters from countless school groups sat on benches, swinging feet and talking at the tops of their voices. A group of German tourists halted before one of the Tiffany windows, loud in their Teutonic approval; their shouted suggestions of where to stand for the best photos were followed by choruses of shutters and flashes and laughter. Out-of-towners proudly wearing sweatshirts from the University of Michigan and the Hard Rock Miami and for the Seattle Mariners swarmed in clumps among the leafy greenery, pointing with upturned heads where the rain battered against the atrium windows. All the noise—weather, laughter, shouting, cameras, the wild shrieking of the high school girls showing off for the boys—echoed and pealed throughout the stone-faced room, bouncing and distorting until its volume seemed heavy with invisible mass.

The din should have been enough to make me cover my ears. For some reason though, no matter how crowded and noisy, I still always thought of the Met as one of the most peaceful places in the world.

When Maya returned with her second cup of coffee, she found me staring out the windows at bare branches beyond. "I've been tiptoeing around the subject today," she said delicately. "But you look like shit. You've been sitting here for twenty minutes being polite without once being real. What's up?"

Four expensive years at a good university, learning rhetoric and persuasive argument, and all I could answer was: "Huh?"

"Our museum get-togethers are supposed to be fun. You sneak in with one of your dozen admission pins." A yellow fold-over tab of aluminum clutched my collar. I'd salvaged it, and several very like, from a garbage can outside the museum long before, so I could bypass the steep entrance fee. "I get in with my tax write-off membership. We buy some overpriced coffee and pastries, and then we drop scorn on other people's outfits. You're breaking routine. It's driving me crazy." She cut off my apology before I parted my lips. "Nuh-uh, I don't want to hear it. Is it the job search? You can't be all mopey about that. Everyone's blue when they're on the hunt!"

I could be, and was. "Nobody wants me!" I told her. "My dad's been slipping brochures from employment agencies under my door. Subtle, huh? I've got applications in with two of them. I've put my résumé on one of those giant job search Web sites and the only responses I've had were from a telemarketer and from a bottling plant wanting me to take over one of their trucks. Maya, I don't drive. And I'm pretty sure the telemarketer was a phone sex company!"

"It can't be that bad!"

"I considered the phone sex operator offer for a good half hour!" I protested, half seriously. "I could have earned them some serious bucks. You know I would've kept those bozos on the line after they'd had their turn and demanded that they pleasure *me*."

"The fact you're making jokes tells me not all's as dire as it would appear. At least, not as bad as your dress-to-depress getup would indicate."

"Dress to depress is how I feel." The courtyard's clamor seemed to grow in intensity when I admitted it. "It's hell, waking up every morning convinced I'm going to have to do some kind of unskilled temp job. I stay awake nights, imagining going back to Seasonal Staffers and begging them to take me back. I could always do some kind of part-time thing, but I won't do that anymore. I guess I could get a job asking people if they want to supersize their value meal, but that's exactly what I wanted to avoid when I started taking the weird temp jobs. My life is—my limitations are driving me crazy!"

"That's you, driving yourself crazy." Maya let that sink in for a long moment before continuing. "All because people have said things that've crawled in your head and burrowed deep." She didn't have to mention any names, but I knew whom she meant: Ambrose. No one had actually said that name to me in weeks. It was as if he'd died and I were a widow grieving his absence, and everyone was afraid to make me cry by speaking aloud his name, so they'd say it with euphemisms: *We're sorry for your loss. I'm so sad to hear of your bereavement.*

For weeks with my friends I'd had to read between the lines. *People have said things?* That phrase meant Ambrose had laid the smack-down on me. *It's a shame we all haven't been able to get together?* Why not blurt out, "Ambrose doesn't want to see you," and get it over with? Perhaps, I suspected deep within, because I really wasn't ready to hear his name invoked. The bruise was still too fresh.

"It's not anything that anyone's said," I told her, deftly skirting around the topic. "I just can't find . . . I don't know. Something. Even Pandora had some hope left knocking around her box, once everything else flew out the window."

"Girl can't go five minutes without showing off her fancy education," Maya teased. "Now I'm going to get all Dr. Phil on you. You need an attitude adjustment, pure and simple. And soon." She seemed to be waiting for some sort of reaction from me, but how was I supposed to respond? None of that was news to me. "You can't shut one door without opening another. It's a scientific fact."

Already I was wincing at the metaphor. "Actually, if you go into an enclosed space like a bathroom and shut the door, to get out you have to open the same—"

"Shut up. And work with me. You've been wandering around the bathroom for six years. It's time to join the rest of us."

"In where, the pantry?"

She raised a finger to cut off my grumpy retort. "At least in the pantry we've got snacks."

I sighed, catching the eye of a man sitting alone two tables over, a coat and open-collar guy in his thirties with a thick shock of blond hair hanging down over his forehead. A newspaper lay spread over his table. His knee propped up his opposite calf, displaying a highly reflective loafer. The man could have been anyone from a Swedish embassy attaché on his day off, to an art historian with Columbia, to a photographer from the wilds of Minnesota—and he had been looking at me. I blinked in surprise. Had he been listening to us, too? No, it was impossible for him to have overhead through the cacophony of rain and voices, even in the relative quiet of the café. The guy quirked his lips in a wry smile of apology, and went back to his reading.

Maybe I should have listened to Maya. She made sense. "I like snacks," I admitted.

"What was it you said to me when I broke up with Jamal, two years ago?"

"The VD clinic's open on Saturday mornings now, you should go get tested?" When Maya glared at me, I pretended to cringe. "That you'd find someone better?"

"And what did you tell me when that crummy Internet start-up company went belly-up?"

My answer was rote. "That you'd find a better job . . ."

She joined in with me. ". . . that I'd really enjoy doing . . ."

". . . with actual stock options," I concluded.

The guy at the other table glanced up and smiled at the sound of our laughter. Once again, his glance lingered before he ruffled his paper and resumed reading. "I get the point," I told her.

"Then darling, please do something about it. We've got a party to go to next weekend and I refuse to let you spend the evening acting like you're Sylvia Plath choking down the last handful of sleeping pills—"

"Sylvia Plath stuck her head in an ov—"

Maya silenced me with an upheld hand. "I *know* how Sylvia Plath killed herself, thank you. I also think you know what I'm telling you, right?"

I nodded. "Lose some of the drama. Enjoy myself more."

"And for God's sake, Nan, stop mourning. This isn't an ending. It's a new beginning. That's how you've got to approach it."

"I know. Thank you."

When we parted so she could return to work, it was with a hug and a kiss and a smile, but down inside I wasn't feeling the Hallmark Moment I pretended. Who ever feels better after getting royally dressed down by a friend, even if she has the best intentions in the world? It doesn't happen that way. What Maya had done was simply to hand me a warning citation: shape up, or ship out. I was a down-in-the-mouth pain in the ass, a doleful reminder of failure and sorrow.

Holy crap. I was turning into my older brother. What a chilling realization.

"Do you mind?" I blinked and looked up to find the blond guy from the other table hovering close by. His voice surprised me with its depth; it was like amber, golden and solid. Before I could answer, he had insinuated himself into the chair Maya had vacated. "Thoughts in a twist?"

He nodded at my plastic coffee straw, which in my ab-

straction I'd managed to tie into several knots. I suppose my
frustration couldn't have been any more obvious if I'd sat
there with small dark personal storm clouds hanging over
my head. At the same time, though, I didn't know this guy,
and I hadn't come to the museum to be picked up by some
perfect stranger. I smiled my most polite and distant smile
and prepared to excuse myself. "I'm sorry . . ."

"I'm sorry too," he replied, pushing his chair away slightly.
"My bad. I know how important personal space is to
women. Particularly with a strange man thrown into the
equation." When he grinned at me, his teeth had the brilliant rainbow sheen of recently-bleached enamel. "Allow me
to introduce myself," he said. "Cameron Jerome. Investigative journalist, communications artist, and writer. Lover, not
a fighter."

Oh. A kook, in other words. At least he seemed a harmless kook. "Cameron Jerome?"

"No, no," he said. "Cameron Jerome." Wasn't that what I'd
said? Apparently not. He reached into coat pocket and withdrew a business card, which he slid across the table with im-
maculately manicured fingers. For a moment when I saw
the odd text, I wondered if he actually was Swedish, after all.

CAmeRON JEROme

NuManity Workshops, Inc.

"The *mes* are never, ever large," he explained. It sounded
like an apology.

Upon hearing the word *workshop*, there are really only
two types of New Yorkers: the kind who instantly begin

twitching for their checkbooks and planners, and then the camp into which I squarely fell. My type just twitched. "Well, Mr. Jerome," I began, ready to excuse myself.

"It's JEROme," he said, using emphasis to imply the capitals. "But call me CAmeRON."

I would sooner have called myself a cab. I know we New Yorkers love our eccentrics. I had tipped the Naked Cowboy in Times Square several times, thank you very much. But we also have our keen instincts of preservation, and mine were telling me not to waste my time on some huckster trying either to sell me videotapes on hypnotherapy or simply trying to lure me into his cult of personality. "You know, CAmeRON," I said, trying to imitate his inflection, down to the almost silent middle syllable. "Nothing against you, but I'm not really looking for any workshops, so . . ."

"Oh, I didn't want to talk about my workshops!" His voice was mild and contained no reproach as he leaned over the table and took back his card. Once more he reached into his coat, this time withdrawing a gold pen and scratching out the offending line. "It's not about me. My mes are never, ever large. It's about *you*." He pointed at me with his Cross, then pushed back the card.

"Me?" I asked, though when I found myself wondering if my me was too large, I backtracked. "I?"

"Would you share your name?" Before I knew what I was doing, I told him. "I'm an observer, Nan. You're an observer too, aren't you? I saw how you noticed me watching you. What would most people have seen if they looked at you? Two women friends enjoying coffee at the museum. What did I see? One woman. Singular. Forlorn. Sorrowful." I wasn't impressed. Stevie Wonder could've been across the room from me and seen that. "And yet, extremely beautiful. Oh yes. Quite beautiful. That's all I wanted to say. It's the simplest, most essential compliment in the world, no? I think you needed to hear it."

From my skin color alone at that moment you could have plucked me up, dropped me down into the conservatory, and called me Miss Scarlet. I'm so unused to anyone calling me beautiful. I'm not beautiful. Cute, fun, lively, smart, perky—at my best, any of those adjectives could be used to describe me. Never beautiful. The word simply didn't fit.

Part of me had been living with a notion that I was ugly inside and out, lately. From a perfect stranger, it felt stimulating to get the news I was . . . well, not doomed to spend my life atop Notre Dame cathedral, scraping the Hunchback's corns. It felt like Bactine for the soul. CAmeRON, or whatever the hell he wanted to call himself, had been a shaft of sunlight in an otherwise dreary stretch of days. No matter how crazy his workshops, I was grateful to Mr. JEROme for that. "I was thinking—" he started to stay.

Little ray of sunshine or not, I wasn't so desperate that I was going to fall for a cheesy pickup line offered by the first Swedish attaché I ran across with anal capitalization habits. "I have to go." I stood up from the table.

"I understand that I must be threatening to you," said CAmeRON. Like a gentleman, he stood up and helped me with my coat. "No worries. Would you, however, do me the indulgence of allowing me to invite you to a party I'm having in a couple of weeks? I'll be having friends of mine there—actors, artists, creative types, New York's best and brightest—and Nan, I would be honored to invite you as my guest. Here." With his pen, he scribbled a few digits on the back of his business card, then stuffed it into my coat pocket. "Think about it, at least, and call me? I'd be happy to see you there. You could bring a friend or two if it makes you feel more comfortable."

"Thanks," I said, trying to sound polite. It would be interesting to see CAmeRON in his natural habitat. There was no way I'd go alone, though, and none of my friends would want to accompany me. "Enjoy the museum."

I heard his voice trail after me as I weaved my way

through the tables. "I think you'd enjoy yourself. I hope you'll call."

Poor guy. It simply wasn't going to happen.

I couldn't help but notice, though, that there was a spring in my step as I made my way through the Egyptian antiquities back to the main entrance. Maybe I'd end this one day out of many still feeling a little more beautiful than when I'd started it.

Kentro Ellinikou Politismou, E. 78th Street
(dry-cleaning bill: $14.95 plus tip)

"It's all Greek to me!" Clark raised his tiny glass into the air and toasted the six-foot cast-metal hanging on the wall. It held the place of honor in the club's reception hall, centered above a platform and podium, swathed on either side with yards and yards of white silk. On its face, a classical figure of doubtful gender stared blankly at the room. Was I culturally bankrupt because I hadn't a clue who he or she was? "God love ya, sentro . . ."

"Kentro," I murmured, trying to keep down both his voice and my own.

"Sentro nellyfoo politico." He swayed uncertainly.

"Kentro Ellinikou Politsmou," I hissed. "Keep your voice down."

Despite my warning, and despite a Trojan horse's worth of Greek men and women standing within earshot, Clark gave it another shot. "That's what I said. Senro gitchygoo spittleismo. Greek to me!"

It had been a long time since I'd seen Maya in a dress, much less with her hair up. She looked gorgeous. Clark looked gorgeous in his borrowed tuxedo. Heck, even I looked semigorgeous in my one decentish black dress, but none of us wanted to be tossed out on our gorgeous asses because of our friend's impending drunkenness. Maya cut in on the conversation, her eyes wide and serious. "Listen up. The Greek-to-me thing? Wasn't funny the first time. Right now, surrounded by actual Greeks, it's bordering on suicidal, okay? So keep your voice down and stick to *Hellenic Cultural Center.*"

"I've been drinking ouzo," he announced, turning his puppy dog eyes on her. A tendril of his long hair unhooked itself from around the back of his ear and fell over his forehead.

She reached up and swept it back for him. "I can tell, honey. Stand here for a minute while I have a word with Nan. Don't talk. And by all that's holy, don't drink."

"What?" There was no reason for me to feel guilty as she dragged me aside, but I somehow managed anyway. "I didn't get him pie-eyed. He was already trashed when I got here."

"I'm not blaming you," she said, all seriousness. "He's still upset because that girl he was seeing dumped him earlier this month."

"Veronica? From New Year's?"

"Monica, I think. He's embarrassed about having to come to Emmett's party stag."

"I'm stag!" I protested. Did she think I didn't feel the sting of being at an engagement party without a date? "You're stag!"

"Regardless. Clark always has a girlfriend du jour. You know that. Help me out. Maybe you could get a plate of food while I try to convince him that the words *open bar* don't obligate him to suck up all the liquor in the building with a sippee-straw, okay?"

Everyone I dreaded talking to at this shindig stood near the food table. "But . . . !" Why couldn't we switch? Why couldn't I manage the Carrie Nation routine while Maya visited the dreaded buffet? Starving though I was, with the Legion of Doom at the room's center, I hadn't helped myself to one little nosh since I'd arrived. At my transparent protest, she fixed me with a look of such iron determination that across Manhattan, refrigerator magnets loosened themselves from their appliances and began to inch their way in her direction. Maya was definitely going to make a great mom, one of these days. "Fine. *Fine.*" I tried not to stomp as I flounced away.

The sure sign of a flop party is when no one will talk to its guests of honor. For the last forty-five minutes, both Emmett and his girl bride-to-be had stood at the center of the large, luxuriously appointed reception hall while groups of their guests hovered in anxious clusters around the edge. To the rear, concentrated around a small bandstand where a twangy guitar/accordion/bass trio wheezed out what sounded like the Goldberg Variations on "Never on Sunday," were the Greek-Americans hosting this sorry shindig. When I'd first arrived an hour before, a half hour into the proceedings, I'd been so certain I'd come to the wrong street address that I'd walked all the way downstairs and back outside to check the street address. But no, the number above the blue and white flag matched that on the invitation, and once upstairs I'd had a nice chat with Mr. Gaitanas, a kindly old security guard sporting the thickest and greyest head of hair I'd ever seen. He was so slow-moving and elderly that he couldn't have chased down the most asthmatic of would-be criminals on crutches and foot braces ever to breach the cultural center's sanctity, but he was more than happy to tell me that yes, the building was where the Dunnigan/LaPlatte party was being held, and that it was being thrown by Isobel's . . . I had to think several seconds before I could remember . . . by Isobel's Greek mother's father's brother-in-law's American cousins, since her own family was so far away. Something like that, at any rate.

The consequence was that while the Kokkinos claimed ownership of Isobel, they didn't seem to know her at all.

With her pale, fine features, her blond hair, and her tilted nose, she seemed as likely to claim kin with the handsome, dark-haired families murmuring in hushed clumps as with Homer and Marge Simpson. Nor did I exactly see her rushing to visit with them, either; she and Emmett clung to each other, seeming anxious to pretend as if they were at some other party. One that hadn't stolen its decorations from a road company of *Zorba*.

They weren't the only group of people isolating themselves, either—from instinct and habit most of our little gang had immediately claimed the area around the open bar as our very own, while nearest the door stood timid bunches of under-forties who looked as if they'd maim, prostitute themselves, and sell their souls for a cigarette at that moment. The women were almost identical in their dark dresses, draped blouses, strappy stilettos, and stark haircuts, while their male companions wore broad-collared open-neck shirts and tight-fitting charcoal suits. Nearly all of them carried smart leather rucksacks, as if they'd stopped by on the way home from the office. Their bored expressions and similar urban uniforms made them look like the Ennui Scouts of America; I gathered they were Isobel's work friends.

Amidst the almost funereal hush, the center of the room was No Man's Land. Individuals might break away from their groups every once in a while to creep toward the lucky couple with congratulations, or to refill their plates from the Greek buffet, but no one stayed long; centrifugal social forces dragged them back to the perimeter again. As the trio struck up another morose rendition of "Never on Sunday," I hoped and prayed my own trip would be as brief. I had three reasons not to visit the center of the room. Roughly in ascending order, they were:

1) Never mind that it was Clark's stomach to which I catered. Anyone who saw me loading up a plate full of food would assume it was all going straight down my piehole.

2) More specifically, Isobel, centerfold of this month's issue of *Binge and Purge Magazine*, was going to see me waddle away with a plate full of food.

3) Ambrose had exiled himself from the rest of the Elizabethan Failures to stand near Emmett's side, accompanied by some unidentified woman.

4) And did I mention the part about Isobel, who had already most likely achieved her complete nutritional daily intake by lightly inhaling the scent of a crushed teaspoon of thyme sprinkled with the juice of a single lemon plucked from a postmodern theorist's tree along the Segura River and couriered to Manhattan from Spain on a pillow of gold sateen, was going to see me? With a plate heaped with food?

"Nan!" Emmett, comforting in tweed and thick wool, had already started smiling the moment I began walking in his direction. Fate seemed grimly determined to walk me over the coals in bare feet, so I gave in and marched toward the fire with a smile on my face. "I don't think I've seen you in a dress in, well, forever! You look nice."

It had, in fact, been forever since I'd gussied up. When was the last time I'd worn this outfit? I think it had been seven years ago, when I'd bought it for the last nice dinner with the others shortly before graduation. I had always liked the thing, but around Isobel and her coterie of fashionistas, I felt out-of-date and dowdy. "You look fantastic yourself, mister!" I told him. Warmth from his praise spread through my chest and up to my face, making me feel as if I'd just downed a whiskey. My own compliment couldn't have been more sincere; he really did look as if he were about to embark on the time of his life. "You guys are really a handsome couple. It's almost as if you were made for each other" I said, trying to include Isobel.

Once the words left my mouth, I realized how sincere they'd been. When had Emmett gone from resembling an innocent kid fresh out of school, a smooth-skinned and bright-eyed pup who had nothing but high expectations of his own future, the kind of kid who would read obscure and artsy authors in public places with the book cover clearly displayed, to an urban sophisticate who looked perfectly natural next to a cool number like Isobel LaPlatte?

"Weird, us being here, isn't it?" His comment was intended for my ears only.

"Well, if your fiancée's relatives are Greek-American . . ."

"I didn't mean this place. This venue. The Kokkinos. I mean, you and me, all grown up like this." For a moment I was startled; I'd been thinking the same thing. "Me, next to the most beautiful woman in the world, and you . . ." My heart nearly stopped. There was no good way to finish that sentence. It had only taken two words, a simple "*and you,*" to make me realize how far apart he and I had grown. "I'm so glad you're here," he finished.

Despite our distance, I was glad too. When he grinned, it was with the same smile I'd seen during so many late nights in his dorm room. No matter how married he was, I'd still be the recipient of those smiles. I could happily live with that. "What do you think of Ambrose's date?"

Glad for a change of topic, I eased sideways to study her. The woman in question had her back turned, but I took in her narrow shoulders and the ponytailed rope of auburn hair that hung between them. Then I shrugged. "Pretty?"

"That's what I thought too." Emmett dropped his voice to a confidential level. "Phi Beta Kappa, Ambrose told me. Fulbright Fellow. Teaches political science. He gave me her whole damned curriculum vitae, for some reason." Because Ambrose knew Emmett would repeat it to me, I realized. I was certain of it.

"Darling." *Dorling.* Isobel had bestowed upon me a look of tolerant oversight she might have given her worst enemy's cold sore, but now she was bored, poor thing. "This party is horrid."

"Ssssh."

"Well, it is. Everyone keeps expecting us to—I don't know. I could *murder* Mummy for talking me into this charade." *Shorrard.* "I wish someone would *do* something."

"They're your relatives, sweet. I'm sure they'll do something soon. Why don't you think about . . ." Emmett leaned over and whispered something into her ear that made Isobel's pretty pink lips purse into a point with a twist. When he moved away, he was smiling again, but there was something fundamentally different between it and the ones he had given me; the one now lingering on his lips was whiter, brighter, wider, a intimate Colgate smile of print ad proportions.

Intimate enough to make me look away. Ambrose fidgeted beyond Emmett, plate in his hand and doing a terrible job of pretending not to notice my proximity. "Excuse me. I've got to get some food. For *Clark,*" I said to the cooing couple, with emphasis. Emmett scarcely seemed to notice. Isobel had already dismissed me the moment I'd stepped up.

Ambrose had thrown down a gauntlet in the shape of a Phi Beta Kappa key. We couldn't avoid each other another month—but I could postpone meeting by a little. I sidled to the buffet and picked up a plate, considering what I might say to him. It was too late to pull an *Ambrose! I didn't see you here!* and I could never stoop so low as to throw myself onto him with squeals and a *Long time no see!* Total avoidance or ignoring him, though, would only justify Ambrose's worst suspicions about me. I wanted to hit the bastard. Hard. Telling me I wasn't self-aware had sent my self-consciousness levels skyrocketing. I'd analyze everything I said and his reaction to it until the wee hours of the morning, damn it.

I didn't know what any of the trays held on the buffet table. All I knew of Greek cuisine was flaming cheese and gyros, and this spread was nothing like a streetcart vendor's. There were a few dishes I could clearly identify as salads, and a couple more containing beets, a food I'd hated since childhood, but to classify most of the others I felt as if I needed the entire *CSI* squad and their forensic equipment. What were those green cigars? And what was the stuff that looked like chicken livers with tomatoes, but smelled like pork? And why did Greek people put peas in everything? So intense was my concentration that I didn't notice the man on the table's other side until he spoke in a deep and resonant voice. "I recommend the dolmas."

I almost gasped aloud at his beauty. The man's long black hair surged in thick cascades of waves down to his collar. His nose was large and masculine, matching the broadly painted brows hovering above his dark eyes. Some poet of the Romantic era had one hundred and fifty years before coined the phrase *sun-kissed* solely for the purpose of describing this Greek god's golden, toasty skin. And he smiled. Specifically, he smiled at *me*. The sure cure for any sour social situation? Attention from a handsome stranger. Now, all I had to do was say something suave. I cleared my throat, ran the tips of my fingers along my temple to smooth down my hair, and sucked in my lips very slightly to moisten them. Batting my eyelashes ever so slightly, I cocked my head and let out the finest quip ever to emerge from my mouth: "Huh?"

Thank God he didn't seem to notice that I was quip-impaired. "Dolmas," he said, his mouth still curved and friendly. "The stuffed grape leaves."

"Oh yes." That would be the green cigars. I positioned myself in front of them, trying not to look like a total gastronomical boob. At the same time, I wanted to hear him talk some more in that husky bedroom voice. "What are they stuffed with?"

"Tender, succulent lamb," he said, lowering his hand to the table. Was he going to grab mine? No, he had picked up the serving tongs and grasped a single stuffed leaf with them. He put it onto my plate, and reached for another. "Chopped onion, pungent and sweet. The juice of the fresh lemon." A third dolma joined the others. "And spices. Magnificent spices—cinnamon and parsley minced fine with the sharpest of blades and mint wakened by the sun." Just the sight of him was the best appetizer ever. I gawped, mouth open, not really certain at that moment which of my hungers was strongest. "All cooked in the oil of the olive . . . do you like olives?"

"Do I?" I murmured. Then I came to with the morning-after shock you feel when you've woken up with someone in your bed and for a split second you panic at the thought of having bed head and bad breath. "I mean, I do! I love olives. Olives are the best. I mean, I could live on olives. They're so . . ." I was babbling. "Nummy." This was not going my way at all. I cleared my throat and tried again. "You seem to know a lot about food."

From his shrug I could tell he was preparing some modest denial. "I run a shop for gourmets," he murmured. He made love to the word *gourmet*. He took it to dinner, invited it home to look at his etchings, served it red wine, stroked it, caressed it, spanked it on its bottom, and the next morning made it breakfast. "I believe in food as a sensual experience."

"Oh my," I replied, trying not to lose my balance. "I like sensual experiences." Again, that was one of those sentences that managed to sound a lot better in my head.

Instead of giving me the look that confirmed me as a genuine lunatic in his eyes, my Greek friend simply took my plate, walked several steps down the buffet, and began loading it up. One by one he named the dishes while I pretended to comprehend, as he ladled onto my plate a spoonful of pink goop, some fishy stuff, a salad of what looked like crumbled soaked green Styrofoam with feta cheese, and then dibs and dabs of cabbage whoosis and a phlegmlike chaser. Okay, so maybe I was a gastronomical boob. What I did know is that when he reached the end of the table, still glancing at me from time to time as I watched him fill my plate according to his tastes, he used a spoon to top off my plate with a dozen different types of olives. "My heart will be broken. I know you won't eat all of this." It sounded like a rebuke.

"Oh, yes I will!" I rethought that response. "I'll try it all, at least. I'm sure it's delicious. I have to feed some to my friend over there." When I looked over my shoulder, Clark was leaning heavily on Maya. It looked as if they were attempting some kind of line dance.

"Ah, a boyfriend," said the man in a way that made me want to give a whole new meaning to the phrase *Mount Olympus.*

"Clark? Boyfriend? Oh, no, no, no. Just a friend. A friend who's a boy. He's had too much to drink. But I haven't. Not that I'm trying to, that is." Worse and worse. Maybe I should make a getaway until I could regroup, restrategize, and return. "But thank you. I wouldn't have known what was best without your help."

At the very last moment, before I edged past the end of the table and made my way to Ambrose and the Brain Trust, he reached out and laid his hand on my upturned forearm. His skin felt like a branding iron on my skin. "I admire a woman with appetites." His eyes bored into mine for a moment before he sauntered off. I gaped after his round little butt.

Why did I feel like I'd just had sex? Heck, that had been better than sex. I didn't even smell. I tried to shake my dreaminess before I turned back around, but again, there's something about blatant flirtation that left a girl feeling . . . floaty. Twice in a week I'd had total strangers speak to me like I was the kind of girl a guy would notice. An *attractive* girl, if I didn't want to go so far as to believe CAmeRON and call myself beautiful. Like sex, the encounters had softened my rough edges and left me feeling human and approachable.

"Hello, Nan."

I didn't startle at the sound of Ambrose's greeting, or

flinch when I saw him studying the heaps of food on my plate. Had my feet moved at all? I didn't remember. Walking felt like being propelled forward on a little puffy cloud. "You are looking fantastic," I replied. He seemed taken aback by how sincere my compliment was. I hadn't considered that simply being friendly might set Ambrose off guard. I actually felt as if I had the upper hand. "And what's your friend's name?" I asked.

"Nan, this is Barbara Wellesley."

The auburn-haired woman added, "Like the college. Hi." As I'd told Emmett, she was indeed pretty, one of those fresh-faced women who cleaned up well. I felt instantly as if I knew her history—Barbara had been the kind of girl who got great grades in school but sat in the back of the classroom, hoping no one would notice her, who wore plain clothing and long mousy brown hair around her makeup-free face until at some point in adulthood, she decided to pretty up with a few color rinses and makeovers and discovered that she liked the way she looked.

"Wellesley, like the college, of course. I've heard such good things, Barbara. Ambrose has been telling all his friends about you." I was surprised how little spite my words carried. I was still too floaty to wish anyone ill. "Have you two been dating long . . . ?" I asked, looking from one to the other.

"Oh, about three weeks?" Barbara looked at Ambrose for confirmation. "We met at book club. We were discussing Cinda Llewellyn's *The Poetics of Artistry* when we . . ." While she talked, Ambrose put an arm around her and smiled. It was a show for me, I felt sure—the whole thing was a show for me. *Look,* Ambrose was saying, *I've moved on. I've gotten over you. I've been seeing someone special and she's here at this special occasion with me. See what you missed out on?*

My whole life lately seemed like a parade of other men's girlfriends. Let's see. There was Brody's spectacularly wrong girlfriend. Then the possible invisible girlfriend of my dad who was making him so much alter his life. Emmett's girlfriend, who had snagged herself the man I'd always pretended I wanted. Now Barbara. More put-together than I. Smarter than I. Infinitely more successful than I could ever be. Barbara was the retaliatory response to our argument at Cask and Carton the month before, a ground-zero, take-no-prisoners strike where Ambrose knew it would hurt me the most.

The thing was, I didn't mind at all. Minding would have been ridiculous. Why hadn't Ambrose found a Barbara years before? She would stimulate him, and not in the obvious ways he craved that I couldn't or wouldn't give. Barbara would probably give him the drive to get out of that terrible job as a barista. Maybe she could get him writing again. Ambrose and I would never have worked: too much sloth in one basket, between us. Ambrose needed someone in his life who would give him a little friendly competition. He deserved something to strive against. "I really hope I'll get to know you better," I told Barbara, at the conclusion of her story. "Ambrose, let's catch up later? I've got to get some food to Clark. He's a little—" I waggled my head from side to side to finish the sentence.

"Oh. Okay." Years of close friendship didn't aid my reading of Ambrose's expression at that moment. Was it relief? Disappointment? Some mixture of the two? "I hope this isn't awkward for you," he said in a lower voice.

"Oh gosh, not at all! Let's talk this week, okay? Maybe the three of us can do dinner?" Then, with exaggerated enunciation, I mouthed the words *nice job!* and glided off without looking back.

Behind me, I heard Barbara speak up. "You have the sweetest friends!"

Sweet. Yes, thanks to a round of harmless flirtation with a gourmet shop owner, I was the sugar tycoon. I'd single-handedly cornered the honey market; I could afford to be sweet that evening. Maybe the friendships I'd taken for granted over the years had changed a little. Perhaps they'd never be the same again. But it was like Maya had told me a while back: When one door closed, sometimes another opened. A solid, well-built Greek door. That really needed to be banged on, hard.

"Took you long enough," said Maya on my return. She gaped once she saw the huge piles of food on my plate. "Did you leave any for the rest of the party?"

"Some of this is for you and me," I told her, holding the plate between us. "Try one of the dolmas." I helped myself to one, plucking it from the pile with my fingers and taking a bite. A complex array of flavors titillated my tongue . . . sweet and savory and highly spicy without being hot. "I think I love Greek food."

I'd only brought back one utensil, and Maya was using it to fork-feed a compliant Clark. "And what's brought on this change of mood?" she asked me. "I saw you and Ambrose in confab. What's wrong with his date?"

"Nothing! She's fine. Very pretty. Very smart. I could like her." These grape leaf things were really good. I ate some more.

"Okay, so why are you gloating? Did the LaPlatte say something stupid?"

How silly. "No! And don't call her that. She's Emmett's girlfriend."

That was enough to cause Maya nearly to gouge Clark's eye as she tried to feed him. He grabbed the fork and helped himself to a stuffed grape leaf, taking tiny bites from one end and working his way to the center. "Nan, you called her, and I quote, 'Lady Wish She Would Just Di,' last week."

"Well, that was childish of me. I'm over it now."

"Are you sick? Do I need to take your temperature? Should I call 911?"

"Stop!" At my protest, Maya crossed her arms and waited. I knew the look. Jericho's walls would have crumbled at that look, even without the jazzy trumpeters. "Okay, there was this *guy*, and he was a little *flirty*, and I might have been a little flirty to *him*, and . . ."

"Mmm-mmm-mm!" Maya shook her head. "Look who is back on the damned horse."

"Oh stop. It was a little eyelash batting, nothing more."

"With one of the Kokkinos family?" Maya wanted to know.

I was more than willing to talk about it. "Yes," I said. "Extremely good-looking."

"Dark hair?"

"Curly and hanging down to his collar. I was at the table and he—"

"Were his eyebrows thick?"

Asking if a Greek man had thick eyebrows, in this room at least, seemed to me a little bit like asking if Donald Trump enjoyed making money, but I went along with it. "Very thick. And black like his hair, too. He was—"

"Was he kind of foxy?"

I took another bite. "That's what I've been trying to tell you. You're not—"

"Because if that's the one," Maya announced, "he's lurking behind you right now. Don't look!"

If there are two words assured to make me swing around and stare, it's *don't look*. Uttering them will guarantee I'll crane my neck, bug out my eyes, prick up my ears, and gape like a corn-fed yokel who's never before seen the hootchie-koo dancers in Kansas City. By the time my brain took over and tried to make me play the part of the hooded-eyed sophisticate who's seen it all, I was already sunk. My Greek friend had seen me. He was lounging, drink in one hand and plate in another, against the open bar, hips cocked. When I turned and gawked, he wrinkled his nose, sipped deeply from his glass, and placed it on the bar. He tilted his head in my direction, acknowledging me.

"Oh crap," I announced.

"Nice going, with your mouth full," Maya replied. "He is a good-looking one. I'd be in a good mood too, after a little flirty-flirty with him."

My mouth had been full, I realized to my horror. "But he likes a woman with an appetite. He told me so." Maybe it wasn't so bad, after all. I turned back around again and showed him the dolma on a fork. Then I smiled and waggled my eyebrows and hoped I was approximating a signal for "Mmmmm, good eats!"

It seemed to work. His eyes smoothed out into slits as the corners of his lips rose into a smirk. I was a monkey's uncle if that wasn't the universal sign language for "Told you so!"

"Okay, steer gently," Maya advised, trying not to move her mouth as she spoke. "You haven't been down this road in a while. Don't get stuck in the potholes."

"Thank you for the metaphors," I said back in the same stilted, motionless manner. "How's this pose?" I leaned against the wall with one of my shoulders so that, if I looked a little to the right, I could still see him standing there, glowering at me like one of those impossibly masculine romance cover models.

Maya murmured, "Casual . . . so make sure you stay casual."

Oh, I was casual. I laughed lightly, as if Maya had told me something funny, then stopped when I worried I had grape leaf caught in my front teeth. A quick tongue-check revealed nothing out of the ordinary, so I took another tiny forkful and chewed. If My Big Fat Greek Hottie liked a girl who enjoyed her food, fine. He would see me enjoying my food!

I was very conscious of the long, languorous way in which I was suddenly chewing my bites, instead of my usual frantic gulping. I usually ate greedily and quickly, hoping to get it over with as quickly as possible; friends didn't call me a compulsive masticator for nothing. Eating as if I was enjoying an epicurean experience made every bite, well, almost sensual. When my glance sidled over again, my handsome friend had raised his plate to his mouth and begun sampling a mouthful of a tomato salad. He stared into my eyes the entire time.

"I think I need some air," I heard from behind me.

Was Clark okay? When I looked at him, he seemed unusually pale. "Air? Or restroom?"

"Air," he gasped out. "Wait. Restroom."

"Red alert, then." Despite my concern, I felt a momentary twinge of annoyance at having to abandon my flirtation. I'd already turned around, though, to help. "No, no, we'll be okay," Maya assured me, as Clark stood up on unsteady feet and put his arm around her shoulder. "You've got work to do."

"Oh please. I'm more worried about Clark."

"Don't worry about Clark."

"But I am worried about Clark."

"*Clark* is worried about *Clark!*" Our friend looked as if he expected very shortly to be tasting that ouzo all over again.

"Ssssh. You stay. Have some fun," Maya commanded. She tucked her purse under her arm. "We'll be right back."

I didn't relax until they'd exited the room without incident. The Greek's eyes were still upon me as I resumed my solitary station. I resumed where I had left off, spearing something at random from my plate, inserting it slowly in my mouth, wrapping my lips around it and pulling it from the tines, and chewing it slowly while I glanced over to see his reaction. I didn't need Maya's help. I could be debonair on my own.

He very deliberately plucked an olive with his thumb and forefinger, inserted it into his mouth, and chewed, pausing only to suck a bit of juice from his thumb. The one little inkling of intimacy made my heart pound more quickly; the skin on my arms tingled as if he'd stroked it with his own broad, coarse hands.

My turn. The instrumental trio reached the climax of a heartrending slow song, making me feel as if I were a character in a foreign-language film. A black olive sat on the edge of my plate, held there only by the glue of a cucumber-smelling white goo. I plucked the olive from its bed and, holding it at both ends, gently inserted it between my lips. I couldn't look at my Greek friend while I did it. I knew I probably appeared ridiculous, and while I was enjoying the hell out of the flirting, I wasn't exactly sure how far I wanted to carry it. Yeah, I wanted to jump his bones, but at the same time, hottie though he was, I only wanted to exercise a few pickup muscles I hadn't used lately. Nothing more. I didn't think of myself as that girl who went to parties stag and ended going home with someone else's date. That girl turns into the middle-aged woman who makes passes at the groomsmen during her goddaughter's wedding.

I munched the olive, letting the tip of my thumb trace the bottom curve of my lip, wiping away a stray trace of imaginary food. Then I turned my head. He had another olive of his own now; he traced it around his own lips as if painting them with the thin film of brine. His tongue lashed out, flicking over the olive's tip lightly and repeatedly. My nipples twinged in sympathetic response, and when he finally took the tiny purple fruit between his lips, I felt slightly breathless.

My turn again. Across the room, there was a scattering of applause. The trio had finished their tragic dirge; the accordion began a livelier tune. I took one of the flatter purple olives from my plate and while holding it between my thumb and middle finger, used the very end of my forefinger to rub a circle against the olive's tip. Then I inserted them both into my mouth and withdrew my index finger. Damn, I was smooth! Feeling a little smug, I bit into the fruit.

Ouch! A pit in the middle of the olive jarred my jaw to the very bone, bringing tears to my eyes. I'd probably broken a molar. And I didn't have even bare-bones dental insurance after last month, either. Fuck! So hastily was I sucked out of my little dozy dream world of flirtation that I stumbled away from the wall where I had leaned, nearly colliding with a small party of Isobel's magazine buddies on their way to the bar. They stared at me as if I were some kind of freak in off-the-rack couture—which I was. When I tried to straighten up and wipe the tears from my eyes, though, I inhaled much too quickly. Something wedged in my throat.

The olive pit, to be exact.

I've had a lot of choking fits in my life, but they've always been of the wheezing and rasping variety, painful but not life-threatening. Never before had I experienced a can't-breathe-in, can't-breathe-out, can't-wheeze-or-rasp-or-gasp full-blown object-blocking-my-airway fit. Weirdly, I felt as if I'd simply frozen. Around me I could see people talking and laughing and taking deep sips from their glasses, but my own functions had completely ceased. My mind kept whirring away, thinking, *What am I supposed to do? Will I have to give myself a tracheotomy? Who in this joint would have a ballpoint pen and a roll of duct tape? Why me? And why do I have to die to this ridiculously jaunty song?* A million synapses fired away in my brain, yet not a one of them would move my limbs.

Around the edges of my vision, I seemed to see small particles swimming, like bacteria under a microscope. My eyes watered, and the pressure in my chest became more and more dire. I stumbled forward another two steps, arms beginning to flail. My plate fell from my fingers.

Crash! The sudden noise of china shattering into a dozen pieces brought me back to my senses for a moment. Beneath my feet were dolmas and *gavros salata* and *pastitsio* and the shards of crockery, but I didn't care. All I wanted was first aid. I looked into the startled eyes of the people around me, willing one of them simply to *help me.*

Instead, I heard the commotion of something else splintering into bits. When my head jerked around, I saw my handsome gourmet had tossed his own plate on the floor. *"Opa!"* he cried, nodding at me with a grin. Next to him, another of the Greeks furrowed his eyebrows, slammed his plate against the inside of a plastic wastebasket to loosen it of its food, and then threw it down. Sounds of breaking crockery and shouts of *"Opa!"* began to resound from the far corners of the room, as more and more of the distant LaPlatte relatives began to get into the act.

My knees began to feel weak. I had to get my Greek friend—anyone!—to understand that I wasn't trying to commemorate his cousin's union. The whooping and sounds of shattering grew, causing the tiny band to respond with increased volume. With both hands I rapidly beat my chest as I stumbled forward, hoping that my gourmet would realize I was in serious trouble. He repeated the gesture and advanced.

Just when I thought he understood, he grabbed my right hand. Someone else grabbed my left, and suddenly I found myself being dragged along in some kind of native line choreography with all the male Greek Kokkinos in the room. They thought I had been encouraging them to dance! The men grapevined, and I stumbled, past the engaged couple. In baritone voices they began singing to the sprightly music while they dragged me along. My vision got blurrier around the edges with all the increased motion. I had barely enough consciousness left to see both Isobel's and Emmett's amazed faces staring at me as we whizzed by.

I wasn't going to die of oxygen deprivation. I was going to be trampled to death. In a last-ditch effort to save myself, I broke free from the dancing, singing line when once more they dropped their hands to pound their chests in time to the music. Water! Someone had to give me water! I careened toward a group of stodgy old Kokkinos women, all of whom beamed as I staggered closer. I needed water! I cupped my hand and raised it to my face several times in rapid succession. Surely no one could mistake *that* gesture!

They nodded, understanding. They were going to help me! Then, *"Yasas!"* cried the women, cheering as loudly as the men. They all lifted their glasses in the air, toasting the happy couple. No! That hadn't been what I meant at all!

"*Yasas!*" The men shouted back, scampering for glasses so that they could join in. Everyone was so busy participating in the revelry that no one noticed when I veered off, close to passing out.

My eyesight had rapidly diminished to a small tunnel of white when abruptly I felt a massive pressure around my middle, as if my insides were being squeezed like a toothpaste tube. Suddenly I could breathe again. I gasped in fresh air; it seemed to scorch my tender lungs with every wheeze. Boisterous noises assaulted my ears as the bedlam of the dancing and cheering and toasting continued. A pair of strong hands held me by the hips. Doubled over, I continued to cough out my lungs.

It took me nearly a minute before I could stand up again. It still hurt to inhale. My midsection throbbed as if someone had taken a hammer to it. "Are you okay?" I heard in my ear.

Ambrose's big hands still supported me, one on my arm, the other on my shoulder. I nodded, my windpipe too raw to speak. After much throat-clearing and eye-wiping, I felt almost well enough to croak out a response. "Thank you. Thank you!" Amazing, the sincerity those two words could hold.

"Yeah, it looked like you choked on something, after you started off those toasts." Ambrose rubbed his goatee. "You're really okay? I hope I didn't break a rib. I've never done the Heimlich before. On a real person, anyway. Just on a Resusci-Annie during CPR and choking training at work."

"Do you need me to call an ambulance?" Like-the-college stood at Ambrose's side, a cell phone in her hand. "You look awful."

Ever quick to soften the blows that landed on me, Ambrose spoke up. "Barbara means . . ."

"I'm sure Barbara's right. I probably do look awful," I said. The backs of my hands were streaked with mascara, which meant my face was probably a mess.

"You should sit down," she told me. What a kind woman Ambrose had found. I let her help me into a chair.

When I turned my head to survey the room, I realized I'd journeyed from one side of the reception hall to the other, leaving chaos in my wake. The men were still dancing, now joined by some of the women, while the small band egged them on with increasingly lively music. Some of the fashionistas stood by, clapping politely and watching the proceedings, while many of the older Kokkinos still called out incomprehensible toasts as they raised their glasses. I'd taken a quiet party and turned it into a free-for-all.

In the middle of it still stood Emmett and Isobel. So pretty. So stunned. Both wore a frightened, uncertain expression, as if afraid of moving and bursting the dream bubble only to find themselves fighting off straitjackets in a cozy little mental institution. They were absolutely going to hate me, after all this.

"I can't stay," I told both Ambrose and Barbara. "I . . . I have to go." Before Isobel flounced over and slapped me, that is, sending my already-existing humiliation from mere nightmare into the lowest of Dante's hells.

"But Nan . . ." I ignored Ambrose as I blundered my way around the edge of the room to the door, wanting nothing more than home and bed. I didn't care to look back into the crowd so I could find my handsome Greek friend, much less care to see him ever again.

Flirting really got a girl into too much trouble.

APRIL

My apartment above Przybyla and Sons Bakers (sixteen stale prune Danishes: free, utterly free)

From the way my brother brandished the telephone receiver at my face when I arrived from my Saturday morning duties in the bakery, you would have thought that he was Dr. Van Helsing with a rococo crucifix and I was Mrs. Dracula, a little peckish after a good day's nap. "Listen," he commanded.

My telephone had to be at least thirty years old and represented everything outdated that I liked about my apartment. Although it featured touch-tone buttons, it still used a mechanical bell that could have woken the dead, was hardwired into the wall, and was the approximate color of water in the toilet, post-Ty-D-Bowl. I was slightly surprised to hear a mechanical and unemotional voice issuing from the cluster of tiny speaker holes: "You have . . . *four* . . . new messages. To listen, press five."

"Prithee, what black sorcery be this?" I asked Mitchell with a bad English accent. " 'Tis a stick that bespeaks itself with the words of a man!"

"It's voice mail."

"I know it's voice mail, you ass. What's it doing on my phone?"

Mitchell pushed a button. From the receiver, I heard,

"Message number . . . one. Friday, eleven . . . oh . . . two . . . P.M. Hallo. Have I rung Nan Cloutier? This is Isobel LaPlatte." I'd known who it was from the moment those BBC intonations inflicted themselves on my eardrums. After leaving her phone number, she continued, "Ring me back, please. I really must talk with you." *Tork.*

"I don't know how in the world you expect any employers to make contact when you wander all over the city during the day and don't give them any way to leave a message." Mitchell spoke with the practiced oratory of a certificate-bearing big brother. "You don't answer the phone when you're here!"

There were too many people I didn't want to talk to. "Employers aren't calling me," I assured him. I could tell from the pity and fear in their eyes after they looked at my résumé that I wouldn't be hearing anything from them more than the sound of snickering behind my departing back. "Besides, you're doing too much for a temporary living situation. What's different in here?" Whenever I'd looked around the machinery room during the last three days, I'd sensed change. It unsettled me.

"I didn't change anything. I cleaned a little. You didn't have dust bunnies—you had dust *wolverines* in here."

"I liked my dust wolverines. I was training them to fetch!"

"Train them to answer the phone and we'll talk." He pushed a button on the handset and held it to my ear.

"Saturday, April first. Nine . . . twenty . . . seven . . . A.M. Hallo, is this Nan Cloutier's flat? If so, please ring me back. I'd like to talk about your role at yesterday's reception, if you please. Thank you. Ta."

The expression on my brother's face was priceless. "Ta?"

"Shut up. I'm not responsible for the way she talks. Next." I wiggled my finger.

"Saturday, April first. Nine . . . thirty . . . nine . . . A.M. Nan? This is Emmett. Is this really your number? Why do you have voice mail?" Hah! At least Emmett knew me. I shot a triumphant look in Mitch's direction. "We're both really anxious to chat with you. If you can't—" His voice dropped down to a whisper. "If you can't bring yourself to talk to Isobel, could you at least call me so we can talk about what happened? Thanks. Bye."

Mitchell cleared his throat. "Should I ask?"

"Probably not." I sensed, however, he still intended to. "I broke a couple of dishes. Just a touch of mayhem, nothing major. Next."

"Saturday, April first. Nine . . . fifty . . . A.M," said the service's mechanical voice. My heart gave a jerk at the rounded vowels that followed, jumping from its normal slow and steady beat into a suspenseful military tattoo. "Nan? It's Colm." I waited for what seemed like months for the long pause that followed to end. Had he changed his mind about calling, only to remember he'd already spoken? Was the voice mail broken? Was that it?

I didn't want to know, though I craved the answer. "Next," I told Mitchell. "Next!"

"I oughtn't have phoned." Through my old handset, Colm's voice was faded, tinny—a diminished version of itself. I longed for the real thing, deep and rich and strange. Who else in Manhattan would use the word *oughtn't?* "My grandfather was released from his duties at the store. They're claiming it's because of infirmity, but in reality they want to make way for a younger replacement. As you might imagine, he's fairly upset. Well." A short pause. "I thought you'd want to know. There's nothing else." A longer pause, this time. At that point, when I noticed Mitchell holding his breath, I realized he was still listening in. "Yes," Colm said at last, drawing out the word as if he wasn't at all sure. "There's nothing else."

Beep. I felt a pang of the what-ifs. Enough weeks had passed, though, that their familiar ache had dulled. Mentally I wrapped up my regrets, tied them with string, and closed them away into an airless cupboard where I wouldn't have to see them.

"Sorry, honey." Mitch spoke as he pushed the button to delete. I shrugged. It didn't matter. At least, one of these days it might not.

The voice spoke. "Message five. Saturday, April first. Eleven . . . forty . . . two . . . A.M."

"Must have come in a minute ago," Mitchell commented. "See, the nice thing about voice mail is that if you're on the phone, it'll still record . . ."

I shushed him. On the other end, someone spat words like machine-gun bullets ". . . *know* you two are up there, you never do anything real before noon on weekends, so pick up the phone and get *down* here already. I've been circling the block for like, five minutes now, and the streets are full of thugs who look like they'd jack the Lexus if I parked it, so . . ."

"Brody," we both said, then put our ears back to the receiver.

". . . *Jesus,* Nan, I don't see how you can *live* in this shithole neighborhood, it's like a war zo—hold on, I have to merge here, it's like . . . hey, buddy, screw *you!* No, screw *y*—!"

My younger brother's voice abruptly terminated. "End of messages," announced the voice. Mitchell and I looked at each other for a moment without expression, and then scrambled for our coats.

I wouldn't at all have been surprised to see Brody's suburbia-mobile wrapped around one of the streetlights, reduced to a smoking heap of char and steel; he's that bad a driver. Save for a few old Polish women gossiping in the front door of the Przybyla's bakery, however, the street was fairly quiet for a Saturday morning. "Maybe he's gone back home," I suggested.

"Maybe we should go back upstairs and see if he calls again?"

Both of us stood staring at each other in indecision, hands deep in our pockets, when from the west we heard a squeal of tires as my brother's silver Lexus rounded the corner. Pigeons scattered as he careened down the street and skidded to a stop. The door locks popped open, and the passenger window rolled down. "Get in! Get in!" Brody yelled.

"No one's going to carjack you in this neighborhood," I said with great reasonability, leaning over. "Not during the daytime, anyway."

Behind us, the old womens' mouths paused in mid-rumor, shocked as he started to lay in on the horn. "Would you hippies get in already?" he shouted between honks. "We don't have time to waste!" Mitchell, doom writ plain across his face, immediately dove for the rear. As if I intended to occupy the death seat with Brody at the wheel? Hardly! I ran around to the other back door and climbed in.

"Crap, Brody, it's forty-eight degrees out and you've got the heat jacked up all the way in here," Mitchell complained.

"I get cold." The car started pulling away before I'd fully situated myself and closed the door. "What took you so long?" Brody wanted to know.

The both of us were too busy frantically trying to latch our seat harnesses to answer. I waved back at Zofia Przybyla, who had exited the bakery at all the commotion and who stared at our squealing departure. I hoped I wouldn't get a lecture about noisy visitors, Monday morning. "*A*, neither of us were aware you were planning to kidnap us, and *B*, we didn't know you were calling because Mitch was trying to teach me to work the answering machine."

"Voice mail," mumbled Mitchell.

"Whatever."

"Oh yeah, I did notice something different about your number. Like, someone actually *picked up*, even if it was a machine. Gosh, Sis, welcome to 1980. There's this totally awesome game you should try out sometime, it's called Pong, and—"

"Spare me your sarcasm. What's all this about?"

"It's Dad. He's in trouble."

Those were the last words I expected or wanted to hear. Kids always think of their dads as Supermen, impervious to death and disease. Brody's panic and rush suddenly acquired a frightful logic. "Oh my God! Is he in the hospital?" All my annoyance disappeared in a rush of adrenaline. "Is he . . . ?" Beside me, Mitchell clutched my hand. "Tell me he's not . . . !"

"He's dead," Brody said, veering so suddenly to the left that my shoulder restraint activated and yanked me hard across the breasts. I cried out from the shock of both impacts. "Yeah, right, like I'd tell you two wusses this way. No, he's not dead. It's worse. You'll see."

Ever since Brody was old enough to walk and talk simultaneously, Mitchell and I had shared a brother-to-sister private expression that we wore whenever we were both thinking the same thing about Brody: *That little shit.* Our lips flattened to a thin straight line, pulled to the sides of our faces. Our eyebrows glowered. Our eyes rolled slightly while we counted to ten and tried not to rip into him. We exchanged it now in the back seat. Brody continued rocketing uptown. "What in hell is worse than death?" Mitchell wanted to know, once we had our anger more under control.

Brody's big eyes seemed to fill the rearview mirror. Of course, he was so short and his seat so far forward that his forehead nearly touched the windshield, anyway. "A woman," he intoned.

Mitchell sank back in his seat and hid his eyes with a hand. "Oh God," he sighed.

Despite the shock Brody had given me mere moments before, I decided to play along. "How do you know he has a woman?"

"I followed him last Saturday." The Lexus lurched onto Eighth and we sped north. "You'll see. It's disgusting."

"You *followed* him?" Mitch sounded absolutely incredulous, and I can't say I blamed him. "Isn't that a time-waster? Why not cut to the chase and snoop through his e-mail?"

"His account's password-protected." At Mitch's throaty expression of outrage, Brody grew defensive. "Hey, don't get all high and mighty with me. I wouldn't have known about today's lunch if I hadn't gone over to check his planner this morning. You should be thanking me."

"His planner? You didn't," I groaned. Was that why he sped through the streets like a driver for Satan's Cab Company who had to make his fare quota on penalty of losing his eternal soul?

Again he looked at me in the mirror, seeming to ignore the tourist pedestrians while he sped around a parked van and through an intersection as the light turned. "Don't tell me you aren't the slightest bit curious," he said. "You, of all people?"

I wasn't sure what that was supposed to mean, exactly, but I couldn't disagree. I was curious. For four months I'd watched my dad transform from academic schlub into the kind of late middle-aged man that a lot of women found very attractive. Young women, even. Sometimes very young women, I realized with queasiness. "It's not a student, is it?" I gasped. Brody would think that a horrible thing, too, and overreact in precisely this way. "Tell me it's not a student! Is she younger than me?"

"Hah." Brody sounded smug. "I knew you'd want to know, but I also knew you wouldn't believe me if you didn't see it yourself. You are so going to owe me when this is over."

"So what if she's younger than you?" Mitch wanted to know. "Wouldn't you be happy if Dad were happy?"

Yes, yes, of course yes. "It would be creepy," I said. "She's not younger, is she?" Brody refused to answer. "Aren't you the *least* bit interested?" I asked Mitchell.

"What are we going to do, barge in on his lunch and go all *Jerry Springer* on them? Huh? Have you thought this through?" Mitchell asked. I suspected he was as intrigued as I, but was still too stubborn to admit it.

"Who do you think I am?" Brody possessed all the primness of an etiquette expert asked if it was more proper to excuse oneself before or after picking one's nose in public. "Of course we're not going to barge in!" He pulled the car to a stop at the curb, only seven inches from wiping out a third of Michigan's Ferndale High School marching band. "We're going to stalk them. Now get out," he commanded, ignoring the angry yells and relieved giggles of the kids in varsity jackets.

Mitchell was only too glad to follow instructions. I was too bewildered to comply. "What in the . . . ?"

Scarcely had the budding question begun to leave my lips when Brody hefted his wrist into the air. With a fingernail he tapped the crystal of his watch. "Tick tock!" he yelled. "Tick tock!" I scrambled out into oncoming traffic so I wouldn't have to hear those two words again.

While Brody searched for parking, Mitchell and I waited aimlessly on the corner of Eighth and 43rd. Mitch bounced on the balls of his Doc Martens, hands plunged deep in the pockets of his army surplus jacket, trying to pretend he was somewhere else; I shuffled back and forth and sighed a lot, torn between wanting to see the woman who'd inspired my dad's transformation, and feeling dirty for my role in this whole sordid affair. Stalking? I wasn't a stalker! Twice I started to speak to Mitch; odd, how I felt compelled to defend my inquisitiveness. Standing up for my feelings, though, would mean assuming some responsibility for Brody. That I wasn't prepared to do. "I'm sorry about all this," I said at last.

"If there's anything I've learned from watching Nick at Nite, it's that you don't blame Ethel for Lucy's escapades," Mitchell sighed after a pause.

I dropped my mouth open, pretending outrage. I was *Ethel?*

"Nick at Nite. It's a *cable* station," he explained with exaggerated care.

"I *know,* doof." I had an urge to hug him, right then, for trying to lighten my gray and confused mood.

"You know Bro's never going to be happy with any other woman Dad sees, now Mom's gone," Mitchell added, more serious in his tone. "That's the way he is. Here he comes." He nodded in the direction of Ninth Avenue, where Brody was jogging toward us on his stubby little legs, breathing heavily.

I nodded. "I know. But we're not like that, right?" When Mitch didn't answer, I asked again. "Right?"

"Why are you guys standing here?" Brody huffed as he joined us. "You should have gone on ahead!" Though he sounded exhausted, his eyes shone with the thrill of the chase.

Mitchell didn't appear at all rushed. "Where are we supposed to go?" he asked. "You never said."

"Man, Mom and Dad sure didn't give you guys any of the initiative gene when they cooked you two up," he said. "I guess they got it right on the third try. It's obvious I have to do *everything* in this family." When Mitchell and I lagged behind in his wake, he looked over his shoulder and urged, "Come *on.*"

The owners of Vamanos! apparently felt that if you decorated a restaurant with enough old Mexican movie posters, reproduction tin signs of Chiquita banana ads and motor oil, and colorful sombreros, then suspended from the beams creaky old ceiling fans, the people of Manhattan might actually think they'd stumbled through a warp in time and space into a genuine Tex-Mex roadhouse—a three-story Tex-Mex roadhouse within shouting distance of Times Square, where every margarita is sixteen dollars and comes served in a thin-necked plastic souvenir mug standing three feet high. Brody breezed right by the cheerful girl brandishing menus standing inside the front door. "We're meeting someone," he announced, barely giving her a glance. Both Mitchell and I gave the girl wan smiles of apology as we skimmed by, but she already had dismissed us and moved on to the next party.

"Lie low," Brody hissed as he sidled through the bar in the direction of the stairs. The instruction was meant more for Mitchell than for me. My older brother was the only one of us who towered above the high-backed restaurant booths. "Let me be the advance scout." He stepped onto the concrete stairs. "Don't let yourselves be seen!"

We let him vanish up the industrial staircase in a hunched-over posture. He peered around as if he were a World War I soldier evading Germans in the trenches. "Remember when we used to try to play hide and seek in the apartment?" Mitch suddenly said to me. "And there were like, only three places to hide? Good times."

"Under the sink, in the hall closet, and in the bathtub." I remembered it well. It was a fair comparison. "Ooo, remember that time you were it and we let Brody hide and never went looking for him?"

Our laughter was cut short by the sight of our brother at the top of the stairs, furiously waving at us to follow. Mitch groaned. "I think this is his revenge."

I felt like a spy. The queasiness at my stomach's center half-convinced me I was wrong to follow, but my legs marched me upward. We'd come this far; backing out would be cowardly, right? I owed it to myself to see who was making my dad rethink his life. Besides, Vamanos! was a public restaurant . . . it wasn't as if we were tracking him down in someone's private hot tub. Right? Were any of my justifications working? It didn't seem so, because the scent of hot fried tortilla chips blasting from the kitchens at the top of the stairs still made me barfy.

"Can I help you guys?" A spiky-haired boy who looked barely old enough to be working bared his teeth at us.

"*Jee*-zus, no," said Brody, recoiling at the sight of the kid's braces. "We're joining someone."

"Oh. I can help you find your party if you'd—"

Brody cocked his head. "Go away, kid. Guys, keep against the wall."

Mitchell lingered behind to slip the poor kid a few dollar bills while I followed. After that encounter, I was more or less afraid not to. Brody was a police dog who'd caught a juicy scent; his bite would only get worse if I ignored him. A few tables of customers glanced our way as we squeezed by, keeping our bodies as close to the wall as possible without actually stepping over the booths and tables. "Look." Brody slipped into an alcove where doors to the restrooms were adorned with artificial flowers. "Over there. Far wall. Act natural!"

Only in a Little Rascals or Three Stooges film is three heads poking around a corner to spy on someone "natural." Mitch and I hung back at the alcove's far wall, twisting our necks so that we could see and trusting that the shadows would obscure us; Brody studied the table like a Hitchcock villain, half his face obscured by the stucco, the other half scowling in Dad's direction. "See? There's a woman with him. *Told you*."

Overzealous he might be at times and evasive at others, but Brody had never really been a liar. Still, I was absolutely, utterly shocked to see that he had been correct. We stared at the woman we'd all come to see, next to Dad on a three-quarter-circle padded bench. We stared at the back of her head, anyway—her blond hair curled gently, like a figure from Botticelli. I couldn't yet see her face. As they talked, her hands smoothed the tablecloth and fiddled with utensils. Though Dad occasionally helped himself to the chips and salsa sitting between them, she only indulged in sips from her water glass. Finally she turned. Her nose crooked at its end, saving her face from being merely good-looking and instead making it interesting; more importantly to me, she looked to be in her late thirties or early forties. "Oh, thank God," I whispered.

Brody turned to glare at me. "You think this is *good?*"

As if to fuel Brody's worst suspicions, at the booth, the woman reached out and stroked the shoulder of Dad's jacket. He was looking almost criminally good for a parent; his sideburns had been fashioned so that they had a bit of a flare at nose-level, his salt-and-pepper goatee had been freshly trimmed, and he wore a spanking white T-shirt under his open-necked, pointy-collared shirt. He resembled, in fact, a lady-killer. The woman made some kind of comment about my dad's face and waved her index finger in the vicinity of his mouth. He blinked at her, stared down at his drink, then returned a wolf's grin in response to something she said.

My dad was flirting. My dad! Flirting! Fascinating as it was, I wanted to avert my eyes—both because it was too personal a moment to eavesdrop upon, and because the whole parental flirtation concept carries a certain "ick" factor. When I turned my head to gauge Mitchell's reaction, he seemed equally uncomfortable. One of his hands completely covered his mouth.

"Look!" Brody rasped.

The woman had leaned forward to rest both her palms on Dad's shoulders, as if feeling the muscles underneath. They slid down over his biceps to his elbows. She touched the bottoms of his sideburns with her fingers, then with briskness traced around his facial hair once more. Then, while we all watched with held breath, she brushed her fingers through his hair, testing the length several times. Dad seemed almost embarrassed at the attention, laughing and trying to pretend it wasn't happening.

"She's a 'ho.' "

"Brody." Both Mitch and I let the reprimand fly simultaneously. I took the lead. "They're both adults." And thank goodness. "She looks like a perfectly nice woman. Not a 'ho.' "

"She's a 'ho,' " said Brody, convinced.

"Who's he?" Mitchell had been keeping an eye on the table while Brody and I argued. When I turned back, a man now lounged by the booth. He was younger by quite a few years than either Dad or the lady; a pretty man with dark eyes and long, liquid hair and a narrow soul patch tickling the underside of his lip.

"Jesus," said my younger brother. "He wasn't around last week. He's probably her husband, catching them before they go off to their dirty afternoon."

Brody's statement made me want to tell him to consider the source. Since Mitch wasn't in on the secret of Brody and Missy, however, I merely commented, "Yeah, I can guess why that would be *your* theory."

He shot me a scowl. "What do you mean by that?"

Oh, he knew. I backtracked before this turned into a squabble. "Nothing. Maybe he's the waiter."

"He's not a waiter. He's sitting down with them." Even Mitchell couldn't deny his interest. "She's introducing Dad. They're shaking hands. He's helping himself to the chips."

"Poor Dad," I commented. When my brothers looked at me in surprise, I explained. "I mean, expecting a nice romantic interlude and having some other guy barge in and ruin it for them."

"Yeah, I can guess why that would be *your* theory." Mitch turned away his head.

"What do you mean?" I asked, thrown by the comment.

"Nothing, of course." He had already returned to his observation. "I don't know about you guys, but I'm genuinely glad that Dad's seeing someone. He's mourned Mom's loss long enough. I think it's high time he moved on and realized that his life isn't over."

Brody and I exchanged knowing glances. It suddenly struck me that when it came to our opinions of Dad and his budding romance, we all were saying more about ourselves than we may have realized. Dad was our Rorschach, a smudge of ink on a blank page. Reading him was up to us.

"Okay," said Mitch, still watching. "I take it back. This is getting weird."

Our heads swung to the table, where the blond woman was once more running her hand through Dad's hair. He stared at the menu and pretended not to be mortified. Then the other man reached out and let his own slender fingers riffle Dad's scalp, mussing the hair several times and then smoothing it down. The woman spoke and again ran her palm down the front of Dad's jacket; the man replied by mirroring her gesture and then opening the jacket front and tapping Dad lightly on the chest, talking all the while. Next, the woman ran her finger around the inside of Dad's collar and T-shirt and then picked up her menu and began to study it; while his mouth rapidly worked in speech, the man ran his hand once more through Dad's hair, then followed suit.

Brody turned around, purple with outrage. It's something of a feat to render my younger brother speechless, but the display of public hanky-panky had managed to do it. "You—you—you . . . !" he said, pointing back at the table.

He was right. I couldn't believe my eyes. I was flabbergasted, and grappled for explanation. "Is Dad one of those nudist guys you see on the news who join those clubs? What do you call them?"

"A swinger?" Mitch shook his head. "Hell if I know."

"You—!" Brody still tried to summon words.

"You're the, um, expert, on men who . . . you know. Other men," I said to Mitchell, deliberately being obscure in the vain hope I didn't upset Brody further. "Does, you know, run in families?" He gaped at me.

"You *swore* he was only *exploring* his *metrosexuality!*" The words flew out of Brody's mouth as if jet-propelled. "And look where it's led! He's a bisexual swinger!"

He'd shrilled the words so loudly that I feared Dad might have overheard, but a quick survey of his table revealed the trio still engrossed in their menus. Mitchell and I grabbed Brody and hustled him back down the promenade of booths toward the stairs. He wrenched himself free once we'd reached the first floor. "I told you he was up to no good!" He was obviously still baffled and angry.

"I'm sure it's okay," I said, trying to be comforting. "We don't know what's really up."

"Yeah, Bro, it could be something completely different from what you think," Mitchell added.

"Yeah, Mitchell. You're absolutely right. Because so many explanations leap to mind why a 'mo and a ho' would be rubbing Dad's muscles!" A few early bar patrons turned around to look at who was shouting over the horse races on television. "I did you both a big favor by dragging you here, admit it."

I didn't want to speak. Was what Brody had done really a favor? His expression demanded an answer. "Yeah," I finally told him. "You did us a favor." Why was he so determined to grab credit for this embarrassing trip?

Though red, he managed to look jubilant. "And you owe me now. You owe me big, right?"

Mitch nodded slightly in my direction, encouraging me to play along. "Yeah," I said. "I owe you big time. Anything you want, ask."

"Hah! And you didn't believe me!" Brody actually swaggered with accomplishment. What had I said to trigger the sudden change in his mood? Maybe he was simply elated at being proven right—Brody loved validation. "Meet me on the corner. I'm getting the car. You two can pony up for parking." The hell! He turned and pointed back at me. "Don't forget. You owe me now!" he caroled.

Brody exited the restaurant with a swagger. Mitchell and I exchanged our look of old. *Crazy little shit,* it said.

Apartment 1907, The Moroccan
(one "When Life Gives You Lemons Make Lemonade" floral bouquet: $39.95)

My cunning plot was this: Aided by one of the building's residents leaving for church, I'd slip into the Moroccan early in the morning with my vase of flowers and my card. I'd leave both outside Mr. Andrew Iverson's door. Then I'd escape without being seen. Admittedly, it was so sharp a plan that were it a knife, it would have sliced through butter only if the butter had warmed to room temperature or perhaps a little beyond, and if the butter were given a firm jiggle during the actual cutting.

It wasn't without pitfalls. Every other time the previous December when I'd arrived at the apartment building laden with Chinese or Thai takeout or parcels of books, the building's other inhabitants had barely given me a second glance when I'd ducked through the doors behind them instead of waiting for Mr. Iverson to buzz me in on the video security system. Murphy's Law dictated that today, of all days, I would find myself confronted, accosted, and hauled away by the NYPD for trespassing.

It didn't happen. The moment I ducked under the Moroccan's tasteful burgundy awning, a young guy exited the inner entrance dragged along by a black Labrador on the end of its lead; he even opened the doors and gave me an *I know you, don't I?* smile when I skipped inside.

Then there was the potential that I'd arrive on the nineteenth floor and find old Mr. Andrew's door wide open, foiling my attempts at secrecy. Or worse—I'd approach the end of the hallway and discover a funeral wreath on the door, or perhaps a squad of paramedics wheeling his lifeless body away while I stood there horrified, clutching a bouquet of inappropriately cheery yellow flowers while Margarita the nurse wept through her hands and sobbed that if I'd only arrived yesterday, I might have said my last farewells.

It didn't happen. There were no mourners in the hallway and nothing on the door save its numbers and a nameplate in the old gentleman's copperplate handwriting, as there always had been.

In movies there's always a disaster right as the heroine attempts some quiet good deed. I could have overbalanced and fallen into the door, causing a commotion. I could have dropped and smashed my heavy water-filled glass vase at the last moment, then watched with horror as the colorful submerged lemons bounced to a stop at Mr. Iverson's feet. Or I could have managed to set the vase on the carpeted floor outside the apartment, and found old Mr. Andrew peering at me inquisitively when I stood up again.

Again, though, none of that happened. Some nobler part of me wanted to knock at the door and speak to the old man, if only for a moment, but the coward in me triumphed. With pangs of guilt, I left the flowers behind and headed for the elevator.

When I stepped through the front door into the wan spring sunshine, I felt as if I should be happy that none of the dreaded scenarios my brain had devised had happened. Like Mr. Iverson himself, my December visits to the Moroccan belonged to a past more colorful than the drab, practical present. Part of me knew I probably wouldn't be coming back again to the stately apartment house with its chintz-draped appointments, or its lobby that smelled of lavender carpet freshener, floor polish, and Endust on old wood.

Of course, my brain hadn't at all considered the possibility that at eight forty-five on a Sunday morning, old Mr. Andrew might be returning from a walk in the park. In a hurry to get back to the subway line and blinded by the sunshine reflecting from car windshields, I didn't notice the three of them until I was nearly halfway down the block, when the grace notes of Mr. Iverson's voice caressed my ear. "Nan?"

My heart leapt, instinctively glad at the sound of his voice. It's difficult to say that Mr. Iverson was in his Sunday finest, because even in the days of his broken arm he'd been nattily attired. There was something especially jaunty today about his pearl grey vest and dark suit coat; it might have been the fresh carnation at his lapel that made him look like Fred Astaire's grandfather, only notes away from breaking into song and dance. Accompanying him a few steps behind was Colm, decidedly un-Astairean in jeans, a dress shirt, and a new leather jacket. Colm's hand had been cradling the shoulder of the woman at his side—a brown-haired girl in a buttoned-up wool coat. Her only distinguishing feature was the downturned corners of her mouth. His hand dropped when he saw me, I noticed. The girl assumed a polite smile that still made her look as if she were sullen.

I don't know which caused more of a chill: the sight of Colm, or the realization that he was now with another woman. If I'd been the star of some cheesy sitcom or melodramatic movie, I could have rested easy in the probability that although I thought now Colm had found a girlfriend, later in the plot it would be revealed she was his sister, or cousin, or Mr. Iverson's new nurse who had moments before suffered a slight dizzy spell and whom Colm was merely steadying. But this was real, and I knew she wasn't any of these things. Colm's casual embrace hadn't been familial or supportive. They had been standing too close to be disinterested individuals. The sensation of a breeze on my face wasn't the spring wind—it was the whoosh I felt as once again I realized the world had moved on while I'd been standing still.

My face hurt, as if it would shatter into a hundred pieces if I pulled its muscles into a smile. I did anyway. "You're walking!" I said to Mr. Iverson, genuinely delighted.

"One tends to, when one is out for a stroll. Aren't you a sight for sore eyes! I'd thought this old man had tried you past endurance, my dear."

I wanted to hug him for his drollery, but I settled for a broad and genuine smile. "No, I've just been busy. Looking for a job, among other things." I dared to shoot Colm a glance. He had moved forward to stand beside his grandfather, wearing a polite and friendly expression. Remaining there before him was one of the hardest things I'd ever done. At the same time, knowing that he'd found someone else to date afforded me a sense of relief. I didn't have to wonder if he were still available. If it hadn't before, hope would have flown out the window, faced with the reality of his new situation. "I got your message yesterday," I said to Colm with a nod intended to thank him. Then, to Mr. Iverson, I added, "I really am so sorry to hear that you're no longer with the department store."

"Well, well, they've been looking for an excuse to banish me." Mr. Iverson clutched the lapels of his suit jacket, refusing to look abashed. "And they've found one."

"Old man, your nearest and dearest have been begging you to retire for years." I had missed Colm's voice most of all; it was the element of him that tied together those odd and unbalanced features, grounding him in the real and the now. "We want you to enjoy your life while you're still in your prime—I didn't say *past it*, old man," he added when Mr. Iverson raised a warning finger. "You put back that lethal digit right now."

An awkward pause followed. In case it had anything to

do with me, I cleared my throat and spoke. "I brought flowers," I explained. "I left them outside your door. I thought they might cheer you up."

"The mere sight of you is cheer personified, my dear." Mr. Iverson's pretty compliments always left me blushing. "We had intended to go from our stroll to breakfast, but I had forgotten—" He stopped, and repeated his last two words, fretful. "I'd forgotten—"

"Your pills," Colm supplied, his voice gentle. "And I was about to go up and get them for you."

"Yes, yes, that was it. I was about to say the very thing." The slip was merely an old man's lapse of memory, but Mr. Iverson seemed upset with himself for making it. "No need to speak for me, boy. Nan, dear, do you know Colm's friend?" When I shook my head, steeling myself for the introduction, he gestured in the woman's direction. "Nan Cloutier, this is—"

"Elizabeth Mercer-Berman," she supplied. Without bothering to wait for Mr. Andrew, she leaned forward and shook my hand. I murmured something back about being glad to meet her. "How do you know—do you work at the store?" she asked me, Colm, and his grandfather simultaneously.

"I used to work at Mercer-Iverson," I said before they could speak. "A long time ago. And you do, of course?"

"I'm a buyer." Of course. I intuited it all, now. They had met on the job. He was an Iverson. She was a Mercer. It was a relationship of which everyone in that near-incestuous morass could approve; Colm had managed not only to regain both families' favor by working for a company he'd once shunned, but had picked one of the preapproved, stamped, and accredited life options the position afforded him.

And why shouldn't he? I couldn't fault ambition. I lacked the prerequisites. "That is marvelous. Really marvelous. Well." Again, I felt awkward. I'd intruded on what truly was a family moment. "I should probably get going."

"My dear, you're more than welcome to join us for breakfast. More than welcome. Isn't she?"

Oh, how I wanted to accept Mr. Iverson's invitation, especially when Colm nodded. "I can't," I said instead. "I really have to get back downtown."

"How's your brother?" Colm said suddenly. Was he trying to forestall my departure?

"Which one? Never mind. They're both crazy," I cracked quickly, winning from him a crooked grin. "Well. It's been nice seeing you." I stumbled aside, waving. As much as I'd hated the thought of meeting, I loathed more the prospect of having to part.

It was as if Colm sensed my unwillingness. "Elizabeth, could you do me a personal favor and sit my grandfather in the lobby?" he asked, hands in pockets, his eyes upon me. "I'll nip up to the apartment and fetch his pills in a moment flat."

For a moment Elizabeth did nothing; then, as if disinclined to grant favors, she let Mr. Andrew lean on her arm as they maneuvered beneath the awning and indoors. "Goodbye," I called out at the last possible second, once again feeling a wave of sadness.

I mourned because this would be it—the interview I'd avoided for so long. So determined had I been to prevent this encounter that I didn't have even the simplest of apologies prepared. There was so much I felt compelled to articulate, yet I knew I only had moments in which to say anything. Barely had I opened my mouth to stammer out something, anything, a verbal placeholder while I thought over what was to come next, when he spoke. "I'm really sorry." He rubbed the vertical worry-crease that rose from the top of his nose to the middle of his forehead, and ran his fingers through his hair. "I think I cost you a job."

"No." I shook my head.

"Sorry to contradict you, but I compelled you to run through Mercer-Iverson in one of the most ridiculous costumes I've ever seen a person wear outside of the stage version of *The Lion King*. It's been on my conscience since."

Why had it been such a relief that Colm had apologized first? I clung to the respite it gave me and answered. "It was me. My legs did the running. I did the hiding, not you."

"But—"

I silenced him. "I know we can't talk very long. You've got a peckish grandfather, and I don't think your girlfriend . . ." I let the word hang for a moment longer than necessary, in case he wanted to correct me. As I suspected, he didn't. "I don't think she wants to be separated from you very long. I wouldn't, if I were her." Colm's lower lip disappeared as he sucked it in and chewed on it. I took a deep breath and continued. "I have to admit I envy her."

"Nan, don't."

"I'm gonna anyway. Here's the thing: I liked you, Colm. I liked you more than I ever let you know, and it's a shame, but I know my shot is gone. Elizabeth's right for you." A pity that her tiny, pointed features gave her a look of perpetual crabbiness, but I felt certain Colm would see beyond that to the Elizabeth within that I was too obstinate to notice. "Way better for you than I ever could have been. I've got a screwed-up life, no job—you don't need any of that. Remember that night you told me why you took a regular job again? It's fine to have something to strive against to fuel your creative drive, but it wouldn't work with a relationship. That's the one place where you shouldn't constantly have to strive to make something happen. In the end I'd always be your oppugnant force."

"Do you truly believe that?"

I took a step back and shrugged. It wasn't a question I could answer with ease. My nose prickled inside, usually one of the sure signs I intended to cry. My emotion, however, didn't spring from the disappointment of what could have been, but from what was. I truly did believe what I'd said about myself. Even if I'd not let Damien paw me that disastrous evening, I would have fouled things up one way or another. It wasn't a matter of not being good enough for Colm—I simply hadn't been ready for him. "So. Okay. That was a rough confession," I admitted, trying to laugh a little while I wiped my nose on the inside of my wrist. "But I got it out. Go to breakfast already."

When he stepped toward me, closing the gap between us, I hesitated, suddenly self-conscious. Was he going to hug me? What if Elizabeth were watching from the lobby? In my head I tried to remember how much of the street was visible through the windows, and whether we'd be in her sight lines. "Don't do anything embarrassing," I pleaded. My ducts itched with tears; I squeezed shut my eyes to squelch the wetness.

First I sensed the warmth of him, so proximate that I could feel the stir of breath from his nostrils on my forehead. Next I smelled the sweetness of the soap he had used that morning, cut by the pungency of fine leather. Then I felt pressure, so gentle that it scarcely betrayed itself, on my right lid. His lips delayed there for a second, leaving behind the slightest whisper of a kiss. Colm shifted, and then his lips weighed lightly against my other closed eye. Finally I felt a soft and lingering kiss between my eyebrows, and then a stir of air around my left ear as he spoke the last words I was likely ever to hear from him again. "Well. I don't believe it, even if you do."

I didn't dare open my eyes for many seconds. When I did, he was gone—a refraction in the shifting glass doors of the Moroccan. While I'd gibbered on, he hadn't disagreed with a word. No shakes of the head, no interruptions, no gainsaying. Not until the very last did I know he'd wanted to contradict me the entire time.

Only now it was too late to do anything about it.

My apartment above Przybyla and Sons Bakers
(new-interview shoes: $29.99)

"Nan Clowter! Nan Clowter!" I was so used to Zofia Przybyla mangling my name that as I stepped in from the alley, I didn't bat an eye when I heard it shouted from inside the bakery's back room. The baker's wife today wore a red sweatshirt decorated with baby rabbits executed in pink and blue puffy fabric paint. Its cheapness contrasted sharply with her fearsome hairdo, puffed and sprayed and shellacked to proportions normally only seen on the drag queens at Lucky Cheng's. I couldn't imagine how many is-sues of *Us Weekly* under the hair dryer it would have taken to make her hair so hard, permanent, and water-repellant.

There seemed to be some sort of dictum that when it came to being inexpensive, comfortable, and attractive, women's shoes could only be two of the three. For my new interview shoes I'd settled for inexpensive and attractive, and the backs of my heels throbbed as a result. "Is some-thing wrong?" I asked politely, as I wrestled off the shoes. The interview had been a bust, anyway. Apparently, the real estate weekly hiring writers to dash off exciting blurbs for their featured homes would rather have hired a trained monkey than me. After reading over my attempt to make a showerhead in the middle of an eight-hundred-thousand-dollar apartment's bathroom sound like a hot, happening feature, I'd been dismissed without as much as a thank you. "Mrs. P.? What's wrong?"

Without warning, I found myself holding a plastic storage box. Mrs. Przybyla stacked another on top of it. Through their milky exteriors I could see what looked like V-necked sweaters, men's shirts, and tidy rolled-up neckties. "Your brother, he leave them with me." She batted her eyebrows in such a bad humor that I expected flecks of mascara to fly from them, like ash from a volcano before it starts spewing magma. "Then he fill up staircase with boxes, boxes, boxes."

I'd been so intent on Mrs. Przybyla's summons when I'd entered that I hadn't noticed the stairs running up to the second-floor apartment; boxes and cartons and wadded jumbles of clothing lay on either side of the concrete steps, leaving only a narrow and erratic trail up the middle. "My brother?" I asked. It was a Monday. Unless he had a school holiday, he was supposed to be at work. "Why would Mitchell do this?" Had he brought more of his belongings out of storage? Why? His room was tight on space as it was.

"It is mess! What if there is—God forbid—health department inspection? They write up citation for fire hazard and then just like that poor Rocky and Zofia Przybyla are out of business, poof!"

"I'll clean it up," I promised, calculating the number of times I would have to make trips up and down the stairs on my already-sore tootsies. "He probably had to get some of his sweaters out of storage because it gets so *cold* up there." For effect, I shook my shoulders in what was supposed to be a shiver, but I ended up only dropping one of my shoes onto the floor. "He's had this cough he can't get rid of. The doctors are worried it might be pleurisy."

Zofia Przybyla stared at me; I stared back. We'd happily ended at our usual standoff, in which she painted me as the careless tenant taking advantage of her good nature, and I sketched her as the slumlord for whom I was doing a favor by not exposing the hellish conditions of my living quarters to the Health and Human Services department and/or the Channel 7 investigative report team. Stasis had been preserved, and we could now go our separate ways until I had to see her again next Saturday morning.

Only at that moment, the back door swung open and Brody stepped in, arm wrapped around one fully stuffed laundry bag and its twin slung over his shoulder. He looked from me to Mrs. Przybyla and nodded. "Hey," he said, before heading up the stairs with his load. It had never occurred to me that Mrs. P. could have meant my younger brother.

That was it? *Hey?* I wanted to throttle the little freak. "What's all this stuff?" I called once the flare of rage in my chest had subsided enough to allow speech. "What do you think you're doing?"

He turned around and shook his head as if the answer were obvious. "What? What! You *owe* me, remember?"

"What do I owe you?" I demanded, grabbing hold of my shock and letting it drag me forward. "Letting you use my apartment as a storeroom?"

"No. I'm not storing stuff, silly. I'm moving in."

"Moving in?" So stunned was I at his answer that I felt rooted in place. But it was a joke. It had to be. Freeze tag— Brody had won that round. "That wasn't funny. Christ, Brody, I thought you meant I owed you . . ." I waved my hands around, searching for an example. "Dinner. Or babysitting. Or at *worst* telling that hellhound of a wife of yours that you were over here when you were with . . ." Mrs. Przybyla seemed very interested in the conversation; she stood in the bakery door with her arms crossed, drinking in every word. "You know. Missy." That name made Brody drop his laundry bags and stagger back down the stairs. "If you want to leave a few things here for a couple of weeks, fine. We could have talked about it and made some kind of deal. But I'd *appreciate* it if you'd at least . . ."

My words trailed off as he reached the bottom of the stairs and stalked forward. What in hell gave him the right to seem as shocked as I? "For one thing, you're my older sister and I'm really, really disappointed that when you swore up and down that you owed me, it apparently came with limitations. Honestly, Nan, that hurts." He took the top plastic bin from my grip, and set it onto the stairs, then smoothly relieved me of the second. "I hope that the day never arrives when you are so destitute and unemployable that you come to me for aid, because if I had to turn you down, it would be a crying . . ."

"Can it," I suggested. "I'm hip to the passive-aggressive thing."

Guiding me by the elbow, he led me a little farther away from Mrs. Przybyla. She responded by following. "Okay, listen, here's the thing," he said, his voice nearly a whisper. "I wasn't kidding. I really need a place to stay." Horrified, I simply took in the abrupt change of his expression, from outspoken to abashed. "Marcy threw me out. I told her last night about Missy."

"What?" Before he could divulge any more detail, I turned and smiled at the baker's wife. "Mrs. Przybyla, could you excuse us?" I asked her. "We'll have all this stuff cleaned off the stairs in an hour."

"I maybe should be charging more rent." She glowered. "For all the brothers you have."

"If you did, you could use some of the money to repair the leaking roof and the toxic black-mold colonies," I said brightly, pretending it was a good idea. She turned and wandered back into the shop.

Brody lurched after. "Hey, Mrs. P., you wouldn't happen to know where I can buy some indoor parking in this neighborhood, would you? I've got a Lexus and . . ." The door slammed shut.

I waited until we were in the privacy of my apartment—*my* apartment—until I started shrieking. "What do you *mean* you told Marcy about Missy? What'd you do *that* for?"

Brody instantly flew to the defensive. "What did you want me to do, lie?" he demanded. "It's fine for you to have guys throwing themselves all over you and sending you flowers all the time for I don't want to know what kind of sick sexual favors, but you can't spare a little sympathy for your poor little brother once he's found the truest, realest, best thing he's ever had in his life?"

When his voice cracked toward the end of his plea, my guilt straight away sputtered, then roared. "But you have kids!"

"I'll always have kids. I'll always love my kids and take care of them. Don't I have to take care of myself, too?" I must have been visibly weakening, for he pressed his advantage. "You don't know what it's like living with a woman like Marcy. Missy's . . . different. Look, all I'm asking is that you let me stay here for a week or so until Missy can talk to her husband and we can find a little place together. Someplace nice, like Hackensack. You can do that, can't you?" A massive lump seemed to have formed in my throat. "For me? Your little brother? I don't ask for much. You won't notice I'm here. I can clear an area on the far side of the room and sleep on your air mattress. . . ."

"I don't have an air mattress." If my tone was sullen, it was because I felt as if I were being strong-armed into letting him stay.

His voice transformed from wheedling to incredulous. "You don't have an air mattress? Jeez, Nan, what kind of life are you living where you don't even have an air mattress for unexpected guests? That's a household staple. Like spare towels or a two-month supply of water and canned goods."

"Wouldn't you be more comfortable with Dad?" I crossed my arms, still unwilling to give in.

"No!" I'd never heard him more vehement. "With the kinky escapades he's up to now? I'd rather live with you two hippies than him, any day." He shook his head with vigor.

"Brody . . ." I threw up my hands, frustrated that I couldn't find any reason to deny him. "I already have one brother leeching on my friends and sucking up all my spare time. No, I'm not saying you'll do the same. I can't . . . you'll have to . . ."

Apparently he thought I was about to demand he leave. He backed toward the door. "Fine. I'll go back home to a loveless marriage and a wife who doesn't want me there and we'll fight in front of the kids all the time and I'll ask them to pass written notes from me to her because we're not speaking to each other. That'll be healthy for them. Or maybe I'll go sleep in the Lexus on the street outside, huh? Okay, so it'll be the last time you see me because this is a crap neighborhood and the Lexus'll be stripped to the chassis before sunset, but at least you won't have to offer your little brother shelter." He looked around at the hulking silhouettes of the baking machines. "Such as it is."

"I'm not . . ."

His face twitched; his eyes narrowed. "You let Mitchell stay. You always liked him better anyway."

He had me. "Don't say that," I warned him. "I love you the same." That was my mom's voice issuing from my lips—her words exactly, from the days when we were smaller and would nag her to name which of us she best loved. How long had Brody been upset because I'd let Mitchell live here? Was that what this was all about, beyond the trappings of needing a place to crash? Feeling left out?

I'd tired of arguing, though I'd said precious little in the last two minutes. Crap. What could I do? "You know you can stay," I told him with reluctance. Before he could gloat, I raised my finger. "A *short* time. Only until Missy tells her husband. Then you go with her. And," I added, "I don't want you treating this place like some kind of love nest for you and Missy. No conjugal visits. And," I added further, "I'll need a month's rent in advance."

I named a figure that exactly equaled what I'd owe Mrs. Przybyla by the end of April. As I'd hoped, he incorrectly assumed I'd quoted a one-third share and mentally tripled it in his head. "That's all you pay for this dump?" he asked, and shrugged. "I guess that's fair."

"Agreed?"

"Agreed."

He rushed at me and hugged my middle so tightly that I felt like a wine grape about to surrender my juices. I felt a fleeting pang of guilt for gypping him out of a few hundred dollars. It was an awkward moment; Brody's not really a hugger. After an instant, though, I relaxed into his grip and squeezed him back. Poor little man.

"Okay," he finally said, breaking away. I caught him wiping beneath his eyes with the back of his hand. "Bring in the rest of the stuff and put it on the far side of the room, would you? Thanks."

I was too flabbergasted to protest. "By myself? Where are *you* going?" I wanted to know.

"Nan, I don't know if you noticed." His voice would have been appropriate for the simple or for very small children. He raised it slightly as the telephone began to ring. "But first things come first. This street you live on is like a third-world country. I've got the Lexus to think of." When I gawped at him, he clapped his hands lightly. "Tick tock. Tick tock! And get that for me, would you? I gave the office your number and told them they could reach me here."

My little scam over the rent didn't seem so dastardly, after all. Producing enough fumes to require an Environmental Protection Agency emergency inspection, I stomped over to the phone. "Cloutier Refugee Center," I announced. On the other end, there was silence. "Hello?" I asked.

"Nan?" I'm not sure exactly how she managed it, but the British speaker on the line's other end managed to make my name sound like two syllables. At the sound of the familiar timbre, my shoulders slumped further. "It's Isobel LaPlatte. I've been trying to reach you for three days."

A luxury loft deep in the heart of Tribeca
(one bottle of Falling Leaf Chardonnay, $17)

"Okay, exactly how many Bed, Bath and Beyonds did they visit to get this many pillows?" Maya wanted to know.

I couldn't blame her. The pillows were the first thing I'd noticed as well—seemingly hundreds of them, scattered on sisal carpet roughly the size of my machinery room back home. As with snowflakes, no two seemed alike. Some had been made extra-large to wrap arms and legs around, while others looked as if they'd been plucked from under the antimacassars from an old maid's fussy parlor. There were fringed pillows and pillows embroidered with old-fashioned sentiments, stuffed cases big enough to be sofa cushions, fuzzy pillows with plush faces of barnyard animals. The pillow fairy hadn't only visited; she'd met with an unfortunate accident and exploded all over the loft.

After having stood downstairs in the street for a half hour, we were already twenty minutes later than intended. I looked around the loft's wide open spaces, gift bottle of wine in hand, feeling damned stupid and out of place. I didn't know a soul. "Do you see Scary Poppins anywhere?" I asked.

As if she'd heard me, from across the room I saw a blond

head bobbing up and down as it made her way in our direction. Every now and then her hand would surface, furiously signaling—not drowning among the partygoers, but waving. "You can't call her names anymore," Maya reminded me, not without a touch of malice. "Now that she's your *best friend.*"

"Maya, darling!" *Dorling.* Isobel seemed to have an extra hinge that for greetings allowed her to bend forward from the middle of her chest without curving her lower back. Her lips left invisible marks in the air on either side of Maya's head, as she ever so gently curved her hand to cup my friend's shoulder. Then, turning in my direction, she tossed her British reserve to the four winds and went for a big ol' American bear hug—only when bears attack, their claws haven't been whipped into shape with a French manicure, and they usually aren't wearing head-to-toe Lily Pulitzer.

Isobel liked me. She actually *liked* me. Those three days of avoiding the phone and her voice mail? Wasted guilt that could so easily have been saved and used on an issue more worthy, like the plight of the homeless or world hunger. She had only wanted to thank me for saving her party and endearing her fiancé and his friends to her relatives. They'd had a grand time after I left, apparently, dancing until the wee hours of the morning. Three days I'd frittered gnawing on my cuticles when I could have been basking in the glow of Isobel LaPlatte, my newest, bestest friend in the whole wide world. "You lot are late!" she announced, not seeming to realize how out-of-place we felt.

"We were waiting outside," Maya explained.

I added, "For you."

"Oh!" Light dawned. "How utterly wretched of me! I caught Suze coming into the building and when I realized this was Madchen Franck's flat, well, I came right up. Everyone knows Madchen!" We didn't. It must have shown, for Isobel covered her mouth in apology and then turned and madly waved her head about again, looking for someone.

"Madchen!" she finally cried out to a woman nearby—a tall, middle-aged culture vulture with short dark hair and bruised-looking burgundy lips who had been walking from one side of the loft to another with several empty wine glasses in her hands.

The woman stopped in her tracks; her hostess smile thinned until it was nothing more than the upcurved lips of someone determined to be polite. "Isobel," she murmured.

"Darling, I want to introduce you to my girlfriend, Nan, and her friend, Maya." *Gullfriend.* "I was just telling them that *anyone* who's *anyone* has been to your flat, though this is the first time I've had a chance to come up and look about. Somehow I've missed out on other invitations!"

Although Isobel spoke with the adoration of a British schoolgirl with a harmless crush on the senior maths lecturer, our hostess didn't seem to be thrilled. "Have you? Fancy that."

Isobel's obliviousness to the woman's aloof comments wasn't solely my imagination; Maya had given me several glances of concern during the conversation. "It's really a lovely loft," I volunteered. "I brought some wine."

"I love all the brushed aluminum," Maya added. "Very sleek and industrial."

Madchen didn't pay a bit of attention to our weak compliments, or to my gift. "Who invited you, dear?" she asked Isobel.

"Guilty as charged," I confessed, raising my hand. My response elicited a raised eyebrow. "I'm a friend of CAmeRON's," I said in response to her unasked question. "He invited me to bring a few friends."

Name-dropping: music to the savage Manhattan hostess' Wonder Bra-clad breasts. Instantly Madchen's posture changed from rigid to relaxed; she eased one of her hips to the side so that her slinky pajama-like pants pooled around her ankles. "Are you? Isn't he adorable?" she asked, suddenly sociable. "I love him. Have you read his book? Of course you have. Isn't it marvelous? It meant everything to me. Oh, sorry," she added suddenly, as horrified as if she'd accidentally passed gas. "I know what you're thinking. Mes should always be small. Of course they should. Slip of the tongue. Is that wine for the party? Aren't you sweet?"

I surrendered the gift. What I'd actually been thinking had been more along the lines of, *CAmeRON wrote a book?* and *Why am I here?*, not to mention, *Am I wearing the right outfit for changing my name to Tanya and robbing banks at gunpoint after the cult initiation tonight?*

Madchen reached out and with her free hand grasped my forearm. "We must talk later. I'll look for you when we're lying down."

A moment more, and the only trace left of her was the scent of vodka. "Isn't she brilliant?" Isobel wanted to know. Maya and I were too busy goggling at each other to answer—not that Isobel gave us a chance. "Oh, there's Suze and her gang. Meet and greet! Suze! Suze!"

Isobel was off, her slender body twisting and sliding through the assembly without once touching anyone. Maya and I followed in her wake, universally ignored. "That was interesting," Maya said, grabbing a glass of wine from a cater waiter's tray. "How'd you manage to invite the hostess's worst enemy to her apartment?"

"Look," I told her, eyeing a tray of cheese and fruit before I passed it by. "Next time, *you* listen to Isobel gush on and on about how wonderful you are and how you should do something like gullfriends do, and we'll see how you fare. How many social events am I welcome to where she'd fit in?" My friend stopped another waiter. "New York's best and brightest are supposed to be here. I had to invite her!"

Maya had no compunctions about helping herself to cheese; I'd always envied her talent of balancing food and a drink and managing to talk at the same time without looking like a hungry oaf. "We could have crashed a wedding reception. Maybe a really upscale one."

"That's our June stunt," I reminded her.

We'd reached the other side by then, where Isobel was already gabbling away to three other women standing at the edge of the pillowed area. Most of the party's thirty or so guests were crowded onto a narrow area of wooden floor at the room's edge; once again I found myself wondering why so many pillows. Was there going to be a trampoline display later in the evening? The loft's ceilings were almost high enough. ". . . really have to meet my gullfriend, the one I told you about. You know," Isobel said to a plain-faced woman with multiple ponytails, who tried to step away. "The one who absolutely *saved* my engagement party from being the *social* fracas of the season." That was precisely how Isobel saw me—the life of the party, up on all the latest Greek dances. The woman's ponytails, tiered like Olympic diving boards, seemed to bob with annoyance. Her eyes darted to and fro as she sought escape.

"Yes, that would have been a pity." Another woman spoke; her words seemed as authentic as her hair's several shades of auburn, or the rigid, perfectly round breasts spilling out of her tight top.

"Jasmine O'Brian," said the third woman, extending her hand to me. At close to six feet tall and completely clad in purplish leather, she was a tower of burgundy. Long hair the color of obsidian hung over her shoulder and halfway down her back. "Isobel's told us quite a lot about you today."

I introduced myself and Maya with a sense of uneasiness. There seemed to be some kind of nasty undercurrent whenever people spoke about Emmett's fiancée, as if everyone knew the word *Isobel* in Swedish meant *eats monkey testicles for breakfast,* and knew Isobel wasn't clever enough to be in on the joke. Although Jasmine's comment hadn't been laden with the contempt the other women had shown, their reactions were still, as Maya had commented, interesting.

Did Isobel simply rub other women the wrong way? Interesting concept. I broke away from my thoughts to catch the rest of Isobel's introductions. ". . . and Suze works at *Charisma* with me as a photographer. . . ." Ms. Ponytail's lips twitched at the reminder. "Jasmine manages an art gallery. And Cam is a . . . beg pardon, I don't remember what you do."

"Funny. I tell you every time we meet," said the busty Cam. She bestowed upon us a look of bare tolerance. "I translate poetry. From the French." Maya and I gave appreciative nods meant to imply that translating poetry from the French was infinitely preferable to translating from any other language.

"My bloody memory!" Isobel laughed.

No one else joined in. Jasmine leaned over to me and asked, "Isobel tells us you worked as a holiday promotional planner?" Whoa. Way to go, Isobel, on the creative job titles!

"In an elf costume?" sniggered Suze, giving her buddy Cam a foxy sideways glance.

It amazes me that no matter how old I am, sooner or later I end up back in the middle-school locker room, enduring the parade of catty comments little girls exchange when they think their parents and teachers aren't listening. Admittedly, I was guilty of that crime myself, but I only indulged when others were out of earshot. Certainly I never made fun of people right to their faces, nor did I follow it up by giggling with my friends. If this was New York's best and brightest, I wanted back in with the dim and the dull. "Elf costumes are so inappropriate for Independence Day. I dressed up as Uncle Sam then."

"Wild!" said Suze.

Cam tittered. "A costume for every occasion . . . your boyfriend must be one happy man."

I didn't like any of the implications these women were making—that I was some kind of nympho with a costume fetish, that my job was laughable, that Isobel and I were Thickie and Thickier, barely able to keep up with their not-so-clever quips and implications. Maya began to bristle beside me, but I was already rising to my own defense. "I enjoyed it, actually. Of course, not everyone's suited for a job where you have to be pleasant every now and again."

"I'm sure you were marvelous," said Isobel, beaming in my direction.

Cam and Suze didn't look at all impressed, but Jasmine broke in before they could say anything else. "I wish I'd known you earlier. My gallery is opening an exhibition of illustrations drawn by children afflicted with muscular dystrophy," she said, touching my arm with cool fingertips. "Some of them are really quite imaginative. It opens the day before Easter, and I would have been glad of your expertise. We have an egg hunt and goodies for the children. In fact . . ."

It sounded as if Jasmine had landed upon a fancy way to ask if I was available to don a costume and hand out chocolate eggs to kids. To be honest, I was nearly desperate enough to do it. Brody's money had slightly eased the financial stress of being unemployed, but Manhattan is an expensive city and every little bit counts. Was I going to have to beg for a job in front of Suze and Cam, though? Maybe there was some way I could get to Jasmine on her own, later. "You know . . ." I began.

From the center of the room came the sound of clapping. Madchen had shucked her flats and tiptoed her way across the field of pillows to stand amidst the acre of stuffing. "Since we're more or less all here now, I'd like to thank you all for coming to this very special event." The crowd made some appreciative murmurs. A handful applauded. I took a look around the guests, since I'd not had much opportunity before. Most of them were on the young side and, as we New Yorkers tended to do, used iconic clothing, jewelry, and eyeglasses to convey in which little urban box they fit: hipster, alternative rocker, art world pretender, socialite. Most had obviously been around the scene for a while. Among them, I faded into the background; I didn't have a neat little box. Very few wore the type of post-work, around-the-office clothing that I'd expected for an early evening gathering. With the possible exception of Jasmine, most were dressed in loose, relaxed garb. Apparently, they'd gotten the same instructions from Madchen that I'd received from CAmeRON when I'd called him the week before: "Wear something comfortable."

Madchen clasped her hands together, smiled with the practiced smoothness of a social maven, then pulled a few three by five cards from her pocket and began reading through a pair of half-glasses hanging from her neck. "I first took notice of this remarkable young man with his first book, *Toms and Harrys Without Being Dicks: A Male's Perspective on the Dating Dilemma.*"

"Good God," I heard Maya mutter. She took a hefty swig from her wine glass and refused to look in my direction.

I turned when someone touched me on my shoulder. "Do you have a moment?" Jasmine mouthed, barely aspirating the words. I nodded. We were at the edge of the assembly, so it was easy to back a few steps away. "I don't want to keep you very long," she said so quietly as she leaned down that it was little more than breath in my ear. "It's my impression that Isobel is not very . . . practiced . . . shall we say, at having female friends. She's very excited to have a girlfriend for the first time and, well . . ."

Yes, that made perfect sense. Isobel had always struck me not as a flirt or a slut or any of those restrictive labels, but someone more comfortable in the company of men. It was men who made her laugh and talk, and men on whom she could work her charm. A lot of women found that quality off-putting. Perhaps I'd been one of them. Though I wasn't getting the vibe that Jasmine and Isobel were the best of friends themselves, I did intuit that Jasmine wanted some kind of assurance. "I barely know her," I confessed. "But she's marrying one of my best friends, and I don't want to hurt him by being mean to her."

Her hand rested on mine for a moment, and squeezed. It

was all she needed to say in response. "Talk after about the Easter event?" she mouthed.

Loath as I was ever to don another seasonal costume, I nodded. Jasmine seemed to be a nice person at heart. I could more easily see decking myself out in her employ than returning to Seasonal Staffers. I sidled back to Maya. Madchen was still talking. ". . . public access cable show, *Spy in the House of Love,* featuring such star-quality guests as Jerry Hall, Emilio Estevez, and Margot Kidder, has for three years provided a once-monthly look at both sexes' right to bear arms—and bare bottoms, too." While the guests tittered appropriately, Maya rolled her head backwards and around, relaxing her neck. When she lolled in my direction, she gave me a lethal stare. "His workshops for men, *Taking the Me out of Come: What Women Really Want from Romance,* were declared to be 'a white flag on the battlefield of the sexes' by *The Village Voice.*" Madchen paused, put down her cards, and beamed around the room. "And I personally am very pleased to have him host the inaugural event of what I hope is a new trend that will sweep the city, if not the nation. So. Without further ado, allow me to present my friend—and everyone's sensual guru—CAmeRON JEROme!" She stepped sideways, nearly tripped over one of her pillows, and applauded in the direction of a screened-off area in the back.

Although I joined in and lightly patted my fingers together like the others, by this point I was having a serious case of the Dorothys—all I could remember was, at that moment, there really was no place like home. It had taken a lot for me to call CAmeRON to begin with; I had to risk him not remembering who I was or turning down my request to see him again. Most of all, I had to gamble on him thinking I was more interested in pursuing something than I at all was.

I'd only really called because I needed some kind of high-class event to bring my new gullfriend to. CAmeRON was only a curiosity to me, someone oddball enough to want to spend more time with for stories I could tell later. A little like my old jobs, in fact. Maybe I was one of those people who liked collecting experiences, just for the living of them. If only that didn't sound too much like Maya's old theory of me being a modern Thoreau. Too heavy a mantle for my shoulders.

I had liked the notion that at a larger get-together I could spend very little time with CAmeRON if he turned out to be more than I cared to handle, even slipping away if I wanted to. I liked that a party situation, especially with friends around, wouldn't lock me into a typical date—even as I resented, right now, that CAmeRON never had a traditional date in mind when he invited me. This sensual guru business only gave me the willies. Surely no amount of oddity was worth it.

Except maybe the sight of CAmeRON JEROme in baby blue footy pajamas, carrying an oversized teddy bear dressed in a women's business suit. Suddenly it was all worthwhile.

"Friends," he said, smiling around. I'd learned a word in the eighth grade as the bonus vocabulary word of the week, but I'd never had an opportunity use it: he was *unctuous*. Maya cackled outright, trying to hide it behind her wrist. I heard other suppressed outbursts, both male and female, from around the room. "No, no, it's all right to laugh. I don't mind in the least. We're all here for one purpose tonight: to have fun. So giggle! Enjoy yourselves!" The invitation took the wind out of Maya's sails. She coughed, pretended to have no expression on her face, and stared straight ahead.

CAmeRON took several steps forward, playfully kicking the pillows as he advanced. "Touch. It's the most essential of needs." He was not a loud speaker, by any means. If anything, he made the choice to keep his voice slightly below a normal level, so that we all had to hush and strain our ears to hear him. Clever, that. Once again, I began to wish I hadn't stepped foot in Tribeca that evening. "Like bread for the body, touch feeds the soul." After he cuddled his teddy bear, he smiled at a tall brunette who looked skeletal enough to be a runway model. "Am I not right?"

She made an uncomfortable face. "I'm off carbs this month."

"Touch is what makes life worth living," he said, moving right along. "Unfortunately, too many of us are too busy with our professional lives to take time to share touch with our friends. Aren't we, Businesswoman Bear?" He addressed the stuffed animal in his hand.

"*That's right, CAmeRON*," said the bear in the high falsetto of the man holding it. Maya shook her head, turned right around, and headed toward the cater waiter standing at the back of the room, in search of more alcohol. "*When I'm through with a busy day's work, I find myself full of stress that Ben and Jerry's can't relieve.*"

He dropped the false voice and continued conversationally. "Well, Businesswoman Bear, that's why I invented Shnuggle Buddies."

"*Shnuggle Buddies? Why, what's that?*"

"Remember the good times you used to have with your best friends, growing up? Remember having sleepovers and cuddling, before sexual intercourse became both an option and an obsession? Shnuggle Buddies is a new program that lets adults, like these good people here, have the chance to return to those innocent days and enjoy each other with nonsexual touch." Businesswoman Bear looked around the audience as if she were impressed by the idea. "What we're going to have our friends do, right here at this very first Shnuggle Buddies meeting, is have them pair up and pick a spot among the pillows to lie down. Come on, everybody! Pair up for the Shnuggle Buddies experience!"

Oh no. That was where Nan Cloutier got off the bus. I didn't clap during folk songs at religious services, I didn't sing along at concerts, I didn't volunteer to jump up on stage during concerts or magic shows, and I certainly, *cer-*

tainly never paired up for a Shnuggle Buddies experience. A few feet to my left, Isobel waggled her fingers and bobbed up and down on tiptoe. "Madchen!" she shrilled. "I'll be your snuggle chum!"

I found Maya by a low counter near the open kitchen, discreetly loading cheese and crackers into a Ziploc bag she kept in her purse. "You ready to go?" The mere look on her face was enough to make me realize it was silly to ask.

"Listen, I apologize. I didn't know it was going to be touchy-feely. Get a couple of the crabby puffy things," I instructed.

I have a theory that you can tell a really long-standing friendship by the complexity of its everyday emotions. Early friendships are all about the simple sensations of joy and excitement and pleasure; the older ones still have those components, but over the years they've acquired texture and depth. As Maya crimped a corner of her mouth and stared at me, her hands still busily stashing away cheese for later, I detected a lot of mixed sentiments. Irritation. Patience. Humor. Most of all, love.

"You didn't know," she said, shrugging. "And I *knew* I should've Googled your friend's ass on the Internet. It's my own damned fault. Now let's get out of here. What about your gullfriend?"

I'd been ready to flee, but Maya's question gave me a whole new empathy for the gentleman forced to choose between the lady and the tiger. Did I abandon Isobel and risk hurting her feelings—and Emmett's by extension—or did I stay, endure the shnuggling, and endanger my own already tenuous sanity? I opened my mouth to provide an answer, still not knowing exactly what I was about to say.

"Ladies?" A soft voice spoke behind us. Déjà vu time, right back to the moment in seventh grade when my math teacher had caught me passing a note as a favor from one cheerleader to another, had read it aloud, and had left everyone with the erroneous impression that I thought Tommy Harris was the cutest eighth grader who'd ever walked the face of the 'plant.' Sic. Sic as a dog, that's what I was as I turned to face CAmeRON. Thankfully, the rest of the class—or guests, rather—were busily finding spots among the pillows. "Nan," he said, recognizing me. He inclined his head to the side, as if we'd known each other for ages and hadn't kept in touch. "I'm so glad you made time to come. Won't you both join us?"

"Maya and I were leaving," I explained, wiping from my lips the remnants of one of the crabby puffy things. "She's had kind of a busy day. . . ."

"All the more reason to relax and enjoy the simple pleasures of what Shnuggle Buddies can offer you," he countered.

"Nan said she wasn't feeling well," Maya parried. "Plus strangers put her ill at ease." She pretended not to see me when my eyes goggled.

"All the more reason that you two should be my special shnuggle buddy partners. Join me, won't you?" Riposte, thrust, jab, and twist. He'd won the skirmish; there was no way we could wriggle from underneath his blade. "Nan, it really is good to see you again. I'm so glad you came. Maya, is it? How lovely to meet you. I'm so glad you could be here." In his hands he clasped one of each of our own, pulling us toward the center of the room like a kindergarten teacher herding wayward children, talking to the group using his same quiet, intimate speaking style. "That's right. Buddy up with a friend, but be aware we'll be switching buddies in a few short minutes. It's all right to have a shnuggle buddy threesome, you know, if you're all comfortable with it." As people settled themselves, the floor became a mass of pillows and writhing body parts that resembled a scene from *Caligula* without the nudity, the sex, or the incestuous bits.

"I'm not comfortable with a shnuggle threesome." Maya sounded as if she'd rather endure a triple root canal.

CAmeRON seemed to be having another of his convenient fits of temporary deafness. "Now, let's not have any actual touching yet. Wait for us to join you." Still linked by his hands, the three of us stepped over several couples, feeling the sisal crunch beneath our feet. More than a few of the pairings had two women and one contained two men, but most were male-female.

Isobel lay near the middle of the room, her back propped up on multiple pillows and her hands neatly folded over the hollow concavity that was her stomach. Her legs crossed at the ankle, like a lady. "Isn't this *brilliant?*" she asked me as we passed. Beside her lay Madchen Franck like a corpse at a wake, only without a corpse's jolly joie de vivre. There was one hostess who definitely wasn't enjoying her own party. Farther away lay Jasmine O'Brian with a strange man I'd not noticed before; she didn't look any more happy about the setup than I did.

"Here we are," CAmeRON finally said, making a space for us toward the back where Businesswoman Bear was already propped. He dropped to the floor in one swift and fluid motion and crossed his legs, gesturing for us to join him. Maya and I exchanged grudging glances, sighed as one, and struggled down to our knees and then our butts. Somehow I'd managed to find the one area of the room with minimal pillow and maximum sisal; my wrist received a slice of carpet burn as I slid down to my side. "Now," he said to the group at large. "Let's start slowly. I want you to turn to your shnuggle buddy and tell them what's on your mind. Let it all out. Let them know what you're *really* feeling. All right? Let's give it a try." As I feared, he plopped on his left side and faced me. CAmeRON had the good fortune to have snagged one of the big pillows for himself. He leaned his chest upon it, laced his fingers and spread wide his elbows, rested his chin on his hands, and blinked. Wearing nothing but a ribbon around his waist, he would have made an admirable Cupid to my candy box heart. "Hi there," he said in a sleepy voice, as if we'd moments before woken up naked in bed together and he was about to follow up with *you were great last night* and then make an excuse to get out as quickly as possible. "Whatcha thinkin'?"

"I have to pee," I blurted out. Honestly, of all the things on my mind at that moment, it was the only one I could say without extensive editing.

"C'mon. You can do better than that."

"You first," I suggested.

"Okee-dokee." He squinched up his eyes as if contemplating. "I'm thinking . . . that you are peerless and that I am glad that our lives are touching right at this moment, for when two lives meet, they make the other all the more blessed for it. Now you." He cocked his head again. "I'm all ears."

I felt as if I'd been sucked into an adult version of *Romper Room,* and that at any moment Mister CAmeRON would pull out the magic mirror to tell all of his audience that they were very, very special. "I'm thinking I still have to pee," I admitted.

CAmeRON sat up. "Now, at this point it's all right to be anxious. It's natural!" he announced to the group. I flushed red at being used as an object lesson. "Not everyone's genuinely in touch with themselves. Years of emotional self-avoidance can dull a person to her—or his—real emotions."

I blinked several times and gaped. Ambrose calling me out of touch with myself was one thing. At least he *knew* Nan Cloutier. One brief encounter in the Met coffee shop did not make CAmeRON JEROme an expert on . . . and in my head I made sure to capitalize it correctly . . . ME. Before I could protest, he'd already flopped back down onto his right side to snuggle close to Maya. The top of his head was roughly level with her shoulders. "I'm thinking," he said to Maya's breasts, "that you are a very unique person with an old soul."

"I'm thinking," replied Maya in a no-nonsense voice I recognized and feared, "that *very unique* is redundant. A thing that is unique is already one of a kind and cannot be more so."

CAmeRON laughed with what sounded to me like unease. "I'm thinking that you are as wise as you are beautiful. You have the primal, almost archetypal beauty of a primitive African fertility goddess."

Maya abandoned her sideways position and sat up, hands on her hips. "I'm thinking that a scrawny little white boy in pajamas just told me I have saggy titties and a big fat black ass!"

I wanted to laugh aloud right then, but instead I sat up too. "And what do you mean, I'm dulled to my emotions? I spend all my damned time thinking about my emotions."

For the first time that evening, CAmeRON seemed to break character. "Hey, quiet down," he said in a normal voice. Then, clearing his throat, he assumed the therapist's tones again. "Let's not disturb the other shnuggle buddies. Many women assume that when a man says something, he says it from a platform of privilege and assumed superiority, but I believe that women are wonderful creatures who should be revered, and I would never intentionally—"

"And that's another thing," Maya interrupted. "I'm not ever taking the *me* out of *come*, no matter how much you ask me to."

"But I meant—"

"I don't get this whole thing about sensitivity classes for men," I said, speaking up despite the fact I was uncomfortably aware of everyone in the immediate vicinity watching and listening to us. Still, complaining aloud was far more satisfying than having to lie on the scratchy rug and share my feelings. "They're deceitful. You're making beaucoup dollars telling men that women are an alien species who have to be studied and dissected before they can be understood."

"But I disagree." CAmeRON sounded genuinely surprised. "Women want fundamentally different things from men."

Maya and I chorused a simultaneous "No!"

I continued speaking. "When you talk like that, you're implying that men's experiences are the norm and what we feel is distinctly different. You're saying that guys have to change themselves and become *abnormal* to understand us. You're saying . . ."

". . . that men have to take classes and capitalize their names all weird to appeal to women," Maya finished for me.

I nodded. "Even this Shnuggle Buddies thing—it's like saying, guys, if you want to get laid or at least cop a feel, you have to do it the long way around, by first taking everything sexy out of sex. Like I said, it's deceitful."

"Infantilizing sex implies that men like you think women are infants," said Maya.

"I don't think you're infants. Shnuggle Buddies is *not* about sex." CAmeRON's tone began to sound defensive. "It's a nonsexualized indulgence. That's the point."

"Then why do I feel so dirty?" I heard from behind Maya. Jasmine O'Brian sat up and struggled to her knees. "I'm sorry, Madchen, but I'm a married woman. This isn't seemly."

CAmeRON had been prepared to deal with defection from a single pair of malcontents, but Jasmine's mutiny left him speechless.

"Jasmine, really. We won't be doing anything of which your husband would disapprove," said Madchen from behind where I sat.

Jasmine's burgundy leather creaked as she pulled herself to her feet. "I can't imagine that there's anything we'll be doing here of which he *would* approve." The woman had incredible posture—I had to give her that. Many women stoop to conceal their height when they're as tall as Jasmine. Not she. "I'm sure it's all good fun, but it's not for me."

"Or for my fertile primitive voodoo African ass," said Maya, using CAmeRON's shoulder as a prop as she hefted herself to her feet.

"Or for me." Peer pressure wasn't what made me ease myself up. This place simply wasn't where I was meant to be. "I'm sorry, Cameron," I told him, pronouncing it without the weird lacks of emphasis. For someone who wanted to deemphasize the *me*, forcing everyone to remember his unusual capitalization requirements was a weird way to go about it. "Like Jasmine said, I'm sure it's a fun regression into childhood, but lately I'm more interested in being an adult."

"But now I won't have a shnuggle buddy," complained the man Jasmine had left on the floor, one of those square-jawed, rugged types who had seemed genuinely anxious to share a little cuddle time with her . . . or anyone with breasts.

"CAmeRON's free," Jasmine pointed out. When both men let quick grimaces contort their faces, she added, "If it's really nonsexual, it shouldn't matter, right?"

To seem churlish at our small insurrection wouldn't suit; Cameron Jerome saw that instantly. "Of course, if you ladies are uncomfortable, by all means go. Maybe sometime in the future you'll find yourselves yearning to release the free spirit within . . ."

I'd already turned away by that point, immediately to halt at the sight of Madchen and Isobel, the first sitting up with her legs bent, the other contentedly curled up like a kitten who'd just filled her tummy with milk. What was I supposed to do about my gullfriend? She'd arrived on her own, so conceivably she could find her way home without my help. Or did the fact I'd invited Isobel imply a responsibility on my part not to leave without her? I decided that it might be simplest to walk away without a good-bye. It seemed almost cruel to make Isobel choose between whatever friendship she imagined herself having with me, and her obvious desire to have an in with Madchen. Maya and Jasmine had already collected their bags and started for the loft's front door; I smiled at Isobel to let her know staying was all right, and followed.

"Wait," I heard. When I turned, Isobel was trying not to topple from a small mound of pillows as she gained her balance. "I'd better go with my girlfriend," she told Madchen, genuine regret in her voice.

"Well, if you must." Our hostess's lamentation was nowhere near as sincere. She could have broken a Guinness record for pillow vaulting in her haste to make her way to Cameron's side.

Apparently they had been big at Godolphin and Latymer on proper farewells. "It was a lovely party," Isobel said to Madchen's back. I could see that the woman had already mentally dismissed Isobel and that any further words would fall on empty ears. Didn't Isobel realize? Was she really that unintelligent? I ached a little for her—and for Emmett, if that was the case. "I'd fancy a tour of your flat next time I'm back," she said.

Poor little girl. She didn't have to leave, and yet she'd cared enough to give up what might have been her one chance to monopolize the hostess's attention and get on her good side. A world of possibilities gone, all for me and Maya. God knows we didn't have anything much to offer her save maybe a pitcher of beer and some filched cheese. Like the Grinch's heart at the end of his story, my affection for Isobel grew a size or two bigger, knowing what she'd given up for us. "Come on," I suggested, holding out a hand.

"Glad to," she said, taking it. Not until we were clear of the pillowed mass and well on our way to the door did she look over her shoulder back at Madchen and sigh, just as Lot's wife might have with regret upon realizing she'd left her best outfits behind in her flight from downtown Sodom. "Rancid old twat," she pronounced. Nice mouths on them, those Godolphin and Latymer girls.

Good. So she wasn't as obtuse as I worried. She and Emmett would be fine.

Przybyla and Sons Bakers
(one Saturday morning's net:
all the day-old bread I cared to carry)

One by one Mrs. Przybyla counted off from the stack of dollar bills, talking to keep time with her practiced rhythm. "And that young Miss Winter! So proud! She works out at gym and now all she do is wear top with no sleeve to show off biceps. Men don't want woman with muscles, do they? No! Look at you. No muscles."

"No man, either." I twirled the garbage bag between my legs while I held it by the neck, then slipped on the plastic tie and moved to the next. Privately, I didn't think that the male sex was what Ms. Winter had an interest in attracting, but there was no use sending my landlady off on another tangent.

Over the last six years I'd become accustomed to the fact that Mrs. Przybyla was a morning person. Like clockwork at five A.M. every day save Sunday, through the thick floors and steel doors I could hear her and her husband arriving in the back alley for work. Ovens and baking sheets and mixers and all the other tools of their trade would whirr and bang and roar to life, and more often than not, I'd pull the covers over my head and ignore it all. What still surprised me was how talkative she always managed to be once the shop pulled down its shades at one in the afternoon. A Saturday morning's worth of customers provided her enough gossip, speculation, and outright calumny to keep her jaws working well until after I'd completed my clean-up duties. "I think she looks too thin. Unhealthy. Like she has some sort of disease."

I could say nothing, so that by Monday morning all the bakery regulars would know that Mallory Winter was inches away from committing herself to the Sloan-Kettering Cancer Center, or I could contradict her. "That's the style these days, Mrs. P.," I said.

"Style! What do they know of style?" It was an ironic statement coming from a woman mixing a Luxor Las Vegas sweatshirt, a button that said *Support our troops!,* and multiple crucifixes, but I let it pass. "Well don't you be going to gym. It will only kill you in the end!" she warned, zipping the day's proceeds into a bank deposit bag.

I finished the last of the trash bags, sighed, and stood up. "At your rates, my rent is more than I can afford, much less gym fees. Don't worry. Speaking of which." I cleared my throat, telling myself not to be nervous. "I kind of need to ask if you wouldn't mind letting me have off next Saturday. I could work Friday instead," I said when she opened her mouth. "I know Saturday's your busy day, and I know it's the day before Easter, but I have this thing I have to do."

"Thing?" In Mrs. Przybyla's mouth, the word sounded bitter, as if she'd tasted lemon juice concentrate spiked with Liquid Drano.

"It's a job . . . thing," I admitted. Why was I so shy about saying the word? "Like an audition."

"Audition? Audition? You are trying out for Broadway musical? You will be in *Cats*? Mr. Przybyla and me, we loved *Cats.*"

If the last time the Przybylas had been to a show was to see *Cats,* no wonder Broadway was always in trouble. "No, it's not an acting job. If I do a good job on this one assignment, I might be able to get the full-time position, see. I've been asked to organize an art gallery opening. So I have to send out the invitations, call the caterers, write up a mini-catalog kind of thing, create an easter egg hunt, talk to the people who . . ."

"Pffffffff. Fancy work. That's all anyone really wants these days! Is sad day for United States of America when people turn up noses at honest living and only look for fancy work!"

In Mrs. Przybyla's eyes, *fancy work* covered everything from performance art to stock speculation to prostitution. I probably fell somewhere toward the latter range of the scale. "It's not paying much money," I said, in case she got the half-cocked notion to up the rent. "I was actually making more at Seasonal Staffers." She said nothing, instead turning her attention to the stale-ish loaf of raisin bread and a brioche I'd plucked from the day-old bin, busily wrapping both in waxed paper and plastic wrap. "I'll come help out two days this week if you want, to make up for it."

"No, no, fine. Is fine." It was too late. I was a fancy-worker, a slacker, she who shunned real labor to fritter away her time with words and ideas and postage meters. "If is not beneath you, trash bags should go out now." She finished wrapping my bread and stalked into the back, muttering to herself.

By the time I wrangled several smelly garbage bags to the street and walked back upstairs, I smelled like the trash myself. I'd been on my feet since the shop opened at eight, I hadn't had lunch, and needed a shower badly. If I'd been a man, I would've grabbed a beer from the fridge, turned on the tube, and blindly watched TV with my hand unconsciously shoved down my pants front, scratching. If I'd lived alone, I would have shucked my clothes piece by piece the moment the door closed behind me, intent on the bathroom and a bar of soap.

But I wasn't a man, and I didn't live alone. I was a woman with no privacy and an apartment ringing with the sound of shouting because I was the proud guardian of two brothers at each other's throats. *"I don't have to listen to anything you say, you fucking fucker!"* I heard from the far side of the machinery room.

A moment later, from my living room, Mitchell's voice yelled back. *"You never do anyway, you little dipshit."*

"That's because you never say anything worth listening to. Fuckchop!" Brody rounded the corner wearing a Big Dogs sweatshirt with the arms cut off to expose his miniature biceps. Mrs. Przybyla would have had a fit. He breezed right past me, not saying a word, until he reached the door of the bathroom. *"Maybe if you had a life you wouldn't be so boring!"*

Mitchell appeared in the living room doorway opposite Brody, still wearing a sloppy pair of sweatpants and a T-shirt so oversized it would have fit a linebacker. It might have been one of Ty's. They faced each other across the bathroom. "Boring? Don't talk to me about *boring*. You're a piece-of-shit accountant who dresses up in a suit every day! You're the *definition* of boring!"

"Oh, because showing filmstrips to private school kids is sooooooo interesting!" Brody turned on the scorn. "I know for a fact I make more money than you. God knows I make more than Nan. I even make more money than Dad, did you know that? Huh? Did you?"

"Hey," I said. The tiled walls of the bathroom echoed their argument hollowly. My temples pulsed and throbbed like mad.

"How'd you find that out? Snooping through Dad's checkbook?" For a moment it looked as if Mitchell might have drawn blood; Brody's face turned red and his mouth disappeared as he sucked in his lips. "You know, it all boils down to money for you. So what? So what, Brody? We all know you took the most boring major in college so you could get the most boring, high-paying job you could, just to prove you were better than any of us. And you know why?" Brody didn't say a word. "You know why you always overcompensate? It's because you're so *short.*"

"Fucker!" Brody lunged through the door and after Mitch, who ran away for safety.

"You're *short,*" Mitchell yelled, grabbing one of the sofa cushions and using it to shield himself from Brody's fists.

"And?"

"You're a short little shit and you know what? No matter how much money you make and how many Lexuses you have, they're not going to make you *any taller!*"

A growl of pure rage erupted from deep within Brody's chest. He charged over the coffee table where I'd stacked three hundred invitations for Jasmine's opening the night before, neatly arranged by zip code and ready to send. "Stop fighting like a pansy, asshole!"

I couldn't help but yell out a wordless warning; the coffee table was rickety enough as it was. Worse, in his television watching, Mitchell had left a giant tumbler of diet Pepsi next to them. Four hours' worth of work could be ruined in an instant. Mitchell grunted at Brody's impact atop him. The sofa rocked onto its back feet, banged against the wall to jar everything on the shelves above, and thudded down again.

"What the *hell is going on?*" I screamed at last.

There was a brief respite as the two of them stopped wrestling. Both of them huffed and puffed as if they'd run a marathon. Mitchell pushed Brody off, stood up, and walked around the table to stand by me and point at his opponent. I didn't much appreciate the way he seemed to assume I'd be on his side. "I found out this tiny little shit has been cheating on Marcy!"

"We're having problems!"

"Problems? You're the problem! It's *you!* I mean, it doesn't take a genius to figure out that when your little brother moves in with you he's got trouble at home, but I thought it was Marcy being her usual bitch self. I didn't know you were the one who totally screwed things up!"

"I'm in love with someone else!"

"So what, Marcy's only a bystander who gets injured because of your romance? Too bad, so sad? Is that it?" Mitchell's voice, already loud, began to crack with emotion. It was the closest he'd ever come to admitting to the rest of us that he'd been in a similar position himself, nine months ago. I ached for him. "So everyone else is supposed to sit back and deal with it? I don't care how big a bitch that woman is. You made a *promise* to her the day you got married. You pledged an *oath*. You promised to love her, comfort her, keep her in sickness and in health. . . ."

Brody had turned a deep shade of red. "I know how it goes!"

"And forsaking all others be faithful to her for as long as you both shall live!" Mitchell paused to let the words sink in. "I know we haven't seen Marcy for a while, but I thought it was because you'd taught her to hate us all. Did she die last year, Bro? Is that why we haven't seen her? Is that why you're suddenly free to drop the vow about faithfulness to fuck around with your little whore . . . what's her name?" Brody didn't answer. "Too ashamed to tell me her name, huh?"

"It's Missy," I said, sick of the arguing. My alcoholic roommates had been more peaceful than my brothers! "Mitchell, for the love of God, please calm . . ."

"You *knew?*" My older brother suddenly reeled away from me, gaping at the two of us the way he would have his worst enemies. Our angry triangle seemed to occupy the entire room. "You *knew* about this?"

I tried to minimize my involvement. "Yes, but . . ."

"For how long?"

"Mitchell."

"*For how long?*"

I sighed. Peachy. If my brother wanted to torture himself, that would be gee-whiz golly-doodle dandy with me. "For a couple of months. Happy now? Yes, I've been hiding this earth-shattering secret from you for a couple of months. I'm the devil, right? I'm sooooo mean to you, hiding secrets while out of the goodness of my heart I let you live with me.

While I let you *both* live with me even though you drive me *up the freakin' wall!*" Grabbing the closest of my boxes of invitations, I moved it to a chair across the room. "So yes. I kept it from you. I didn't know Brody was going to take it this far. I didn't know he was going to leave Marcy. I didn't know if this thing with Missy was going to last or whether he'd stop thinking with his dick and go back home."

"Hey," said Brody, offended.

"I didn't know Brody and Marcy would split, Mitchell, because I'm not Jeanne Dixon and I'm not Miss Cleo and I'm trying not to be a damned judge, either. Okay?" I grabbed the second box and stacked it atop the first. Only two more boxes—and a special invitation I'd prepared myself—still remained on the wobbly table.

Mitchell's voice was deadly quiet. I'd either splashed cold water on his anger, or he was in the middle of a slow burn. "Did Dad know too?"

"No," said Brody.

"Yes," I said at the same time. Brody's head jerked in my direction, his eyes flying open. "Oh, give him some credit, Bro," I snapped. "You're the one who brought Missy to that dinner like she was some kind of trophy."

"You've *met* her?" Mitchell bellowed, losing his temporary calm. "You had *dinner* with her?"

"We didn't give anything away that night!" Brody protested, sounding strident. "We acted like colleagues!"

"He *works* with her? That is so clichéd!"

"Give me those," I said to Brody, pointing to the third of the boxes of envelopes. He obediently bent over to pick it up and pass it over the coffee table. "Dad isn't stupid, Brody. He has a PhD. He figured it out pretty much like, immediately." I felt better with most of my invitations out of harm's way. "I didn't confirm it either way, but trust me, he knew."

Mitchell continued his grousing. "I can't believe everyone knew before me. That's so typical of this family! Nobody has any consideration for each other."

"Oh, grow a spine," was Brody's contribution to the collective peace.

"Grow up, both of you! I didn't say anything out of consideration for you, Mitchell." I was good and tired of both my brothers at this point. "What was I supposed to do, tell you Brody was having an affair? Exactly how would you take that, after Ty abandoned you for some other guy on the other side of the country? Exactly like this, that's how. I knew it wouldn't be good, Mitchell. I know how sensitive you are!"

"Don't." Mitchell's eyes began pooling with tears, their surface tension yet unbroken. One blink, and they'd start cascading down his face. "Don't presume. You don't know a *thing* about how it feels. You've never been serious about anyone in your fucking life." I'd been reaching for the last of the boxes, but Mitchell's verbal blow stopped me in midbend. My hands moved to my abdomen, as if I'd been punched. "And neither have you," he said to Brody. Finally he blinked. A bead of moisture ran down his left cheek, followed by another on his right. "You were never serious about Marcy. Not really. Not if you could throw her away this easily."

Brody wrenched his neck to the side to crack it, then looked up at Mitchell with hostile eyes. "So because Ty left you after seven years, all of a sudden in your eyes I was never serious about Marcy. Shit happens, asshole. Shit happens between two people, and when it happens to others it's not about you and it's definitely not about the precious little hurty boo-boos you've stored up through the years." He'd spoken the last few words in a mockery of baby talk; it seemed to me over the edge. "Other people have lives, you know."

"Brody," I pleaded. We all were in too much pain to continue. I hated our arguments. They left me drained and miserable, no matter how I scored.

"They do!"

"Stop!" I ordered.

Brody turned on me. "Stop what, telling him the truth? He's the oldest! If I'm the overachieving youngest and you're the fucked-up middle child, he's supposed to be the one with all the willpower! He's got no spine! He's a jellyfish! Oh, look at me, I'm Mitchell Cloutier, I had my widdle baby feelings hurt by a big mean man."

Mitchell's cheeks were wet, but he tried to sound gruff. "Shut up."

"You sure can be high and mighty when you want, but don't dish out what you can't take, butt-wipe." That should have been enough. Brody never knew when to stop. Let that be enough, I silently appealed to the Kwan Yin. As ever, she maintained her porcelain repose and scorned response. "You want to know why Ty left you? You want to know? It ain't all about height, you know. It's because you're a whiny . . ."

"Brody," I warned him.

". . . self-centered . . ."

"Stop it." Mitchell wiped his face with the back of his hand.

". . . arrogant mopey little kick-me that Ty couldn't take anymore because you're so stupid and *boring*, Mitchell. Christ, even Nan thinks you're boring. She says you hang around here with no fucking life and mooch away all her friends. . . ."

"Brody!" I yelled, absolutely furious with him for having shared my confidence. Especially since I'd kept his for so long!

At the same time, Mitchell pounced. His big feet caught on the coffee table, sending it pitching sideways. One of its legs creaked and splintered; the box of envelopes slid off and with it, the papers, and the tumbler of soda. Brody lurched away to avoid our brother's attack, his shoulders dislodging the lowermost of my living room shelves. Then Mitchell made his tackle, shoving Brody up and back. My pulp paperbacks, my snow globes, my old college textbooks—all of them began to rain down on my two battling brothers, tumbling into the whirlpool of disaster on my floor.

"Stop it!" I yelled, closing my eyes so I wouldn't have to watch. *"Stop it!"*

Over my own scream I heard the smash of porcelain that brought everything to a halt. With my eyes still squeezed shut, I heard my brothers' heavy breathing, the faint fizz and pop of spilled soda, and the thud of my own aching heart. I should have walked away, then, still blind, so I wouldn't have seen the destruction. I could have imagined for a time that my living room hadn't been savaged, that everything was still intact and unbroken.

But I couldn't. I was surprised how tightly my fists had clenched when finally I blinked and looked around. My silly paperbacks lay everywhere, their colorful, outrageous covers now bent and trampled. Half of the last box of invitations had spilled. They lay on the floor, smudged and trampled, still threatened by the spreading tide of Pepsi and sparkly snow globe fluid. "Shit." I stumbled forward, numb.

Mom's figurine of Kwan Yin had broken, the seamlessness of its delicate blue and white glaze fractured into three parts. Collecting them in my hands felt like picking up pieces of my own broken heart.

My lower lip trembled with sorrow as the bits clinked against each other. Neither Brody nor Mitchell would see me cry, though. Weeping was an intimacy I wouldn't share with anyone I disliked—and I hated my brothers right then. I regretted ever letting them into my apartment, my life, my world. They'd run roughshod over my peace and my relationships, and now they started in on my possessions as well. "Everything that means anything to me," I said, slowly and quietly, barely comprehending my words, "you've destroyed." I placed the Kwan Yin on the armchair, letting its ragged seat cushion cradle her pieces.

I knelt on the floor in the pool of carbonated brown liquid, with wet fingers fishing the labeled and stamped envelopes from the encroaching wave and tossing them back into their box. One envelope lay face down in the puddle's center—the one envelope I'd hand-addressed and set aside from the others, while I still tried to decide whether or not to place it in the post office box. *Colm Iverson,* read the spikes of my printing when I turned it over. The ink of my pen had run and blurred in the wetness, but the Morningside Heights address was mostly still legible. "Everything you touch of mine, you ruin."

Mitchell had begun quietly taking the other spilled envelopes and wiping them on his sweatpants to remove any droplets before they could pucker and discolor any more. Brody watched me as I knelt there in the puddle, staring at the ruined invitation. "So one guy doesn't get his invite. It's not a big deal, right?"

"This wasn't for just anyone," I said slowly.

"You can make another one. You've got extras, right?"

"I can't." I looked up at him and shook my head. "No extras. There were none.'"

"You could buy a card and handwrite . . ."

"Brody." Mitchell's voice was hushed. From the corner of my eye I saw him shake his head.

Many of my books were already waterlogged, their decades-old pages absorbing the brown liquid and beginning to curl and swell. How long would it take before the invitation card inside Colm's envelope would be completely saturated? I imagined how the ink of my personal message would bleed until it was nothing more than a black and veiny smudge, no longer legible. *Colm—Please come. Nan.*

"I'm sorry," I heard Mitchell say, from a long distance away. When I finally rose, my jeans were damp and my fingers sticky from the evaporating soda. I wandered back to the armchair and collected what was left of Kwan Yin.

Brody looked from me to Mitchell, and back again, over and over. "Hey, it'll be okay, won't it? It's always okay."

I had to get out. "I'm sorry too," I told them both before I left. "I don't think it'll be okay this time."

99th near West End Avenue: In my dad's apartment (car fare: $8.75 plus tip)

On my old walls hung posters I barely remembered buying in my early teens. Nirvana. Pearl Jam. Soundgarden. Grunge rock had been in, and I'd bought the CDs and the band paraphernalia because all my friends owned them. I hadn't particularly liked grunge rock, mind you, and it was years before economic necessity made grunge of the more mundane variety part of my daily life. But in seventh and eighth grade the goal is to make it through the school year without ever once letting on that the guys of your dreams aren't any different from the guys in the dreams of all your friends. We'd loved Kurt Cobain when he was alive, and mourned him when he died, but now the only time I really thought of him or any of that music to which I'd once dutifully listened was when I stepped into my childhood room.

My bedroom was like a time machine. The posters were the same; only the cellophane tape holding them seemed to have yellowed. Old Betsy-Tacy and Narnia and Laura Ingalls Wilder books still sat on my shelves in the same places they'd occupied since I'd received them for various birthdays and Christmases; stuffed animals I'd once genuinely loved still perched at the back of my dresser. My narrow twin bed was made up with old Snoopy sheets I'd used from the time I was thirteen. None of it was as comfortable as it had been a decade before. The things might have been mine, but they weren't home.

Two taps sounded on the door before it swung open. My father poked in his head. "Um," he said.

From where I lay curled on my side with my arm under the bed pillow, my head resting squarely upon dancing Snoopy's tummy, I said in a very small voice, "You can come in." Dad had left me alone for several hours while I'd cried myself out. He now eased through the door and sat on the bed beside me; I waited until the old bedsprings stopped groaning under our combined weights before speaking again. "I'm sorry about earlier." He didn't say a word, or move. Maybe he wanted more of an apology for the awful thing I'd said when I'd earlier burst through his apartment door—or maybe I was feeling badly enough about the afternoon's argument that I wanted to make apologies where I could, warranted or not.

"You were upset, honey," he told me. With his hands hanging between his legs and his shoulders slumped, he seemed almost helpless. "I know you didn't really wish I'd never f . . . made love to your mother." Another moment of silence passed. "If I hadn't, we'd never have had you."

"Yeah." I barked a laugh full of bite. "The world would really have mourned that, all right."

"Honey." Amazing, really, how a single word could carry so much of equal parts reproach, disbelief, and amusement. "I talked to your brothers, you know." I didn't know. I didn't care. "They called." I rolled my eyes and buried my face in the pillow. "I didn't tell them you were here, if you were worried."

"To be worried would imply that I gave a damn," I said to Snoopy's midsection.

"What?" He pulled at the denim of my shirt. When I repeated myself, he only once more repeated, "Honey."

"Why is it that my room is the only one that's untouched?" I asked him abruptly. The question was a bit of a dodge from the disappointments of the afternoon and his need to talk about them, but nonetheless I wanted an answer. Mitchell's room had become my dad's at-home office before I'd gone off to college. Several years ago he'd stripped Brody's old bedroom of its Cindy Crawford memorabilia and furniture and turned it into an exercise room of sorts, the home for his treadmill and exercise bike. "Why is my room a shrine?"

"Don't talk silly, Nan. Your room's not a shrine. There are no candles in here."

"Hah. Funny. Not. Is it because you thought the boys would be fine on their own, but pathetic little me was always so close to financial insolvency it was inevitable I'd come back? You didn't think I could make it, after all?"

"Mary Tyler Moore."

I blinked several times at the non sequitur.

"You're gonna make it after all." He'd evaded my question, which was as good as answering it. I turned my face away for a good sulk. "Sweetheart, you're not pathetic. Sit up and talk to Daddy. That's it. That's a good girl. All the way up." I let him maneuver me like a rag doll into a sitting position, at which point I flopped onto his shoulder. "Don't ever call yourself pathetic," he told me. "God forbid I should ever hear that word coming from your mouth."

"I bet you heard it from both their mouths," I said, meaning my brothers. "I bet they had a lot to say about me on the phone."

His cheek rested against the top of my head. The prickle of his goatee bristles against my scalp was an old, familiar feeling; more than anything else in the room it brought back the sensations of being a little girl again. "Mmmm, not really. They had plenty to say about themselves, but not much about you." When I refused to answer, he encouraged, "I think they're pretty penitent."

"They ought to be!"

"Mom's Kwan Yin makes an unfortunate casualty," he commented.

Simply acknowledging that loss made me shake. "Dad, that was the last thing she ever gave me!" He squeezed my shoulders a little more tightly. "I mean, they could've bashed in the TV. They could've burned my books or ruined my bed or shredded all my clothes. I wouldn't have cared. But the two things that meant the most to me in that apartment were the ones they had to ruin in their stupid, *stupid* pissing contest."

"Two things?" I shrugged, not wanting to talk about the other. "So tell me about the Kwan Yin," he finally asked. When I looked up at him through my hair, not comprehending, he murmured, "Tell me why she meant so much to you."

Fine. He was determined to depress me further. "I don't know. I remember looking at her as a kid when she was on Mom's desk, and I remember Mom explaining how Kwan Yin was the bodhisattva of mercy—hey." Suspicious, I pushed myself away and cleared the spots where dried tears had glued hair strands to my cheeks. "Is this going to be one of those stupid lessons where it all ends up with you making me realize it would be better to honor Mom's memory by clinging to the spirit of compassion and mercy rather than to a stupid statue?"

Dad laughed, hard enough to make the bed jiggle. "No. I didn't have that in mind at all. But if you made that kind of leap I must've done something right in raising you."

"Good, because it pisses me off when someone uses sense and wisdom to guilt me out of a bad mood." I went back to leaning against him, though this time without burying my entire face in his rib cage. "Is it wrong to be mad at them, even if they're sorry?"

"Well. This should be an opportunity for me to talk about forgiveness and love thy neighbor and all that kind of stuff. Not that forgiveness isn't a good thing." My father sighed heavily. "I'm kind of mad at them myself, though. What were you kids arguing about?"

How much did I really want to get into issues of which I was already sick? I ticked off my index finger. "Brody has fallen in love with another woman."

"That Missy creature?"

"So you knew?"

"Honey, Daddy's not stupid."

Glum as I felt, I wasn't immune to a fever flash of triumph. "That's what I said!" I ticked off three more fingers as I outlined the rest. "Mitchell found out and got upset. Mitchell finally admitted that Ty left him for some other man. Brody went ape-shit when Mitchell accused him of having a Napoléon Bonaparte complex."

"Well." Dad paused. "He does."

"Yeah, stop the presses. And then all hell broke loose."

A deep sigh broke loose from Dad's chest. "I thought we all knew that Ty had left for someone else."

"Only because Ty called me after it happened to let me know! Mitchell only talked about being deserted, not about the reasons. None of us *talk* about stuff, Dad."

"Honey, don't say such things."

"But it's true! And it's not fair to me!" I felt pressure building up in my chest once again, as if my father and I were actually arguing. "You guys all have your secrets and what do you do with them? You drop them on me! Why not? Nan's not doing anything! She'll take good care of those secrets, yessiree!"

"I've never . . ."

"Are you a bisexual swinger?" I asked, not bothering to be anything other than blunt. "Come on," I told him. My question simply didn't seem to have registered. Dad's expression was alert, but distant, as if he had a thousand thoughts firing at once within the recesses of his brain. "Are you, or are you not, a . . . you know. Bisexual swinger?"

"Why in the world," he finally asked, his voice creaking like a rusty hinge, "would you give your daddy a heart attack with such a question, baby?"

"Yes or no. It should be easy."

"Why are you asking?"

"Yes or no!" He was evading the question. No wonder I'd spent a lifetime hiding—hiding grades from myself, hiding myself in costumes . . . hell, even hiding from people *inside* the costumes. I'd been born into a family expert in concealment. We might never have been able to get up a good game of hide and seek in this apartment, but we knew how to play where it counted—on the inside. I was sick of it.

Anger vaulted me to my feet. "The reason I'm asking?" I marched from the room, leaving the door open behind me and calling back loudly enough for him to hear. "You want to know the reason I'm asking?" Down the hallway I marched, past the exercise room and home office and around the corner past the bathroom. For a moment I feared he might not follow me, but he shuffled behind to catch up.

"This is why," I announced, flinging open his closet doors . . . so to speak. "Oh my God." What lay within surprised me. I'd expected a rack full of new clothing—but not the array of shiny black shoes that glittered at me from the floor. Six or seven pairs, there must have been, all neatly set onto a low shelf along with some boots and slippers and what looked like genuine patent leather tuxedo shoes. Not a one resembled the ratty old loafers I'd grown up assuming were standard-issue dad-wear.

Belts, glossy and new, hung from hooks. They still swung from the violence with which I'd chucked open the doors. The belts framed a veritable men's clothing store of sweaters, pants, suits, socks, and neatly rolled underwear. At some point my dad had installed a new compartmentalized closet system to replace the old wooden rod that over the years had bowed from the combined weight of all his and Mom's clothing. I don't own a ton of clothes myself, but my mouth watered at the sight of all the shelves and cubbies and nooks, each with a specific purpose. There were people all across Manhattan who would have paid eighteen hundred dollars a month to *live* in that closet.

Even as I continued to lust in my heart after his closet, Dad still pretended to be baffled. "You think I'm a bisexual swinger because I bought some new clothes?"

"Some new clothes? *Some* new clothes? Dad, this is *all* new clothes. It's a whole . . ." There weren't enough hand gestures in the world to say what I needed, though I went through a good few dozen before I found my tongue again. "We *saw* you, Dad. We *all* saw you, in the restaurant, with those *people,* and they were all over you like you were hot meat in the fondue pot, and . . ."

Dad shook his head, baffled. "What? I don't like fondue."

"At the Mexican restaurant! Vamanos! You were there with a man and a woman! You were wearing . . ." Seized by inspiration, I turned to the closet and riffled through the rightmost compartment, a little longer than the others, where dad's new designer suits hung, their shoulders squared and neat. "You were wearing *this* charcoal jacket," I said, pulling it out. Another garment followed, its long train clinging to the fabric. I stopped cold and let the jacket fall back onto the rack with a metallic click of the hanger. Then I pulled out what lay behind it: an Empire-style cocktail dress, black trimmed with the palest pink around the top, its fabric elegant and smooth to the touch. "Oh my God."

I took the dress hanger from the rack and held it out in front of me, utterly aghast. "Well, now you know all about *that,*" I heard from behind me. When I turned, my father's expression was both impatient and cross.

"You mean . . . ?" It might be difficult to ask one's own father if he was a bisexual swinger, but that question was child's play compared to the words I had to force out. Hadn't I already been through this once before with Brody? "You're a bisexual . . . cross-dressing . . . swinger?"

"Nan." My father had adopted the classroom voice he used whenever he needed to chide a student who'd fallen behind. "I bought this dress for you." When I responded with mute shock, he added, "Don't give Daddy the lecture about how you don't need his help. I bought it for you to wear at your party Saturday. You don't have any good clothing. You need a grown-up dress if you want to make an impression." When I continued to gape, he added, "I thought you could accessorize it with a nice scarf. Maybe polka dots. In a contrasting color. I'm thinking you don't like it. I can return it. I'll return it tomorrow."

"No!" I said, holding out the dress and looking at it again. "It's perfect!" I didn't know whether I loved my dad more at that moment for thinking of buying me the perfect dress, or for imagining that his little girl was a size six instead of the size ten she really was. Perhaps a little of each. I'd exchange it myself so he'd never know. I couldn't wait to try it on.

After draping the hanger on one of the hooks, I ran and grabbed Dad around his middle and squeezed. It was a satisfying moment for us both, until I realized I'd still never gotten an answer to my questions. "But what about your girlfriend? What about your boyfriend?"

Chuckling, Dad sat down on the armchair by his bed and patted the mattress to tell me to join him. "First off, I want to know which one of you decided your poor old daddy was a . . . bisexual swinger." I cringed at hearing the words thrown back at me. "Let me guess. My youngest?"

I couldn't help but confirm it. "I think he was the first one to say the words."

As if he was nibbling on the inside of his lip, Dad nodded. "If you ever repeat this, I'll totally deny it. But sometimes, Nan, your brother can be a little shit. I think he's been snooping around in my checkbook." I didn't say a word; this was one of those areas where my mouth was better left shut. "Okay. I'll tell you who those people were if you won't laugh at me."

"It's funny?" I couldn't believe it. "It's a comedy?"

"Kind of." The expression on his face was half-shy, half-apprehensive. It was the closest I've seen my dad look like a little boy since Mom's funeral. "It's a television show." My mouth flew open, but no words came. "You're going to think it's silly. One of my former students got a job with the Discovery Channel. A pity, really. Her senior essay on the role of frontier expansion in Elizabethan court politics was publishable. I always thought she'd . . ."

"Anyway," I prompted, curious as hell to find out the rest of the story.

He took the cue. "Anyway. She said they were putting together a new show called *The Ultimate Self-Help Manual*. It's about single men in need of a makeover. When she was trying to think of guys she knew who needed a makeover, the first to come to mind was, well . . ."

"You," I guessed. He nodded. "You don't think that's kind of mean?"

"I'm not telling it right. She didn't come right out and use those words but the meaning was there. I'm not saying she was wrong, Nan. I've been in a rut for years. You always commented on the holes in my sweaters, Brody would go on and on and on about my shoes—even Mitchie said I was looking a little frayed around the seams, and you know when Mitchell says you're dressing badly . . ."

"Definite pot-kettle syndrome there."

"Exactly." He cleared his throat and then averted his eyes when a wild grin broke out on my face. "So the show's about taking ordinary, maybe underachieving guys, giving them a crash course in how to buy clothing and what looks good on them, how different types of hair styles might make them look, skin care, exercise, that kind of thing . . . and then letting them go. They don't buy anything for you, they don't take you to any stylists, they don't send a squadron of gay guys to make you over. You're supposed to take over, make your own choices, and do it all on your own. Then every few weeks they send cameras to see how you're doing. So those people you apparently saw were a producer and a consultant who were looking at the progress I've . . . what? Don't laugh at your daddy, honey."

"I'm not laughing," I told him, so happy for him that I wanted to bounce. "I think it's fantastic!"

"Do you?" Again, the shy, uncertain look. "It's not . . . vain? I'm not a young man anymore. You don't mind a daddy who's working on changing himself, inside and out? Everyone needs a change, once in a while, right?"

"Oh Daddy," I said, loving him with sweet certainty. "How could I mind? You know I think you look fantastic. When are you going to be on?"

"They follow your progress or lack thereof for six months. I don't know how long production takes. In the autumn, I imagine. You're really okay with your daddy looking like an idiot on television?"

"Don't ever call yourself an idiot. God forbid I should ever hear that word coming from your mouth."

He shook his finger in my face. "One of these days you are going to have a daughter who turns your own words against you and your daddy is going to sit back and laugh."

I couldn't help but lean forward and hug him. "I am so proud of you." He colored a little at my praise, making me squeeze him again. "I wish you had said something to me! To all of us!"

"I meant to." Embarrassment oozed from him like sap from a sugar maple, slow and steady. "It was difficult, and the more things changed . . . the more difficult it became." I understood his sentiment all too well. I'd felt it every time I'd withdrawn or stumbled into some kind of difficult situation; silence was often the easiest option. "Besides, you said we all burden you with our secrets."

"Yours is different," I said quietly, wishing I'd never opened my mouth.

"You're not entirely forthcoming about your personal life yourself, young lady," Dad told me, growing almost stern. I bristled at the unfairness of that accusation, though in my heart I knew it to be true. "What was the other thing your brothers ruined this afternoon? You said there were two."

Once again I opened my mouth and tried to speak, but found no words. I'd been much happier talking about him than returning to the tired old topic of myself. "I know it's not only the Kwan Yin that's eating at you, baby," he finally said.

Wordlessly, I withdrew the ruined invitation from my back pocket. Body heat and the passing hours had long ago dried it. Under my fingers, the paper felt gritty and rippled. The address was barely legible. What had once been a smooth ivory envelope now looked as if it had been left in a gutter on Broadway during a February thaw.

I watched as Dad peered at my handwriting on the front. "Who is Colon?" he finally asked.

"*Colm*," I growled. He showed no comprehension. "He was at my New Year's party."

"Oh." He put down the card and cocked his head at me. "Is he special to you?"

"He was." I'd never exerted such effort to expel two simple words.

"So mail it."

I looked at him with astonishment. "It's stupid. Nothing's going to happen."

"The stamp's still on it. I can make out the address, just about. They'll deliver it."

"Even if I did, nothing would come of it. It's useless. I'm never going to find anyone. You were married and had Mitchell by my age."

"Sweetie, you can't hold yourself to anyone else's calendar. Mail it."

The moment that invitation had fallen into the spilled soda, I'd known there were a dozen alternate ways I could have asked Colm to attend Saturday's event. I could have written a postcard. I could have phoned. I could have gone over to his apartment and left an invitation written in shaving cream on his door. Somehow, though, the irony of his being the only invitation ruined hadn't escaped me. I'd thought it an omen, a warning against meddling with something best forgotten. Dad's suggestion seemed so simple, so unabashed, that I wanted to follow his advice.

"Will that make things better between you and your brothers?" Dad wanted to know.

Pain twisted my face. "I can't go back there tonight," I said, shaking my head. The thought of returning to my apartment now or tomorrow or even the day after that brought back too much sorrow. "I'd have to see all that mess, and I'd think about the Kwan Yin, and I'm afraid I'd say something I shouldn't, and, oh hell." I sighed. "I'm such a baby."

"You know what you need?" Dad asked. "I've got an idea. Don't say no, because I'm already thinking it's a good thing. You need a little vacation from your life. Stay here for a few days. Stay here through next Saturday. Seriously." I'd thought it a goofy idea the moment it sprung from his mouth, but he wouldn't let me naysay the suggestion. "Do your daddy a favor. We'll swap places. I'll spend some quality time with the boys. Get Brody to talk to me about that Melissa woman, maybe see if Mitchell will talk about Ty. You can spend the week here, get your work done, use my computer to work on your catalog. Nope. It's done. Daddy says so."

I grinned at him, both liking the idea and finding myself afraid to accept it. "You're crazy, you know. *They're* crazy. They'll *drive* you crazy."

"That's what kids do to their parents, honey," he said, pulling me to him. "So consider that settled. I'll pack a bag and head over in the morning and I'll whip those boys into shape for you. The only thing I ask in return, though," he said, growing stern again, "is that you mail that invitation to your young man friend. See what happens."

"You think he'll come?" I asked, wanting the answer to be a yes.

"Why wouldn't he?"

For a hundred reasons, I thought to myself.

"So that's a yes? Run down to the post office and mail it right now, before the last Saturday pickup."

I almost nodded, but in the end I had to shake my head. "I'll take you up on the offer of staying here," I told him, standing up and walking over to his dresser mirror. My face was blotchy, but passable; a few minutes outside in the cool air would return it to normal. "But I can't mail this yet. There's one thing I have to do first."

"What's that, baby?"

Could I explain to him? If I tried, I might chicken out, or let him convince me not to. Our family would have to bear one more secret—at least for now. "I'll tell you later," I said, kissing him on the cheek. I had to get out and do this while I still had the urge and before my nerve faltered.

There was no way around it: I had to earn the right to mail that invitation.

Planet Microphone
(bottled water: $4; Chex Mix: free)

"Watch it, sister!" barked the brute with the long red side-burns and the redder mustache. The lip underneath that mustache rose up in a sneer that would have done Elvis proud. "Clumsy bitch."

Yes, there's nothing like being called a bitch by one of New York City's finest drag kings.

We'd collided shoulders moments before, when I was try-ing to push my way through the crowd to the front of the room; she'd been on the way back to a table of similarly dressed friends carrying several bottles of beer. He? She? Which was the correct pronoun for a biological female who'd glued fake facial hair to her face and dressed herself convincingly in men's biker duds? In the end it didn't mat-ter. I wasn't at the bar to make friends.

I wasn't there to drink, either—a fact driven home every time someone had passed by my solitary spot at the club's rear, near where the bartenders dispensed alcohol to their patrons. I'd seen a parade of bottles and pitchers, tray after tray of shot glasses passing by. Though I longed for a slug to bolster my resolve, I abstained. I had to do what I'd come to do completely sober, or else it wouldn't mean a thing.

I'd been the lone female in the back corner, where creepy older guys with comb-overs sat watching the hot young things closer to the center of action. When it was my time to rise and cross the room, it felt like the longest walk I'd ever taken. An entire hour I'd spent eating away at myself with nervousness and worry; it was only when I finally stood up and crossed the room that I noticed how truly diverse were the bar's patrons that night. The party of drag kings had taken over some of the tables at the back, but they were joking and laughing and leering at a number of younger club kids downing shots of sour apple schnapps. Dowdy middle-aged women flirted with lonely looking middle-aged men who played pattern-matching games on the video monitors; a table of gay guys talked loudly over each other near the front. Young people of both sexes and all persuasions hung out everywhere, some of them listening to the music, some drinking their way into a bleary-eyed stupor, most talking and eating the Chex Mix. On any other night, I would have enjoyed the different crowds knocking elbows.

That night, though, my brain scarcely registered them as I pressed forward.

From the front of the room someone called my name a second time, more insistently than the first. I'd almost reached him, though. Soon he would see me, and in that moment my fate would be sealed. Once our eyes met, I wouldn't be able to back out; I couldn't revoke the consequences of where a moment's impulse had led me.

Finally I was past the bar's end and into a stretch of clear space. It was there that he noticed me. "Nan! There you are!" I heard him say. Then I found myself stumbling in his direction, pretending to smile, fingers outstretched, accepting what he pressed between my hands.

"Thanks," I whispered. My voice had gone to gravel. Could I go through with this stupid, foolhardy plan at all? Fear seemed to have clogged my every artery, preventing blood from entering my poor, dizzy brain. Could I remain standing?

I had to try. Once again the loudspeakers boomed out a bright, bouncy tune it seemed I'd known since birth—and suddenly the entire world was reduced to me, the microphone, and a series of block letters on a small television screen. I took a breath, brought to my lips the large black mic the karaoke jockey had given me, and dove in. My voice—my thin, reedy voice—caught in my throat, then as I tried to catch up to the beat it wailed out, "Once I had a love, and it was a gas . . ."

In the four beats of silence that followed, I had an epiphany of the sort I've always craved, but with which I'm rarely gifted. With perfect foresight I saw how my attempt at karaoke would play out. I would sing "Heart of Glass" while a few people listened and the rest regarded me as background noise at best. I'd fumble some of the lyrics. A few of the notes would sound sour from my untrained pipes. I'd be far, far from perfect. I might even suck.

Yet I would have taken the chance. Afterwards there'd be a smattering of applause, and I'd grin, my soul and pride properly mortified. Then I'd leave the bar and head back to my dad's place, knowing the world wouldn't come crashing down around me despite my many imperfections.

Then, the next time, risking and failing would come more easily.

Chelsea: Luminous Egg Gallery
(income: $600;
aspirin, breath mints, and coffee: $8.35)

The framed and matted artwork in front of me was the gray of cement, or of old twine left out to weather. I couldn't stop staring. Though from a quick glance one would have thought the piece a single-colored expanse and nothing more, closer inspection proved that it was every color in the crayon box—the most delicate swirls of purple and orange and red and blue, overlapped and crosshatched until they had achieved a combined shade and consistency of their own. Arcing across the topmost layers of color were words, faintly traced in white crayon: *Love. Hate. Hunger.*

"You did this?" I asked the little girl in pigtails who sat nearby, watching from her wheelchair. Jasmine O'Brian consulted her clipboard and then posted a small placard beside the work. *Rose Avergne,* it read. *My Thoughts.* I blinked at the price, perched high in the three-digit range. When the little girl nodded timidly, I exclaimed, "That's fantastic!"

"It be chizzlin', no diggity?" Jasmine asked, leaning down and smiling at Rose. "Props for pimpin' a killer bomb that'll bring in the chips! Gimme skin?" She extended her thin and elegant hand in the air and waited for a response that never came, no doubt because neither I nor Rose, who had that well-bred air of a kid raised in an upper middle-class family, understood a slang word Jasmine had enunciated in her clear and cultured voice. "She's shy, poor thing," Jasmine confided to me as we moved on to the next work. "I have a stepdaughter at home—fifteen. She adores it when I speak in the parlance of today's teen. Yo, peeps!" She addressed a small group of kids. "Wha's crackulatin'? Y'all ready to do your thizang today? We gonna be off the hizzle, hmm?"

It was a bit like listening to Julie Andrews read the collected lyrics of Ol' Dirty Bastard. Suddenly I felt very sorry for Jasmine's stepdaughter. "You know," I told her, trying to sound helpful. "I can take over the cards if you have something you'd rather be doing."

"Oh. Lovely! Are the nibbles set?" She handed over the placards and smoothed down her hair. It was almost criminal how effortless Jasmine's beauty seemed; dressed in a vintage cocktail sarong gathered at the waist by a bow, she looked as fresh as the flowers of its pattern.

"The caterers are setting them out now." I'd found over the past week and a half that Jasmine and I had diverging notions of *nibbles*. To me, the word conjured up images of Cheese Nips and beef jerky in front of the television late at night, or at a party maybe chips and spinach dip. To Jasmine, however, it meant sautéed endive with Cointreau *jus gastrique* cut with lobster butter, snow crab flakes with cream of nettles garnished with white almond crisp, miniature noisettes of venison with a bitter chocolate and juniper berry sauce, and "just for fun," Barbary duck sautéed in pecan oil with an accompanying mushroom mousseline enhanced with beet caramel.

"I do hope they brought the pumpkin cake with *Beaumes de Venise* compote. The last caterer thought he could fob off on my guests a crème brûlée with muscat sherbet. It's not the same, is it?"

Like I would know? "No, of course not," I assured her in a soothing voice. Jasmine's gastronomic appreciation left me both a little awed and, frankly, worried. "Um, I hope you don't mind, but I know that kids are sometimes picky about their food." Particularly deer, duck, and crab, I thought to myself. "So I took the liberty of ordering some . . ." What had the caterer called it? My French was as bad as ever. "*Cornettes au fromage*. And miniature *Pissaladière*."

"Macaroni and cheese? And pizza?" She laid a hand on my arm. For a moment I was terrified the jig was up and that I'd be bounced from the gallery. "Nan, what a brainstorm! I knew I could rely on you. Did I tell you how smashing you look today, by the way? That dress is marvelous! I'm not sure I would have recognized you!" I knew I shouldn't let compliments go to my head, but I'd so rarely had a job in which I received them. I kept the preening to an internal minimum. Jasmine gave my arm a squeeze to thank me. "Let me take one more look around and then I'll open up the doors to the public. I'm sure everything's the lick!"

Was "the lick" good? I surely hoped so.

Jasmine would find everything shipshape, of that I was sure. I'd poured my heart, soul, and all my time into ensuring that everything Jasmine wanted, Jasmine got. Nibbles? I got her nibbles, with a few more for the kids. Programs? I'd negotiated an acknowledgment for the printing company so that, as a charitable donation, they bumped up the program from black ink on beige paper to full color on glossy white stock. Appearance by the Easter Bunny? I'd hired a fuzzy suit and arranged with my old work chum Amanda to appear. Thinking of which, she was running late.

Easter egg hunt for the junior artists and their brothers and sisters? Set up in the tiny sculpture garden at the gallery's rear, laden with colorful plastic eggs filled with finer milk chocolates. Press releases? Well, Jasmine had written and sent them out to the foundation officials and to arts organizations and papers before I'd been asked to take over, but I'd followed up with cheery little phone reminders and some broadly dropped hints about the nibbles.

Cleanup after the party? I'd contracted with the crew the gallery usually used for special events. I'd managed to come in over seven hundred dollars under my budget, too, thanks to the savings on printing.

Affixing a few placards to the wall would be nothing, after all that work. For the thousandth time I blessed my dad for allowing me to turn his place into Operation Get Nan a Job. For six days his apartment had served as my little oasis of peace and bliss, freeing me from both the abrasive presence of my younger brother and Mitchell's ever-present, specterlike attendance. True, after tomorrow, who knew whether I'd work with Jasmine again? The only certainty I had is that Monday I'd have to head back downtown to the shambles of the life I'd cobbled together for myself, and try to make do.

Although a good amount of the kids' artwork was of the draw-an-outline and color-it-in variety favored by kids, there were a few like Rose's that showed a good degree of sophistication; I'd seen far worse in the conceptual gallery openings Maya and I would haunt for the free hors d'oeuvres. I'd put up the last of the cards when Jasmine's assistant, Felix, sauntered in my direction. I felt slightly guilty; Jasmine had needed my extra help only because Felix had spent the previous two weeks in his home state of Minnesota looking for employment. It was his job I coveted. "Nice work," he drawled. "You've done just what I would have told you myself. Give Jasmine what she wants, then give a little bit more."

"Thanks." I blushed. Felix was a beautiful young man, a Pixy Stix-thin Asian-American with his hair dyed blond and his mint-condition clothes so perfectly retro that they seemed purchased from a Sears Roebuck catalog from 1974. "Coming from you, that means a lot."

"I know." Felix looked the slightest bit smug. I didn't mind; I suspected he deserved it. "Anyway. You had a ringie-dingie. Thought you'd like to know." He handed over a slip of

cream-colored paper on which, written in tiny letters styl-
ized to look like the Greek alphabet, were a phone number
and the words, *Call Amanda*. "She said she's only got five
more minutes of break time."

Break time? Amanda wasn't supposed to be working.
She'd told me she was taking today off for this event. "Shit." I
had a bad feeling.

Felix raised his eyebrows and wrinkled his nose. "Uh-oh.
Better use my phone," he said, pointing to the back where
his little office protected Jasmine's own larger inner sanc-
tum. "And close the door. Little pitchers!"

There weren't enough big ears in the world to fill with all
the curse words I wanted to say. I'd *known* something was
going to go wrong—this was my life, after all. Nothing
worked out right. Once the door slipped shut, I plopped
down behind the warm cherry veneer of Felix's desk—a
desk I'd hoped might be my own. That possibility seemed to
be slipping through my fingers rapidly. I punched out
Amanda's number and rapped my fingers while I waited for
her to pick up. When she did, it was in midgiggle. "Brandon?" she asked.

"*No*, this is not Brandon." The giggle died. "What the hell is
going on?" I asked.

"Okay Nan, this is going to sound bad, but DeeDee called
me in to work. We're doing a thing at Radio City Music Hall
and they're short a few people. You know how the newbies
always quit the day before the holiday."

"But you promised to work for *me* today!" I reminded her.
"You made a commitment!"

"Sorry, but I can make more money here than I could for
you. A lot more." I was too busy fuming and hyperventilating
to reply. "Oh come off the high horse, Cloutier," she said.
"You would have done the same thing back in the day."

I would have liked to think I wouldn't. But yes, if I'd been
starved for funds, I would. "What am I supposed to do?" I
asked.

"I've got the costume in a bag nearby. Get someone else to pick it up and take over. Don't get all bent out of shape. Any monkey can wear a costume."

Where was I going to get that monkey, though? The sludgy, hot feeling I experienced—was it my blood pressure reaching the boiling point? And why was I stabbing Felix's message pad with his scissors? I don't know what I expected to find in Felix's desk drawer; maybe part of me wondered if he kept a spare rabbit impersonator in there. I slammed it shut. Shit! There was no way I could MacGyver my way out of this situation with a pink marking pen, a roll of Scotch tape, and a pad of Post-its.

Ordinarily I would have rationalized away the obstacle—told myself that in the large scheme, an Easter Bunny appearance wouldn't matter. There was plenty else for people to enjoy. Today was different. If Jasmine wanted a bunny, there was no way in hell I'd let the day end without her getting a bunny. Even if I had to produce one out of a hat.

Who else did I know with costume experience? Three times I hesitated before dialing a number I hadn't used in a long, long time. The first ring ruined any hopeful fantasies of hearing a recorded message that the line had been disconnected; the second reminded me I'd best take a deep breath. By the fourth ring I was actually praying that he wouldn't pick up, but then I heard a flurry of static, and a bedroom voice asking, "Wassup?"

"Damien?" An unnecessary question. I knew his voice. I could imagine from the sleepy way he spoke that he was lying down, probably in bed or on his sofa, probably naked, probably unshaven.

"Who's this?"

I was unsure why the question irritated me. "Nan Cloutier." I tried not to betray emotion. I suppose every girl likes to cherish the illusion that her former sexual hobby can pick out her voice from all others, that he'll remember it forever and have her name always on the tip of his tongue.

At least I didn't have to provide any more clarification. That would have been humiliating. "Nan," said Damien. "God. Nan. God!" A pity he couldn't hear me raise my eyebrows while I waited for him to finish his religious epiphany. "Your brother told me you were mad and didn't want to ever talk again or something. Couldn't stay away for too long, huh?"

In my dad's library, among his historical books, we found, growing up, an old Victorian acting manual that featured woodcuts of a man and woman making every silly expression known to mankind. If Damien expected me to be wearing the pursed lips and sideways glance of the illustration accompanying *coyness,* or the wide-eyed goony stare over the word *earnest,* he would be sorely disappointed. In fact, I looked more like dour Queen Victoria herself at her most unamused. "To be honest, I had a proposition for you. I'm kind of in a jam. . . ."

Wait a minute. Why had I called? Why in the world had I picked up the receiver and dialed the number of the one man in the world whom I did not want at the Luminous Egg Gallery that afternoon? Once again, like the last time I'd had a bad encounter with Damien, I was reacting with animal instinct before I'd even opened my eyes.

I was going to have family and friends here. Jasmine would be watching me. Most of all, though, I hoped against hope that Colm would come. I wanted to show him what I could do when I set my mind to it—not to flaunt once again *who* I'd done when I'd lost my mind years ago. Parading my mistakes before him wasn't likely to . . .

To what, Nan? I thought to myself. Win him back? That was unlikely, and besides, he'd already moved on. Show him up? That wasn't at all what I wanted to do. Make amends? That was perhaps the closest I'd come in my conscious mind to admitting what I wanted. Self-horror and fear had set me in motion and kept me running, that night last January.

Maybe I wanted Colm to see that it hadn't all been in vain.

A moment's silence was all Damien could endure without hearing himself talk. "I think I know what kind of proposition you've got for me." In the background I could hear him moving around to sit up. His next words, though soft, were stronger and more supported. "It's probably been a long time for you, huh? Alycia's gone for the weekend. Want me to come over? Saturday afternoon delight?"

A long time ago when I'd been feebler, his voice would have worked on me. I had been a weak, weak girl then. "Business proposition."

"Monkey business?" he immediately replied. "Aw, Nan. Don't be snitty. You know how it was. You'd come listen to me DJ sometimes but we were never *friends,* right? Not really. You'd call me up, I'd do what I do best, and you'd be happy for a few weeks until you were ready for more. I can live with that kind of arrangement."

I couldn't. "Why am I not tempted?" I asked. Sexy as he was, no matter how outlandish his facial hair might have been this season, the old attraction was over. Way over. I wasn't even remotely intrigued. Months before, I'd emigrated from a world that included Damien and I seemed to be discovering that I didn't mourn his loss.

"Aw, come on, Nan."

"My brother was right," I told him. "Pretend I never existed. Goodbye, Damien."

I put down the phone with a pang of regret—not for alienating my former hobby. Oh no, not that at all. I mourned because I'd hung up on the one person I knew who had any experience dressing up in stupid holiday costumes.

The only person, that is, save one.

I've never been certain what hemming and hawing actually were, but if they involved rapidly tapping a pencil onto a message pad until the point broke, accompanied by biting the lips and blinking rapidly at the ceiling, I indulged in them. Finally I stood up, sighed, and spoke aloud. "Oh, why the hell not?"

Riding the 1 line in a cocktail dress and heels? Not really recommended. Even on a really nice spring day it only makes you feel as if you're prancing around Manhattan in nothing but lingerie, as if you're some sort of lower-mid-level hooker who can't afford carfare. That's amusing for a couple of minutes, but when you have to navigate the stairs and then run down 50th Avenue at top speed, you'd rather have on sweat clothes and sneakers.

I recognized the costumes worn by the Seasonal Staffers as a model I'd worn two years before—pastel tights that led up to the bottom half of a giant eggshell right below the buttocks, and above the belly button, a feathery body and beaked face topped off by a remnant of jagged-edge eggshell worn as a hat. It was supposed to resemble a chick hatching. Wearing it, I'd always thought I looked more like a nightmare vision out of Hieronymus Bosch by way of Hello Kitty. The crew of four busily passed out cards advertising Bergdorf Goodman's Easter sale.

I marched right up, yanked a pale green Amanda by the tail feathers, and pushed her against one of the lit-up poster display windows. "Hey!" she protested at first. Her expression changed when she recognized me. "Cute dress!" she exclaimed. "Did you cut your hair?"

"My dad recommended his stylist," I said, forgetting for a moment my displeasure. "He picked out the dress too."

"Nice!" I could practically see the dollar signs register in her eyes. "Your dad's single, right?"

That comment brought me back to business. "Where's the costume?"

"There's no need to be so *rude*." Amanda jerked away from me and began digging under the yolky padding of her lower eggshell. "Doing you a favor here, after all."

"Some favor!" Amanda had let me down for the last time.

"Quitting on me at the last minute and dragging me all the way midtown so I could do the job myself."

"You're awfully high and mighty lately, you know. Like you're suddenly too good to put on a bunny suit?" From the compartment built into the outer extremities of the eggshell, Amanda produced a small red and white ticket. "That getup of yours is as much a costume as what I have on."

"It's not the costume I mind. It's that you made a commitment and let me down." When had I developed a work ethic? I wondered. The words coming out of my mouth surprised me more than if I'd grown a second head without warning. "What is that?" I asked, when she shoved the ticket in my hand.

"Luggage check. Sheraton Towers." When I didn't reply, she added, "I've got an ex who works there. Well, what did you think I was going to do, bring it with? Oh, and ask Tony if he wants to get a drink after his shift, when you make the claim."

"I'm in the middle of a job here! I'm not looking for pickups!"

Wearing the charitable face people adopt when they're reminding themselves to be kind to the slow, Amanda smiled. "Ask him if he wants to get a drink with *me.*"

What did I look like, the Dolly Levi of 50th Street, matchmaking people for the hell of it? "Yeah. Sure." I stomped off muttering curses.

"Smell ya later," I heard her call out behind me.

Not bloody likely. Though from the state of that particular bunny suit, there was a distinct possibility I'd be smelling myself all afternoon. By the time I got to the Towers, I'd been gone from the party for nearly an hour. That in itself was fine; Jasmine had told me that once the doors opened, all I really had to do was mingle, eat nibbles, and enjoy myself. My family was supposed to be coming, though, and some of my friends. Would they stay long enough to wait for my return?

Did I actually want them to? It didn't matter. I could bear the humiliation, exactly as I had all the other years when they thought it amusing to drop by Seasonal Staffers events and poke fun at me. I could even toss back my hair at the luggage check desk and pretend that I was claiming a Gucci travel bag rather than a plastic hanger trailing six feet of pink acrylic, complete with floppy ears. I had dignity. I had dignity enough to allow me to change in the lobby restroom, and to ignore the sudden silences that would fall whenever talking pairs of women would enter to discover me peering into the mirror, applying whiskers to my cheeks and fixing a pink latex ball on the end of my nose.

I had such poise that I could walk through the lobby of the Sheraton Towers to the street with my shoulders back and chin lifted high as if I'd been wearing silk and leather instead of plush pile, the straps of my heels dangling from one big pink mitt and my purse hanging from the other, while I ignored the whistles and catcalls coming from a crowd of consultant conventioneers. My composure was unruffled as I tripped down the stone steps toward Seventh Avenue, nor did I falter, cower, or apologize as I stood in the midst of marveling New Yorkers and tourists, hailed a cab, and gave the driver instructions back to Chelsea. I'm just that kind of unflappable, devil-may-care girl.

Of course, I did get slightly flustered when I realized I couldn't get into my purse with the enormous mitts of my one-piece suit for the cab fare and I had to enlist the help of the driver to fish it out, but as we say in showbiz, them's the breaks.

When I finally careened back into the gallery, by the artful fixture of squiggles and dots hanging over the back doorway I could see I'd been gone for one hour and twenty-five minutes. Through the glass front I'd seen that the event was already in full swing; inside I saw a mix of patrons peering at the artwork and at each other with equal interest, preteen artists and their proud parents, and the arty-farty filler types who will attend any opening to which they're invited and provide interesting conversation and perspective until the booze runs out. Felix met me at the door. "Good timing," he murmured. "Jasmine was beginning to wonder where you'd been."

"Did you cover for me?" I asked.

"Now, what kind of assistant would I be if I didn't? Give me those," he added, nodding at what I carried in my paws. Heading uptown I'd felt something like a hooker, but now that I was back in Chelsea I more resembled a children's TV show character who'd carjacked that hooker for her purse and shoes. I handed them both over to Felix before any of the kids noticed.

"Nan!" I heard from a dozen feet away. Jasmine had pivoted around once she saw me; the fringes overlying her long dress flew out at she turned and glided over. "My dear!" When she held both my mitts in her long and elegant hands and looked me up and down, from my fuzzy pink feet and the elephant-leg folds of fabric hanging above them, through the white pom-poms on my belly and between my breasts, to my exposed, flushed face with my ball-nose and my plastic whiskers, and then up to the pink ears quivering above my head, I very much felt like the Elephant Man receiving the sympathy and pity of a fashionable society lady.

"I'm sorry I had to scoot," I told her. From the corner of my eye I could see Emmett and the love of his life breaking away from the Elizabethan Failures and wandering over. I tried to scan the room, looking for other familiar faces, but Jasmine distracted me with a squeeze. If she was preparing to fire me or let down my hopes for a more permanent position, she was going about it in the gentlest way possible.

"You do know?" she asked, looking into my eyes, "I did

make it clear, didn't I? That you weren't expected to come as the Easter Bunny yourself?"

I couldn't help but laugh; she looked so mortified for my sake that it was the only reaction I could really summon. "I don't mind," I told her. "Really. I don't mind at all."

Jasmine, however, kept objecting. "I know you were trying to come in under budget and I appreciate the gesture, but I wanted you to enjoy the party after all your hard work!"

Once more I tried to scan the crowd, but another voice interrupted me. "Nan!" Isobel took over squeezing duty on one of my paws. "Emmett, darling, look at her. Isn't she amazing?" *Dorling.*

Emmett's high-voltage smile could have lit up the room. It was intended mostly for Isobel, but I no longer minded. "I've long thought Nan amazing," he said, winking at me.

Isobel sighed. "I wish I weren't so self-conscious. Nan is always such *fun.*"

"Well," Jasmine was still saying, this time to Felix, who'd returned from the office after dropping off my shoes, "I'm seeing to it that this is definitely the last time she wears these getups."

I held their comments close to my heart, deep inside. "Thank you," I said to Isobel, glad to have a gullfriend who thought silly costumes were a lark. "And I don't mind!" I said to Jasmine, meaning the words.

"The kiddies are waiting," Felix whispered. He handed over a wicker basket stuffed with transparent grass and eggs like the ones hidden in the sculpture gardens.

A crowd had formed behind him of the younger children—both the artists of the show and their brothers and sisters, as well as kids of the various guests. Even the less savvy among them knew I wasn't the real Easter Bunny, but their eyes were already shining at the thought of both the excitement and the sugar they'd been promised. Isobel reached up to adjust my nose for me; while she fussed over my whiskers with the same care she would have shown for her own makeup, I kept scanning the crowd.

There were my other friends, Maya and Jack and Clark, liberally helping themselves to the free nibbles. Ambrose stood with his back to me, peering at one of the pieces of art. My dad hovered near the back of the crowd, while my brothers skulked behind him. Almost everyone's face, friend or stranger, had turned in my direction, waiting.

There, toward the back! My heart started to thump at the sight of a tall man with dark, straggling hair and a five o'clock shadow spreading across his lean face. He lifted his fingers to adjust his glasses and looked my way. . . .

Yet it wasn't Colm. For one split second I'd desperately wanted to believe he'd come. His look-alike—well, he didn't. The hair was the same shade, the rims of his spectacles were dark and thick, but this guy was too angular, too refined, to have the same offbeat charm I'd admired in Colm. I wouldn't have mistaken the two if I hadn't been thinking so much of the original.

Maybe it was as Colm had suggested. With its parade of millions, in New York City there were some people impossible to avoid, and others with whom you never could connect. I knew then, with so little time left in the afternoon, that Colm wouldn't come. I'd spend a lifetime disturbed by resemblances of him in the crowds, half-seeing his face in some of the people I might encounter. We'd had too many missed opportunities; our paths simply wouldn't cross again.

I couldn't think of that now, though. "Hey kids!" I willed my voice to project enthusiasm. "Are you ready for some fun?" A few of them bit their fingers; others swayed shyly from side to side, while more nodded. "I didn't hear you!" I said, more loudly. "Are you ready for some *fun?*"

"*Yeah!*" they chorused back.

"Then let's go!" I'd run all over town that afternoon. I'd

donned a costume I dreaded. I'd released a friend into the wild, never to be seen again. They were nothing, however, compared to the disappointment I had to stifle as I skipped in the direction of the garden, pretending not to have a care in the world.

My apartment above Przybyla and Sons Bakers
(flowers: $36)

Paris took Helen to Troy; despite a childhood suckled by a bear, he'd grown up recognizing a good prize when he saw it. Native Americans used to collect scalps after a battle and carry them back to camp to prove their prowess. Napoléon plundered Egypt and came back to Josephine with the Rosetta Stone in his grubby little hands. Even my great-grandfather in 1944 brought home from France a pineapple grenade that sat on a bookshelf in his study in Vermont. For years it was such an object of horror and fascination for me and my brothers—something explosive! in the house! that could detonate at any moment!—that when we later discovered it was inert, our disappointment sported fangs.

My spoils of war were four. First was the wrapped bundle of daisies I'd purchased on impulse earlier that morning. I'd gone to a nearby market only looking for roses so I could thank my dad for the use of his apartment, but I'd been so entranced at the thought of daisies in my own place that I'd found myself plucking them from the bins, red and yellow and purple, until I'd amassed an armful. The roses I'd arranged in a vase in my dad's foyer, so they'd be the first things he'd see when he got back home. After a week with my brothers, he'd probably welcome something cheerful.

The second was a sheet of letter-sized paper illustrated with a large pink blob that I'd tucked into my bag two days before. One of our young artists had a little sister inspired at seeing her brother's artwork in a public exhibition; when she'd received as one of her gifts from the Easter Bunny a packet of colored pencils and a drawing pad, she'd immediately set to and produced a minor masterpiece.

i loev the buny, was its title. It was going onto my refrigerator.

Best of all was the third spoil of war. Not only had Jasmine O'Brian the day before couriered over a large bottle of kosher sparkling strawberry juice (accompanied by a lengthy note that explained it should have been champagne, but a small kosher deli had been the best she could find open on Easter morning), but tied around its neck in an envelope had been a set of W-4s.

Starting next week, I actually had a job. A full-time job. I'd train with Felix for a month until he left for the frozen wastelands of Minnesota, but Jasmine liked my work enough to trust me with writing catalogs and press releases and helping book the gallery and plan events. Because, she said, I was so adaptable.

Me. Adaptable. I liked the sound of that word.

I couldn't remember the last time I'd had a real vacation—I think it had been sometime before I graduated from college. There were those who might argue I'd spent the last decade in a state of perpetual vacation dosed with occasional bouts of work, but the last week had been different from those years of moping around, looking for free ways to kill time and bum free food or drinks. I'd had occasional fun, but as my dad had said, everyone needs a change once in a while.

Seven days living somewhere else had cleared my head. Even if Dad's apartment did merely lie uptown among the same concrete sidewalks and avenues surrounding my own home, the benefit it paid me was as good as if I'd traveled halfway around the world. I still remembered the reasons I'd fled from my own home, but the anger and pain had ebbed so that they seemed little more than a red-tinged memory. When the cab pulled around the corner from the bakery next to the back alley, I actually was eager to be back. In fact, from the pounding of my organs it felt as if my stomach were hosting the freakin' Preakness in my alimentary tract. My senses seemed to detect extra textures and colors to the things I'd for so long taken for granted: the blacks and terra-cotta reds of the cragged old brick beneath the graffiti, the yeasty aromas wafting from the dumpster, the almost startling closeness of a bird's cry when it echoed from the alley's other end. I can't say anything was really prettier, exactly, but somehow it seemed renewed—or maybe I was renewed, and seeing things the same way I'd glimpsed them when first I'd walked down the alley years ago.

My haul was almost too much for me, with the daisies taking up most of one arm. The smell of the morning's breads and pastries filled my nostrils when I unlocked and swung open the steel door. I threw inside my purse and the duffel bag containing my mostly dirty laundry, then scampered back to the alley's entrance to collect the rest of my stuff, including the bagged cartons containing more leftover noisettes than I'd ever be able to eat in a lifetime. I wasn't a big fan of venison, truth be told, but it was free food and if I pretended they were beef—weird-tasting beef with chocolate sauce—I could gulp them down. The fact that I had two brothers who'd retained their adolescent appetites wouldn't hurt, either.

Over the duffel bag flew the pink rabbit suit; I'd have to return it later that afternoon or lose part of my deposit, but for now I didn't bother to handle it delicately. It fell over the bag and spilled onto the floor like some kind of Pepto-Bismol-colored area rug. Onto the bottom stair went Jasmine's leftovers. Finally I hauled over my shoulder the old college backpack containing all my work-related files, hefted the daisies once more in my other arm, and started up the stairs.

Then I stopped short at the sight of Colm Iverson, his back pressing into the corner of bricks opposite my apartment door. Behind the lenses of his glasses, his eyes darted from my face, to the flowers in my arm, to the side, and then to my face again. The longer we regarded each other, the more his expression changed from anxious to sheepish, as if he suspected he looked foolish. There was something in his hand. He saw my eyes taking it in, trying to figure out why it looked so familiar.

"You said to come," he said, holding out my invitation. The card nestled in the envelope's flap, both folds of paper stained the color of old parchment. Used disposable napkins wadded up after a banquet retained more of their original color and crispness. "So I came." His head bobbed; he nervously pushed up his glasses by the bridge. "Perhaps it's obvious I'm tardy."

"Better late than never?" The words sounded lame the moment I hazarded them.

He didn't seem to mind. "I . . . I've been here a while. I imagined you were inside," he finally said after a long moment of silence.

It was Colm. It really was Colm, standing in front of me, rubbing his distinctive jaw with the back of his hand. I'd hoped to see him more than anyone else yesterday, even if all we could have done was talk for a last time. Here he was, actual and real. Though I didn't know what, I had to say something, simply for the pleasure of hearing him reply. "Why didn't you knock?"

His lips pulled into a grimace. "I originally intended upon doing so. When I leaned in, though, I heard—well, happy sounds."

"Happy sounds?"

He nodded, then intuited I wanted more of an answer.

"Someone laughing. Some people talking. Sounding happy. Happy sounds." His hands slipped into the pockets of his jeans as he raised his shoulders, half-apologetic. "I hesitated because I know you . . . when I've seen you . . . well. I didn't want to be the bearer of bad news on a happy day."

Happy sounds. What kind of happy sounds could my family be making on a Monday morning? I knew Mitchell's school was out for the week, and Brody could have taken off from the office. But happy noises? Brody hadn't brought that mistresses of his after I'd forbidden her visits, had he? I was so engrossed in the possibilities that it took a moment for the full import of Colm's words to sink in. "Bad news? Not your grandfather? Oh God!"

I could barely hear his gentle contradiction over my racing heartbeat. "No, no. Nothing in the least like that! That old gentleman's too determined to outlive all the other Mercers and Iversons, at this point. No worries there. And no," he said, upon noticing I still wore my stricken expression, "I've not come down with anything terminal, nor has Mercer-Iverson burnt to the ground in a massive conflagration that took all of your former coworkers with it. I merely meant . . . whenever I'm around, you seem to experience . . ." He seemed to be choosing his words carefully. "Regrets and self-recriminations . . . that I'm not certain are wholly deserved."

After the reassurances, I luxuriated once more in the sound of his voice. My indulgence in that particular pleasure had over the months gone from a mild comfort through satisfaction and all the way to serious aphrodisiac. Having him here in front of me made me want to do things. Weird things. Adolescent things, like lick his ear to see what he'd do, or steal his cotton sweater so I could turn it into a pillowcase and have his smell near me. I wanted to bounce up and down and jubilate with cries of, *You're here! You're here!* and then call all my girlfriends, Isobel included, to giggle about it. So bewildering and childish were my responses, in fact, that I had to blink several times and remind myself that he was still in serious mode. "But you came," I pointed out, trying to keep from springing into the air. It might have been to deliver a final good-bye, but still he had come.

Once more he looked at the envelope. "Indeed." He waved it in the air. "I hate to impugn the competence of our civil servants the postal officers, but it seems as if they allowed this particular missive to fall into a handy pile of toxic waste."

My first instinct had been to explain what happened. Obviously I needed not to listen to my first instincts. "Mmmm."

"And then it seems they routed it through the Arctic. I didn't receive it until Saturday, and by then it was too late. I suppose—I suppose I wanted to ask you—actually I'm not sure what I wanted to ask you. Are you an under-twelve budding artist with muscular dystrophy, or did you know someone working with the foundation, or . . ." He searched for another explanation. "Was it one of the venues you frequently visit for free snacks?"

"Four dozen venison noisettes at the foot of the stairs would seem to indicate so, wouldn't they?" I grinned. This was the least awkward I'd felt with him in . . . well, months. "But no. I got a job, Colm. A genuine, respectable, full-time job. I put that shindig together. I got *paid* for it."

I suppose this is the moment I'd wanted most to share with him, but I didn't expect his reaction in the least. Instead of applauding or showing any excitement for me, he cocked his head, slapped his hand to his forehead, then removed his glasses and rubbed his eyes against the back of his hand. He was laughing at me! "Oh lord," he finally said.

"I'm not joking. I really did get a job. You're the first I've told, in fact." My backpack had grown heavy; I let it slip down to the floor. The paper surrounding my flowers crinkled as I bent over. Was he making fun of me? Colm enjoyed his jokes, but he'd never before been deliberately cruel. "Is it that unimaginable?" I finally asked, worried.

"No, Nan. It's not unimaginable at all. I suspected you would find a niche. It's . . ." He shook his head and once more wiped the silent mirth from his eyes before replacing the frames on his nose and pushing up the bridge in that adorable, predictable way. "In an ironic twist worthy of O. Henry, I've lost my position. Or more exactly, I've given mine up." I could only blink. Was he pulling my leg again? "No more Mercer-Iverson," he explained again, trying to catch me up.

"I got that part. But why? What are you doing instead? And what about your grandfather?" Now that his news had begun to sink in, a hundred questions sprang to mind. Feeling more employed than someone else was something of a novelty.

"I very seriously doubt I could have made the move without my grandfather's tacit approval. His feelings toward the families aren't all that positive at the moment." Without warning, he suddenly unattached himself from the wall and stepped forward, his hands outspread. Need I mention that my heart suddenly started to pound? I had to tell him I wasn't ready, that I really couldn't . . . "I thought I might divest you of those flowers," he explained, cradling them in his arms as he might a baby. "Polite thing to do."

With any luck, the flush on my face might not show. "Oh. Thank you."

He leaned back again. "Family of sorts or not, the thought of thirty-five or forty more years working for a concern that was as likely to do to me what they did to the old man—well, it wasn't the most heartening prospect to greet every morning. Besides . . ." His fingers rose to pull aside the flower's cone of paper so that he could look at them. His head ducked from shyness. "I couldn't stop thinking about what you said."

"What I said?" I asked in astonishment. What in the world could I ever have told Colm to inspire him to quit a job?

"You suggested that one day I'd run across an unfinished

painting in the back of my closet." The words were familiar to me. I'd snapped them out when I'd been at my most fearful, hoping they'd sting. Hearing them again only made me cringe. "And that I'd regret selling my soul for a train pass out of . . ."

"Morningside Heights, yes, I remember. That was mean of me. I *like* Morningside Heights."

"I like Morningside Heights too. Last week I liked it enough to give up a regular salary, health insurance, dental, and all the other benefits that came from a promising career in the Mercer-Iverson family." He made a wry face. "All the benefits."

Did he mean . . . ? I couldn't bring myself to ask. "But why?" I asked.

"Because," he said more softly, "I didn't want our paths crossing when we were the old man's age and having you remind me through your dentures that you'd warned me," he said, not without mischief. "When I got your invitation— well, I felt I owed it to you to thank you for the kick in the trousers."

"I intend to keep my teeth for life, thank you very damned much," I announced. "Do you really think I would have said *I told you so* like that?"

"Let me consider that pertinent question from the woman who booed her own brother while he sang. Hmmm." Colm tapped a finger against his lips and pretended to cogitate.

I couldn't help but laugh. I once again felt oddly happy at how smoothly we'd fallen into our banter again, but in the back of my mind I needed to know whether or not I could hope for more. It would be unfair to myself to indulge if this were to prove to be the last time. "What about . . . ?" I couldn't remember her name right away, though I could instantly picture the pinched, narrow features of her face. "Elizabeth?" I finally supplied.

Colm lifted his head and stuck out his chin, as if trying to think how he should answer. "I told you I lost all my benefits when I left the company. Although," he added, "Elizabeth Mercer-Berman should more properly be called more *duty* than *benefit*. As you might have guessed, I intensely dislike being ordered about, and she . . ."

"Colm," I told him, knowing I'd not say my next two words very often. "Shut up." He obediently closed his mouth. "Come here," I ordered.

"Yes'm," he mumbled, the corners of his lips twitching. This time when he approached with his hands spread out, I didn't back away. I stood on tiptoe; he leaned down. Our mouths met somewhere in the compromise zone between our heights, touching tentatively at first and then pressing together. I felt more than heard the crinkle of the floral paper on my back, where the daisies pressed into the small of my spine as we held each other, eyes closed, tasting what we'd denied ourselves for far too long.

The up side? He was a far, far better kisser than Damien had ever been. Part of me didn't mind having waited three months to find that out.

Moments, days, or weeks—it was still far too soon when we each finally pulled our faces away from the other. I stared into his brown eyes while he cleared his throat and spoke. "I've always liked you, Nan," he whispered. "I'd like to like you better."

I was glad of the hair falling in my eyes, right then. It gave me an excuse to pretend I was brushing my hand over my eyes for a reason other than the tears springing there. "Me too," I managed to choke out. "I sang karaoke. For the mortification of my pride!"

He didn't seem at all put out by the non sequitur. "We obviously have some catching up to do," he told me, still holding me around my waist. "Start with this new job of yours. How fantastic is that? Tell me . . ."

We both jumped at the sound of the door opening immediately beside us. I hadn't heard anyone draw the bolts from the inside. "Dad, I'm taking down the last of this . . . trash,"

Brody stuttered. The Hefty bag he lugged in both arms looked nearly his weight and size, and at the unexpected sight of us, it sagged from his arms and fell on the floor. "The hell," he said.

Much as I didn't want to, I let my hands unclasp and separated myself from the warmth of Colm's chest. While we disentangled, Brody watched with attention. "Dad," he finally called back. "Nan's doing it with some guy in the hallway!"

I was in too good a mood for much arguing. "You little shit," I said with affection. "Take in my backpack, would you? Colm, come on in and let's—"

I looked over Brody's shoulder into my apartment and stopped. My eyes, expecting to see the hulking shapes of dark old machinery, saw only space and light. No cranks, no gears, no mammoth old oven hoods casting shadows across the floor. The room had been emptied of all the old hulks abandoned by generations of bakers.

"What in the world . . . ?"

I stepped forward, weightless. Each step felt as if I walked on the moon. Vast expanses of barren wood planks spread before me. A large area rug had been spread in the floor's center, but the room's sheer immensity dwarfed even it and the small arrangement of furniture hauled in from my living room and set around the rug's perimeter. I approached the little circle of chairs and sofas and reached out in wonder to caress the leaves of a tall potted plant. I recognized the floor covering after some furious memory searching—it hailed from Mitchell's apartment and had been in storage—but where had an actual live plant come from? And where had everything else *gone?*

"Honey," I heard from behind me. When I turned slowly, feeling as if I were walking underwater, I saw both Mitchell and Dad standing in the doorway of the kitchen alcove. A new clock hung over the archway's center, ticking off the seconds. "You're home earlier than I thought."

"Home?" I asked. This couldn't be my apartment. The brick walls had been repainted. It was light and airy. I didn't live here.

Colm had come in bearing the daisies. Against the starkness of the white brick, they seemed obscenely colorful. "You've really fixed up this place!" he told me.

Before I could decline credit, Brody spoke up. "We did it. Her family," he added with hostility, as if drawing a line of demarcation between them.

"It was Dad's idea," Mitchell said, stepping forward. He still held a dish towel in his hand—a dish towel I'd never seen before, completely free of the tattletale gray of my own. "He said a change would do you good. Don't you like it?"

I couldn't answer. *Like* was too mild a word to sum up all the conflicting impulses shooting through my synapses. "Nan's smart enough to know she couldn't live here the way it was," said my father.

"The old living room's my bedroom now," Brody announced. "Well, Dad's been sleeping in there, too."

I couldn't find words to express my feelings. Hell, I couldn't manage a grunt. "Oh my God," I repeated over and over, like a mantra. Everywhere I looked was something new. I wandered to the wall, where in the bricks they'd fixed braces and sturdy planks of wood for shelving. Some of my old pulp paperbacks rested on their surfaces, along with the few snow globes that had escaped damage during the purge of the week before. There were photographs now, too. One of Mitchell and Ty back in the happy days, and one of all the family with Mom and Dad from when we were younger, and one I'd posed for two days before in my bunny suit. They were all framed and arranged between the piles of books and knickknacks. And in the center, smiling serenely, sat a figure I'd thought I'd never see whole again. "The Kwan Yin!" I breathed.

"Dad glued her back together." Mitchell had come to join

me; I could feel his nervousness. When I picked up the porcelain bodhisattva and turned her over and around, I could spy the thin tracery of lines where she'd been fractured. If I hadn't been looking for them, I would never have noticed.

"Dad's apparently been watching a lot of HGTV," Brody said, clapping our father on the back. "He's got quite a lot of decorative flair. Who knew? And I support that one hundred percent," he added quickly. "Just like I support Mitchell's lifestyle choices."

"Thank you, son." Dad sounded like he was trying not to laugh.

"Because that's the kind of person I am," Brody added, chest swelling.

When Mitchell winked at me, I got a vague inkling that while my older brother might have been clued in that Dad was not a bisexual swinger after all, the pair of them were keeping it from Brody—probably as punishment. I was still too taken aback by all the changes around me, though, to enjoy the joke. "Where did everything *go?*"

From the doorway I heard someone loudly clearing her throat. Mrs. Przybyla stood there holding my pink plush bunny suit by the very tips of two fingers, treating it with the revulsion she would have accorded the death shroud of a bubonic plague victim. She let my bagged cartons of leftovers drop unceremoniously onto the floor inside the entrance. "Floppy thing was on stairs!" she keened. "If health inspectors stop by and see absolute pigsty fire hazard, my husband and I will be forced out after so many years working in—"

"No prob, Mrs. P.," said Brody, reaching for his pocket. He withdrew a money clip and unloosed a ten-dollar bill. It made its way from his fingers into hers. "We were right this minute going down there to clean up Nan's mess." I noticed the way he stressed my name. "Don't you worry about a diddly-darned thing. Okay?"

The baker's wife, who wore an Orange County Choppers T-shirt sporting an American flag motorcycle splayed out in front of what looked like a burning pentacle, sniffed. "And this is for *her,*" she said with a nod, handing an envelope to Colm on her other side. Colm smiled and nodded; she sniffed in his direction as well. I watched as she looked around the room's expanse, turned, and started carefully down the stairs.

After her exit, Dad started walking in our direction. "It only took a little initiative, honey. Your landlady was a big help. All your daddy had to do was contact a couple of dealers about buying scrap machinery, and they took care of all the heavy lifting. Your Mrs. Przybyla let us keep some of the proceeds to pay for the paint and the light fixtures and the shelving and the ceiling fan." I looked up. I hadn't noticed all the new hardware over my head. "Then I got the boys to hunker down and put their shoulders to the grindstone, and—what's wrong?"

Halfway through his speech, I had started to stagger away from him. I was having enough trouble believing that all of this change was real. When he mentioned my landlady, however, the entire situation gained a new layer of surrealism that, exactly like beet caramel in a mushroom mousseline, left a bizarre taste in my mouth. "You talked to Mrs. Przybyla about all this?" I asked, panicking. It sank in that my landlady had moments before *been* here. She'd already seen the results. "You let her help *pay* for it?"

"Well of course, honey. She's your . . ."

I'd already sped back across the room, Colm my goal. On his face I could see delight on my behalf; he actually thought this transformation was great. They all did. They all thought they'd done me a wonderful, brilliant favor for which I'd be eternally grateful—and they had, only . . . I took the envelope from atop the daisies.

"Don't you like it?" I heard Brody ask again, a faint note of complaint in the question.

My finger tore a jagged slash through the paper back. The envelope fell to the floor in gentle swoops while I read the short note attached.

"Brody, stop asking her that," I heard Mitchell warn. "She's—"

My laughter interrupted whatever emotion he'd been about to attribute to me. "Nan?" I heard my dad ask.

"What's so funny?" Mitchell wanted to know

"She's hysterical."

My younger brother was closest to the truth. "You never, *never* should have let Mrs. Przyblya see any improvements up here," I told them, helpless for breath. I displayed the word-processed letter from her husband. "Do you know how many years it took me to convince her this place was a violation of every health code?"

"Nan," said my father. "She was quite helpful."

"She's decided to rent this space as a luxury loft." I folded up the note, then stooped to pick up its envelope. "With roughly a five hundred percent increase in the rent, starting June first. No wonder she was helpful!"

"What about your lease?" Colm's question was low and urgent. I could tell he worried for me.

"I never had a lease." Didn't they understand the joke?

On Brody's face I could see confusion as he multiplied by five the figure I'd mischievously tripled when he'd moved in. The calculation registered blank disbelief. "I love the apartment," I told them all, certain of my affection for the gesture and my love for them. "But you've improved me so much that you got me evicted from paradise." I found myself with a choice between laughing and crying, and I couldn't help myself: I chose the laughter.

"Honey," I heard my dad say to the wall, trying to fumble for an apology.

"Oh man," Mitchell added, shaking his head and looking at the floor.

"Shit," was Brody's abrupt reply. He stared at the ceiling.

Only Colm looked at me. His long hands set the daisies onto the back of my sofa, then reached out for mine. "Will you be all right?" he wanted to know.

Free as my apartment now was of the dark outlines cast by the vanished machinery, to me it seemed that my life was the more cleared from gloom. Best of all, no shadow of Colm parting from my side darkened my future. "Don't you worry about a thing," I assured him. "Everything's going to end up just fine."

NOVEMBER

Malamute's Bar & Grill
(beer: $13.75; unlimited stale popcorn: still free)

"Did I ever tell you I used to love that man?" I asked. Emmett stood near the jukebox, using the bottle of beer in his hand to drive home a point to my older brother. What were they arguing so amiably about? Politics, maybe; ever since Emmett had discovered that one of the Kokkinos was considering a run for city council, he'd thrown himself into the budding campaign with vigor. From my spot at the table I watched their mouths move and eyes dart.

Despite the autumn chill, Ambrose hitched up the arms of his sweater and patted the back of my hand. "A hundred times, sweetheart." He paused to swill down the last of his beer. "But you can keep doing it."

"Did you really?" Isobel asked from across the table. One of Emmett's oversized sweatshirts dwarfed her tiny frame. After work, she'd come to my place to change into her jeans before we met Maya for dinner. "Nan, you are *so* funny. Isn't she funny, Ambrose?"

"She's our Nan," he said, smiling at me.

"Did he love you back?" Isobel wanted to know. After the margaritas we'd downed with dinner, she might have had a little too much to drink. "Or did he make you cry? If he made you cry I shall be very cross with him and spank his bottom when we're home."

"Can I watch?" Maya wanted to know.

She received a light slap to the hand for the remark. "Naughty!"

"I'm just saying, if I'd known Emmett was going to be into the kinky stuff when we were in college, I wouldn't have gone in on those leather pants we got him for his birthday, senior year. Oh! Speaking of leather pants! When's your dad's show on?"

"Thursday night," I told her. "Thanksgiving evening. And he's not going to be wearing leather pants in it!" I didn't think, anyway. Unless Maya knew something I didn't.

"Well," said Isobel with an air of authority. "I'm terribly excited for him. I've put it on to TiVo and I've told all the single women at work to watch. All the ones over thirty, that is. The older ones."

Maya and I exchanged a secret look of amusement. Isobel seemed convinced she would stay twenty-five forever. "I'm going to check on the guest of honor," I told them all, rising. "Back in a sec."

Ambrose looked at his watch. "Yeah, we really should be starting soon. You've got to work in the morning." I didn't need the reminder. It had taken me two and a half months of sluggish rage and regret to get into the habit of rising before eight, much less get myself groomed and out the door before nine. Thanks to the holiday, though, the work week was two days shorter; I could afford to be a bit sleepy the next day. "Hey, can you get Barbara for me?" he said when I eased myself from behind the long table.

"No problem." Ambrose's girlfriend stood at the far end of the bar between both Jack and Clark. When I approached, she was listening to them explain in excessive detail the plot to a supernatural movie. I leaned up on tiptoe to whisper in her ear, "Your boyfriend can't live without you."

"Thanks, Nan," she said, pausing long enough to squeeze

my arm before turning back to the conversation. "But I don't understand how he can be a child psychologist if he's dead. Doesn't he know he's dead?"

"No, no, no," said Clark excitedly. "That's the whole twist of the movie!"

I left them at it and waved at old Rosie where she sat with a whiskey in the corner, talking to the bartender. The back hallway was one of the quieter places in the building; I opened my jaw to soothe my ears after the din. "Hey," I said, rapping on the men's room door. "Honey? You in there?"

The door cracked open slightly—no more than a millimeter. "Yes," a miserable voice said.

"Aw, what's the matter? C'mon, let me see you."

"No." Colm's answer was as curt as any schoolboy in a sulk. "It's horrible. Are you sure I have to wear this?"

"It's all part of the initiation, my dear."

"Your friends are going to laugh at me."

"I think you're overlooking the fact that laughing at you is the entire point of this exercise," I informed him with a great deal of Mary Poppins briskness. "Have the wisdom to accept the things you cannot change."

"Thanks bunches. Your pep talks should be recorded and distributed on CD," he moaned.

"Come on. Just a peek." I shoved at the restroom door, but he'd wedged a foot at its base. It no more than wobbled from the pressure.

"Go away."

"Fine," I said. "I'm going to see you in thirty seconds anyway."

"That's thirty seconds less laughter I'll have to endure."

"You big baby," I teased. "Hold on."

"Don't forget that we can't stay out late," he warned me before I left him. "You've got work in the morning."

Apparently, a major entrepreneurial concern had employed everyone to remind me of that fact at every turn. My friends deserved bonuses for the numerous reminders they'd been giving me all evening. "I know."

"And we promised to stop by the old man's on our way home."

"I know," I repeated.

There was a pause before he spoke again. "And I love you."

Third time really was the charm. "I know," I said, wanting more than anything to hug him, no matter how silly he might look.

He pounced. "If you *really* loved me you wouldn't make me . . ."

"Shut up. You're still being initiated." I stalked away from the door and underneath the elk's head hanging above the back hallway entrance, waved a signal to Emmett. From across the room he grinned, nudged Mitchell, and started toward our table, where he assumed his place at its head.

That was my cue. I turned and rapped on the men's room door once more. "Are you ready?" I asked. "It's time for your entrance."

The door swung back, tentatively at first and accompanied by a deep sigh. Colm stepped out, dressed from toque to the long, pointed toes of crakows in an Elizabethan reproduction costume Emmett had once worn as Lodovico in a college production of *The White Devil*. The outfit had seen better days; the fussy hat had deflated over the years, the codpiece was positively ratty, and the velvet pantaloons looked as if they'd been smashed in a trunk since the last initiation. The tights were Colm's own, purchased specially for this occasion. I laughed at his expression of absolute misery. "If you make me wear this tom-frippery all the way back to our apartment, afterwards . . ." he said in warning.

"You don't think your grandfather would get a kick out of it?" I asked, guiding him down the hallway. "You look positively Sir Walter Raleigh-ish."

By then we had stepped into the room. Hoots and catcalls began to fly in our direction, not only from the Failures, but from the bar's other patrons as well. I could feel Colm's spine stiffen at the attention. "I loathe costumes," he forced out through gritted teeth.

"Consider to whom you just said those words," I reminded Colm as I settled him at Emmett's side. With a quick kiss on his cheek, I stepped away.

Emmet had been speaking, his glass held high in the air as he orated with perfect enunciation. "To explain what an Elizabethan Failure is," he began, "let us contrast it with its opposite: the Elizabethan Success. Take, for example, that extraordinary Renaissance man in every sense of the word—Sir Philip Sydney, the very embodiment of grace, courtesy and heroic virtue . . ."

I sat down next to Barbara Wellesley, taking a moment to lean over and wink at Maya. "Hands off," I reminded her. "All mine."

"I gave up men in tights a long time ago, girl," she said. "Nice calves on him, though."

Barbara, in the meantime, had cupped her hands to her mouth in utter horror and embarrassment for Colm. "Oh no!" she said, unable to believe his mortification as he stood there, grimacing through Emmett's lengthening speech.

"You might want to reconsider that thing with Ambrose you've got going," I told her. "Your initiation's next, you know."

When she audibly drew in a sharp rush of breath, Ambrose leaned over to squeeze Barbara tightly. "Hey!" he warned. "Don't be scaring her off! She's only just got me broken in!"

I couldn't help but grin. Maybe it was contagious. From his spot by our leader's side, Colm fixed his eyes on me and returned my smile. He only had to stand there for a few more moments and allow us to toast him and welcome him as one of our own, an Elizabethan Failure of considerable proportions in his own right. There'd be laughter and jokes and—oh yes—photographs. There would be photographs aplenty.

Colm and I would tumble into a cab and head back to our home in Morningside Heights, stopping only to say goodnight to old Mr. Andrew on our way. And at the very end of the night we'd slip into bed together while he reminded me I couldn't stay frisky for too long. I had work in the morning, after all.

Months and years from now, Colm would resent the embarrassments of the evening no more than I would relish them; in the end, the memories of the laughter we shared with good friends would be what lasted. That was the nicest thing about costumes. No matter how terrible they appeared and no matter how miserable they were to wear, in the end they could always come off.